Bring the Fire

The Wisdom's Grave Trilogy, Book Three

by Craig Schaefer

Cover Design by James T. Egan of Bookfly Design LLC.
Author Photo ©2014 by Karen Forsythe Photography
Craig Schaefer / Bring the Fire
ISBN 978-1-944806-15-6

CONTENTS

PROLOGUE

"A trilogy," Carolyn said, "has rules."

"Aren't you going to turn around?" her interrogator asked.

The floor of the interrogation chamber thrummed under Carolyn's feet, carrying the echo of mighty engines far below. The cramped brick walls, painted a shade of pea-soup green from one of her childhood nightmares, closed in around her as the last wisp of cool air fled through the open door at her back. The heat stole her breath, her voice, as beads of sweat gathered on the prickled skin of her arms.

"I thought you wanted to meet the King of Rust," he said. "Demanded it, no less. It's a little late for second thoughts."

One corner of his mouth curled, cruel and eager.

"Go ahead. Turn around."

She braced her cuffed wrists against her legs and slowly turned in her chair.

There was no one behind her. The bulkhead door hung open, gazing out upon a desolate corridor of corroded metal sheeting and thick, black-iron rivets. She looked back at him. The interrogator's hooked beak of a nose twitched as he snickered.

"You should see the look on your face," he said. "Sorry, couldn't help myself. Destroying hope is just a thing we do around here. A little parlor trick to pass the time. No, I'm afraid the king is far too busy to waste his valuable—"

He paused. Frowning now, as he touched a finger to his left ear and stared down at the brushed-steel face of the table between them.

"My lord? Yes. Yes, of course. Right away."

The interrogator blinked and looked back to Carolyn.

"I stand corrected. Get up. He has an opening in his busy schedule. He's not coming here, though. We're going up to see him. This is a rare honor. For your own sake, I suggest you behave appropriately. Good things come to those who please the Kings of Man."

The legs of Carolyn's chair squealed as they slid back. She offered him a wry smile, mustering some black humor to cut the edge of her anxiety.

"Trying to offer me a little more hope, so you can yank that away, too?" she asked. "Please. Like I told you, I already know how this story turns out. I die at the end. Well, not the very end. Probably a chapter or two before the final page. Someone else is going to have to write that part. Hopefully a better writer than me, just for posterity's sake. I'd like to be eulogized by someone who *isn't* a hack."

"There are all kinds of deaths," he told her. "Fast and easy ones. Slow ones. Very slow ones. Play your cards right, maybe you'll get to choose."

Her cuffed hands gestured at her glass of water. Only a tepid half-inch remained in the glass, with a paper-thin slice of wilted lemon riding on the surface.

"Can I bring my water?" she asked.

He rose to his full height. A long-nosed Luger pistol rode in his shoulder holster. An obvious affectation, she thought, the weapon of choice for every Nazi on the silver screen.

"There's barely anything left. Why not drink it here?"

She scooped it up between her hands, carrying it close to her chest.

"I'm not thirsty yet," she told him. He shrugged and led her out.

When they brought her in, she'd had a bag over her head. Now she saw the labyrinth her captors had walked her through, an endless maze of sheet-metal corridors with hard grilles lining the floors and oblong bulbs, penned under wire-frame cages, shedding dim white light down from above. Corrosion seeped through the slabs of metal, turning the edges mottled yellow and orange, like some vast corruption festering behind the walls was trying to force its way in. Bulkhead doors sprouted here and there like metallic blisters, no symmetry, no rhyme or reason behind their pattern.

The engines thrummed in the distance. And above their drone, muffled behind rust-tinged walls and almost too soft to hear, a man screamed until his voice gave out. Carolyn clutched her glass closer to her chest, gripping it like a talisman, and kept her eyes straight ahead as they walked.

The interrogator gave her a sidelong glance. "I'm curious. Have you figured out where you are yet?"

"I was brought in on a helicopter," she mused. "But we didn't land so much as move...*sideways*. Ezra Talon, the Salesman, created an engine that could open a gateway between parallel worlds. He based it on a design that one of his former incarnations had built into a suit of armor. I think you people came up with similar technology and incorporated it into your vehicles. It's the perfect kidnapping scheme: even if an eyewitness sees you snatch your victim, good luck tracking you once you've left the planet."

"Correct so far," he said.

"So we're not on *my* Earth, not anymore. That humming sound, the vibrations I've felt since we began—that tells me we're on a vessel of some kind. An ocean liner? An airplane? No. There's no ocean sway, no turbulence. We're in motion but through a medium that's utterly still."

She gave him an uncertain look.

"Given those facts," she said, "I might guess we're in outer space."

"And if you did, you'd be close. But wrong."

They turned at a junction and he led her down a flight of corrugated metal steps. He gestured with a sweep of his arm, inviting her to face a long gallery window set into the wall, reinforced glass framed in rusted steel. Carolyn turned, staring out into the dark, and froze.

"Now do you see?" he asked.

An infinite darkness thundered beyond the glass. There were no stars, but there was light. A storm in the vast distance, painting the darkness with streaks of putrid yellow lightning and auroras that shimmered in venomous green. The lightning took the shape of runes, sigils the size of planets, before flickering dead. When Carolyn closed her eyes she saw their aftermath imprinted on her eyelids, brutal shapes in pale white that reminded her of dinosaur bones.

"Of course," she whispered. "What do you build for the monster who has everything? You create a ship that can go *anywhere*."

"The kings are far too grand, too vast to be confined to a single world," the interrogator said.

"Ezra's machine moves people from Earth to Earth, passing through the Shadow In-Between. The ocean of potential, of raw magic, the space between everything that is and everything that might be." Carolyn pointed to the window. "But we're sailing *inside* of it. Inside the Shadow. You're a tiny hop away from any world in all of creation."

He led her along the gallery and drew her attention to the window on the other side. They weren't alone. Two more vessels, vast as battleships, sailed through the darkness. They were cut from the same mold: bulky bodies with sweeping metal wings and long, thin necks leading up to a bulbous deck, looking like bloated, cancerous swans. Ribs of jagged metal festooned one of the ships, spears and blades bristling from every blister in the steel. Ragged crimson pennants trailed from spear hafts, drifting in the void. The other ship was caked in rot. Furry mold clung to the steel, patches of bilious corruption that turned Carolyn's stomach, and every surface untouched by mold was buried under layers of grime and neglect.

"Flagships," the interrogator said. "The King of Wolves and the King of Lament. The others will be arriving soon. It's rare for them to meet in person like this, but under the circumstances..."

"Circumstances?"

"The reason we took you. The story we all want to hear." He flashed a toothy smile. "The story of the death of God. We want—we need—to know how it happened. And what became of Marie Reinhart and Vanessa Roth after they committed the ultimate murder."

"I never said that's what happened, did I?"

"Are you claiming it isn't?" he asked. "Remember, as I've already demonstrated, I'll know the second a lie passes your lips. You don't want to make that mistake again."

"I claim nothing. Only that this is the last story I'll ever tell, and if you owe me anything, it's this: let me tell it the right way. No jumping ahead, and no spoilers."

His nose wrinkled. He held his silence.

"As I was saying," she explained, "a trilogy has rules. The first book sets up the characters, the stakes, the setting. In the second book, tragedy strikes. We see our heroines face their darkest hour—in this case, the destruction of Deep Six. As the station collapsed, Nessa barely escaped. And she escaped without Marie, who was sucked out into an alien ocean. The dimensional gateway fell shut at Nessa's back, never to reopen."

"But Reinhart wasn't dead—not yet, anyway. Correct?" he asked.

"That's right. An emergency return built into her armor whisked her to another parallel Earth. Lost, alone, but alive. Of course, Nessa didn't know that. And she was dying, infected by raw Shadow. The spell book she'd been given by her unknown patron was revealed to be a death trap, designed to kill her the moment she started mastering magic. She had three vials of a serum that could hold off the infection's progress. Three vials, three days left to live. Three days left to live, and her lover, and her entire life's purpose, had just been stolen from her. She had nothing left. Nothing but her hatred."

"What did she do?"

"A trilogy has rules. And while things take a turn for the worse in the second book, they have to get even darker as the third begins. This is the last time I get to do this, ever, so let me start it correctly."

"If you must," he replied.

"Once upon a time, a little girl was fascinated by fairy tales. She saw how they existed to teach important lessons. To be courteous to strangers. To stay to the path and walk with caution. And to never ever steal from a witch."

"Not the opening I expected."

"Then she grew up," Carolyn said, "and discovered she was one. Not just a witch, but *the* Witch: a fictional character brought to life and doomed to an endless cycle of rebirth and violent death. Her faithful knight was gone, presumed dead, lost across the wheel of worlds. Her unseen patron turned out to be a traitor, and the book of spells she thought a priceless gift had poisoned her body and soul. Once again, just as it had in every lifetime before this, all that she loved had been stolen from her. But Nessa remembered those fairy tales. And she remembered what always happened when someone stole from a witch."

"Which is?" he asked.

"Retribution. Merciless, cruel retribution. With three days left to live, Nessa resolved to make the entire world pay for her pain, starting with the man who had sent her and Marie on the run in the first place. And after him, she had a long list of people who needed to die for their sins against her, and she'd burn as many as she could before her light went out. If she could manage it, she'd wash her hands in the blood of every last man on the list. All the way up to the top..."

Act I

Are You There God?
It's Me, Nessa.

ONE

Dawn broke over the desert. The news broke on its heels, electronic transmissions racing faster than the sunlight.

The woman on the screen was pushing thirty, with a peroxide smile and blond hair that came in a bottle, and she was wondering how she'd ended up here. Stuck in the boondocks of morning television, with no way to climb up the ladder and a line of identical clones waiting to take her job if she ever fell down a rung. So she smiled, she read the teleprompter, she smiled more, and she prayed she could get through the week without another zoo-animal special interest segment. Last week an ostrich had pissed on her sandals while her smug cohost kept a safe distance on the set.

"Here's something a little offbeat to spice up your morning coffee," she said to the camera. "Everybody expects to see flying saucers zipping around the Mojave, but do the guys at Area 51 know about *this*?"

Smug Cohost gave her a grin. "That's right, Sandy! We just got this footage courtesy of our affiliate in Spanish Springs. And it appears to be…well, just take a look for yourself."

The footage came from a cell phone, one of a half dozen held up in a tight cluster of witnesses. The camera jerked, taking in the spectators along the street, cars stopping, people poking their heads and their phones from the doors of tract houses. Then up to the sky, zooming in on what they were all murmuring about.

The object in the sky only held in clear focus for a couple of seconds. It was a small, dark blur; then the light hit just right and the camera captured it in perfect clarity.

A woman in a long, dark dress, riding sidesaddle on a broom.

The broom flew overhead like a comet. The phone shook, the flying woman's image dissolving into a blur once more. Then she slipped out of sight behind the rooftops.

"Looks like Hollywood is at it again," the cohost chortled. "Viral marketing, anybody? No word on what they're promoting, but I'm sure we'll be hearing all about it in a couple of days."

Sandy stared at the monitor. The prompter was feeding her the next line, something about how they were doing amazing things with computer graphics these days, but she wasn't reading it.

"Or," she said, "we just saw a woman flying on a broomstick."

He blinked at her. Then he turned up the wattage on his smile and tried to cover.

"Boy, they're doing amazing things with those computer graphics these days, huh?"

"We should say that the footage came in five minutes ago," she said to the camera, "and it's one of dozens of pieces that have just been submitted to our affiliate station. All of which, as far as we can tell, were filmed by ordinary area residents."

"*Heck* of a publicity stunt," he said.

She didn't know why she couldn't play along. She'd seen more than her share of hoax footage. Pie-tin flying saucers, furry-suited would-be Sasquatches. The footage couldn't be anything but a trick.

Except.

Except for one fleeting tenth of a second, in the middle of the moment of clear focus, the woman had looked down and fixed her gaze on the camera. Her face was still a blur, too distant to make out, but Sandy *felt* her stare as if it had pierced through the lens, across the miles of hot dusty desert and shimmering air, out from the monitor and straight into her eyes. A secret message, one the man beside her couldn't see.

"We have no other information at this time," she said to the camera, "but we'll keep you updated as the situation progresses."

"But it's obviously a hoax."

His smile didn't reach his eyes anymore. It felt like they were playing psychic tug-of-war. As much as she wanted it to be real, for reasons she couldn't give voice to, he needed it to be a lie.

"We have no other information at this time," she repeated.

Her cohost took a breath. His eyes went bright again, his grin plastic.

"Moving on, right after this commercial break it's time for another visit with Zookeeper Brett and his wacky, wonderful animals!"

* * *

Storms brewed over the Midwest, and a C-130 Hercules carved its way through the roiling gray clouds. The cargo plane rocked on a shudder of turbulence. Inside, the armored belly of the hold had been converted into a mobile command station. Screens lined the walls, giving readouts, scrolling status reports, tracking glowing pins on a vast neon-green wire-frame map of the United States. As Harmony Black paced the padded floor, chin down, fingers pressed to the throbbing ache behind her forehead, a young man's voice echoed over tinny speakers.

"Okay, so our contacts at NBC are squashing the Roth footage, and Senator Mundy is on the phone with FOX right now. Looks like they're on board too. CNN is running it with the morning news cycle. I mean, that cat's *way* out of the bag. CBS is running it, too, but the good news is pretty much everyone is treating it like a viral PR stunt."

Harmony's partner passed her, pacing in the opposite direction, fingers poking at her phone.

"It's already on YouTube and half a dozen UFO sites," Jessie said. "Footage going viral in three, two—yep, here we go. Think we should start issuing takedown notices?"

Harmony stopped pacing. She tapped at her forehead.

"No. No, if people start thinking the government wants the footage erased, that'll make it ten times worse. We go the opposite direction. Ride the momentum." Harmony looked up to the speakers. "Kevin, call off the dogs. No squash orders, formal or informal. Let it play."

"You sure?" the voice asked.

"Buy up a website, brooms-don't-fly-dot-com or something. Make it look like a professional skeptic's site and tear that footage apart frame by frame. Show every possible way it could have been staged. Get it online, get it trending, spread it to the media, and by tonight I want seven or eight more websites parroting the same information but reading like different people wrote them and came to the same conclusion on their own. Spam it across skeptic and believer web forums, too, under at least a dozen different accounts. Can you handle that?"

"You got it, boss. One disinfo campaign coming right up. If you need me, I'll be down on the troll farm."

Harmony turned toward the main console. April sat in her wheelchair, the Irish woman's eyes sharp behind her steel-rimmed bifocals as her thin hands caressed the keys. On the wide map screen above her, a curving parabola in yellow light traced a line from Pyramid Lake. A cup of tea, cold and untouched, rested at her side.

"We need to know where Vanessa Roth is headed," Harmony said. "Doctor?"

"I'm building a trajectory model by pinpointing every sighting thus far," April replied. "Won't take long. She's not exactly being subtle."

Jessie stood at Harmony's shoulder and lowered her voice. "This is a problem, and beyond the obvious one. Vanessa is *alone*. Only one reason she'd leave Marie behind."

Harmony stared up at the map screen, watching the flight path as it arced downward, across the desert.

"Marie Reinhart is dead. Which makes Roth a ticking time bomb. More than she already was."

The overhead speakers trilled.

"Agent Black?" asked a nasal voice. "Operator from Pennsylvania Avenue, section four. We have an urgent call incoming from SAC Brannon, authorized under a one-four-three. Should I put her through?"

"Do it." She paused as the speakers clicked. "Special Agent Brannon? This is Harmony Black."

"Good to hear your voice," said the older woman on the line. "I don't know if you remember me. We liaised last year, during that attempted bombing on the Vegas Strip."

"Of course," Harmony said. "What can we do for you?"

"I wish I could tell you. We have a situation here, and it's...strange."

Bars of light flickered on the map screen as April attempted different combinations, trying to connect Nessa's trajectory to Las Vegas. She looked back over her shoulder and shook her head. That wasn't the witch's target.

"Strange in what way?" Harmony asked.

"My office handles all Bureau activity in the state of Nevada. I've just been contacted by the Carson City mayor's office to verify a call they received about a planned CIRG group exercise at the Carson City Federal Building. Said there was going to be a simulated terrorist attack for training purposes, and they were asked to keep police and emergency workers clear from the area."

"Not the first time. When is it scheduled for?"

"This morning," Brannon said. "ASAP."

Another curving yellow line flickered up on the screen and locked into place. April gave a thumbs-up from her wheelchair. Nessa was headed for Carson City.

"That's...short notice for a major training exercise," Harmony said. "The Critical Incident Response Group normally gives at least a month's warning."

"Exactly. And nobody contacted me about it, either. So I reached out to the CIRG offices over in DC for confirmation. Next thing I know I've got some mid-level flack from the DOD on one line and Senator Cheng from Ohio on the other, neither of which have any reason to call me, let alone know I exist, and they're both telling me to call *you*, pronto. You want to tell me what's going on here?"

April was one step ahead of Harmony's racing thoughts. A side monitor flashed, switching from a tactical map to a listing of the occupants of the federal building. The third entry down strobed, lit in a bar of lime-green light. Senator Alton Roth rented an office there.

"Keep everyone clear," Harmony said. "Everyone. Police, EMS, your people. Treat that building like it's radioactive until I say otherwise."

"So you're...confirming that this is a tactical exercise?" Brannon asked.

"I'm confirming that you need to stay clear, on my authority."

"Last I checked, Agent," Brannon said, "I outrank you."

Harmony clasped her hands behind her back. April was still racing ahead; on a third monitor, she pulled up a flight plan, filed with the FAA eight minutes ago. Alton's private jet was being fueled up for a last-minute trip back to Washington.

"Ma'am, I believe you recall a number of...inconsistencies in Bureau operating procedure the last time we crossed paths. Inconsistencies you were later contacted about by your own superiors and encouraged not to include in your official reports, for the well-being of your career."

Brannon held her silence for a moment before she replied. "I do."

"I believe you were also assured that you would be insulated from any negative fallout, as a result of your cooperation."

"That's right."

"You will be insulated," Harmony said. "Keep the area clear. I'll be back in touch shortly."

They broke the connection. April pulled on her wheels and swiveled her chair around.

"Senator Roth is her target," April said. "But he saw her coming. He issued the bogus 'training exercise' order, and now he's fleeing the city."

Jessie squinted up at the screen, watching the slowly bending line of light trace Nessa's flight path.

"Only one reason to do that. Calypso, the senator's personal demonic genie, is calling in the heavy reinforcements. Alton won't be there when she arrives, but his shooters will be."

"Damn it." Harmony went back to pacing. Her migraine spiked like an ice pick behind her left eye as the cargo jet's floor shuddered beneath her, riding hard on the storm. "We're too far, we'll never make it in time. Do we have anyone in the area?"

April turned back to the console and typed fast. She shook her head. "Nearest team is on a mission in Sacramento. It'll be at least two hours before we can get them geared up and on the scene."

"It'll be over by then."

Harmony walked up to the tactical map. The screen cast her upturned face in glowing, shifting geometries of light.

"Vanessa Roth is flying right into an ambush. And she's on her own."

TWO

The Carson City Federal Building was a long, tall slab of beige stone and tinted rectangular glass. It had been a post office once, before its conversion into rented office space. This morning, with the sun rising in the arid desert sky, shadows painting the city in shades of dusty turquoise as the sky came to life, it wasn't anything at all: the parking lot stood empty, save for a few lonely cars scattered here and there, abandoned since the night before.

Nessa came in for a landing. The broomstick swooped down above the building's facade, arcing like a child's swing, and yanked to a sudden stop. She hopped down, her buckled shoes landing gracefully on the pebbled rooftop. She stared out over the edge of the roof, one pale hand cupped over her eyes to cut the sun's glare, and frowned.

There should have been people here by now. Office workers, maintenance people, upturned faces along the broad walkway below to witness her arrival. She didn't need an audience for what she had planned, but she didn't like being denied one.

The building had been evacuated before her arrival, and it wasn't hard to guess why. After all, Daniel Faust had been adamant about the need to keep magic a secret from the slumbering world. A rule she no longer cared about, if she ever had, but Alton still thought he could survive this. And if his pet demon was planning to flex his muscles in Alton's defense, he'd want to do it outside the public eye.

An access stairwell stood at the edge of the roof, with a locked door barring her way. Nessa twirled her fingers and produced an antique skeleton key. It felt like a lifetime ago, back in Manhattan, when she'd just awakened to her true nature. She'd found the long, heavy key at an antique shop and enchanted it in her workroom, a tool to gain access to her traitorous psychiatrist's private office. It had served her well then, and now it would help her to put a second traitor in his rightful grave.

She pressed the key to the lock, cold antique iron bumping against modern stainless steel. Now, as it did then, the words of the incantation rose freely to her lips, driven on a spear of raw willpower.

"No man's design will bar my path. No locks, no wards, no hopes, no dreams. I am the night wind."

Wispy clouds slid across the rising sun, casting the rooftop in a long, slanting patch of shadow.

"I am inevitable consequence," Nessa whispered, "and I will not be denied."

The steel of the lock ran like hot mercury, melting aside as the skeleton key slowly, impossibly, slid inside for a perfect fit. She gave it a twist and the lock clicked. The door swung wide. She strolled down the stairs, down to the top floor of the office building, looking for her father-in-law. Thanks to the occult disease in her veins, her hourglass was running low. Alton's, on the other hand, had just run out.

*   *   *

Nessa wasn't the only hunter in Carson City.

A spotter, watching with binoculars from a distant rooftop, saw her land and gave the signal. They rolled in heavy, a mismatched convoy of vans, SUVs, and pickup trucks, anything they could scrounge or steal at short notice, pulling up against the concrete bollards that lined the pedestrian walkway. Doors swung open, trunks popped, and combat boots hit the ground running. They formed packs, some charging the main entrance while others circled around the building, cutting off every exit.

Some of the men were human, urban mercenaries with prison ink who would pull the trigger on anyone for a buck, called in on a last-second contract they were promised would be easy money. Cannon fodder. The other hunters, the ones with eyes that ran like rancid egg yolk and bruise-blotched fingernails, hung back and moved with caution. They knew what they were up against. Or they thought they did.

In a parked minivan, a woman in black leather, her platinum-blond hair coiled in an elaborate, waist-length braid, leaned back in her seat. She watched the action unfold, pensive, her eyes shrouded behind jet-black Wayfarers. One of her men paused. He glanced back at her as he jumped down onto the sidewalk.

"Ma'am? Are you coming?"

Nyx's fingers stroked the collar of her biker's jacket, the slick leather clinging to her bare skin. Just above the valley of her breasts, under a dangling zipper, purple veins spread like shock waves from an impact crater and offered a hint of the concealed horrors below. Damage she was still healing one agonizing quarter-inch at a time. She'd taken eight high-velocity rounds, shells designed to plow through engine blocks and turn armor to confetti, straight to the chest and belly. The last crumpled slug had wormed its way out of her intestines, shredded tissue mending itself in its wake, just before dawn.

"This one will supervise from here," she said. "When you capture our prey...this one will join you inside for a chat."

Calypso had called her an hour ago. She'd never heard the bargaining demon's voice on the verge of panic before. It was a pleasant sensation, but Nyx only had one question for him: she wanted the cop, the one who had shot her. Calypso didn't know where Reinhart was, but he knew who would. Vanessa Roth. And once she was in Nyx's hands, her skin peeling one slow and ragged strip at a time, Vanessa would tell her anything she wanted to know.

* * *

Alton wasn't here. Neither was his demon. The senator's rented offices, on the third floor, stood empty, papers scattered and a cardboard cup of coffee—still warm against Nessa's fingertips—left abandoned on a receptionist's desk.

"*Coward*," she hissed under her breath. Fine. He couldn't have gotten far. She strode into his office and paged through his desk calendar, looking for a lead.

Sudden movement and the muffled sound of squealing tires drew her attention. She glanced out the window and saw the convoy pull up, the mob of hired guns rushing the doors, men circling the building to cut off the exits and pen her in. Alton had called his friends for help.

"Oh no, we're trapped." Nessa rolled her eyes. "Honestly, as if they didn't just see us literally fly in on a broomstick. What do you think, Marie? Should we—"

The words died on her lips. So did the ghost of her lover. She could have sworn Marie had just been standing beside her. She'd caught her outline in the corner of her eye. Now she stared at an empty doorway.

She was alone.

She took a deep breath and it felt like she had broken glass under her skin. It shifted, filling her lungs with cutting shards as she curled her hands into fists and stalked out of Alton's office.

For just a moment, she thought she could invite the delusion back in. She could escape the agony of grief, wrap herself in the comfort of madness, if she just believed hard enough. She pictured Marie's face, her smile, the warm soft feeling of her hand.

"What do you think?" she asked out loud. "Shall we face them together?"

No. Madness rejected her courtship, and even her hallucinations had abandoned her. She was always alone in the end.

Down in the parking lot, one of the vehicles hadn't been completely abandoned. Nessa's eyes narrowed to slits as she gazed out the hallway window, down at the woman in the back seat. Nyx seemed to sense her. She looked up.

"I came for Alton," Nessa said. Her voice was a razor-thin whisper, but she had a feeling Nyx could hear every word. "But I'm starting with you. You and your hired help. We'll call it an appetizer. A little taste of things to come, so that the entire world can see what happens to people who cross me. I'm going to make an example of you. It's going to be a very long morning. Very red. Very *wet*."

She was practically a blur at this distance, but there was no missing the mocking, shark-fanged smile that split Nyx's face in half. Or the slow beckoning of her flame-blackened fingernails.

"I'll be down in just a minute," Nessa told her.

Dark, fluttering wings beat against her breastbone and wove a magic spell. Alchemy. Transforming her loss, her grief, her pain, into a lit-gasoline trail of rage. She had enough pain to share, to spread to the entire world.

If Marie was dead, then so was Nessa. What remained was the Owl. A creature of perfect cunning and perfect hate.

And the Owl wanted to hunt.

*   *   *

Deshawn was a triggerman out of Reno. He worked two or three times a year. Most of his targets were cheating spouses, or ones that were just too much trouble to divorce. He'd make the kill look like an accident—he was good at accidents—and split the insurance payout with the happy client. It was a decent life. Still, he knew there were better opportunities out there. Bigger targets, bigger paydays.

He'd gotten the call-up to the big leagues just before dawn, the trill of his phone hauling him out of a whiskey coma. He wrestled off his hangover and downed a lukewarm bottle of water while this guy, a bartender who kicked referrals his way now and then, gave him the good news.

"Get your shit and get down to Carson City pronto. This

client's got me calling all the local talent I can muster up. There's a target on the move with a very small window of opportunity—as in, this has to get wrapped up before lunchtime—and the early bird definitely gets the worm."

Now he was bracing his steel in a two-hand grip, rounding the third-floor stairwell with cold sweat on his face, and feeling for the first time in his life like he might be on the wrong side of history. The nameless loser-to-be in the kind of battle where historians only talked about the winners.

"Just put my mind at ease, man," he said softly. "Tell me what I just saw out there in the parking lot, because I know I did not see some bitch riding a motherfucking *broom*."

His partner of the moment was a tight-lipped man with a beetle brow and a Desert Eagle. The gun was bigger than he was, and it swung in his grip like a drunk trying to walk a straight line. He spat a curse under his breath.

"You're not even a member of the Order, are you? Local talent. Great. These assholes are trying to get me killed. You screw up one job—"

"Hey," Deshawn said. "Hey. Talk to me. What is this?"

They emerged onto the landing. The third-floor hallway was a silent stretch of doorways, half shut and dark beyond the pebbled glass, half yawning open on either side of the gauntlet ahead of them. Corkboards and nameplates decorated the drab beige walls. Beetle-Brow slowed his footing, careful now, eyes faster than his feet as he scanned for threats.

"Target's a witch," he whispered.

"This a joke? Y'all are pranking me, right?"

"Target's a witch," Beetle-Brow repeated. "She's not immortal. One bullet to the head, two to center mass, she goes down like anybody else. We get the drop on her, we live. She gets the drop on us, we die. Simple as that."

"Agreed," said the voice at their backs.

Deshawn spun around just in time to meet a gust of glittering, sandy dust. It scorched like he'd rubbed his face, with eyes wide open, against a roll of insulation. His eyes teared up, blinking fast, and he tried to squeeze the trigger on the blurry outline of a woman in black—but his finger wouldn't obey him. Beetle-Brow was down on the ground, his legs kicking, the rest of him motionless as a rock.

Deshawn rubbed at his eyes with his other hand, frantic, until he could see again.

His partner wasn't moving at all now. And in his place, where the man had fallen, was a statue of green glass. He'd been immortalized in a moment of horror, scrambling back on his hands and feet, crystalline jaw gaping wide.

Deshawn looked to his gun hand. His partner couldn't scream. So he screamed for both of them.

His gun was a frozen sculpture. So was his hand. And his skin burned like it was pressed to a hot griddle as Nessa's spell wormed its way up his arm, twisting flesh to glass. He felt one hip turn white-hot, then his other leg, his belly, his skin erupting in spontaneous rashes that became frosted windows into his body. Spreading, consuming him from the outside in.

He ran. Something inside of him turned to glass and then broke as he hit the top of the stairwell. It chimed like a crystal bell and set off a nova of agony deep in his guts. Nessa's laughter followed him, soft at first, then erupting into a full-throated cackle of glee.

THREE

Lenny and Zed had met in the service and bonded over their half-demon blood. *Half* was a stretch. Like most cambion, they inherited a few drops of the infernal red along with just enough power to make them a nightmare for anyone who crossed their paths. When they learned they had a knack for killing, and that they could make more in private practice than they ever could on Uncle Sam's payroll, there was no turning back.

They were part of the second wave. Twelve men on the second floor, spread out to cover every exit. Lenny and his partner stood post on the east side of the building, rifles trained on a lonely stairwell. They kept their lips tight and their ears open, listening for the sounds of gunfire from above.

Instead, they heard a string of echoing hollow thumps and a high-pitched whistling sound, trilling again and again as it came closer.

They shouldered their rifles a little tighter and put their fingers on the triggers.

The thing that rounded the bend, stumbling down the stairs, was almost a man. Half of his body was a sculpture of sea-green glass, from his dangling and frozen jaw down to one motionless leg. The whistling was the sound of him trying to scream through a throat they could see through, air escaping a tiny hole in the heart of the glass as his trapped lungs struggled to draw breath under a cage of frozen ribs. One of his cheeks was a window into his mouth, wet tongue squirming against fractured crystal teeth. His good hand flailed at them, begging for help, as his fingertips shimmered like ocean waves.

"Stay back!" Lenny shouted. "Whatever you've got, man, we don't want it!"

Deshawn's frozen foot hit the bottom step and fractured. His eyes bulged, rolling back, as the nonstop whistling pierced their eardrums. He kept coming. Zed framed him in the iron sights of his weapon.

"Stay! Back!" Zed barked.

He took another step. Both muzzles erupted, spitting three-round bursts. Deshawn's chest exploded into frosted green shards, blasting across the steps behind him and coating the floor in razor-edged glitter. What was left of him collapsed at their feet, a mass of bloody skin and broken glass.

Zed covered his mouth with his arm and coughed into the crook of his elbow. He shook his head as the last gunshot echoed into silence.

"The fuck," he breathed. "Call for backup. Target's on the move."

Lenny plucked a radio from his belt. He had it to his lips, about to make the call, when they felt the air shift. Pressure grew, their ears popping, and a sense of raw velocity made their balance go sideways. Like they were on a jet rising from the runway hard and fast, taking off for a one-way flight. The temperature rose ten degrees in the space of a breath, turning the office-building corridor into a sauna as their vision dimmed.

"What the—do you feel that?" Lenny asked.

Zed was the first to change. His right arm jerked. It felt like something hot and slimy worming its way around his bones. Then his skin split down the middle of his bicep, shredding his bird-and-ball tattoo and spitting blood across Lenny's fatigues. The sudden rush of agony stole his breath as his tendons tore, muscles ripping loose and snapping like whips from the open wound, moving with minds of their own. A slippering length of scarlet meat lashed out, curling around the muzzle of his partner's rifle and jerking it to the floor. Lenny pulled the trigger on instinct, another three-round burst chewing into the floor tiles and spewing jagged chunks of laminate across Deshawn's corpse.

Lenny looked down and watched his stomach swell. In the space of three heartbeats he'd gone from a tight, muscular abdomen to looking like he was nine months pregnant, his shirt tearing and buttons popping to expose the distended, veiny skin of his belly, flesh stretched so thin it looked like wax paper.

He fell to his knees, howling, as his belly burst open. A ragged rope of intestine whipped around his throat like bloody rawhide and began to squeeze. His partner was down on the floor beside him, kicking and spasming with white froth running from his gaping mouth and *something* clawing its way out of his bulging throat, a creature born from chunks of broken bone and organ meat.

The last thing he saw, before his air ran out and his vision faded into crimson and black smears, was the Owl as she glided down the staircase. Her feet hovering an inch above the glass-strewn steps, pale hands open at her sides, a figure of dark majesty.

* * *

Nessa's traitorous spell book was gone, lost with her lover at the bottom of an alien ocean, but she didn't need it anymore. Her creator had endowed her with an intuitive grasp of magic, its weaves and its ways, and all she'd learned—from the book, and then from her adopted daughter, a fierce witch in her own right—had empowered her grasp. Magic was a dance. A waltz at reality's edge, one foot always on the brink of an abyss, flirting with the endless void. The Shadow In-Between could fuel a witch's craft or damn her in a heartbeat.

Nessa was already damned. And with raw Shadow corrupting her body, burning in her veins like a lit trail of gasoline, she had no need for wards and protective measures. Nothing could save her life now. And that meant there was no reason to hold back.

Other witches flirted with the void; she embraced it, straddled it, and rode it hard and fast, turning the endless crashing tides of Shadow into fuel for the furnace of her rage.

She floated through the carnage, turning an approving eye to the mutilated bodies at her feet. Not enough. She wanted more.

Boots tromped in at the far end of the hall. Two more men in tactical gear, one already shouldering his rifle while the other barked into a walkie-talkie.

"Eyes on target! She's on the second floor, east end, all teams move to—"

Nessa's black fingernails gleamed as she flung out her hand and batted the air, like a cat swatting at a mouse. A heat-mirage shock wave rippled through the air, swept both men up, and slammed them against the wall, human toys in an invisible fist. Bones snapped, jutting through torn fatigues, and necks cracked against cratered drywall. One was dead before he hit the floor. The other crawled on his belly along the blood-streaked laminate, dragging himself on his good arm, like he still had some faint hope of survival.

She extinguished it with a giddy laugh and a twist of her hand. His spine buckled backward until he was folded in half, his eyes staring up at the ceiling tiles, his mouth frozen in a soundless, eternal scream.

Maybe soundless. She couldn't hear, not with the roar of blood pounding in her ears like a waterfall as the unleashed Shadow boiled inside of her. She was fuzzy-headed, muscles spasming, crimson dots speckling her vision.

Too much, she thought. *It's slipping out of control. Won't be able to—*

More gunmen rounded the far bend. She stared down the muzzle of a shotgun, her magic fumbling loose in a shower of sparks from her fingertips. She threw herself left, through an open office doorway, as the weapon roared and buckshot peppered the air.

Nessa landed hard on her hip. Her legs kicked in a sudden seizure as she gulped down air, struggling to get herself back under control. She'd pushed too far, stolen too much of the stuff of Shadow, and now it was fighting to swallow her whole.

She fumbled for one of the long, slender vials filled with Hedy's elixir. She yanked the cork with her teeth, threw it back, and gulped it down, the spicy broth flecking her lips and dribbling down her chin. It smelled like apples and tasted like hot cigarette ash. As the alchemical serum did its work, fighting the fires raging inside her body with a wave of cool wind and ocean water, she heard voices arguing in the hall.

"She's cornered, no way out of there. Go in and finish her off."

"Hey, fuck that and fuck you too. You see that horror show by the stairs? I'm not ending up like those guys."

"Well, *somebody's* gotta go in there."

"Uh-uh. Get on the radio, call up whoever brought the Molotovs. We'll either flush her out or roast her alive. Either way's smarter than charging in blind."

The spasms and tremors faded as Nessa pushed herself to her wobbly feet. She felt drained, empty and aching, like she'd just run a marathon, and the Shadow had faded with it. Still in her veins, black specks in her blood like termites slowly eating her from within, but the storm had passed.

She eyed her stock. Two vials left. If she went all-out like that again—if she was even capable of it right now—she'd need to drink another to keep the Shadow from swallowing her whole. Every vial gone meant one less day to live. So she'd save them, guard them like her most precious treasures. One vial would keep the disease at bay tomorrow and give her time—if she was cunning, if she was quick—to track Alton down and corner him.

She'd use the last one, if she needed it, to borrow the strength to kill anyone who still dared to stand with him. Then she'd invite the Shadow into her body one final time. What was it that Daniel Faust had told her, his theory about how they were living in the last days of a secret world? *It's only a matter of time before somebody does something stupid,* he'd said, *something that can't be written off as special effects or a hoax or a mass delusion. Somebody's going to conjure a demon on the Vegas strip, or fight a magical duel on Broadway in front of a few hundred witnesses and a live TV camera. At which point we're all good and screwed.*

The right moment, the right place and time to unleash her full power, and this entire world would awaken to the reality of magic. They would know that witches walked among them. Some would learn the meaning of fear. Some would learn the meaning of hope. *There are worse ways to commit suicide,* Nessa reasoned. She leaned her palms against a desk, breathing deep as her heartbeat slowed from a gallop to a steady, confident stride. She would die, but her legacy would be a world forever transformed.

She thought of her apprentice, her adopted daughter. *A world that Hedy and her coven can rule,* she thought. *My parting gift.*

But none of her grand plans meant a thing if she didn't survive the next ten minutes. The office was a dead end. One way out, back into the corridor and the shadow of a loaded shotgun. She checked the windows. Tempered glass, not built to open. Men were milling on the asphalt below, like ants with guns. Nyx still reclined like a queen in the back seat of an open minivan, eyes shrouded behind her Wayfarers as she tilted her chin up, waiting for her hunters to bring back a prize.

Nessa curled her fingers, feeling a pulse of raw magic like static electricity, invisible pins dancing on her palm. She could manage a little spellcraft without going all-out again, if she used it wisely. That meant playing defense. As much as she wanted to turn this entire building into a chorus of dying screams, all that mattered right now was escaping in one piece and without squandering any more of her precious elixir.

Out, then. Up and out, the same way she'd arrived.

Nessa hurled herself through the open doorway, left hand

raised in a claw as she spat dimly remembered words from the pages of her spell book. Phantoms erupted from her hooked fingers, the air bursting in a twisting cyclone of darkness. The hunters threw themselves to the floor as shadows of tortured men, flayed and shrieking, boiled over their heads. Illusions, harmless, but they didn't know that—and as the images dissolved on the air, Nessa was already on the run, her buckled shoes pounding the steps as she raced back up to the third floor.

She rounded the bend, emerged onto the landing—and leaped back as bullets chopped through the air, chewing into the wall and spitting shredded plaster and chips of beige paint. Four hunters were covering the hallway, two of them taking a knee, two standing tall at their backs, forming a firing squad.

No escape. Nessa wheeled around, looking back the way she came, only to hear boots pounding as the men on the second floor closed in. The stairwell had just become a killing box, guns at both ends and no other way out. As soon as the hunters drew straws and decided who was going to make the first move, they'd flush her out and cut her down.

Not dying here. That's what she and Marie said to each other when times were tough. The words were a talisman, a magic spell that worked until the night it suddenly didn't. Now they were all Nessa had left. She steeled herself for a fight and crouched low on the steps beneath the third-floor landing.

"Not dying here," she murmured through gritted teeth.

At the far end of the hall, calling out from behind the hunters' backs, a woman's voice answered her.

"Got that right."

The shooters turned, confused by the sound. A dark, limber woman strolled from an open office doorway, her dreadlocks brushing the shoulders of her worn olive utility jacket like swaying serpents. She cradled a jar of white soapstone in the crook of her arm. Nimble fingers gave the silver cap a twist.

"*Identify*," one of the shooters demanded. "I didn't see you in the convoy. You one of Nyx's people?"

"I'm gonna paraphrase a line from the lady down the hall," the new arrival said. "Y'all made a lot of stupid-ass choices that brought you to this moment in life. I'm the fallout."

She plucked off the silver cap. A cloud, roiling, black, buzzing, boiled from the soapstone cask and billowed down the corridor like a torrent of living smoke. Muzzles flashed in the sudden darkness, guns barking, stray shots plowing into the walls and blowing out a window. The gunmen were reduced to silhouettes, fumbling, flailing—then screaming.

The cloud was made of insects. Gnats, no bigger than a speck of soot, washing over the shooters' bodies by the thousands. The tens of thousands. Nessa stared, unable to look away, as one of the men flopped onto his back at the cloud's edge. His head poked out of the churning swarm, baring a skull stripped of its scalp, white bone gleaming, and a single lidless eye. His mouth hung open on a broken jaw, and gnats swarmed over his tongue, devouring the stringy meat.

In less than a minute, it was over. The living sandstorm gusted, whirling in the air like a fist of smoke, and swarmed back into the cask. The woman screwed the silver cap back on. She gave the soapstone cask an affectionate pat.

She and Nessa stood twenty feet apart, the remnants of a massacre between them.

"You going to stare all day, or do you want to get out of here? Name's Dora, by the way."

"Nessa," she replied, edging her way closer.

"I know. You've got an appointment with my coven sister in Vegas. And seeing as her pet gangster failed spectacularly, delivering you safe and sound just became my job. C'mon, there's a utility stairwell right around the corner."

Nessa followed her down the bare concrete steps, glancing

back over her shoulder. "I appreciate the help, but you're wasting your time—"

At the bottom, Dora held up one sharp hand. She put her ear near a bland, windowless door. Her amber eyes seemed to glow from within, like candlelight behind stained-glass windows.

"Shh. Wait. Listen."

Nessa fell silent. She heard the tromp of steel-toed boots, at least five men, running fast. They froze until the echoes crumbled to silence. Dora waited one more second, nodded to herself, and pulled open the door. They sprinted down an empty corridor lined with dark office doors and bulletin boards, took a left, then another, guided by Dora's intuition.

The next door opened onto hard sunlight and the arid heat of a desert morning. Nessa cupped a hand over her eyes, squinting, as they emerged into the fenced enclosure behind the building. Utility trucks gathered dust and baked in silence, scattered across the mostly empty lot. The hunters had left a sentry. His black Kevlar stretched over his potbelly and a rifle dangled on a strap over one shoulder, festooned with gadgets: a comically long banana-shaped magazine, two scopes stacked on top of one another, a pair of laser pointers, and gadgets she couldn't begin to guess at.

His sleepy eyes went wide and he fumbled with the rifle, struggling to bring it up as the cluster of gimmicks and toys caught on his overstuffed utility belt. Dora sighed as her free hand snaked into her jacket. She came out with a cheap little snub-nose .32 and shot him three times. Two copper-jacketed rounds plowed into his body armor, and the third smashed through his left cheekbone. He pitched to the asphalt on his ruined face and stayed there.

Dora barely lost a step, hustling across the lot. "Twenty pounds of tacticool bullshit on his gun, not one hour of training. That's a positive sign, you know. If they're calling out the scrubs, either they're running out of hired guns, or the really good hunters are starting to turn down your contract."

"Nyx is out front," Nessa said. "You want to call her a scrub?"

"To her face? Nah, some other time. I pick and choose my battles, which is a skill you might want to think about acquiring at some point. You've got work to do."

"I told you, you're wasting your time. Whatever you and your friend want, I can't help you. I don't have *time* to help you."

Their destination was a battered VW bug, faded cherry, with a crumpled back bumper and a windshield wiper held together with a twist of silver duct tape. The doors squawked. Dora jumped in and drummed her fingers on the steering wheel until Nessa got in on the passenger side.

"Trust me, at this point, shit's gonna go down fast. You could call this a point of critical mass." Dora gunned the engine and stomped on the gas, steering for the open gate in a dead sprint. "Everything's getting ready to change. Or blow up. Or burn down. In any case, we can't throw this party without you and your girlfriend."

Nessa squeezed the armrest. The VW jolted out onto the street, swerving left and barreling past the empty convoy out front. In the rearview, men were poking their heads out, pointing, running for their cars.

"Listen to me," Nessa said. "My knight is dead. I'm dying. Whatever you wanted from me, whatever you had planned—"

"She's alive."

The words froze on Nessa's tongue. She stared at Dora. She couldn't even blink, like she was afraid the slightest movement would shatter the promise of those two tiny words.

"Your girl's alive," Dora said. "She's out there, on her own, lost, and she needs you. Almost as bad as you need her. My sister can help you out. *If* you're on board for this, and if you're ready to throw down like you never have before. There's a fight coming, the fight to end all fights, and you're gonna have to bring every scrap of strength you can muster. It's going to cost everything you have. And then some. You ready for that?"

Nessa said the only thing she could say.

"Let's go."

FOUR

Three miles outside town, at the moment Nessa was claiming her first victim of the day, her father-in-law jerked to a stop in the back seat of a stretch Lincoln. Alton leaned against the leather-wrapped armrest, clinging to it like it might slow the gallop of his heartbeat. He had promised his chauffeur a fifty-dollar bonus if he could get them to Carson Airport in ten minutes or less, and the man had delivered in spades.

"Pay him," Alton said, giving Calypso a nod. "I'm not carrying any cash."

His "campaign manager," dark as midnight in a tailored linen suit the color of a sandy desert drift, arched one eyebrow.

"Bad etiquette, baby. You bet he couldn't make it on time, and you lost. Never expect another man to pay your gambling debts."

Alton shoved the door open and staggered out into the harsh, hot light of the desert morning. Calypso let out a barely audible sigh as he dipped his fingers into his breast pocket. He passed a hundred-dollar bill, crisply folded, through the driver's partition.

"Keep the change," Calypso told him.

He ambled out, following Alton onto the tarmac. The senator's private jet—a sleek white Dassault Falcon paid for with a mix of lobbyist money and campaign-fund overflow—was fueled up and ready to go. He hadn't skimped on the décor: the jet's interior was a span of snowy white with gold trim, seats done up in leather softer than a baby rabbit's fur, complete with a glass-enclosed minibar stocked with Rémy Martin and eighteen-year-old Glenlivet whiskey.

He didn't usually have a stewardess. Not that the woman in the emerald sheath dress, her skirt cut at a sharp angle like a hard-edged jewel, looked like she was part of the crew. She stood in the aisle, tossed her scarlet hair, and looked past Alton like he wasn't even there, locking eyes with Calypso.

"We need to talk," Caitlin said, her voice a cold Scottish burr.

"Right." Calypso put his hand on Alton's shoulder. "Go sit up front. Watch some cartoons. Grown-ups need to have a discussion."

Alton wasn't budging, trapped somewhere between confusion and anger.

"This is a private plane—"

Calypso's hand tightened, hard enough to shut him up.

"This," he murmured in Alton's ear, "is the right hand of the demon prince of the West Coast, baby. We're on her turf. And when the lady wants to talk, a smart man *listens*. Go up front. Sit down. Give us a minute."

The senator edged around Caitlin, making his way up the aisle. She watched him like an entomologist studying a dead bug. Then she swung her attention back to Calypso. She gestured to a pair of white-leather chairs, facing each other across a small tabletop.

"Shall we?"

"You know," he said, easing himself into the high-backed chair, "when a woman tells me we need to talk, that's usually the prelude to her walking out the door."

She took the other chair and primly folded her legs.

"I'm not here to give you material for a new song."

"Then I'm all aflutter with curiosity."

"You invoked the Order of Chainmen," she said, "and sent them after a pair of mortal women. Vanessa Roth and Marie Reinhart."

"I know, I know, I should have given you a courtesy call before they started tromping on your turf." He held up his open hands, placating her. "But it's infernal law, baby: the Chainmen hunt where they *want* to hunt. They don't have to respect princely jurisdiction. Plus, I've got Nyx heading up the particulars. Girl's a wild child, and not generally inclined to report in at regular intervals."

"I don't care about the hunt or the hunted. I'm more concerned with the side effects. Nyx and her people attacked the Bast Club in Chicago."

"Chicago ain't your problem, last time I looked at a map."

"Daniel, my human paramour, decided—for reasons beyond me, just like most of the things he does—to *involve* himself. He spirited Vanessa and Marie out of the club, right under Nyx's nose. You see the problem."

Calypso's manicured fingernails drummed on the lacquered table.

"Infernal law," he mused. "You interfere with the hunt, you *join* the hunt. On the wrong side. Your boy just brought a heap of trouble on his head. Until the job's done, he's any demon's meat."

Motes of copper gleamed in Caitlin's irises, swirling like burning ash on a hot desert wind.

"Which makes my problem," she said, "your problem. Because you and I both know that those women did nothing to invoke the Chainmen's wrath. According to every record I could dig up, every avenue of information, they never even *met* one of our kind before the night we started hounding them. How did you do it?"

Calypso shrugged. He glanced down, like he could escape her unblinking stare. "Been around as long as I have, people take your word for solid credit. Told 'em Vanessa had a contract with me and broke the deal, and Marie helped her run. That and a bankroll was all it took to get the ball rolling."

"You lied. You lied to the Order and filed a false writ."

His gaze dropped lower, down to his lap.

"You don't know what's at stake here."

"My lover's life," Caitlin replied. "Nyx already wants Daniel dead. Now she has an ironclad excuse to kill him. The law is the law. I can't stop her. I can't even retaliate. The only thing that can stay her hand is the end of the contract."

His nails rapped the table, sharp. He found some scrap of strength and used it to lift his chin, looking her in the eyes.

"I need those women dead and buried. So yes, I called in the Order. Face it, when it comes to putting people in the ground, they work faster than rat poison in your martini."

"Why?" Caitlin shot a hard look over her shoulder. Alton was on his phone, hunched low, muttering orders. "For Alton's petty little revenge? You know the consequences of filing a false writ. Why would you risk yourself like that?"

Calypso snorted and leaned back in his chair. "Hell with *his* revenge. His son was a disaster waiting to happen; if Vanessa and Marie hadn't done him in, I would have killed the boy myself sooner or later. That's not the revenge I'm worried about."

"The women. They're gunning for Alton's head."

"Wouldn't you?"

Caitlin pursed her scarlet lips, thinking it over.

"In a heartbeat," she said. "Have you considered giving it to them?"

"Can't do it."

"Can't, or won't?" She dropped her voice, leaning toward the table. "This entire situation is spiraling out of control. How long have we known each other?"

"Centuries," Calypso said.

"Centuries. And you were right, that night on the Chrysler Building: something is happening here. Something profound. History is about to change, change in a way we have never seen before, and it's far too late to stop it. The dominoes are falling, faster and faster. Stand in the way, you're going to get crushed."

"I'm just asking for a little more time."

"You're asking me to choose between our friendship and Daniel's life," Caitlin said. "Don't put me on that spot. You may not like the outcome."

Calypso jabbed a finger at Alton, on the far end of the motionless plane. "I banked everything on getting that man into the White House. Everything. I'm a bargainer, baby, this is what I do. You can't pull a bigger coup than this. Come Election Day, I'll be legendary. And to do that, I've got to keep him safe, sound, and scandal-free."

"You're already legendary in my book. And to be fair, Alton was already a politician when he sold you his soul."

"A failing one. Without me, he'd be lucky to be elected city dogcatcher at this point. But I have to take him all the way. If I don't, I'll be a laughingstock. All my credit, all my wins, all the stories about the Man of the Crossroads...gone." He waved a hand like he was shooing away a fly. "Just gone. I'll be busted, broke, and back at ground zero like a fledgling. A nobody. I'm too old to be a nobody."

"So you'll chase your pride straight off a cliff," Caitlin said.

"I just need a little more time. I can still pull off a win *and* get your boy off the hook, trust me. It'll make the story even better in the end." He paused, glancing out the porthole window. "People don't get it, what we're all about. It's not about conning mortals out of their souls. Hell, if I was about quantity, I'd just hang out a shingle on Fifth Avenue. So many humans chasing that next hit, that next high—money, sex, power—I could reap a dozen by lunchtime."

"It's about the legend," Caitlin said.

"Everybody knows the story about how Johnny bet his soul for a fiddle made of gold, and played the devil down. Fables. Legends, the kind that mortals never forget."

Caitlin held up a finger tipped with a blood-red nail. "Ah. A battle you lost, I recall."

"A battle I *threw*, and everybody downstairs knew it." Calypso flashed a smile. "Not remotely the same thing. That boy couldn't play the fiddle worth a good goddamn. See, nobody remembers the facts. Nobody knows. Nobody cares. How about Robert Johnson? Gave the world the Delta blues, a gift for all mankind. And what does the folklore say? Not that he was a natural talent or that he practiced until his fingers bled, no. They paint him as an artist who wanted the music so badly, *needed* it, aching with every beat of his heart, that he went down to the crossroads at midnight and struck himself a deal."

Caitlin didn't reply. She stared at him, her inhuman eyes still glittering, as if she could see down to the core of his being.

"What?" he said.

"I know you," she said. "There's a chip in your armor. A hitch in that old, polished swagger. You're trying to sell yourself on a bargain you don't entirely believe in. And I suspect I know what's worrying you."

"There's a legend unfolding before our very eyes," he said.

Caitlin nodded back over her shoulder, to the man with the blue suit and the American flag lapel pin.

"Not his," she said.

"I'm used to being the star of the show," Calypso said. "And I'm feeling, more and more with every passing hour, like a bit player. I saw something when I met Vanessa Roth. Something I couldn't define, couldn't understand. Something telling me I'd best get on the right side of this story. And now it's too damn late."

"How's that?" Caitlin asked.

He slid his jacket sleeve back and glanced at the golden watch on his wrist.

"Because right about now, I expect whatever's left of her is being buried out in the desert. The last domino fell this morning, baby, and it's shaped just like a tombstone."

Alton pushed up from his seat, ambling down the aisle toward them with his phone pressed to his cheek.

"Just...keep me updated," he snapped, then hung up. He shot a glare at Calypso. "I thought these people you hired were professionals."

"You may stand corrected," Caitlin murmured.

"That was the mayor's office on the phone. Your shooters turned a block of federal property into Swiss cheese, and Vanessa just walked out right under their noses," Alton said. "No sign of her, no body. Actually, no, plenty of bodies, just none of them *hers*."

"I should be going." Caitlin rose gracefully from the white leather chair and looked to Calypso. "Still time to change your mind. Don't squander it. By the by...just Vanessa? What about Marie?"

Alton scowled. "Dead, according to Vanessa. Good riddance."

"That doesn't make sense." Caitlin glanced between them. "No hunter's staked a claim, demanded their pay for taking her down?"

Calypso sank deeper into his chair. He steepled his fingers like a chess player pondering his next move.

"It's a combination contract. You take both their heads, or you get nothing." He frowned at the table. "And no hunter would bag one of them without making damn sure they were in a position to claim the other. We would have heard somebody bragging about it by now, at the least."

"You think Vanessa's lying?" Caitlin asked.

"I think," Calypso said, "the fate of this whole shindig hinges on one very important question: dead or alive, where *is* Marie Reinhart?"

FIVE

Miami—or at least the bizarre looking-glass Miami that Marie had found herself in, jettisoned across space and time in a shattered suit of armor—woke from the top on down. The first rays of dawn struggled to touch ground. They pushed broad gossamer fingers through a canopy of ash and bilious brown haze, the sun nothing but a pale smear of light rising above the impossibly tall skyscrapers. The spaghetti-soup tangle of the aerial roadways, suspended fifty stories above her head, painted the streets below in a twisted mask of shadows.

Marie had spent the night slumped in the doorway of a liquor store, shoulder pressed to a graffiti-shrouded metal shutter, her back against crumbling stone. The sound of trucks and cars rumbling high above stirred her from what little sleep she'd been able to snatch, a couple hours' reprieve at best. It was starting to rain. The sparse droplets felt hot and oily against her skin, leaving specks of wet soot behind, and an electric ozone stench clung to the humid air.

Her stomach was growling, but that was the least of her problems right now. Her armor, invented by this world's version of Ezra Talon, was a smoking, sparking ruin she'd abandoned in an alley four blocks away. The "return fail-safe" was just that: a one-way trip back to the suit's origin point, a world she'd never seen before.

Not in this lifetime anyway.

But she'd been here. The bum who took one look at her face and ran in a blind panic told her that much. So did the statue she'd found on the next block, a larger-than-life shrine in towering bronze depicting a woman with her face. An inscription laid down the law in stark, bold words:

Even in Death, She Watches Over You.

Even in Death, She Watches You.

OBEY.

Priority one, above getting her bearings, above filling her empty stomach and finding some painkillers for her stinging ribs and throbbing head, was getting out of sight. Whatever she'd done, whoever—whatever—she was to these people, she couldn't show her face in public. Marie pushed herself to her feet, biting back a fresh lance of pain that hit her chest like a whip. Her final battle with Scottie Pierce, or the ink-mutated monster Savannah Cross had turned him into, had left her with fresh cracks along her rib cage, a swarm of pulled muscles that jabbed at her like hornet stings with every move she made, and a tapestry of oil-paint bruises that smeared her skin from her breastbone to her left hip. Right now, just walking in a straight line was a challenge. She gritted her teeth and made it work.

At least Scottie was dead, one less threat to worry about. She couldn't say the same for Savannah. There was a good chance the mad sorcerer-scientist had drowned in the wreckage of Deep Six, but until she saw a corpse with her own eyes, Marie didn't dare count on it.

The canvas tote bag, covered in tiny craft mirrors and enchanted by Nessa's hand, still dangled at Marie's shoulder. It had accompanied her across two worlds now, unseen. That was the magic her lover had laid upon it: to go invisible and unnoticed. Marie took a quick inventory. She had Nessa's spell book—worthless to her, even if she hadn't discovered how dangerous the trapped text really was—and the ornate copper bell they'd taken from the cathedral beneath Deep Six, along with the sapphire shackles that had bound its dead guardian's wrists. Nothing she could use, nothing she needed. It just made her think of Nessa's face and feel a fresh ache, deeper than flesh and bone.

Nessa had made it out. Marie saw her there at the portal arch, arm stretched out, hand reaching for her—until the window shattered and the cold alien ocean swept Marie out into the dark, drowning her hopes. But Nessa had made it out. That, she could count on. Marie cupped the thought in her hand, like it was a glowing ember of warmth, and pressed it to the bruises over her heart.

"Out" didn't mean "safe." There were still hunters, human and inhuman, hot on their trail, and they wouldn't stop. And Nessa's life was still an hourglass with its sand almost gone. If Marie didn't make it back to their world in time...

She felt the hands of despair wrapping around her ankles like ropes tethered to wet sandbags, dragging at her every step. Her resolve was a sword. She sliced through the ropes with a single sharp thought: *no*. She'd come too far, fought too hard, to fail now.

Marie was the Knight. And the Knight found a way.

As above, so below. The streets at ground level grumbled to life, answering the echoing engines and rumbling, impossible ribbons of the skybound highway. Marie kept to the shadows, ducking into alcoves, head down and eyes hard. The pain kept her alert. Pedestrians were taking the sidewalks now in ones and twos, and cargo trucks—bigger than the ones on her world, tall and boxy with featureless steel sides and opaque windows—spat plumes of black smoke in their wake. Most of the people in the open huddled under umbrellas and wore surgical masks; it reminded Marie of a documentary she'd seen once about Tokyo in flu season. People crammed into close quarters had to work extra hard to keep disease from spreading, and the masks were a basic courtesy as well as a measure of self-protection.

The masks were common enough, down here, to become a fashion statement. A few were plain, white, disposable, but most bore a dazzling array of colors, patterns, even logos she didn't recognize. More importantly, they were ubiquitous enough that she could wear one without drawing a second glance—and cover half of her face, from her nose to her chin. In her life as a cop, she'd seen bank robbers get away with weaker disguises than that.

She ducked into an alley, letting a pack of pedestrians hustle on by, keeping her back turned and head bowed until they passed. The rain pattered down, leaving her scalp stinging as the hot, dirty droplets rolled down her tangled hair, leaving wet smudges on her shoulders.

On the far side of the street, a steel shutter rolled up and a neon light flickered to life behind rain-slicked glass. *Pharmacy*, it read, *Sundries, Scrips*. Marie waited until the coast was more or less clear, a red light on the corner holding back the traffic, and splashed through a puddle as she darted across the broken pavement. She shouldered the door open and got out of the rain.

If she squinted, the store could have been a bodega back home. It was about the size of a shoebox with dusty shelves offering everything from chips and candy to toiletries and over-the-counter medicine to a glass case displaying a dubious assortment of sandwiches shrouded in plastic wrap. The brands were all wrong, though. Along with a ubiquitous Triumph brand—generic versions of everything in the store with plain black type and unadorned white plastic packaging—Marie was lost in a world of Peppa Colas, rainbow-colored Cloudburst snack cakes, and cups of instant noodles with labels written, she was almost certain, in Sanskrit letters.

A small television set, perched on a bracket over the checkout counter, played a commercial under a wash of grainy static. Two young lovers ran hand-in-hand on a sunny beach, leaping in slow motion, while a voice-over spoke and fine print scrolled at the bottom of the screen.

"—the Center for Disease Management is anticipating another

WES-V outbreak this fall," the announcer said in a soft, reassuring voice, "and it is every citizen's duty to minimize the risk of infection. Meloproponin can lead the way. Ask your barber if Meloproponin is right for you. Don't take Meloproponin if you're pregnant, nursing—"

Marie turned her attention from the screen to the young woman behind the counter, who hadn't even glanced her way. The cashier—maybe twenty, with her violet hair greased into a crown of quills and black gauges stretching her earlobes—was focused on a plastic tablet in her hand. She poked her finger at animated gemstones, making them explode.

Marie glanced from her to the cardboard box on the counter, piled with mounds of surgical masks. *Stay healthy!* read a hand-lettered sign in black marker, *Masks 3.99 ea.*

There was no ethical way to do this. Marie wouldn't make it another block with her face in the open, and she didn't have any money that would spend on this world. She was going to have to take what she needed. She had never stolen anything in her life, and she didn't want to start now, but she didn't see an alternative. So...grab a mask and run? Try to slip one into her mirror bag, where it would disappear along with everything else inside the enchanted canvas? What was the least worst way to do something wrong?

She cleared her throat. "Excuse me," she said.

The girl looked up. Then she staggered back, eyes going wide. A rack of liquor bottles, single-serving sized, rattled against her shoulders. The tablet dropped from her open fingertips and clattered on the dirty linoleum.

"I'd tell you that I'm not who you think I am," Marie said, showing her open hands, "but I don't think you'd believe me. Look—I need one of those masks. Obviously. As soon as I figure out what you people use for money, and get some, I'll come back and pay you for it. I promise. Okay?"

The clerk's head gave a tiny, almost imperceptible nod. Her lips parted but no sound came out. Marie wished she'd just grabbed what she needed and run, never showing her face. *God*, she thought, *she's terrified. What did I DO to these people?*

She picked up a teal mask and slipped it on, elastic bands snug around the backs of her ears. A display of travel umbrellas, small enough to fit in a purse, drew her eye. She picked one up.

"I need some aspirin. Tylenol?" The clerk answered Marie with a look of petrified incomprehension. She tried again. "Painkillers. Something that won't make me sleepy."

For the first time, the young woman spoke up and pointed a trembling finger at the medicine rack. "E-Z-Go. The blue box, s-second shelf."

Marie grabbed two boxes and slipped them into the mirror bag. A fresh pang of hunger drew her eyes to the snack display. She looked for the cheapest thing on the wire racks and picked up a Triumph-brand chocolate bar.

"Are these good?" she asked.

"They're edible," the clerk said.

"I'll be back," Marie said. "I promise. I'll pay you back for all of this."

The clerk stepped closer to the counter, just long enough to tap a button on her cash register. It sprang open with a chime. She jumped back again.

"Take what you need," she said.

Marie tilted her head, glancing between her and the open till. "Are you sure?"

"Please," the clerk said, the word coming out in a strangled squeak.

She doesn't want me to come back, Marie realized. She dipped her hand into the till, snatching a few worn and wrinkled bills. She backed her way out of the shop, slow.

"I'm sorry about this," Marie told her. "I really am. You won't see me again, okay? I'm sorry."

Out on the street, the bottom of her face shrouded in the

thin cotton mask and the rest shadowed under the brim of her umbrella, she walked as fast as her wounds would let her. The city was bustling now, coming to life, and she found a measure of anonymity in the growing crowds. She moved with the flow of foot traffic, no destination in mind as she worked out her next move.

The street opened onto a canyon of stained concrete and onyx glass, the skyscrapers strobing with towering LED displays. It reminded her of Times Square. She found an alcove where she could stand out of the way and catch her breath. She tore open one of the boxes of E-Z-Go and wrestled with the childproof cap while she watched the morning news on a screen five stories high. Loudspeakers carried a jaunty synthesizer riff across the man-made canyon as a scarlet logo blazed the letters S U N.

"Good morning, Loyalist America!" chirped a perky blonde behind the anchor's desk. "I'm Petra Harpsichord—"

"And I'm Lawrence Fifteen," said her smiling partner. He wore a suit made of what looked like purple vinyl. "You're watching State Unlimited News, and we're here to bring you the caffeinated truth."

Marie tapped a couple of blue gel caps into her palm, added another for good measure, and slipped them under her mask. She winced, throat aching, as she dry-swallowed them one at a time. Then she tore open the wrapper on the Triumph bar and took a bite. The clerk's description, "edible," was about all she could say for it as she chewed on waxy, bitter chocolate and miserly slivers of peanut. Fine. All she needed, right now, was fuel to keep fighting.

"It's sweeps week," Petra said. "Is your favorite show riding the cancellation bubble? *Washington Heights*, *Sneaky Camera*, and *Sexy Nurses in Danger* are all up for renewal, so don't forget to tune in if you want more. Remember: every watcher is watched, and every screen is counted."

"Meanwhile," Lawrence said, "once again, TAG leads the way!

Talon Armaments Group has unveiled its new weapon in the war to rebuild and reclaim America."

Marie watched, gazing up at the towering screen, as the image shifted to an aerial view of a devastated cityscape. The circling camera captured shattered skyscrapers, flame-scorched streets, and rubble. Construction cranes dotted the skyline like beacons of hope in the debris, and at their heart stood a mammoth machine on four stout steel legs. Workers scurried like ants across its long, flat back, the deck a staging ground for building supplies, while vast mechanical arms lowered girders into place.

"TAG's new Slepneir construction mech, the brainchild of Ezra Talon himself, was deployed in the ruins of New Amsterdam yesterday. Block by block, street by street, we're bringing the city back to life. A government proclamation has commanded the deployment of twelve more Slepneirs by next Summer Solstice, meaning more hours on the production lines for loyal and hard-working citizens—"

The empty wrapper crumpled in Marie's hand as she swallowed down the last grainy mouthful. She was already on the move, eyes on the street, hunting for anything that looked like a taxi. One came trundling along between a pair of smoke-belching cargo trucks, thick wire cages over the windows and its yellow paint pitted by acid erosion. Marie stepped to the corner and held up one hand, hoping the gesture translated between parallel worlds.

The cab pulled over. She hopped in back, sliding on the rain-damp vinyl bench seat. The car smelled like cheap aftershave and cigar smoke.

"Where ya headed?" asked the cabbie.

"I need to go to Talon Armaments Group, or…wherever their local office is. Is it far?"

He stepped on the gas and hauled the wheel around, lurching away from the curb. "Nah, get you there in a jiff. You new in town?"

More new than she could say. She had a hundred questions about this place, but ninety percent of them would make her sound like an alien invader. *Which I sort of am*, she thought. But now she had a direction, and a mission. Ezra Talon had studied interdimensional technology. He'd even sent a care package to her own world's version of Ezra, ensuring the young man started off on the path to science and riches.

If anyone could send her home, he could.

"Just got in this morning," she said. "I've...got a job interview over at TAG. Engineering. I'm a little nervous, I guess."

The cabbie whistled. "Nice work, if you can get it. Off to see the wizard, huh?"

"Excuse me?"

"Ezra Talon. That's what everybody around here calls him. The guy's a recluse, has been for years, but the stuff that comes outta his head? Pure genius. He's gonna save us all." He paused a moment, his bloodshot eyes darting left and right, like he'd just belched in church and wasn't sure anyone had heard it. He quickly kissed his fingertips and touched them to the dirty sun visor. "Praise the Overlord. I mean, of course."

"Praise the Overlord," Marie echoed, settling back into a nervous silence.

Nessa's hourglass was running out. Recluse or not, Ezra was going to meet with Marie, and then he was going to send her home. She didn't plan to give him any choice in the matter.

SIX

A hot white spotlight swept across the desert flats, sending night creatures scurrying. Helicopter blades churned in a ceaseless war-drum beat as the corporate chopper—jet-black and emblazoned with the Talon Worldwide logo in glittering gold—slowly circled beneath a canopy of stars.

The light jerked to the left. Freezing in place on two weary figures down below. One hunched over against his cane, the other waving her arms to catch the pilot's attention.

The helicopter touched down. The side door rattled open and the two refugees clambered on board. They strapped in, pulling on headsets to talk over the noise as the chopper lifted off again.

The copilot's voice cut over the din with an electronic crackle. "Glad we found you, sir. It was a little touch and go there."

Ezra Talon—a world away from the incarnation Marie was hunting—clutched his silver-capped cane between his knees and cradled the raptor claw sweep of its ivory handle. His white whiskers twitched as he stared out the window, dour and silent.

Rosales, beside him, was already relaxed. Her inhumanly turquoise eyes studied the desert flats. They picked out tiny, luminous details in the dark—the endless dance of predators and prey—that Ezra's couldn't perceive. She stretched out her legs and got comfortable for the long flight home.

Escape had been easy. Nessa's ragged coven had shoved her and Ezra into a geodesic tent, down on the blood-soaked shore of Pyramid Lake, while they waited for their mistress to pass judgment. Nessa had taken off instead—literally—and thrown the whole camp into chaos. Rosales sliced a hole in the back of the tent and they slipped through the torn fabric, making their way to safety; their captors probably hadn't even noticed they were gone yet.

Rosales was a little put out by the whole ordeal, but not overmuch. She didn't do revenge. Generally it was too much work for too little satisfaction. She was a woman of simple tastes and took her pleasures where she found them: she ran, she hunted, she fucked, she killed, she ate. All the good things in life, and her place on Ezra's payroll ensured the good things would keep coming with minimal effort.

Except.

Except Ezra wasn't the only man who foolishly thought himself her master, and now she had to file a report with the other one. They'd found something, down in the ancient stone cathedral beneath Deep Six. A mummified corpse bound in sapphire chains, a remnant of a long-dead and alien race. An inscription on the sarcophagus called him the "first of the three faithful thrones" and threatened damnation upon anyone who disturbed his rest.

So of course Vanessa Roth plunged her hand into the creature's desiccated rib cage and plucked out a prize. An ornate copper bell, inscribed with runes in a forgotten tongue. The bell that *Rosales* was supposed to retrieve and bring back. And she'd let it slip right out from under her fingertips.

Pain in my ass, she thought. *This whole thing. Pain in my—*

She blinked, suddenly aware that somebody was talking to her. "Hmm?"

The voice of the chopper's copilot crackled in her ears. "I said, looks like you had a long night out there."

His cheap aftershave flooded the cabin and rankled her nose like curdled milk and gasoline. She knew from experience that it'd make his skin taste bad. For a second, she entertained the thought of tearing his throat out anyway, just for kicks. No. She didn't need Ezra more agitated than he already was. Old man would probably have an aneurysm, and then it'd be bye-bye to one of her two meal tickets.

She bared her teeth at the copilot in the least friendly smile she could muster. He turned around and minded his own business for the rest of the flight.

They landed on the rooftop of the Peregrine Building, Talon Worldwide's corporate headquarters. The executive elevator paused on the forty-third floor, the twenty-first, and the eighteenth, Ezra's small entourage growing with each stop. By the time they disembarked at subbasement two, seven more people walked in a pack along an ivory corridor lit with azure-blue piping: Bran—Ezra's wiry-bearded chief of engineering—and his six most trusted subordinates. Their plastic clean-room suits rustled as they marched, eyes forward, translucent helmets cradled in their arms.

The procession stopped at an oval vault door set into the wall, forged from titanium steel. A gridwork of green lines swept across the face of an electronic scanner just left of the door.

"At the risk of beatin' a dead horse," Bran said, the Irishman standing aside to give Ezra some space, "gotta tell you, boss, we'd get a lot more done if you'd let us work on the project when you *aren't* here to supervise. You don't need to have your hand in every second o' the day."

Ezra pressed his palm to the scanner. The lines strobed and swirled, and a crisp chime echoed down the antiseptic corridor. Unseen tumblers clanked into place. With a groan of pneumatic valves and gears, the vault door began to open.

"Pardon me if I prefer to keep our research on a short leash." Ezra shot a sharp glance over his bony shoulder. "I mean, we're *only* cracking holes in the fabric of the universe and tearing open gateways to alternate dimensions down here."

"Well," Bran said, "when you put it that way."

The vault door clanked to a stop. They stepped through the oval of steel and into a laboratory that looked like the command deck of a battleship. Mottled olive railings ran along ramps and raised platforms, while cold amber lights blinked from server racks in the shadows. Reel-to-reel tapes clicked, spinning behind shrouds of bulletproof glass, while automated pens scratched spidery readings onto spools of engineering paper. The technicians spread out, carefully stepping over fat hoses and extension cables as they took their stations, getting to work.

The fruit of their labor stood upon a rounded dais at the heart of the chamber, held up by a derrick and chains. Ezra clutched his cane in both hands as he stood in its shadow, gazing up like a man venerating a holy image. One of his former incarnations, in another world, had pioneered this project. His prototype had made its way across the wheel of worlds. Lost now, destroyed when Deep Six was swallowed by the ocean, but the research remained. Now it was Ezra's turn to perfect the design.

He'd dubbed it the Golden Saint, though the armored suit—segmented like an insect's carapace, gleaming plates set off by jet-black joints, strong enough to stop anything short of a fifty-caliber bullet—took on a copper shine under the hard laboratory lights. The rounded "halo" above the helmet, reflected in its onyx visor, wasn't just an aesthetic choice: it pulled in broadcast signals, battlefield telemetry, satellite transmissions, and navigation data.

Part of the breastplate and the coppery armor along one sleeve had been removed for maintenance. Beneath, a coat of sigils and runes carved with laser precision shone with faint violet light. Spells of warding and binding, designed to carve a channel between worlds and keep the suit—and its wearer—intact in the process. The Golden Saint was the perfect fusion of occult art and modern technology, a tool for exploration like none other. And a weapon of wars to come.

"She's beautiful, isn't she?"

Standing at Ezra's side, Rosales shrugged.

"It's all right," she said. "You need me for anything? I should get back to my office, start running background on Vanessa's 'coven.' I want to know who these people are, in case they decide to come gunning for you later."

He barely answered, just gave her a nod and a wave of his hand. He was distracted. She liked him when he was distracted.

Rosales's office was in the security wing up on the penthouse floor. She wasn't there much. Being that high in the air made her restless, nervous, and she kept the floor-to-ceiling windows shrouded under venetian blinds. Her empty bookcases and the kidney bend of her glass-topped desk stayed cloaked in shadow. Her turquoise eyes could see in the dark just fine, and on the rare occasions she had to deal with visitors, she liked how uncomfortable the cold and desolate office made them. She'd had the obligatory chairs for guests removed as a not-so-subtle message: she wasn't a fan of long meetings.

She slouched into the only chair left, hers, and booted up the desktop PC. Then she slotted a slim black USB stick and rattled off a quick chain of keystrokes. Programs embedded on the stick, custom-designed, wormed their way through Talon Worldwide's security and carved open a channel to the outside world without leaving a trace.

A ball-shaped webcam, clipped to the top of her monitor, woke with a soft green glow. Her screen popped open a video-chat window. She'd made the call. Her secret patron answered.

The man on the screen had a squat bald head, cauliflower ears, a boxer's nose, and cruel, wormy lips. He looked unfinished, like a crude bust formed from clay by an amateur sculptor. He didn't say anything.

"Good news and bad news," Rosales told him.

Adam, the master of the Network, held his silence. She hated this. And she knew that he knew she hated this. *Asshole*, she thought. He could probably read her thoughts, but she didn't care.

"You were right," she said. "One of those trinkets you've been looking for was hidden under Deep Six. The bell."

"And yet it isn't in my hands."

"Hey, shit went sideways, and you can blame yourself for that."

Adam arched one bushy eyebrow. "Oh?"

"I had the situation on lock, and then somebody crashed the party. Savannah Cross and some psycho covered in congealed black goo. Last I checked, Cross is on *your* payroll. For starters, she and her boy carved their way through Ezra's topside security force. Not that I care, but dead bodies make my life complicated. I agreed to pull this double-agent routine in exchange for one simple request: that you *not* make my life *complicated*."

Adam stared at her, nonplussed. "Tell me about the bell. Did Dr. Cross secure it?"

"Don't you know?" Rosales tilted her head. The tip of her nose twitched. "She hasn't reported in, has she? Your mad scientist is on the loose."

"Tell me about the bell."

"She didn't get her hands on it. Shit went sideways, fast, and Cross literally vanished in the middle of a beatdown. Vanessa Roth grabbed the bell and passed it to her girlfriend. Problem is, Deep Six is nothing but a bad memory: the station collapsed, and Reinhart got washed out to sea along with Cross's pet monster. Good news is I overheard a little something before I got Ezra out of there. The cop is alive. Not alive on *this* world, but alive. So the bell is still in play."

"I'll notify our agents. And Mr. Talon's progress?"

"On the Golden Saint?" Rosales held out her palm and waggled it from side to side. "Seventy, seventy-five percent done, if I understand the eggheads in the lab."

"Good. Continue to watch and report. We will step in when the project is complete and...take ownership."

"Explain that," Rosales said. "As far as I understand it, you Network guys—you're like the interdimensional Mafia, right?"

Adam's brow furrowed. "We are not petty criminals, Ms. Rosales. The Network is a holy order."

"Oh, so...ink? The drug epidemic you unleashed from coast to coast? That wasn't a criminal act?"

"We aren't *petty* criminals." He folded his fat, piston arms and shifted in his chair. "What of it?"

"Why do you need a suit of armor that can jump across worlds if you're already operating on a dozen different planets?"

"We can communicate across parallel Earths, sending targeted transmissions," he explained, "and move inanimate material. Anything more than that requires extraordinary sacrifice and resources. Or the aid of a Cutting Knife—and there are only nine of those in the entire universe. In any event, we can do it, but the cost rarely justifies the benefit. The ability to mass-produce a suit that allows simple, reliable, and streamlined travel would be invaluable to our cause. The savings in—"

He paused. His eyes darted right, studying something offscreen. One corner of his wormy lips twitched, unreadable.

"Excuse me. I believe we've just located the errant Dr. Cross. Stay on the line for a moment?"

"Whatever." Rosales slouched back in her chair and kicked her heel against the floor, spinning in a lazy circle. "You're paying me by the hour, and the meter is running."

SEVEN

Ezra's helicopter hadn't been the only one sweeping the desert, casting a searchlight along the edges of Pyramid Lake. Another, branded with a fake network-news logo and a Denver registration, had been honing in on a tracking signal.

Every executive inside the Network was fitted with a spinal chip. Ostensibly to rescue them in the event of an abduction, but no one was fooled. And when Savannah Cross's chip went offline shortly after it was implanted, Adam didn't even bother talking to her about it. The woman was a scientific genius and a magical prodigy; whatever tricks he used to keep her under his thumb, she'd just find a loophole. He was forced to resort to his least favorite tactic. Trust.

So when the chip suddenly sprang back to life after a year of dormancy, giving off a strong and clear signal from a spot about a hundred yards northwest of the ruins of Talon Worldwide's lakeside camp, there was no hesitation. Adam scrambled a rescue team, skilled shooters trained in everything from hostage recovery to close-quarters combat, and told them to be ready for anything.

With dawn still an hour away, a Maglite's beam strobed across the sand. A cloud of steam danced across the shaft of hard white light, curling like cigarette smoke.

"Jesus," the team lead breathed into his headset.

The chopper's pilot, hanging back and prepping for launch, asked a question in his ear: "You find Dr. Cross?"

They'd found her tracking chip. And her spine.

And almost a skeleton's worth of femurs, ribs, finger bones, scattered and jumbled in a bubbling pool of black tar. The rescue team slung their weapons and stared at the steaming puddle. It stank of sulfur, the rotten-egg stench slipping under the leader's visor and turning his stomach.

"Orders, Captain?" one of his men asked.

"Get a body bag," he said. "And a shovel."

"Captain? You can't be serious—"

"All of it. Scoop up all of it. The bones, the...whatever the hell that goo is. We can't leave it for some hiker to stumble across. We'll take it back to base. Adam will know what to do."

Which was how the remnants of Dr. Cross came to be zipped in a body bag and laid out on a stainless-steel slab in her own laboratory, black Mylar gleaming under the nightingale-blue lights. The doctor's work surrounded her, her formulas still etched upon long whiteboards, tanks and tubes piping fresh batches of the drug she'd dubbed "ink" as white-coated technicians worked to refine her formula. Her legacy.

Mr. Smith had been the first Network official on the scene. The bland man, in his bland gray suit, wanted a firsthand look at the remains. The lawyer wasn't qualified to render a medical opinion; he just wanted to make sure she was dead.

Adam's face loomed from a video wall. "You seem pleased," he said.

Mr. Smith primly adjusted his gray necktie. "I won't lie. The woman was a thorn in my side from day one. *Our* side, sir. We're better off without her."

"That remains to be seen. Though I did warn her about taking the power of magic too lightly. I suspected her ambition, while admirable, would devour her in the end."

One of the technicians slowly backpedaled, his eyes going wide. "Uh, Mr. Smith?"

The lawyer ignored him, focused on his opportunity to butter up the boss. "You are rarely wrong about these things, sir."

"Mr. Smith?" The voice rose an octave, turning into a strangled squeak. "You need to see this!"

Smith turned on his heel, then froze.

The zipper on the body bag slithered down, one slow tug at a time, drawn by a tether of black slime. The glossy plastic folds parted, and the thing inside sat up. It was a thin armature of a human body drawn in jagged lines of ink, dripping, drooling like blood on razor wire. The technician staggered back—then hurled himself to the laboratory floor as a liquid whip lashed through the air, smashing a tank of freshly processed ink. Shards of glass tumbled to the floor, crashing onto the man's huddled back, as the liquid drug latched onto the whip—and held there, suddenly turning gelatinous.

"That's...not good," Mr. Smith said. Adam watched safely from the screen at his back, silent and curious.

Another whip-tendril fractured a second tank. Gallons of ink pumped along the line, draining from the fractured glass like a milkshake being greedily sucked through a straw. The shape in the body bag took on figure and form as its mass grew, fed by the drugs.

One wet, shimmering foot touched down on the laboratory floor. Then another.

Savannah Cross's skeleton floated inside a rough parody of her human form, a body made of pure ink. Her eyeless skull bounced and leered with a death's-head grin from within the murky broth. Her blob arms lengthened, sprouting hands, then tendrils filled by her shattered finger bones. Wire-thin whips sprouted from her shoulders, hungrily lashing the air like a cat-of-nine-tails made from living oil.

She had no mouth, but her voice echoed through the laboratory, crisp and clear as a crystal bell.

"Mr. Smith. Adam. How lovely to see you again. Tell me, are you familiar with the story of Theseus's Paradox?"

Adam held a pensive silence. Smith could only manage a slow

shake of his head as she took a step toward him, leaving an ink-puddle footprint on the ivory tile.

"It's been attributed to Plato," she said. "I've always found it fascinating. It goes like this: the hero Theseus sailed his ship through many great and terrible battles. Its mast snapped in a storm, so he replaced it with a new one. Its bow was scorched black by enemy fire arrows, so he replaced that as well. Every splintered plank of the deck, every barnacle-ridden strip of wood beneath the waterline, was eventually torn away and rebuilt anew."

"I don't understand," Mr. Smith managed to say. He edged backward, his shoulders bumping against the video wall as she advanced on him.

"If the entire ship, every last piece of it, is eventually replaced with new material, is it still the ship of Theseus? The same ship he went to war on, back when he started? If the replacement happens steadily, slowly, over time, the materials renewed but the *nature* of the thing unchanged, would you even know the difference?"

She curled her oil-sheen fingers, brushing the bones that floated, disconnected and bobbing, inside the slimy blob of her chest.

"Now take the figure before you. Dr. Cross was the victim of an ill-timed and rash dimensional transition. Her brain was utterly destroyed. Her heart, her lungs, her nervous system, all annihilated. But slowly, steadily over time, she had been replacing her organic body with infusions of ink and using its alchemical powers to keep her alive. That ink slowly took on her memories, her thought processes, patching her damaged neurons and picking up the slack as her gray matter rotted away. Which brings us to this moment. Everything that made the original person who she is, is now gone. And yet here I stand. Show off that fine legal mind of yours, Mr. Smith, and tell me: am I Savannah Cross? How could you ever know for certain?"

His fingers fumbled with his tie. Behind Savannah, the technicians were scrambling for the door in a dead panic. Smith took a breath.

"I would say," he started, careful with his words, "that who a person is—emotionally, internally—doesn't really matter. What defines a person is what they do. The actions they take, and how they impact the world around them. So in your case, we would have to go by existing knowledge and see if you behave the way the former Dr. Cross would if she were in your current...situation."

"Diplomatically put," Savannah replied.

She swung her shoulder toward him, bending boneless and liquid, and a whip of ink sliced through the air. It coiled around his throat with a whiplash snap—and then a hollow cracking sound as his head violently jerked to one side and his neck broke in three places.

The whip uncoiled, slithering back into Savannah's body. Mr. Smith's corpse collapsed to the laboratory floor. Her grinning skull bobbed as she turned her eyeless face toward the video wall.

"There was no doubt in my mind," Adam told her. "For the record, that was unnecessary and excessive. But forgivable. Welcome back, Dr. Cross. Can I hope you'll be returning to your duties?"

She left black puddles on the tile as she strode toward the screen.

"I'm afraid not. Our interests are no longer mutual. You want Roth and Reinhart for petty revenge, because they burned your interests and offended your so-called kings. I want the power they contain. They are connected to the fabric of reality itself, the engine of creation. And now, so am I. You know, you chided me for not respecting magic. And I hate to admit it, but you were right. There's a universe of magic out there just waiting to be understood, to be tapped, to be mastered and devoured. And I want *all* of it."

"Reconsider," Adam warned her.

"Consider this my formal resignation," Savannah replied. "I'm afraid I can't give you two weeks' notice—rude, I know, terribly sorry—but you can keep my old research. I've progressed to a bigger and more important project. Now if you'll excuse me, I have science to do. Stay out of my way."

*   *   *

Adam sat in darkness, arms resting on his wingback leather chair, gazing at a bank of a dozen glowing screens. He punched a key. The laboratory feed died. Then he hauled a gooseneck microphone, vintage chrome like a relic from a 1940s radio show, closer to his frowning lips.

"Security. Send a kill squad over to lab one. Dr. Cross has mutated and gone rogue. Please send *expendable* troops; their guns won't hurt her, and she's probably going to tear them to pieces."

"Sir? Um…why are we sending them, then?"

"Because she's smart. And if I don't make a token effort to stop her from leaving, she'll be watching even harder for the surveillance team I'm sending to follow her. I'm also going to need a dummy surveillance team to cover for the real one and draw her attention. Again, expendables. They won't be coming back."

He didn't wait for the reply. A second keystroke opened a fresh feed. Rosales appeared on the screen, spinning in her office chair in slow circles with her head tilted back as she stared at the ceiling.

"In the midst of crisis," Adam said, "opportunity. For you."

She stopped spinning. "Didn't go too well, huh?"

"Dr. Cross is pursuing her own agenda, and Mr. Smith is dead."

Rosales shrugged. "So defrost another one. Not like that freak hasn't died on the job before."

"No time. I need you in the field."

"And I want to do this why, exactly?" She paused. "Before you threaten me with dire consequences, how about maybe don't, and save us both some time."

"I'll pay you."

"You already pay me."

"Vandemere Zoo, in upstate New York," Adam said.

That caught her interest. "What about it?"

"The Vandemere Lodge is dead—"

Rosales puffed air between her lips, blowing a half-hearted raspberry as she cut him off. "Poseurs. Not one of those guys actually had wolf blood. Bunch of wannabes offering lame-ass, no-risk sacrifices to the King of Wolves hoping he'd puff up their stock portfolios. It doesn't work that way."

"As they learned, to their great misfortune," Adam replied. "But the fact remains, their old killing grounds now lie vacant. And in need of a new owner."

"You're offering me a zoo?"

"I'm offering you a hunting preserve of your very own. Spacious, secure, remote from civilization—oh, and needless to say, owned by a shell company and it's yours completely tax-free. Do what you like with it. Turn it into a vacation spot. Open a petting zoo. Use it for a body dump. You're a resourceful woman."

Rosales drummed her fingers on her glass desktop.

"I might have a few days of vacation time coming," she said. "All right. I'm in. What do you want done, exactly?"

"We were already pursuing Reinhart and Roth for destroying our New York operations. That they crossed paths with the relic is...an opportunity. Find them. The bell is your top priority. Take it and bring it to me. If you can capture the women alive, do so and I'll throw in a sizable bonus. If that's not practical, kill them both."

"Oh, it's plenty practical. I'll start with Vanessa."

Adam lifted his chin, studying her through the feed. "I thought you said Ms. Reinhart had the bell?"

"And I know how those two think. I've smelled their pheromones. I already made a mistake once, taking one of their buddies hostage. Turns out Vanessa doesn't give two shits about anyone in the universe except for Marie, and that probably goes both ways. I get witch-girl on a leash, the cop will do anything I tell her to."

"Do you know where to start looking?"

"I know Vanessa took off, out to murder her father-in-law." Rosales shrugged. "No judgment. Everybody has a bucket list. Anyway, the good Senator Roth's in bed with the powers of hell. Normally I don't fuck with demons—that's exactly the kind of complicated I don't need in my life—but it *does* give me an idea or two."

"Get on it," Adam told her.

"Got another edge. Vanessa's running with a coven now. My best guess is she brought 'em in from a parallel Earth. Believe it or not, that's a point in my favor." Rosales tipped her chair back and raised her arms high above her head, arching her back while she stretched. "They're going to stick out like sore thumbs. Where can you hide a gang of witches from another planet without drawing attention?"

EIGHT

At that moment, there were countless places Daniel Faust would rather be. Brunch at the Metropolitan, enjoying a garlic-butter lobster omelet and a glass of champagne. His usual table at the Tiger's Garden, starting the day off right with tandoori chicken and a Bloody Mary. Sleeping with his girlfriend. Most of his daily ambitions boiled down to some combination of gourmet food, expensive alcohol, and sex, possibly at the same time. In any case, on the list of what he wanted to be doing, wrestling the stiff driver's wheel of a stolen school bus and trundling down the Vegas Strip didn't even make the top fifty.

His passengers mostly had their faces pressed to the windows. Vegas never really slept, and while it'd be a long, breath-stealing desert day before the sky went dark and the neon blazed, the Strip was still a sight to see. A medieval castle in dirty white concrete stood shoulder to shoulder with an Egyptian pyramid, its smoky glass face catching the morning sun and turning it into a white-hot beacon. Costumed buskers walked the packed sidewalks dressed as superheroes and cartoon characters, charging five bucks for a photograph, while jets of water performed a choreographed dance in a crystalline lake.

"I know," he said to no one in particular. "It's a little much, even for us natives. Just wait 'til sunset, you're really gonna lose your shit. But when you need protective camouflage, Vegas is the place to be. A metric ton of weird goes down around here and nobody bats an eyelash."

All but one, he knew by their coven names. Butterfly, Vole, Roach, Mantis, Badger. Gazelle, the long-legged and lanky woman up front, was some kind of aide-de-camp for the woman in charge. She'd gotten everyone changed into thrift-store clothes and bundled up their masks of intricate bone, carrying them in the Nike-swoosh-branded duffel bag that rode on her lap. Her crew could almost pass as ordinary solid citizens, instead of witches from another dimension. Daniel had to give them credit: for people who had just discovered the existence of electricity and indoor plumbing, not to mention TV, airplanes, and the Internet, they were coping pretty well.

The leader of the pack sat just behind Daniel's perch, off to his shoulder. They called her the Mouse, or the Dire Mother. Nessa called her Hedy. She had a heart-shaped face, the first traces of crow's-feet around her eyes, and a thousand-yard stare. Watching the scenery drift by, but her mind was somewhere else. Carson City, maybe.

At least one of his passengers was a local. Carolyn Saunders sat in the back of the bus, eyes on the notepad in her hand as she scribbled away with a ballpoint pen. She'd been writing for hours now, ever since they hit the road.

She's writing another fucking book, Daniel thought. *Great. Can't wait to read about what "Donatello Faustus" gets up to next.*

He knew better than to try to discourage her. Ever since she'd turned his stint behind bars into a pulp fantasy potboiler—portraying the confines of a privately owned prison as an evil wizard's fortress—her readers had been demanding more. He turned his attention back to Hedy. She looked like she needed something, some kind of reassurance. He wasn't sure he had any to give her, but he had to take a shot.

"She's probably all right," he told her.

Hedy shifted her gaze. Somewhere up ahead, a light flickered red, and the conga line of molasses-slow traffic ground to a stop. Daniel shoved his foot down on the brake.

"Everybody was talking about the 'flying woman' this morning," he said. "But we know where she landed and we know what she was out to do. Nothing on the radio about a dustup in Carson, much less a senator going dead or missing."

"You think she changed her mind?"

"I think she missed her shot," he said. "I guarantee Calypso hustled his boy out of there before she hit the city limits. Which I could have warned her would happen. Just like I explicitly told her not to do the thing she went and did. Flying on a fucking broomstick in public. Nice job."

"My mother does as she pleases," Hedy said, her voice dry. "I've known her in two incarnations now, and it's a reliable trait."

"This is a real problem for me. You get that, right? The number-one rule of the occult underground is that you don't pull the kind of thing Nessa just pulled. Ever. She's damn lucky people are already writing it off as a marketing stunt. All the same, there's going to be some pissed-off magicians looking to make sure she doesn't do it again. Possibly friends of mine. Former friends, if they find out I've been helping her."

"Bring the carriage to the side of the road, then," she said. "I'll take my coven and go. We won't inconvenience you any further."

Daniel stared at the distant traffic light, red glow shimmering in a heat mirage. He slapped a frustrated palm against the steering wheel.

"Regardless of what anyone might tell you, I'm not that big of an asshole. I'm not stranding you people on an alien planet. It's fine. I've got a plan. Sort of. First priority is to get you and your pals stashed someplace safe. Then I'll put out some feelers—very discreet feelers—and track Nessa down."

"Safe" was a subjective concept. He considered and discarded a baker's dozen of destinations before settling on the Flamenco. The resort was pure Vegas vintage, a slim tower of white and hot pink with a star-studded marquee that hadn't changed since the days of Sinatra and the Rat Pack. They abandoned the stolen bus in the dusty parking lot of a hot-wings restaurant next door, outside the sweep of a security camera. Daniel didn't plan on playing chauffeur again, and if he did, he'd find a cleaner ride.

The witches followed him like wide-eyed ducklings. Glass doors whisked open at their approach, and the lobby welcomed them with a gust of perfectly cooled air and the chime of slot machines. He left them to whisper on the tropical-patterned carpet, banana leaves in scarlet and green, while he laid down his credit card at the front desk.

He came back ten minutes later with a handful of pink plastic key cards in white paper sheaths. He spread them in his fingers like a poker hand.

"Ground rules," he said. "Two witches to a room, no premium movies, no freaky blood-sacrifice shit that's going to get you kicked out, and do not touch the minibar."

"Great," Hedy replied. "What's a minibar?"

"Where's mine?" Carolyn asked as he passed out the cards. Daniel arched an eyebrow at her.

"I figured you were going home on the next flight back to Illinois."

"My home. From which I was kidnapped by Ezra Talon's psycho bodyguard. The place where they know to look for me, and would no doubt try to abduct me again. Are you seeing a flaw in this plan, or do you just have a fetish for rescuing people?"

Daniel sighed. He dug his wallet out and looked back to the check-in desk.

"I'll be right back. And you, especially, stay out of the goddamn minibar."

"I just spent a week peeing in a prison cell with see-through walls, eating nothing but bologna sandwiches and cartons of lukewarm milk," she called after him. "If you think I'm not going to be shit-faced drunk within the next twenty minutes, you are *sadly* mistaken, young man."

The elevators were on the far side of the casino floor. Daniel and his entourage cut a path down the middle between aisles of flashing, whirring slot machines. It was too early for table action—cards and dice would have to wait for the afternoon rush—but early birds were already camping out at the penny slots with drinks in one hand and plastic tumblers for their tokens in the other.

"So this is a thing you people do for fun," Hedy said.

"Mostly people who are bad at probabilities. So, ah, in all the chaos last night it never really came up. Did Nessa have a plan for getting you and your people back home?"

"This is our home now."

Daniel rubbed the back of his neck. His muscles felt like knotted ropes under his skin.

"Suppose I can't blame you for wanting to stick around—"

"We will find my mother before the Shadow sickness takes her, we will find Marie, and we will reunite them." Hedy's lips pursed in a bitter line. "And if that fails, I'll return to my studies. So we can find their next incarnations and intercede sooner next time. We *will* get it right. Next time we'll get it right."

Gazelle put a hand on Hedy's shoulder. Carolyn just shook her head, trailing in their wake.

"I've been around this block more than a few times," she told them. "I'd love to tell you there's a way to get Nessa and Marie out of this mess, but the story is the story. It never changes."

Gazelle shot her a razor-edged glare. "If you don't have anything useful to say, no one will mind your silence."

The slots on Daniel's left went dead. In the heart of a casino, the sudden gulf of silence was more jarring than a bombshell. His head turned and he stared into a void: the slots weren't just quiet, they were gone, carved out of reality. Nothing but a pie-shaped wedge of tropical carpet remained, under lights that flickered and went dark.

"Hold up." He raised one open hand and the procession jolted to a halt, dead center in the cavernous room.

He glanced right, then left. The machines were back, trilling out their carnival-barker calls, as if nothing had happened.

"Mistress," Gazelle snapped. She pointed in the opposite direction, three o'clock on the dial. Another pie wedge of the room—machines, empty card tables, a few gamblers—flickered into nothingness. No one else seemed to notice. The farthest edge of the room, lights dead, was swallowed by shadows too thick to be real.

"Seems our enemies never rest," Hedy said. "Very well. Let them come. No mercy for fools."

She made three quick, sharp gestures with her left hand, a silent language the others understood. The witches scurried, forming a circle, shoulder to shoulder on the casino floor. Daniel shook his head, turning slow and taking it all in as another two wedges of the room vanished and a third flickered back again. Reality fractured all around them, struggling to hold itself together under an onslaught of silent magic.

"No, no, no," Daniel muttered, "we have *rules*. People do not *do* this shit in the middle of Las Vegas—"

The perfectly regulated air-conditioning buckled and broke like a shield under a barbarian's sword. Clammy heat washed over them, carrying the scent of fresh-tilled earth and distant spices. One of Daniel's shoes stood upon soft carpet. The other, rough stone.

Then the overheads all died at once and plunged them into pitch darkness. The last chime of the last slot machine stretched out, warbling like a note held for too long until it finally shattered into static.

Candles flickered to life. Dozens, then dozens more—votives, tea lights, stout pillars of melted white wax, winding around stalagmites and set out upon outcroppings of rusty red stone to cast a shifting yellow glow across a cavern floor.

At the heart of the light stood a small wrought-iron table bearing a china tea set. And there sat a woman in white, her face concealed behind a mourner's heavy veils, her fingers—too slender, too long, bending and twining like serpents—under opera gloves.

"Sister of the Noose!" Gazelle shouted. *"Kill it!"*

The clammy air erupted in a storm of curse-craft. Death magic took on shape and form, spat from a half dozen twisting tongues, and blazed across the cavern. The woman raised a languid hand, her boneless fingers bending into an arcane knot. A pearl of raw will, like a bubble of perfect glass, encased her. Bursts of violent purple light and living, raging glyphs shattered upon the glass and blasted into showers of sparks.

"Whoa, whoa!" Daniel shouted, waving his arms. "Cool it! She is *not* your enemy. I think. Shit. I hope. Just...let's all just calm the fuck down, okay? Just for a second?"

"A fine notion," the Mourner hissed. The opalescent shield rippled around her, then slowly faded away. "Your confusion is understandable. I did once belong to that less-than-august company. Unlike my dear sisters, the prospect of an eternity enslaved to the King of Rust did not appeal to me. I'd already given my eyes, my womb, and my heart in exchange for power. Those weren't too high a price to pay, but my freedom? That was a different matter. We share a common foe, you and I."

Hedy held her hand open out to her side, fingers spread. Easing her coven back as she squared her footing on the rough, sandy stone.

"We've heard of this 'king' the Sisters serve, but I thought it was just a myth."

"No myth," the Mourner said. "And if he is not the source of your woes, he is unquestionably a factor in them. But hold. I feel my coven sister approaching."

Shadows boiled on the far side of the cavern, then broke like a curtain of billowing steam. Two silhouettes emerged from the darkness. They took on form, then color, as they crossed the border of flickering candlelight.

"I brought the Owl," Dora said. She slapped her soapstone cask on the table next to the tea service. "Let's do this shit."

Hedy broke into a sprint, running across the cavern floor and leaping over a curling line of votive candles, pulling Nessa into a desperate hug. Nessa let out an awkward laugh that turned into a rasping cough, and cupped a hand over her mouth until it passed.

When she pulled it away, flecks of blood dotted her palm.

"She's alive," Hedy said. "Mother, she's—"

"I know." Nessa squeezed her hand. "I know. And if we can find her, I may have just enough time to say goodbye."

She kept Hedy's hand trapped in hers as she turned her gaze to the Mourner.

"As I told your friend, whatever it is you want from me, you're too late. I'm a dead woman walking."

"We are merely willing instruments," the Mourner hissed. "It was not we who called to you."

Nessa squinted at her. "Who, then?"

A gust of hot wind rippled through the cavern, making the candlelight dance. Somewhere in the muffled distance, down a twisting tunnel in the dark, came the braying of dogs.

"Our queen," the Mourner said. "She arrives anon."

NINE

Another breeze, hotter, faster, made the candles flicker. The open flames took on a sheen of dark color, like an oil-slick rainbow. Even as the flames grew, wicks trembling as the candle fires stretched tall, the circles of light around them began to shrink. The fiercer they burned, the less light they shed, until the candles were droplets of pale light floating in inky darkness.

A hush fell over the cavern, an abyss of silence, broken only by the faint tapping of high heels upon the ancient stone. A new figure sauntered forth from the shadows, a vision of the Jazz Age draped in a scarlet torch singer's gown. A wave of raven-black curls spilled across one tailored shoulder, and an antique key dangled from a chain at the hollow of her pale throat. Her head slowly turned and she locked eyes, just for a heartbeat, with everyone in the room one by one.

The Lady in Red's gaze came to rest upon Nessa's face.

The Mourner and Dora both inclined their heads, hands folded before them, in a gesture of quiet respect. Nessa lifted her chin a notch higher and crossed her arms, eyes sharp behind her glasses.

The Lady made her way between the spheres of light. Where she walked, some candles burned brighter, others flickered and died. She stood before Nessa and appraised her like a piece of fine art.

"You've got some color in those cheeks," she said. "Do you know what causes that?"

"Hot blood," Nessa replied.

"We've met several times before. You don't remember, but I could hardly forget. I've found your previous incarnations to be charmingly cunning, if stubborn. Ruthless. Inventively sadistic at times."

"Just wait until you see the brand-new me," Nessa told her. "I've got two days to live and only two items left on my to-do list: I'm going to find my lover, so I can say a proper goodbye, and then I'm going to kill an awful lot of people. Who are you?"

The Lady was silent for a moment, holding Nessa's gaze. Her voice went soft, just for the two of them.

"You know who I am," she said.

"You just said I don't remember meeting you."

"All witches know my name. Give it time. It'll come to you." The Lady waved a pale hand. "But that isn't important right now. Time is not a resource you have in great abundance, and while you've weathered every trial in your path so far—"

"You've been watching me," Nessa said.

"And, through my coven daughters, offering a bit of aid where it was needed. We engineered the means for you to receive Hedy's message, warning you of your true nature. And your curse."

"The black mirror," Nessa said. "*You* sent it to me. What about the rest? Someone posed as me and hid a tarot card at the Bast Club a year before Marie and I ever set foot in the place. We were able to use it to reach Hedy's world."

"And the *book*," Hedy said, acid-tongued as she moved to stand at Nessa's shoulder. "Spells laced with death traps. Was it you?"

"Don't play the fool," the Lady replied. "If I wanted your mistress dead, girl, she would *be* dead. No. Those gifts came from another hand. One that seeks to manipulate you into doing their bidding."

"You know who it is," Nessa said. A statement, not a question. "Tell me. Why all these theatrics, this subterfuge? Whatever it is you want from me, why not just come right out and say it in the first place?"

The Lady raised a manicured fingernail, scarlet paint matching the amused bow of her lips, and tapped her chin as she studied the woman before her.

"You needed to be tested. Tempered. Your dull edges made razor-sharp. That's the kind of lesson only hard experience can teach. If I sheltered you, coddled you, you never would have made it this far. Look back at the ordeals you've survived, Nessa. You were a timid, abused housewife, afraid of her own shadow. But you found the strength to fly free. You shattered your shell and broke your chains. You learned to spread your wings and blood your talons. Most importantly, you learned to trust yourself, and to trust your lover. You and Marie, together, are stronger than anything this paltry world can throw at you. I took no pleasure in watching you suffer...but I take great pleasure in watching you triumph."

Nessa's arms unfolded. She spread her hands at her sides. "So why show yourself now? Why end the game?"

The Lady in Red turned, strolling over to the wrought-iron table. She flashed a wicked smile.

"Oh, this game isn't nearly over. Not yet. But you've earned a gift. And with your knight lost, storm-tossed across the wheel of worlds, it's one you very much need right now."

With a nod from the Lady, Dora lifted the lid on the china teapot. Wafts of white steam gusted up, breaking like waves in the open air as they spiraled At her side, the Mourner's boneless fingers squirmed as they slid into her rags. She tugged out a kitchen knife. Then she held it out, over the open teapot, and let go.

The knife hung there, slowly turning, suspended weightless on a pedestal of steam. It wasn't much to look at. The blade was dull and pitted with rust. Cracks shot through the slender wooden handle, wound with a strip of black electrical tape to keep it from falling apart.

"Oh, hey," Daniel said. "It's the knife I nearly died trying to steal from a restaurant full of cannibals out in LA. Got my ass kicked on my way out. Got stabbed, too."

He paused, expectant. No one answered him.

"You're welcome," he added.

"This is a Cutting Knife," the Lady said to Nessa.

"Seems redundant," she replied. "A knife that can't cut isn't much of a knife at all."

"You are familiar with the Shadow In-Between. The primal well of power that exists between all things. Between all places and times. Between all worlds. Countless Earths, hanging suspended in that moonless and eternal midnight like pearls on a string." The Lady's scarlet fingernail trailed along the rusted blade, and it quivered in response. "A Cutting Knife can carve through the Shadow itself. And open a doorway to anywhere you want to go."

Hedy frowned at the knife. "I don't understand. My coven uses those. We have for generations. But they're useless if you haven't already been to the place you're trying to go. And they don't work across worlds. Believe me, Butterfly and Badger both *have* theirs. Cutting a doorway to our old covenstead, just to see if we could do it, was one of the first things we tried. Their knives are powerless here."

The Lady favored her with a faint smile.

"What you have are imitations, with only the faintest spark of the original Cutting Knives. I suspect that at some point in the distant past, one of your forebears came across the real thing and made an effort to recreate its magic. A spirited attempt, but one that fell short. This is an original. Only nine exist, and only nine ever will. Tell me, what do you know of the Kings of Man?"

Nessa glowered at the knife. "I know that my ex-husband and his 'lodge' gave their allegiance to something called the King of Wolves."

"And on our world," Hedy said, "we were plagued by the

Sisterhood of the Noose, and their devotion to the King of Rust. Two sides of the same coin?"

Daniel put his closed fist to his lips and cleared his throat. He stepped up, the rest of Hedy's coven watching in silence at his back. Carolyn was a quiet silhouette at the edge of a candlelight globe, pad open in her hand, her head bowed while she jotted feverish notes.

"Not a coin," Daniel said. "More like a pair of dice, and every way they land is a losing bet. The Kings of Wolves, Worms, Rust, Silence, Lament—I don't know the others' names. I do know that they're not human, and they're not demons, either. They're something else. And the Network is how they get shit done; it's half crime syndicate, half cult, with mortal agents doing their dirty work on a whole bunch of parallel worlds. Bad news, and they've got a knack for burying anyone who gets in their way."

The Lady's fingers slid along the knife's cracked and taped-up hilt. The blade gave off a low, throbbing hum, like the peal of a tuning fork.

"Once upon a time," the Lady said, "nine beasts dreamed themselves kings and carved out fiefdoms within the Shadow In-Between. They infested it. Corrupting the very essence of raw magic and bending it to suit their own warped souls. And those who called upon that power were, in turn, warped by it. They were—and are—an infection at the heart of creation. A living cancer. So nine of my strongest daughters—war witches, proud and true—set out to hunt and slay the nine Kings of Man."

"Considering the kings still live," Nessa said, "I don't imagine this tale ends with 'and they lived happily ever after.'"

"There was an ambush. My daughters were taken. Not slain, no. The kings instead chose a far crueler fate than death. They were *remade*, stripped of their voices, their bodies, their authority. Refashioned into new vessels that could be used, held, and commanded by any man who wished it. It was the greatest insult they could devise."

Nessa's lips parted. Her eyes widened behind her glasses as she pointed to the knife.

"You mean, that..."

"Is the witch Clytemnestra, my beloved daughter, lost to me for centuries. She has been trapped in this form, passed between lackeys of the kings, treated as a bargaining chip and a possession. Forced to employ her magic in the service of her worst enemies. Daniel did us a valuable boon, freeing her from her latest captor."

"But you're going to change her back now," Nessa said. Her voice went hard, unyielding as her feet on the cavern-floor stone. "You *are* going to set her free."

"Me? I'm not going to do anything at all."

The Lady in Red held out a graceful hand, beckoning Nessa to her side.

"You are. Now come closer, so you and my other wayward daughter can get a good look at each other."

TEN

Nessa approached the wrought-iron table warily, leaving the sanctuary of candlelight. The table had illumination of its own, a faint gossamer glow that boiled from the open teapot and raised shifting bands of silver upon the steam. It smelled of honey and strange spices.

The black electrical tape upon the hilt unwound on its own, one end swaying like a serpent's tail. Slowly it peeled free, twist after dirty twist, to fall away. The cracks along the hilt made faint sandpaper sounds as the wood began to mend. Fractures closed, a road map of disrepair drawn in reverse as flakes of dirt and rust rained down from the blade.

"You're healing her," Nessa breathed.

"She is healing herself," the Lady in Red replied.

Beneath the rust, beneath the wear of centuries, steel caught the candlelight and gleamed like a newborn sun. Hard, unyielding, and sharp enough to cut the skin of the world.

Nessa stood transfixed by the reflected light dazzling her eyes. She floated toward it, drifting off her feet, away from her flesh, and the knife loomed large in her vision. It turned, becoming a frozen beam of hard steel light. Nessa stood upon the beam. She wasn't alone.

A woman, dark-haired, long of face, in olive Grecian robes and leather sandals, stood before her.

"Clytemnestra," Nessa said.

"And you...in you I see a thousand names across as many lifetimes." She squinted like she could see them under Nessa's skin, written along her bones. "Shall I call you the Owl? It seems the name of which you're most fond."

"That would be fine, or Nessa will do. I think I'm supposed to set you free, but honestly, I'm not sure how."

"Hardly," she said. "Do you not have eyes to see? I've been free since I was delivered from captivity and returned to our queen's grace. The simple fact that I'm speaking to you is proof of that. I could abandon this cursed form anytime I please."

"Then why don't you?"

Clytemnestra gave a humorless chuckle.

"Because I spent one lifetime in a human body, and many, many more than that in my current form. One can become accustomed to the worst of conditions, given enough time."

"What I've always considered the folly of hell," Nessa replied. "After a thousand years in the lake of fire, you'd forget what not burning felt like."

"But your tormentor is more creative than that, isn't he?"

Nessa tilted her head, studying her in the steel-beam light. The world around them was a shifting gray void, pale lights strobing in the distance like a smog-shrouded aurora borealis.

"What do you know about me?" Nessa asked.

"That you and your lover are condemned. That this is either a natural and inescapable consequence of your creation or a curse that's been inflicted upon you, depending on who you talk to and what tales you believe. I know you've been tricked this time around, infected with a fatal illness, and your time is fast running out." Clytemnestra offered a demure shrug. "Our queen favored me with two gifts. One is the gift of prophecy. I see many things, some clear and strong, some through a glass darkly."

"What is your other gift?" Nessa asked.

Clytemnestra held her gaze.

"Poison," she replied.

"A valuable skill for any witch. So if I'm not supposed to heal you or free you, what am I doing here?"

The woman closed the gap between them. She took Nessa's hands in hers.

"I haven't had a voice in so long," she said. "Will you hear me?"

"I'm listening," Nessa told her.

"I can carve through the doors of reality. Blaze a trail across the wheel of worlds, a path to your knight. Among other talents. I can aid you in your ambitions. And I think that you could help me with mine."

"Which are?"

"First," Clytemnestra said, "you need to understand. To see what I've seen. To feel what I've felt. It's the only way we can be truly bound together, to amplify one another's—"

Nessa cut her off. "Yes, yes. But you *can* take me to Marie? You can help me save her?"

"I can. But this is nothing to take lightly. There will be pain. More than most could endure."

One corner of Nessa's mouth curled in a bitter smile.

"Don't confuse my quick decision for rashness," she said. "My hourglass is running out as we speak, and being bloody, bold, and resolute is the only way I can get anything *done*. You have the power to help me save Marie. I want it. I'll pay your price."

Clytemnestra seemed almost regretful as she extended one gentle hand.

"Then join me. Enter me. And understand."

Nessa took her hand. The steel beam under their feet turned to a pool of molten metal. Breath gusted from her lungs as she dropped, and the liquid swallowed her whole.

*   *   *

Nessa was (*not Nessa*) freezing, exposed, strapped by unyielding bands to a slab of metal. Rust flakes scoured her naked shoulders as she tried to squirm free. Her vision was a faded smear, distant pin lights stretched to gauzy yellow strips. Blurry figures shambled around her, elephantine and hunchbacked under ragged gray coats. Someone, someone she knew, someone she loved, was whimpering in the dark.

She flexed her bound wrists. Couldn't move. Couldn't help. Couldn't do anything but wait for her turn.

Failure swept over her like waves thundering down on a stormy beach, washing away the sand. She had failed her sisters. She had failed their queen. Words echoed in her mind. Her thoughts, but Clytemnestra's voice.

Purge the kings. Purify the Shadow In-Between. It was my idea. My sisters weren't certain. I cajoled them, pushed them, argued their fears away until they agreed to join my crusade.

"It was my fault," Nessa whispered. A rusted iron band fixed her neck to the table, holding her head in place. She felt it squeeze her throat as she struggled to breathe.

I led them into the ambush. We were taken alive. My fault. What happened to them was my fault.

A high-pitched mechanical squeal, the whine of a dentist's drill, echoed through the blurry darkness. Then a woman's scream. Shrill, louder than the drill itself, going on and on until her breath gave out. Nessa's heart shattered.

Circe, Clytemnestra thought. Nessa's hands twisted, fingernails digging against the unyielding slab, shards of rust stabbing under her broken fingernails. *Circe, my love. I'm sorry, I'm sorry, I'm sorry—*

Crude voices grunted in the dark. Laughing. They were laughing. And the pain and grief and loathing, the tempest in Nessa's broken heart, began its slow transformation into a feeling she knew all too well. Rage.

Do you understand? We were the Lady's first daughters. Magic was our life's breath, our wine and bread. The kings did more than occupy the Shadow. They corrupted it. Turned it toxic. Poisonous. I had to act. I had to do something—

Clytemnestra's desperate thoughts broke against another wail in the dark, her sister, her first love, ending on a ragged torrent of tears. Wheels scraped against a filthy tile floor. One of the hunched figures swayed as it shoved a cart alongside her slab. It had been positioned so Nessa could see the instruments upon it. The drills, the pincers, the scalpels, all caked with blood and dirt. Other tools, ones she couldn't guess at, shimmered with blood-red runes and the promise of cruel magic.

It was her turn.

A presence loomed, glowing white-hot at the edge of her blurred vision. A hand with three long fingers, skin luminous, the air crackling around it. The fingertips traced Nessa's cheek, the curve of her chin. Then they slid downward. Trailing between the valley of her breasts, down to her stomach.

"This one," a voice said, ethereal as its glowing hand. "Has this one been claimed yet? Have my brothers spoken?"

The huddled figure answered with a phlegmatic grunt.

"Then this one shall be mine. Begin the treatment."

The figure's hand, sheathed in a moth-eaten glove, lifted a pair of corroded pincers. Nessa took the deepest breath she could manage, with Clytemnestra's words on the tip of her tongue. She was going to defy him, curse him, swear that she would see him dead—

—then the three-fingered hand fell upon her face. And she shrieked into his palm as the flesh of her lips began to melt, running like candle wax. He took her mouth away, leaving a blob of twisted scar tissue and her breath, her rage, her words, her truth, trapped inside of her chest forever.

"You have nothing to say," the voice calmly told her. "You are an object."

The pincer closed on the flesh of her hip, scarlet runes flaring under a crust of dried blood as it twisted in the hooded figure's grip, pulling at her flesh. The voice only said one more thing as the luminous hand pulled away.

"Reshape it," he said, "and educate it."

Then her skin tore, a ragged wet line welling up and drooling onto the rusted iron slab, and white-hot agony burned her thoughts away. There was nothing left of her but a scream, a scream she couldn't let out.

She lost her hands. Her arms. Her legs. Her face. Everything peeled and scoured and drilled and sawed away as a barbed net of alchemy transformed what remained from gristle and bone to wood and metal. Her magic, the gifts of her queen raged inside of her, no longer hers to control.

A calloused hand squeezed her hilt. A thumb caressed her body. She saw a woman running, recognized her. Another daughter of the Lady in Red.

Her magic crackled free, the tip of her blade flaring. A bolt of occult lightning blasted a hole in the woman's back.

She cut ragged holes in the fabric of the universe, making doorways between worlds. Openings for monsters, for assassins, for the servants of the kings.

Her blade sawed through human meat. Sometimes dead. Sometimes alive and screaming. They used her power to preserve their victims' lives, to keep them awake, suffering, begging for death. She was an accomplice in every crime. And as she was passed from hand to hand in a whirlwind of endless depravity, the faces of the fallen burning into her trapped and helpless mind, she had one constant companion: the scream she could never let out.

*   *   *

Nessa knelt upon the beam of steel, in the hazy world of flickering gray smog, back inside herself. She clutched at her arms, shuddering. Her eyes were wide, cheeks wet, mouth dangling open as the pieces of her mind fell back together like a mirror shattering in reverse. Still broken, still fractured into razor-edged shards.

Clytemnestra's hand rested upon her shoulder.

"You hear me now," she said.

Nessa swallowed hard, throat sore, searching for words. Language came back to her in fits and starts.

"I understand," Nessa rasped. "I saw—I *felt*—"

Clytemnestra's hand tightened. "And as you walked through the hours of my pain, I walked through yours. You listened, and you understand. Now we are in true rapport. Our magic can work as one, a whole greater than its parts. Now we can form a pact, if you wish it."

Nessa ran the back of her hand across her mouth. It came away sticky with spit. She shoved herself to her feet and stood on wobbly legs.

"You haven't told me what you want in return for your help," Nessa said. "And you know I'm dying, right? Can you cure my illness? If not, this will be a short-lived bargain."

"That power is beyond me, I'm afraid. But..."

The faintest smile quirked on Clytemnestra's lips, lighting her amber eyes.

"I told you my particular gifts. I am an accomplished mistress of poisons."

"A worthy skill," Nessa said, "but I don't see how that helps either of us."

"I think you'll find that our ambitions are actually one and the same. Would you like to learn a secret?"

Nessa's faint, sly smile mirrored Clytemnestra's. She lifted her chin, just a bit.

"Always," Nessa replied.

Clytemnestra opened her arms and embraced her. Pulling her close, softly. She brushed aside Nessa's hair and bent her head, putting her lips to Nessa's ear.

Then, with their hearts beating as one, she whispered the secret of poison.

INTERLUDE

"Well?" the interrogator asked. "What was it?"

He and Carolyn had been standing in the viewing gallery while she continued her tale. They gazed out through the long windows and into the endless inky depths of the Shadow In-Between. Another flagship had joined the two hovering alongside the starboard bow. This one was a winter galleon, its worm-eaten beams sheathed in arctic ice, ragged canvas sails coated with unmelting snow.

The Kings of Man were gathering.

"What was what?" Carolyn asked, all innocence. She cradled her glass of water between her cuffed hands.

He turned toward her, impatient. "The *secret*. Obviously. What did the knife tell her?"

"You mean the woman. Her name was Clytemnestra."

He rolled his eyes and flicked his fingers at her. "What did she say?"

Carolyn shrugged. "I wasn't there."

"Seriously," he said.

"Seriously," she replied. "You can tell when I'm lying. We've established that to your satisfaction, yes?"

"Yes. And?"

"And when I say I wasn't there, I wasn't there. You know that I had to recreate most of this story—all the moments I wasn't personally present to witness—in the aftermath. I can only share the details I was able to dig up. And considering how many facts I've managed to piece together, I think I've done a damn good job so far."

"But you *were* there," he said. "You were in the cavern with the others."

"Everything that passed between the two of them, their communion, it was over like that." Carolyn snapped her fingers. "From our perspective, Nessa reached her hand out, she touched Clytemnestra's blade...and then in a blink, it was finished. I only know what happened, their little mental tête-à-tête, from talking to Nessa after the fact."

"So you don't know what the secret was."

"I wasn't there," Carolyn said.

"You know, the only reason you're still alive is because we need answers. If you can't assemble the missing pieces, we don't have much reason to—" The interrogator froze. He put a finger to his earpiece. "Yes, my lord. We'll be right there."

Then he snorted and nodded toward the end of the windowed gallery.

"The King of Rust is ready to see you now. You may regret getting what you asked for. I think you'll find that I was a much easier audience, and far more tolerant of your...quirks, than *he* will be."

Carolyn squeezed her glass tight, fighting off a tremor in her hands. She took a breath and pushed her shoulders back.

"We'll see," she said. "I'm told I can be charming when I make an effort."

ELEVEN

Razor-edged steel flashed, held high in Nessa's hand as she returned to her body. The blade caught a dozen points of candlelight and threw them back, stronger and brighter, lighting the rust-red cavern in a vibrant glow. The wooden hilt felt like living flesh against Nessa's palm, flesh over a beating heart.

Clytemnestra stood at her side. Her body was translucent, crystalline and ocean blue, a projection for all to see. Her voice emanated from the open air, thrumming off the ancient stone.

"Our pact is struck," she said. "We are in accordance."

"We are," Nessa agreed. "And we have work to do. Hedy."

Hedy stepped forward, Gazelle at her side. "Mother?"

"We're going to carve a tiny hole in the fabric of reality. Then we're going to go get my knight. Then we're going to wash our hands in the blood of anyone and everyone who ever crossed us. Do I have your coven's support?"

"Your coven," Hedy replied.

"No." Nessa held her gaze, her eyes grave. She waved a hand, taking in Hedy's followers as they watched in reverent silence. "I told you before, I didn't come to replace you or to take away what you worked so hard to build. The Pallid Masque is *your* coven now. So I'm not commanding you to aid me. I'm asking for your help."

One of Hedy's witches, a sallow-cheeked woman who called herself the Mantis, spoke up. "And we're saying you have it."

The others murmured their assent. No argument.

"Don't misunderstand, I have no plans of stepping aside," Hedy added. "But by right of seniority, by right of coven lineage, you are still the Dire Mother. Admittedly, the rules weren't written to take reincarnation into account, but I feel safe in making a judgment call. Where you lead, we will follow."

Nessa nodded, sharp. "Good. Make yourselves ready for travel. Daniel—"

He eased back a step, the sole of his Italian loafer sliding on the worn stone. A gust of humid air whispered through the cavern and made the candles dance.

"Actually, I have plans tonight," he said.

"You certainly do," Nessa said, suddenly smiling, suspiciously agreeable. Then her smile vanished. "Your plans for tonight are to obey me without question. We're going to need resources. Funding. Precious metals. Possibly weapons."

"Aren't you rich? I thought you were rich."

"My husband was wealthy. We don't exactly have time to wait for the reading of his will, and as long as I'm a fugitive, I can't show my face in a bank. Also, we need your local contacts. Access to a secure and private ritual site."

"Outdoors," Clytemnestra's shimmering projection chimed in. "Finding a pathway is easier under the open sky. Elevated is better, too."

"Outdoors is easy. Elevated? You noticed we're in the middle of a desert, right?" Both women stared at him, silent. Daniel showed them his open palms. "Fine. I'll see what I can do."

"We'll need something of Marie's, to find her across the wheel of worlds," Clytemnestra said. "Blood is best."

"I had a few drops, but I used them up back at Pyramid Lake," Hedy told her. "That's how I figured out she's still out there."

"Something personal, then. Intensely personal. Something she treasures, close to her heart."

"Easily done. Leave that to me." Nessa looked back to Daniel and held up a finger. "One other thing. I understand you have certain influence with the powers of hell."

"Told you back at the Bast Club, I can't get the bounty called off. Once it's in play, it stays in play."

"No," Nessa said, "but you have avenues of intelligence, yes? Useful information?"

"Well, I don't mean to brag, but I *am* kind of a big deal in the infernal courts. I'm in tight with the right-hand woman of a demon prince."

Behind him, Carolyn put her hand to her mouth. She proceeded to let out a delicate string of fake coughs, softly muttering between them: *"He's sleeping with her."*

"You know what?" Daniel said. "I really don't like you when you're sober."

"Do something about it," Carolyn shot back.

"My main concern is that we won't be interrupted," Nessa said. "I'm hoping we lost Nyx and her friends back in Carson City—and encouraged a few of them to consider early retirement in the process—but we're leaving too much up to chance as it is. Can you place tabs on them?"

"I'll see what I can do," he replied.

"Good. Carolyn, as the eternal Scribe, your job is to do exactly that. Follow at a safe distance, watch, listen, and record every detail. There's a very good chance that you'll have to tell this story after I'm gone. I want it told properly."

"Oh, good," Carolyn said. "I was going to do that anyway, and I'm way too old for sneaking around and pulling Nancy Drew crap."

To Nessa's left, Dora and the Mourner sat side by side at the wrought-iron table. Dora's lethal cask sat out, securely capped and silent, beside the china tea service. Dora poured for the two of them, and the Mourner's gloved fingers snaked around the delicate white curve of her teacup. The cup vanished under her veils. As Nessa looked their way, Dora leaned back and shook her head.

"Uh-uh." Dora sipped her tea. "You don't give orders in this corner of the room."

"Actually," Nessa started to say. She clenched her hands in front of her, shifting from foot to foot. "Actually, I wanted to thank you. It's not...easy for me to admit weakness, but I don't think I would have made it out of Carson City without your help."

"Duh. So, you too proud to take advice?"

"Not today," Nessa said.

"You've got passion, and passion is good. Passion makes shit happen. What you had in Carson City, though? That was desperation. Not the same thing. Look around. Life is chaos, right?"

"Unquestionably."

Dora set down her cup and reached for the teapot.

"Most people go their whole lives like a loose sock in the dryer. Tossed around, flipped upside down and sideways. They don't act, they react, never in control. This path of ours, though? Being a witch is all about calling bullshit on that and *taking* control. You lose your head and go off half-cocked on some death-or-glory rampage, that's when the chaos wins."

"I see that now," Nessa said. "I came to the edge of losing everything, letting the Shadow swallow me whole for the sake of petty revenge. And it wouldn't have saved Marie or served my ambitions. I'm better than that."

Dora lifted her teacup. "Damn straight."

At her side, the Mourner's breath made her faded lace veils shiver.

"My sister is correct," she hissed, "as she often is."

Dora gave her the side-eye. "Often?"

"You have more freedom than you think," the Mourner added. "The first storyteller cast you in this role. Authored your existence and your doom at the same time. But there are as many ways to be a witch as there are witches. And with every life, every reincarnation, you are free to reinvent yourself. What kind of witch are you this time around, I wonder? Are you letting this world define you, or have you made a choice?"

Nessa thought about that for a moment. Her mind drifted back across the journey, back to her earliest hours with her book in hand, sewing poppets, filling mason jars with iron nails and spit and menstrual blood. Baby steps. She remembered her fumbling attempts at magic on the edge of Inwood Hill Park, a tiny spot of primeval wild in Manhattan. She'd conjured there, a timid doe emerging from the wood to tease her with the promise of enlightenment before dashing off, again and again.

She'd found enlightenment, all right.

She had found it in betrayal, in the poison that her "doctor" fed her and the poison her husband poured in her ear. She found it at her own breaking point, the moment when her timidity and fear shattered on the anvil of her fury, and she decided she wasn't going to take it anymore. The moment when the phantom doe died on the edge of her blade and her true guide, the Owl, swooped down to land upon her outstretched and blood-soaked arm.

Fury alone wouldn't have brought her this far, though. Fury had limits, and it could leave her blind. Her magic, powerful as it was, wouldn't win the night without focus and intuition to guide it. Nessa had a fresh spark of hope, but to kindle it into a flame she would need to rise above the forces in her way. To be smarter, faster, more cunning, more ruthless, willing to do what her enemies wouldn't and go where they feared to tread.

The sarcophagus under Deep Six had threatened damnation upon anyone who disturbed it. She hadn't hesitated to reach inside. And why not? Anyone who wanted to damn her would have to get in line.

She had two days left. Two days to save Marie's life. Two days to shake the heavens and make the universe remember their names.

A tiny smile rose to her lips.

"What kind of witch am I?" Nessa said. "The unrepentantly wicked kind."

A slithering chuckle drifted from under the Mourner's veils.

"Then do not hesitate," said the Lady in Red. She favored Nessa with a smoky-eyed glance and a lift of her pale chin. She nodded at Clytemnestra. "You've earned yourself a suitable weapon, Nessa. When the time comes to strike, strike without mercy."

Something about the Lady set the cavern to spinning. Her jasmine perfume wrapped an invisible and silken tether around Nessa's throat, dragging her off her feet. *I know you*, she thought. *Where do I know you from?*

The Lady's voice echoed inside Nessa's mind: *A daughter knows her mother's face.*

"Will I see you again?" Nessa asked aloud.

"When the work is done, on the far side of the coming storm. Your education is not yet complete. I've given you what aid I can; the rest is in your hands."

Hedy's witches were clustered behind her, whispering, nudging Nessa's apprentice. "*Ask her,*" one said. Hedy took a deep breath.

"Mother? We have a request. A…it's a tradition, really, for the Pallid Masque. I know you don't remember, but it's important to us."

Nessa turned to regard her. Her coven clustered around, wide-eyed, their anticipation electric.

"Of course," Nessa said. "What is it?"

"A question. One we've been asking for generations, and generations before that. It's…a blessing, sort of, or maybe a ritual for good fortune. But it's the question that guides our coven's purpose, and I—we—need to hear your answer. Your truthful answer, from your heart. Please."

Nessa put her hands on her hips. "Very well. Ask your question."

"Dire Mother," Hedy said, "will you lead us to Wisdom's Grave?"

Nessa didn't hesitate. She had decided who she was and what she wanted. That meant there was only one answer, and in a breath, she committed to it.

"Yes," she replied. "I will."

*   *   *

Janine Bromowitz didn't know the meaning of surrender. She did, however, know the meaning of running out of vacation days. Her supervisor had been burning up her phone all morning, wanting to know if and when she was coming back to work. Her scheduled shift had started at nine. Considering she was holing up in a Travelodge in downtown Chicago, eight hundred miles from the library, she wasn't going to make it in. Tomorrow, then? She'd see what she could do.

She tossed her rolling suitcase into the back of their rented SUV, the front bumper crumpled like a wad of chewed-up bubblegum. Tony Fisher, her impromptu road-trip partner, wasn't happy about letting her drive after their little "incident" out in New Jersey but with his arm in a sling, still healing from a bullet, he didn't have much of a choice.

"Technically I don't *need* my job," she told him. She eased his overstuffed duffel bag off his shoulder, black nylon with an NYPD crest, and loaded it in back. "I mean, without a roommate I'm going to lose the apartment in a couple of months anyway, so realistically, staying out here and finding Marie should still be my first priority."

Tony shook his head at her, somewhere between exasperation and sympathy.

"C'mon," he said. "We gotta be real about this. Wherever she is, you getting fired isn't going to bring Marie home any faster. We tracked her this far, but a dead end is a dead end. It's time to pack it in."

"We know where she is. She's in Nevada."

Janine brandished her phone at him, cued up to a single frozen frame on a YouTube video. A gauzy black blur hurtled through a cloudless sky.

"You saw the footage. It's Vanessa Roth, Tony. It's Vanessa Roth *flying on a freakin' broom.*"

"Okay, no. First of all, you can't even make her face out. Second of all, that's fake as hell." Tony countered with his own phone. "Did you read this? Brooms-don't-fly-dot-com. Guy breaks down the video frame by frame. It's totally CGI. You can see the pixels."

Janine sighed. "On a website that was bought, registered, and went up an hour after the initial footage. You know what that sounds like?"

"Healthy skepticism?"

"A cover-up."

"There are twelve other websites saying the same thing," he replied.

"A massive cover-up. You know who does that, Tony? The Illuminati."

He squeezed his eyes shut and pinched the bridge of his nose. "Please do not."

Janine's rebuttal died on her lips as her phone rang. Her mouth fell open when she saw the caller ID.

"Holy shit. Holy *shit.* Hold on." She tapped the screen and pressed the phone to her ear. *"Did you fly on a broom?"*

Nessa's chuckle drifted over the line. "Good to talk to you too, Janine."

Tony leaned in. "Is that Roth? Where's Marie? Is she safe?"

"Where's Marie?" Janine echoed. "Is she with you? Is she okay?"

"That's…a complicated question. And the reason I'm calling. I need your help. I need something of Marie's—something special—and you may be able to retrieve it faster than I can. I know she tried to deter you from following us. She didn't succeed, did she?"

"Of course not," Janine said.

"Good. Are you anywhere near Chicago?"

"We're kinda there right now. At least until our plane leaves in a few hours."

"Cancel your trip," Nessa told her, "and listen carefully. We abandoned our car in the parking lot of a nightclub. Marie's luggage is in the back seat. That paperback she loves—*Swords Against Madness*—should be inside."

"Her favorite, I know." Janine squinted. "What about it?"

"I need you to retrieve it and bring it to me in Las Vegas as quickly as possible, on the next available flight."

"Uh, mind telling me why?"

"You wouldn't believe me," Nessa said.

"Try me. I believe a lot of things."

"All right," Nessa replied. "Marie is lost on a parallel Earth. The book is a sympathetic link to her spirit, and an ancient witch in the form of a knife is going to use that link to carve a doorway between worlds."

"What did she say?" Tony asked.

Janine pressed the phone to her chest. She stayed like that for a moment, starry-eyed and searching for words.

"She said that life is *awesome*. And we're going to Las Vegas. Please don't ask me why or we're going to get in a really big argument." Janine put the phone back to her ear. "You wouldn't lie to me, right?"

"If I felt like it, of course I would," Nessa said. "But at the moment I'm telling the truth. Marie's life may depend on you retrieving that book. Are you up to the task?"

"For Marie?" Janine said. "Anything. We're ready."

"Good. I'm going to give you directions to the club—"

Janine pantomimed writing notes on an invisible pad of paper. Tony swung the back of the SUV open and unzipped his duffel bag, rummaging fast.

"This is where things may become complicated," Nessa

continued. "These directions will get you close to the club, but they won't take you all the way. From there, you're going to have to keep your eyes open. This is going to sound odd, but…watch for a suspicious crow. If you see it, follow it."

"A crow," Janine replied. "That's not a metaphor, right?"

"Not a metaphor."

Two minutes later they were on the road. Janine took the wheel, eyes high as the SUV cruised beneath the shadow of the elevated train tracks. Tony navigated from the crumpled scrap of notepaper in his hand.

"Nothing about this isn't crazy," he said. "You know that, right?"

Janine took a left at the next light, breaking away from the train tracks, gazing up at the overcast sky. Brackish clouds left a soiled, hazy smear across the afternoon sun.

"Embrace the crazy," Janine said.

"And what's with these instructions? 'Look for a friendly crow'? Like, a sign with a crow on it?"

Up ahead, black feathers ruffled. A row of birds perched along a laundromat's dirty yellow awning. Six pairs of glittering onyx eyes turned as one, watching the SUV as it stopped at the red light on the corner.

One plump specimen, its coat faded with age, shoved itself from the awning and took flight. Then it plunged down, landing on the hood with a *thump* of rough claws. It stared at Janine through the windshield, tilting its head. She stared back and tilted hers. It shook one wing, then the other.

"What. The," Tony breathed.

"That," Janine said, "is not normal bird behavior."

The light turned green. The crow launched itself into the air, catching the breeze as it winged in a slow, beckoning circle above the rooftops just ahead. Tony and Janine shared a glance.

"Embrace the crazy." Tony sank into his seat with a sigh of resignation. "Right. Follow that crow."

TWELVE

Marie slid across the skin of the world next door in the back seat of an armored taxicab. Stiff springs dug into her back as she bounced on the vinyl bench, transmission squealing over every jagged pothole. She had a million questions she couldn't ask. She kept an eye on the glowing blue meter and compared it to the spread of rumpled bills in her hand. The money was a reassuringly familiar green, but all the presidents were wrong—Dixon, Mulraney, Clinton, the latter a doe-eyed black woman encircled by laurel wreaths—and instead of ones, fives, and tens she had threes, nines, and fifteens. At least the painkillers had kicked in, muting the ache in her ribs to a dull throb.

The cabbie was a talker. She tried to keep up with his stream of patter, injecting murmurs of assent and empty words to make it sound like she understood. Their shared language was a lie; the invisible barrier between them was the grind and assumptions of average, everyday life. As an out-of-towner, she could ask him about local events. But when he said his sister-in-law got her hair done last week and everyone agreed she'd been blue-carded, his tone made it clear that everyone—*everyone*—knew exactly what that meant. The question stayed frozen on her tongue, threatening to betray her.

Marie gradually realized, lobbing the ball of conversation back and forth through the scarred plastic divider, that her life in the NYPD had prepared her for this. Interrogation was a skill. She was good at it. Most people, even people looking down the barrel of a prison sentence, didn't need much encouragement to talk.

The right gaps of silence, the right prodding, and they'd offer up answers to their own questions without even realizing it.

"So where you from, anyway?" the cabbie asked.

"Well, I'm applying for a job at Talon Armaments," she said. "I'll give you three guesses."

"Brixton?" He squinted at her in the rearview. "Nah. St. Lancier. All you brainy engineering chicks come outta Saints University."

She flashed a smile and conceded his victory, safe in the lie he wove for her.

The cab took a right turn into a wasteland. Towers of skeletal steel wore shrouds of glazing and tape over their shattered faces, the sidewalks glittering with constellations of broken glass. Polished granite walls bore scorched moon-crater scars. Construction crews were out in full force, and men in lime-green vests waved traffic to the far left side of the roadway to make room for cranes and lumbering two-story machines—baby cousins to the giant construction robot Marie had seen on, the television—ferrying supplies and men to the heart of the damage.

"Fuckin' Fivers," the cabbie muttered. He gestured up at the sky. A dark zeppelin sailed between spires tall enough to slice the grimy brown smog. "It's gonna be fine. You see all those eyes up there?"

"Sure," Marie said. "There aren't usually that many?"

"Nah. Means somebody big is coming to town. Revolutionary Council, maybe." He kissed his fingers and touched the sun-visor again, that reflexive gesture of prayer. He dropped his voice, conspiratorial. "My brother over at the con-con says he saw a black VTOL touching down at Narragan. You *know* what that means."

She had no idea, but she rode his tone and mirrored it back at him. "Better be careful."

"Damn right. Still, don't wanna worry you none. You might get looked at a little hard, being new in town, but you'll be fine as long as your papers are orderly. And the Fivers aren't gonna start any trouble with all these eyes around. They know better."

Papers she didn't have. She doubted her New York State ID would pass muster around here. The cab rattled to a stop at the curb. One side of the street was a construction yard, wood fencing around the looming spire of a brand-new skyscraper, bare girders stretching for the grimy clouds. On the other side, a tower of purple-tinted glass and chrome, wet from the rain. Marie leaned toward the window and craned her neck to read the vast letters T-A-G, struggling to shine under the light of a muffled sun.

The meter stopped at fifty-two dollars. She wasn't sure if people tipped on this planet, and it was one of the questions she couldn't ask. She took a chance, handed the driver a few Dixons and told him to keep the change. He broke into a dirty-toothed smile.

"Hey, thanks! And good luck in there. Make us all proud."

Marie adjusted her surgical mask on the sidewalk, making sure it covered as much of her face as it could. She wasn't alone. On the far side of the revolving doors, the lobby of the TAG building—floored in sandstone polished to a mirror sheen—churned with workers and visitors. A good three-quarters of them were wearing masks, most in jet black and emblazoned with a tiny copper TAG logo in one corner. Marie wasn't sure if they were showing company loyalty or if the office just handed them out for free. It didn't matter, so long as she blended in and didn't have to show her face.

She waited in line at the reception desk, shuffling forward a couple of feet at a time. Displays ringed the lobby, a mini-museum of small video screens, posters, and glass display cases, depicting the dizzying span of Talon's achievements. Androids and vast machines, pure science fiction to Marie's eyes, but the locals barely seemed to notice. Eventually she reached the front of the line, and a receptionist in a blue plastic dress gave her a two-second glance before turning back to her computer screen.

"Purpose of your visit?" she asked.

"I need to see Ezra Talon," Marie replied.

Now she got a longer look. And a colder one.

"No one 'sees' Mr. Talon, honey. If you're press, pass your inquiry through the media office and they'll send you his response, if he responds, within a week or so. Next?"

The man behind her was already trying to push ahead, expecting Marie to stand aside. She held her ground. Talon—this world's version of Talon—was the only person who could send her home. Her only chance at finding her way back to Nessa and her friends. She couldn't fail now. Marie thought fast. She took what she'd picked up from the news broadcast on the street video wall, from her cabbie's running patter, and wove it into a story as she leaned across the counter.

"Listen to me." She pitched her voice like she was still on the force, backing up her words with authority and a badge. "I have information about a planned Fiver attack on the Slepneir construction facility in New Amsterdam."

The receptionist blinked at her. "This isn't—I mean, you should really be speaking to the authorities—"

"No time. All I need you to do is pass a message to Talon. If you do, I'll provide all the information. If you don't, the facility will be destroyed—possibly in the next two hours. And he's going to know, *everyone* is going to know, that *you* could have stopped it from happening. A black VTOL landed at Narragan this morning. Do you think that's a coincidence? Do you?"

The receptionist slid back in her chair. "A message," she echoed.

"Tell him, and use these exact words, that the Knight—with a capital K—is here and she needs help getting home. She was sent here by a different Salesman, with a capital S. One he helped out a long time ago."

Marie watched the receptionist write it down and checked it over.

"I don't understand—"

"You don't have to," Marie said. "He will. I expect you'll be hearing from him very quickly, and he'll be very grateful to you. I'll wait."

As Marie walked away from the front desk, a riot of emotions swirled in her stomach. Once this world's Talon found out another character from the first story was in town—one who knew another of Ezra's own incarnations, no less—she had to imagine he'd want to meet her. And that depended on him getting the message. Marie knew her limitations. She was a bad liar, always had been, but she was good at authority. Hopefully she'd worried the receptionist badly enough that her story would hold up.

Nothing she could do now but wait. Marie browsed the exhibits along the lobby walls. Her feet carried her to the far corner of the room, to a display the other visitors avoided like a bubble of reverse magnetism was pushing them away.

A suit of black armor stood in a display case. It was the dark twin to the powered suit that had brought her across the wheel of worlds, sleek and hard and cold as an arctic drift. That suit had been a clunky prototype; this was the real thing, refined, venomous-spider elegant. A scarlet cloak rested across its broad shoulders, joined by a golden braid that made Marie think of Roman emperors.

A dusty placard at its plated boots read: *REPLICA of custom Valkyrie armor designed by Ezra Talon for Lady Martika (requiescat in pace)*.

A video screen beside the case invited the touch of her finger. The panel rippled to life with a patriotic anthem and a strange flag, American stars and stripes tinged with green and the wrong numbers of each. Then Marie stared at her own ghost. The woman on the screen had Egyptian swoops of black mascara at the corners of her eyes and a jagged scar along one cheek, but it was her face, her voice echoing from the speakers.

"There are barbarians at the gates," she said. "And a barbarian only understands one thing. War. The second war of revolution has become the war of purification. Degenerates, radicals, foreigners, and traitors seek to undermine our way of life, the values we hold dear, and we must do more than hold the line. We must *win*. And how do we measure our victory? By the depths of the graves we force our enemies to dig."

She punched a steel-jacketed fist into her armored palm. Marie swallowed down a wave of nausea as her stomach battled her eyes and ears. *This isn't real*, she thought. *That isn't me—*

"But success does not rise from righteousness alone. It rises from the gifts of Talon Armaments Group. From the new generation of Valkyrie armor to the Odin sky-carrier, TAG forges the tools of next-generation warfare for the armies of New America. Discipline. Obedience. Purity. These are the virtues that define our nation. This is our battle. And Talon leads the way."

The music swelled, then faded to silence as the image dissolved into a company logo. Marie took a step back on wobbly legs. She turned and stared across the lobby.

This place, Jesus, what did I— She bit her bottom lip. *No. That wasn't me. This is a trick, a mistake, it's not what it looks like. That wasn't me.*

This was taking too long. Marie felt exposed, an alien on hostile ground. And mask or not, too many people were staring at her. They'd turn away when she made eye contact, but she felt their gazes in her peripheral vision. The receptionist was on the phone, talking a mile a minute. She and the man leaning down next to her were watching Marie like a pair of hawks.

Outside the purple-tinted glass, a long black car swooped up to the curb. Men in dark suits and dark glasses stepped out, the rain-kissed wind pushing back their jackets and baring the guns on their hips.

Every muscle in Marie's body told her to start running. She walked instead, breathing steady, chin high, trying to keep it casual as she made a beeline for the revolving doors. The receptionist called out behind her.

"Ma'am? Ma'am! Please, wait just a few more minutes. I have Mr. Talon on the phone. Ma'am?"

Security guards were closing in on her from both sides. One of the suits on the sidewalk was muttering into a walkie-talkie as they approached from outside the wall of glass. Marie pushed through the revolving doors.

Then she ran.

Horns blared and tires screeched to a stop. Marie dodged a truck's bumper, inches from clipping her, as she sprinted across the pothole-littered street. The suits were fast on her heels. One held a badge high, its metal tinted crimson, as he followed in her wake.

"She's running," shouted the one with the walkie-talkie. "We need a cordon at 59th and Price, and get a grind-hound up here, fast!"

Marie bolted through an open gate and onto the construction site. Her shoes dug into wet dirt, kicking up mud as she sprinted around piles of rebar and rain-slick plastic pipe. A towering construction mech, squatting on four piston legs and stretching crane arms across the yard in all directions, thrummed loud as a jackhammer. One of the arms, sweeping low and swinging a ten-foot length of steel girder, was coming right for her. She heard the shouts from the workers as she threw herself onto her shoulder, hitting the mud and rolling under the girder's shadow as it swung over her head.

Something pulled in her back, a sudden red-hot branding iron stealing her breath, and her injured ribs were like a spear digging into her chest. Marie scrambled on all fours, pushing herself to her feet in a clumsy sprinter's start, fighting to keep her footing in the mud. She couldn't stop now. Couldn't give up. She jumped and landed on damp sheetrock in the skeleton shadow of the girders overhead. The first few floors were halfway done, a labyrinth of drywall, exposed beams, and rough, naked wood. She dodged around a corner, running blind, just trying to put some distance between her and her pursuers. If she could make it out the other side, then get lost in the tangle of streets—

She jolted to a stop as two more suits loomed at the far end of a drywall corridor. They had a dog, or something that had been a dog once. It was a creature of black fur and soot-stained iron, with scarlet diode eyes and a saw-toothed jaw. It strained against its leash and let out grating electronic squawks as it jumped and gnashed at the air.

Marie broke left. Nothing ahead but a stone staircase, leading her up with no promise of a way back down, but she didn't have a choice. She left muddy tracks as she took the stairs two at a time. Her legs were aching, every breath a gout of fire in her lungs. She turned left, right, up another flight of stairs.

The third floor was a vast and open gallery, no walls yet, nothing but pillars and slow progress. She spotted another stairway down on the opposite side and ran toward it, stopping short as the suits thundered up the steps. She doubled back. More on the other side, their dog-thing leading the way, desperate to slip its leash.

Marie backed up, panting for breath as she made her way toward the building's edge.

"Give it up," one of the men called out, brandishing his crimson metal badge. "You've got nowhere to go."

That wasn't true. She looked over her shoulder. It was a three-story drop to the construction yard. People had survived falls worse than that, hadn't they? She'd read something about that once. She wished she could remember the odds. She wished for a lot of things. The men closed in, slow, and she took a step back for every step they took forward until her heel brushed the concrete lip and there was nothing but brown sky and mud and pain at her back.

The roar of an engine turned her around. She staggered back from the edge, pushed by a torrent of heat and the stench of burning diesel.

Three suits of black armor rose up and hovered before her, riding on plumes of flame. The Valkyries came in for a landing. The one in the middle, standing before Marie, reached up and tapped a fingertip against the base of her helmet.

The helmet opened with a tide of machine-gun clicks, segmented black metal folding in on itself in strips as it peeled away, exposing the face of the woman beneath. Marie recognized her—her bright eyes, her cinnamon hair worn in an undercut that was long and wavy on top but buzzed to the scalp on the sides. They'd met at the Bast Club in Chicago. She'd introduced herself as Tricia and claimed she and Marie had gone to college together.

As one, the other two armored figures dropped to one knee, their heads bowed. Tricia curled her gauntleted hand into a fist and struck her shoulder in a salute. The echoing clang of steel on steel rippled across the open floor.

"Lady Martika," she said. "We've been waiting for you."

THIRTEEN

Alton Roth was back in DC. Back in his element. He usually felt right at home in the marble halls, the grinding gears of government, the sloppy and rough machine that could transform lip-service notions of public service into raw profit. He had polls to tell him his principles, a stream of lobbyists at his office door bearing position papers and discreet checks, and a guardian angel just down the hall.

His angel had been quiet. Alton hadn't understood half of the overheard discussion between Calypso and the redheaded stranger on his private jet, but he got the gist of it. Calypso had crossed a dangerous line, protecting Alton's interests, and the woman was calling him to account for it.

We've got a contract, he told himself for the hundredth time, pacing the goldenrod carpet of his office. *He busts the deal, he loses everything. No. Doesn't matter what kind of pressure they put on him, Calypso's my guy. All the way to the White House.*

Some men turned to diamonds under pressure. Some cracked like coal. Alton needed more than a demon's word of honor. If his time in the Washington trenches had taught him anything, it was that sometimes a man needed to get his own hands dirty. Elbows-deep in the dirt, if he had to.

"Do me a favor," he told his assistant on the intercom. "Pull Mr. Scratch's call logs for the last week. Inbound and outbound. Be discreet. He doesn't need to know about it."

He knew Calypso had been heading things up with his lead hunter, that woman, Nyx. *She* looked like somebody who could get things done. And in a few minutes, Alton would have the number he was using to reach her.

"Right away, Mr. Roth. Also, you have a visitor. She's not on your appointment sheet; do you want me to pencil her in?"

"Constituent or lobbyist?"

"Angelica Rosales, says she's the director of corporate security for Talon Worldwide."

He knew the name. Not hers, but Talon was a big player in DC—and a big spender. Curious. He wasn't on any committees that dealt with arms appropriations, wasn't sure what he could do for her, but this smelled like an opportunity.

"I've got a little time. Send her on back."

Rosales let herself in and shut the door behind her. She prowled his office, taking in the nautical knick-knacks on the credenza, the framed portrait of the president alongside Alton's two diplomas, barely glancing at the man behind the desk. Her fingertip trailed along the buttery wood of a bookshelf.

"Nice digs," she said. "You didn't skimp on the decor. Look, I'm going to cut straight to the chase and save us both a lot of time. If you could cooperate by not playing stupid, I'd really appreciate that."

Alton stared, momentarily speechless. She took off her copper-tinted glasses, her turquoise eyes flashing, and gave him a smile.

"You're trying to kill Vanessa Roth and Marie Reinhart. Hey, fine, your business, I truly don't care."

"I don't—I don't know what you're suggesting—" Alton started to stammer. Rosales held up a finger and wagged it at him.

"Uh-uh. Please. You're doing that thing I asked you not to do. I'm going to keep talking as if you didn't. Now, me, I'm supposed to retrieve a special object in Marie's possession. And I know where she is. Well, sort of roughly where she is. My problem is that I've got two bosses, and one of them—Ezra Talon—wants Vanessa and Marie taken alive. He also wants that special object I mentioned, but my other boss wants it more. And I'm doing a playing-both-sides thing, so I've got to at least make an effort at looking loyal, or I'll only be getting one paycheck instead of two from now on. And that would suck for me, because I like getting paid a lot of money for minimal effort. Are you with me so far?"

Alton sank back in his chair, feeling more of his world fraying apart at the seams. First a demon had walked right onto his jet and confronted him and Calypso about their hunt. Now an executive from one of America's biggest arms dealers was standing in his office, doing the same thing. He was naked, his secrets on full display, all semblance of control slipping out from under his fingertips.

He needed to get it back. More than anything, he needed to feel like he was in control again.

"I'm listening," he told her.

"I'm proposing a little tag-team action. My intel and field support, your shooters. Your people do the dirty, take 'em out, and I get to pick Marie's pockets before you dump her in a shallow grave. You get what you want, I get what I want, nobody knows I was ever involved, and we pretend none of this ever happened. Sound good?"

Alton steepled his fingers. His gaze fixed on hers, steady, as he weighed his options.

"What kind of support?" he asked.

*   *   *

She gave him the address of a private airstrip, a stone's throw from the Potomac. The setting sun painted the sky in pastel pink and drew long shadows across the runway. She was waiting in hangar four.

Alton came alone. He had concocted a story for Calypso, a private dinner with a generous donor, but he hadn't even asked. The senator took his guardian's silence as proof that he was doing the right thing, making his own moves. He and Rosales waited for their third guest.

Nyx didn't come alone. She brought a posse with her, eight

men in urban camo who spread out like a firing line at her back as she strode through the open hangar door. She kept her Wayfarers on, turning her shrouded gaze from Alton to Rosales to an empty patch of floor.

"Someone is missing," she said.

"Calypso doesn't need to be involved," Alton told her. "You're dealing directly with me now. There's been a failure of management from the start of this operation, and I'm here to fix it."

Nyx moved close, black leather glistening as her hips swayed. She had two inches of height over Alton and pointedly looked down at him while her lips curled, amused. She raised a hand and flapped her thumb against her fingers as she spoke.

"Yap, yap, yap. That is what this one hears when humans talk. They rarely have anything interesting to say."

Alton cast a glance at the men backing her up. They stood like soldiers at loose attention, but they weren't cut to any official grooming standards. Beards, long hair, neck tattoos. They were either bargain-basement thugs or real operators, and he couldn't tell which.

"I'm surprised," he said. "Thought you lost all your men in Carson City, when Vanessa chewed them up like reheated leftovers."

Nyx's smile vanished.

"This one still has resources she can call upon."

"Not like mine," Alton replied.

He gestured to Rosales. Her fingers trailed across the face of a drab olive crate, rough plastic with a heavy-duty lock and a fingerprint sensor. One of a half dozen boxes just like it, laid out along tables that lined the hangar wall. Nyx didn't care about the crates. She zeroed in on Rosales's eyes.

"Wolf blood."

"Blame my father," Rosales said.

Nyx looked to Alton. "You know what she is?"

"An enterprising self-starter," he said. "My kind of woman."

"You fraternize with a servant of the kings."

"I'm a servant of myself," Rosales said. "I know the courts of hell and the Network have their little back-alley feud going on, but honestly? I don't care and I don't want to care. It's real simple: we work together, we get this done, we all walk away happy."

Nyx folded her arms, glowering. "This one needs no help from a human, or a wolf."

"You sure about that?" Rosales replied.

She pressed her thumb to the sensor. The lock snapped open with a high-pitched beep. She lifted the lid, inviting Nyx to take a look inside.

Sleek rifles, fully automatic and built for a battlefield that didn't exist yet, nestled in beds of black felt. They had company. Matte-black handguns and cylinder-shaped grenades filled out the crate.

"Are these…?" Nyx trailed off.

"The latest from Talon Worldwide's brand-new summertime catalog," Rosales said. "These crates just mysteriously fell off the back of a truck this morning. No idea how that happened. And of course, once our deal is done, you get to keep the toys. Call it a parting gift."

Nyx almost reached into the crate. She paused, looking at Alton with fresh suspicion.

"This one has seen your contract. Going behind Calypso's back? Making deals with an agent of the Network? This puts you in violation. He could call the contract forfeit." Faint waves of heat shimmered off her alabaster skin as she leaned close to him. "You do understand what that means, yes? This one could claim your soul, here and now. Drag you straight to hell."

Alton pushed his shoulders back and tried to keep any hint of fear from his face. *Clean and cool*, he told himself. *You're in control.*

"He could, but he won't. I assume demons understand the concept of sunken costs? Calypso has invested way too much time and effort into bringing me this far, just to punch my ticket over a little legalese. He wants me in the White House just as badly as I want to get there. Hell, he wants it more than I do. He'll fall in line."

Nyx's nose wrinkled. She turned back to Rosales.

"Did you bring more than weapons?"

"Intel," Rosales said. "No more reports of a woman flying on a broomstick since Carson City, so Vanessa left the scene using ground transportation. Good bet she's trying to reconnect with her weird-ass coven buddies. Plus she's got a little help from the mob."

"Faust." The name was acid on Nyx's tongue.

"Which means Vegas—"

"Too obvious," Nyx said, cutting her off. "Faust would expect this one to search there first. He would never hide her in his own city."

"And given enough time to shuffle her elsewhere, you might be right. But when he took off from Iowa, Faust stole a school bus. My people have been combing through police dispatches all over Nevada. Want to guess where the bus just turned up, a couple of hours ago?" Rosales pressed her thumb against a second case. The lid swung up, offering another bounty of weapons. "They're in Las Vegas. And if he's reluctant to stash Vanessa and her crew in any of *his* hangouts, knowing you're going to come looking eventually..."

"They're hiding in a hotel," Nyx said. One hand curled into an eager fist.

"Your men, my weapons and tactical oversight. Oh, and my corporate plane, which is fueled up and ready to go in the next hangar." Rosales gestured with her thumb. "Wheels up in ten minutes. We can be there in four hours, before he has a chance to relocate the targets, and we get this done *tonight*. What do you say?"

Nyx turned to her men. She pointed a black fingernail at the plastic crates.

"Load the weapons onto the plane," she told them. "This one gets first pick."

FOURTEEN

A storm was coming to Las Vegas. Nessa watched it from her hotel room, a razor line of roiling darkness creeping just ahead of the sunset.

The plan had been set, the orders dispatched. Nothing to do now but wait. She wasn't good at waiting. So she paced, and watched the clouds crawling toward the city, and listened to Hedy and Clytemnestra debate. They were on the far side of the suite, past a king-size bed with a mountain of fluffy pillows and a stretch of hot pink carpet. Daniel had scrounged up a tablet with Internet access. It sat on the kitchenette counter beside Clytemnestra's blade; the ancient witch had emerged from hibernation again, her human form projected in a shimmering blue outline.

"The problem is, my herbcraft is admittedly prodigious, but just like you I didn't learn it on this world. Different herbs, here. Different names for things." Her luminous finger tapped at the screen and passed through it, blasting the pixels with a wash of static. Hedy pulled the tablet a little closer to her side of the counter and advanced the page herself.

"Let me, you're going to break it." Hedy paused. "Are you sure you wouldn't rather just…stop being a knife? You can change your form anytime you want."

"I have my reasons."

"Suit yourself. And same problem here. I know exactly how Nessa's serum is mixed, how to concoct it, the precise herbs—I just can't *get* them on this world. We're down to three flasks—"

"Two." Nessa held up a pair of fingers. They both looked her way. "I pushed myself too hard in Carson City. Had to drink one just to stave off the infection and keep it from killing me."

"Two," Hedy echoed. She looked to Clytemnestra, eyes wide as inspiration grabbed hold of her. "So let's go *back*. You can open a doorway, right? We'll hop over to my workshop, grab what we need, and we'll be back before sunset."

"I can open a doorway, but not easily." Her projection raised an open hand, as if weighing the cool air in her palm. "There's a reason I asked for an ideal ritual site. Have you *felt* this place? This world is..."

"Muffled," Hedy said. "I know, it's amazing the natives even discovered magic exists. Their greatest sorcerers do card tricks."

"It's a sound strategy, though. Nothing says we can't make more than one jump. We'll leave tonight, pass from here to your home world, secure the herbs for another batch of elixir—"

"You're forgetting what's waiting on the other side of that door," Nessa said. "The Sisters of the Noose will be on us like sharks on a blood trail."

"We don't know that," Hedy said.

"The odds are your entire covenstead's been burned to the ground by now. That or they've made it their new lair, infesting the place, just waiting for us to come back so they can finish what they started."

"Mother," Hedy said, "you don't *know* that."

"I know how many of your followers died in Mirenze when the Sisters attacked. I'm not asking you to put yourselves in that kind of danger again. I won't allow it."

Hedy fell silent for a moment. Then she folded her arms and fixed Nessa with a cool and steady gaze.

"As I recall," she said, "you made a pointed statement, no less than twice, that you have no intention of usurping my position as the leader of the Pallid Masque. Therefore, you are not in a position to dictate what dangers my students and I choose to subject ourselves to. According to your very own words, the decision is mine to make."

Nessa stared back at her.

"You really are my daughter, aren't you?"

Hedy nodded. "Mm-hmm."

"I'm very proud. Annoyed, but proud." She pointed to the window, to the distant red rocks and the darkening sky. "Marie is out there. Right now, as we speak, she's out there, alone—"

"If my workshop isn't compromised, it'll take me less than ten minutes to grab what I need."

"*If*. And if it is, it's a death trap." Nessa took a deep breath, steadying herself, grasping for calm. "All right. Let's compromise."

"I didn't think you knew that word," Hedy said.

"Don't push your luck. Look, I have two days' worth of elixir, so I'm not in any imminent danger. We hunt for Marie first. If we can find her right away, all is well. If not, we keep searching. When I run out, then—and *only* then—we risk a return to Mirenze."

A crisp knock sounded at the door. Hedy let Gazelle in, then waited while she leaned against the wall, gasping for breath. Her tanned skin glistened with a sheen of sweat.

"Sorry," Gazelle panted, "just ran up twelve flights of stairs."

"I showed you how to use the elevator," Nessa said.

"Lock myself in a cage? A cage that moves without magic? Oh, no. Not for me. Stairs are fine." She gulped down air. "Daniel went to pick out a ritual site, buy a new deck of cards, and talk to his contact in the courts of hell. Butterfly and Mantis have acclimated the best out of any of us, so they're doing some local scouting, trying to source precious metals for the trip. Roach and Vole are still having trouble passing for natives, so I have them in their room, watching the talking box."

Nessa shot a glance at the television. "That may or may not be a good idea."

"And Badger?" Hedy asked.

"Down in the hotel bar, keeping an eye on Carolyn, who is drunk. Also!" Gazelle sprinted over to the long credenza across from the bed, crouched down, and pulled open the minibar. "Have you seen this? It's a tiny tavern. In your room. Carolyn says that if you drink all the little bottles, the staff just comes back and replaces them all the very next day. And these things in the shiny bag are called 'barbecued potato chips' and I love them. I think we should make our new covenstead here."

"We'll see," Hedy told her. "We have a lot of decisions to make and a lot of problems to solve in the very near future. It'll keep until...after."

After. The word hung in the air like a bad smell. They couldn't see it, but they could feel it, driving out the oxygen, suffocating everyone in the room. Gazelle deflated. She shut the minibar door, flicking a glance at Nessa.

Even a fresh batch of elixir would only delay the inevitable. Nessa was dying.

"Can we have the room, please?" Nessa asked.

Gazelle murmured something about checking on the others and made her way out the door. Clytemnestra simply nodded, grave, and her projection shattered into motes of sapphire light. Her knife-body sat silent upon the counter. Nessa turned to the window.

"We spoke, Clytemnestra and I," she said. "We have a plan. A theory, more than a plan, really. It's a long shot."

Hedy took an eager step toward her. "Then let me help! Whatever you're going to do—"

"It is a *cosmic* long shot, Hedy. A gamble of astronomical proportions. I'll bring you in when the time is right, but for now, I want you focused on the task at hand. Even in a best-case scenario, I don't have much longer to live."

"We don't have to talk about that."

"Yes, we do, because I need to make sure you understand me."

Nessa turned to face her, putting her back to the gathering storm. "Everything we've learned about the first story, and Carolyn's backed it all up, tells us that the Witch and her Knight die together. Either we die together, or I die and Marie follows me soon after. Usually by her own hand."

"Suicide," Hedy breathed.

"Not this time. Marie lives, do you understand me? No matter what happens to me, Marie *lives*. You make damn sure of it."

"I'll protect her like she's one of my own," Hedy said. "And we're not giving up. I'll continue my experiments. I'll find your next incarnation, we'll try again—"

"Task at hand, Hedy. All well and good, but right now, only Marie matters." Nessa glanced down at her phone, distracted by an incoming text. "Janine and Tony just boarded their flight at O'Hare. They have Marie's book and they'll be here in...just under four hours. Daniel should have the ritual site secure by then. As soon as they land, we get to work."

"Have you decided who you want on the rescue team?"

"As few people as possible. I'd say that Clytemnestra and I would go alone, and her only because she has to open the way for me, but—"

"But you know there's no chance I'm letting you go without me," Hedy said.

"As I was about to say, yes."

"Gazelle wants to come. I think it would be wise. She adores Marie and she'll fight harder than anybody to protect her. I mean, anybody but us. Good to have in case...you know. Something goes wrong."

Nessa nodded. She turned back to the window.

"Fair. I'd say bring everyone, if I wasn't half-certain we're walking into a trap."

Her eyes captured the clouds and reflected them back out into the desert. Growing dark, as cold and ominous as her frown.

"I have an enemy, Hedy." She pointed, her fingertip tracing the sky. "Somewhere. Out there among the stars and the deeps. They *gave* me that tainted book of spells. Made damn sure I'd poison myself. But I'm already doomed to die, and doomed to come back again, so why go to all that trouble? It's a murder with no purpose."

"They also left you that card to open the way to my world, and made sure you'd find it," Hedy pointed out. "You didn't know what Shadow infection was until we were reunited. You would have died without ever realizing why you were sick."

"So was it a simple twist of the knife? A little bit of extra cruelty, making sure I could see my death coming but do nothing about it?"

Nessa fell silent. She studied the clouds.

"No," she decided. "And that's what worries me about tonight. Not one thing, not one element since Marie and I first crossed paths, has been random. My enemy has a design. Intricate, elaborate. Terrible. And I fear that somehow, when we open that door tonight and set off across the wheel of worlds, we'll be doing exactly what they want us to do."

"What's the alternative?" Hedy asked.

"There is no alternative. We know it, and they know it too. All we can do is expect the worst and be ready for anything."

Hedy crossed the pink carpet and stood at Nessa's side.

"I'll be with you. Every step of the way."

Nessa squeezed her hand tight, then let it go.

"I know," she said. "I really am proud of you. You know that, right?"

Hedy quirked a tiny smile. "Careful with the compliments. Don't let anyone hear you say that, or they might think the Owl is going soft."

"I should spread some pain and suffering, just to make certain they don't misunderstand me."

"I know a good place to start," Hedy replied. "Because somebody, and I don't care what kind of master manipulator they think they are, deliberately made you their enemy. They chose this fight. Talk about *asking* for pain and suffering..."

"And I will deliver." Nessa took a deep breath. "But first things first. Marie is out there. Damn the costs and damn the consequences. I'm bringing her home tonight."

FIFTEEN

Marie had expected handcuffs, shackles, maybe a summary bullet to the head. Instead, the men on her heels stood down with a wave of Tricia's hand. Her jet-black armor hissed softly as she gestured to the stairs and her two companions, both down on one knee, rose back to their full height. Their helmets peeled open, metal folding in on itself. Both of them were women, one with rich brown skin and deep eyes, the other with signs of a faded sunburn on her freckled cheeks. Marie didn't recognize either of them.

Tricia, though, she couldn't forget. She remembered how the woman had approached her at the Bast Club, feeding her a story about how they'd gone to college together—and how for just a moment, before she regained her composure, she looked crushed that Marie didn't remember her. Tricia watched her with that same tremulous expression now, half wonderment and half fear.

"I'm not who you think I am," Marie told her.

"It's really her, though," said the freckled woman. She looked to Tricia. "It really is."

"It really is," Tricia echoed.

"There's been a mistake," Marie said. "Look, Ezra Talon can clear all of this up, if you'd just let me talk to him alone for five minutes."

The women shared sidelong glances and a soft chuckle, sharing an inside joke. Tricia took a step closer to Marie and held up her gauntlets.

"Relax. No one is going to hurt you here. You're among friends now. Old and dear friends, I promise. I know you don't remember, but it's okay. We're going to fix you. We're going to make you all better."

"Ma'am?" The man with the crimson metal badge, standing at Marie's back, spoke up. "Will you need support on your way to the extraction point?"

Engines roared and the brown sky lit up with pinpoints of fire. Two more Valkyries blazed in on their shoulder jets, afterburners hissing as they landed like birds of prey on the lip of the building.

"Does it look like I need support?" Tricia sniffed at him. "Take your men and disperse. We've got it from here."

They walked Marie across the street, back into the TAG building, onto an elevator. Not to visit Talon's office, though: their final destination was the top floor, where a bulbous and black turboprop jet was waiting. Marie ended up squeezed between a pair of the women, with Tricia and her two companions in the seats facing her. The door rattled shut, sealing them in. The concealing enchantment Nessa had laid upon the mirrored shoulder bag still held strong; even pressed right up against Marie's side, the woman on her left didn't seem to notice it was there. Not that anything inside the bag could help her now.

Tricia tried introducing the others, but her words washed over Marie like the thrum of the rotors as the plane lifted off, lurching straight up from the pad and into the turbulent smog.

They were all smiling, looking at her with expressions ranging from genuine friendliness to open awe. Tricia kept leaning forward while she talked, touching Marie's knee for punctuation. It didn't stop her heart from pounding, didn't stop her from having to take deep breaths to keep the panic at bay.

Tricia had called her Lady Martika. The name from the armor display in the TAG office lobby. The woman who spoke with Marie's voice as she called for death to the degenerates, the radicals, the foreigners. Marie had tugged down her surgical mask so she could breathe a little easier, but she wanted to cover her face. Or wear a different one.

She wasn't that woman. This was a mistake.

"I didn't entirely lie," Tricia was telling her. "We did go to college together. Just, you know, on *this* world. Speaking to you at the club was a protocol breach. I wasn't supposed to make contact at all, just observe and report, but when I saw you there...I couldn't help it. I hope you're not mad."

"I'm telling you, you're confusing me with someone else."

Marie didn't even believe the words. She wasn't a good enough liar to fool herself. All the same, she had to say them. As long as she kept protesting, this wasn't real.

"Oh, no. No mistake." Tricia beamed at her. "Do you have any idea how long it took us to set this all up? And that was before half the plan went sideways on us. I spent months shuttling back and forth between parallel Earths just to keep tabs on all the pieces in play."

"Missed the entire new season of *Golden Voice*," said the dark-complexioned woman at her side. Tricia had introduced her as Kiyana. "Don't worry, I recorded it for you. And adjusted your news feed so you won't see any spoilers until you're caught up."

"Best lieutenant *ever*," Tricia said.

On Marie's left, the one Tricia introduced as Ines—with ice-white hair and features sharp enough to cut glass—wrinkled her nose.

"*Golden Voice* is bourgeois trash. It should be banned from the airwaves for the public good."

The woman on Marie's right snorted into her hand. "'Trash,' says the one member of the squad who never misses an episode of *Sexy Nurses in Danger*..."

The cabin erupted as they all began shouting at each other, more or less good-naturedly, until Tricia flapped her gauntleted hands and waved them back down into silence.

"The point is, my lady," Tricia said, "we're all honored to have you back."

"My name is Marie Reinhart, okay? I'm from a place called New York City—"

Tricia arched an eyebrow at her. "C'mon, Martie. Really? I already told you I've been following you for months. You know perfectly well who and what you really are. *Obviously* you died and reincarnated on that other Earth. I mean, come on, duh? But you're still our Lady Martika. And though you don't remember—which I'll be honest, hurts a little, but I know it's not your fault—the real you is still in there, deep down inside. We just have to bring her back out again."

The others were smiling, staring, with the kind of laser-intense certainty only found among the zealous and the mad. Marie squirmed in her seat. She was hemmed in, and the view outside the window offered nothing but a wasteland of roiling smog. She had nowhere to run.

Then she had a thought. A suspicion, deep in her gut.

"You said...keeping tabs on all the pieces in play."

Tricia nodded. "That's right. I can't complain too much. I enjoyed your world for what it was. But there's no place like home."

"What do you know about Nessa's book of spells?"

"I know that it took forever to get her to notice it. I must have followed her to half a dozen used bookstores, rushing ahead to prop it on a shelf at every single one of them, just waiting for her to finally buy the darn thing—"

Marie lunged for Tricia's eyes. She threw herself across the aisle, screaming, kicking as the women at her sides grabbed hold of her arms and pressed her back against her seat. Kiyana gently slid in and laid one onyx boot across her thrashing legs. The powered armor effortlessly pinned Marie in place while Tricia tried to talk her down.

"No, hey, it's okay, it's *okay*—"

"You killed her," Marie shouted. "She's infected with Shadow. You fucking *killed* her—"

"No, I wouldn't, I swear," Tricia said. "Listen to me. Mart—I mean, Marie, listen to me, okay? I would never ever hurt her. Never in a million years. You just haven't seen the big picture yet. But you will. Just wait until we land and it'll all make sense, I promise."

Marie fell silent. She bristled, locking eyes with Tricia, but she stopped fighting. Her seatmates still clung to her, their steel-gloved hands gentle but firm.

"I don't like the way you're looking at me right now," Tricia said.

Marie's voice dropped to a graveyard whisper.

"You had better," Marie said, "have a way to cure Nessa. Or her blood is going to be on your hands. And yours is going to be on mine. That's a promise."

Tricia broke into an eager smile.

"*There's* our Lady Martika," she said, her voice soothing like she was trying to calm a frightened animal. "You feel it, don't you? You feel it already. That's your nature, rising to the surface. The *real* you."

"Our Lady Fear," Ines murmured.

"You said she even became a lawbringer on that backwater planet?" Kiyana asked.

Tricia nodded. "They call them 'police,' but yes. You should have seen her. No Valkyrie armor, nothing but a semiautomatic pistol with primitive ammunition, and she still led the way into battle. It's in her blood. And now she returns, to lead us once again."

The jet banked hard, veering left, and the smog broke. At first Marie thought they were circling over another skyscraper, but she hadn't felt any descent, only a swift and steady rise since the moment they took off. She stared at vast sheets of dull gunmetal, the thunder of engines that blazed like Vulcan's forge.

It's a ship, she thought.

"*Odin Platform One*," Tricia said, answering her unspoken question. "Or as we like to call it, the *Triumph*."

*   *   *

They led her across a flight deck and through an open bulkhead, down sheet-metal halls that thrummed with the vibration of the engines. Marie ended up alone in a small, spartan room with padlocked cabinets and a doctor's exam bench, a fresh strip of antiseptic paper laid out over the cold vinyl. A new arrival wore spotless white scrubs and peered at her through cherry-tinted glasses only slightly bigger than her beady eyes.

"I'll need you to undress, please."

"Excuse me?" Marie said.

"Oh. I'm sorry. Right, the amnesia, they told me about this."

She brandished a slim black wallet, like Marie's old detective shield, and flipped it open. The woman's badge was a symbol of a pole, striped in red and white, set onto a field of shining gold.

"I'm a barber, by official appointment. *Your* barber, to be specific. Well, your entire squad's." She let out a nervous, distracted giggle. "I swear, m'lady, if you could remember how many times I've patched you up. You had six bullets in you after the Battle of Philadelphia. So if we could just get this examination underway—"

"I'm fine," Marie said. "I don't need any help."

The lies were rolling off her tongue today, but they weren't getting any more believable. Her body was a wreck, punishing her with jolts of pain every time she took a breath or turned her hips. All the same, she could live with it. She was already vulnerable here, already powerless.

The doctor shot a glance over her shoulder, to the closed door. She fumbled with her glasses.

"Please," she said, barely a whisper. "Don't do this to me."

Marie shook her head. "To you?"

"I've been instructed to give you a medical review. If you refuse, your...comrades are going to come in here. They're going to make you undress, and they're going to hold you down until I finish the procedure. But I'm the one they're going to be angry at, and I'm the one who's going to get punished for it."

While she talked, she folded her glasses and set them on the counter. Her hands were shaking.

"Okay," Marie said. She unbuttoned her blouse. "Okay."

After that she was gently poked and prodded, wore a blood-pressure cuff, breathed deep while the doctor jotted down notes on a clipboard. Her body was a quilt of bruises, some fresh and some old, black and blue and yellow all blurring together like oil paint.

"Definitely fractured here and here," the doctor murmured. "Raise your arms for me?"

Marie winced as she held her arms up. A plastic corset filled with blue gel snaked around her ribs. It felt like it had just come from the freezer, and the cold sent a shiver up her spine. The corset hissed and contracted. Not painfully tight but snug, like it had been tailored for her body, and it flexed along with her breath.

Not painful at all, she realized, as the ache in her ribs faded to a distant and almost ticklish tingle.

"Adaptive plastic," the doctor explained. "It uses intelligent compression to speed up healing, along with a time-release anesthetic to keep you comfortable in the meantime. Keep it on, and we'll change it in four days."

"Tell me something," Marie said.

"Hmm?"

"What was she like? Lady Martika."

The doctor studied her for a moment, holding her thoughts in. Then she spoke.

"At first I thought this might be some kind of a trick. Or a loyalty test. They're big on loyalty tests around here. You really came back to life somehow. And you really don't remember anything, do you?"

"I'm not her," Marie said.

"I almost believe you."

"I'm not her."

The doctor turned to her clipboard. Marie realized that she hadn't actually made direct eye contact with her, not once, always glancing down or turning away when they spoke.

"Early on," she said, "there was a hotbed of rebellion down in Austin. Some people in district eighty-four were caught harboring protesters and stockpiling munitions to fight back against the New American Militia."

"What happened?" Marie asked.

"The Valkyries came. And at Lady Martika's command, the culling began. They killed them. Slaughtered their way from one side of the district to the other. She wanted to make an example. Show the rest of the city the price of rebellion. Not everyone. A few, those of us with valuable skills, were taken for punishment and reeducation."

"You were there," Marie said.

The doctor stared at her clipboard. She'd stopped writing.

"My family was there," she said.

"They brought you here. And put you to work patching up the same people who killed your..." Marie could barely get the words out. The room was tilting, growing smaller, squeezing the air out. "That's...fucking *sick*."

"Every time she came back from a mission, Lady Martika made a point of telling me how many rebels she'd executed that day. She made me look her in the eye when she said it, so she could hunt for any sign of disloyalty on my face. I learned to be very good at not feeling anything at all."

"I'm sorry," Marie said.

For the first time, just for a passing heartbeat, the doctor locked eyes with her.

"Why?" she said. "If you aren't her, you don't have anything to be sorry for."

She gestured to a folded pile of fabric on the edge of the counter.

"They brought your clothes. We're finished here. I'll see you for a follow-up in four days."

The blouse was midnight black, edged with delicate scarlet twist cord along the crease of the razor-sharp collar. Matching black breeches accompanied a belt, textured like snakeskin, with a slim silver buckle. Marie's feet slid into high, polished leather boots. She wriggled her toes.

"They know all my sizes," she said.

"They're your clothes."

The doctor opened the door and stood aside, staring at her clipboard. Tricia was waiting in the hall. Marie tried not to flinch as Tricia put a hand on her shoulder, gently guiding her along as they walked.

"Now there's the Martie I remember," she said. "Looking sharp and ready for duty."

Marie bit down on her tongue before she could speak her mind. She knew that anything she wanted to say would probably just get the doctor in trouble. Instead, she dug for answers.

"Tell me if I've got this right. So, Ezra Talon—*this* world's version of Ezra—invented the technology for jumping across worlds."

"Bookmarks," Tricia said. "Stable portals—well, eventually stable, we had some false starts."

"So he founded Talon Armaments Group. At some point he realized our worlds were unusually synchronized and figured out another one of his incarnations was a teenager on my Earth. So he sent him that care package loaded with schematics and advanced technology. Our Ezra grew up, founded his own version of the company—Talon Worldwide—and followed in his footsteps."

"Batting a double nine, so far." Tricia paused. "Um, batting a thousand, I think you'd say? Your world's version of baseball is weird. I didn't really understand it. Anyway, yeah, 'unusually' synchronized is an understatement. You have to beat lottery-winner odds to find two worlds where multiple incarnations of the first-story characters are alive and overlapping each other. The whole space-time continuum has to pretty much bend in on itself and twist sideways. Ezra showed me a diagram, ages ago. Baked my noodle for a week."

"So your Ezra got the idea to build his world-jumping tech into a prototype suit of armor. He didn't realize that Carlo Sosa, this world's incarnation of the Scribe, had infiltrated TAG as a technician. Carlo was communicating with Carolyn Saunders, our Scribe. And he wanted to come over for a personal visit, so he stole the suit."

They walked down a flight of steel-clad steps. Men in flight uniforms snapped to attention as they passed, fists to their shoulders, beads of sweat on their motionless faces. Tricia's eyes twinkled, full of mischief.

"Ah, there's where the plot thickens." Tricia hooked her fingers in the air. "Sure, Carlo 'stole' the suit after he 'found' the heavily guarded key code to get into the massively defended hangar. Honestly? He didn't even pass the preemployment interview at TAG; we twigged to his game the second he applied."

"You set him up," Marie said.

"We set him up to succeed. We handed him the opportunity to steal that prototype, practically pushed him to do it, then we stood aside and whistled with our fingers in our ears until he got away with the goods. Dumbass thought he was some kind of super spy. But this is a fine example of the plan...not going right. He was supposed to take the suit to your planet, get together with Carolyn, and then we'd pull strings to steer them—and it—in your direction. We didn't expect he'd go joyriding first and get himself killed on a plague world. Thankfully, we were able to stash the suit at a roadside attraction and draw your Ezra toward it. Lots of spinning plates, but things more or less worked out."

"Sure," Marie said. "Ezra's motivated. Both versions are. He's the Salesman."

"And he knows it. Being doomed does drive a man's ambitions. I'll be honest, I don't understand all this magic stuff past the surface, but that part's simple enough. Tell somebody they're fated to get their hands and their tongue cut off and die in a prison cell, he's going to work hard to make sure it doesn't happen."

"Imprisoned by a tyrant," she said, echoing Carolyn's words.

She took in the sweep of the corridor, the men standing frozen at attention, the steady onyx eye of a security camera in every corner of the hall. A tall pair of double doors loomed ahead, unmarked and coated in glossy blood-red steel.

"And this is what he did," Marie said. "Your world's Ezra. This...'New America,' this fucking nightmare you people built. To escape the tyrant, he *became* the tyrant. What I don't get is the endgame here. Why go to all this effort? He has to know I'm not your 'Lady Martika.' I'm not going to just jump on board and lead his happy little death squad. What is he, obsessed with me or something?"

"Ooh," Tricia said. "*So* close. Swing and a miss. You were right on track, right up to the end there."

She put her hand on the crimson door and flashed an excited grin.

"Use those detective skills of yours, Martie. You know what this is all about. You know exactly why you're here."

Marie had been piling lies upon lies like a house of cards, weaving a blindfold of pure desperation so she wouldn't have to stare at the naked truth. But she'd added one card, one lie, one denial too many, and she watched them all flutter to the ground at her feet.

Tricia pushed the doors wide, but Marie already knew what she'd see on the other side. The throne room, scarlet and ebony, lined with Ionic pillars and dangling tapestry pennants. The honor guard, a dozen silent soldiers in black dress uniforms, flanking the long red carpet. The throne.

And Nessa, her lips painted plum and curling in a hungry smile as she extended a beckoning hand.

"At long last," she said. "Welcome home, my love. Welcome home."

SIXTEEN

For a moment Marie was back in the tunnels under Chicago as they made their escape from the Bast Club. They'd waded along a flooded tunnel, braved stagnant, freezing water and snakes. She had gone first and talked Nessa through the ordeal by telling her a story. Just a silly story. She remembered how Nessa landed in her arms, shivering, both of them soaked to the bone.

Let's do it, Nessa had whispered in her ear, her voice trembling. *Let's conquer the entire world. And when I'm in charge, they'll never be able to hurt us again.*

"How?" Marie breathed.

This Nessa wore a tailored jacket of black raw silk, with delicate silver buttons and a calfskin holster on the hip of her riding breeches. Instead of a pistol, it cradled a gnarled wooden wand tipped in sapphire, swaying at her side as she rose from her throne. Her right hand was slender and pale, her left encased in a gauntlet of silvery metal, a sheath of mercury that bent and rippled with the curve of her fingers.

"The Owl recorded her warning in Mirenze, trying to stop the cycle of death and rebirth. You and Nessa assumed you were the first and only incarnations to receive it." She shook her head. "I was twelve years old when I dug a crack into the Shadow and saw my fate. By the time I met you, eight years later, my plan was already in motion."

"The rebirth of a nation," said Tricia, standing at Marie's side.

"It wasn't that hard. I simply worked my way into the government and placed my loyal followers—thank you, Tricia—where I needed them for the day the dominoes fell. The first one tumbled with the sound of a bullet. A beloved president, felled by a foreign sniper. An exercise of emergency powers, the 'temporary' suspension of elections, a few more carefully targeted assassinations, and we were off to the races. Meanwhile, I had Ezra Talon pumping out interdimensional technology and the best minds of the occult underground—the ones I allowed to live, after rounding up every witch and spell-slinger with a spark of talent—lending supernatural support. Science and sorcery, weaponized and united in my grasp. We couldn't lose."

She came down from the dais and strode toward them, slow, like a hunting cat. She stood before Marie.

"Once they called me Secretary Fields. Now they call me the Overlord." She winked. "But you can call me Nadia."

"It was you," Marie said, putting the pieces together. "You wrote Nessa's book of spells."

"Bit strange, teaching another incarnation of myself how to be a witch—*the* Witch—but I did my best to give her the tools she'd need."

"You *poisoned* her. She's going to die."

"Not yet, she isn't. She has work to do first. All according to the plan. Besides, didn't I make sure she was properly warned? Didn't I give her the resources to keep herself alive a bit longer?"

"When did you—" Marie fell silent. Her next words came out in a whisper. "It was right in front of us. This entire time, it was right in front of us."

Nadia opened her gauntleted hand, palm upward. A window blossomed in the air above it. A hologram, tinged in shimmering sapphire, rippling as it projected footage from a security camera. Marie watched her lover standing at the coat check of the Bast Club, handing over a crow-feathered coat.

She turned, looked directly into the camera, and flashed a wicked grin before walking away.

"It wasn't someone disguised as Nessa, impersonating her," Marie said. "It was you. You planted the coat there—with the tarot card and the note inside, warning Nessa to hang on to it. Then you talked to Freddie Vinter and made sure she'd remember you, so she'd draw us to the coat when we showed up."

"A year later," Nadia said. "All the while, we'd been manipulating the messages between Carlo and Carolyn, knowing Carolyn was writing everything down—writings that would eventually fall into your hands. She wasn't even talking to Carlo half the time. That was me, posing as him."

"And her writings would lead you to that mall in Iowa, and your world's Ezra, with the technology we made certain he had access to," Tricia added.

Marie watched the dominoes tumble. "Then we'd use his technology and that card to travel to Mirenze and find Hedy, who would know exactly what was wrong with Nessa and what caused it. And how to make the elixir to keep her alive."

Nadia squeezed her fingers shut like she was snatching the world in her grasp. The hologram flickered and died.

"And everything old is new again!" she said with a gleeful laugh. "I hope it wasn't lost on you that the Owl of Mirenze created that elixir in the first place. All of my incarnations, working together in perfect concert, just as it should be."

"Why? What are you trying to *do*?"

"Same thing I always have," Nadia told her. "Try and find a way to beat the system. To break the wheel. And with a little help from my other lives, I'm going to be the one who finally does it. And you're going to be right at my side, beloved."

Marie's stomach twisted in knots. It was her lover's face, her lover's voice. It was Nessa, standing right in front of her. And it wasn't. Half of her wanted to pull Ness—no, *Nadia* into her arms and hold her tight. Half of her wanted to start throwing punches. Or run. Run until she was anywhere but here.

"I'm not Martika," was all she managed to say.

"Of course you are." Nadia reached out. Her mercury fingertip tapped the side of Marie's head. "They're *all* you. The Knight, eternal. Just like I'm Nadia Fields, and I'm Nessa Fieri, and I'm the Owl of Mirenze. I'm the same woman you fell in love with, Marie. Different lifetime, same woman."

"No," Marie said. "I'm not. You're not. From what I've seen so far? You're a monster, and it sounds like 'Lady Martika' was a fucking *bitch*."

Tricia's eyes went cold. She curled her hands into fists. Nadia just shook her head and pursed her lips, amused.

"Oh, darling. I knew this was going to be difficult, but you're really going to make me work today, aren't you? First of all, of course I'm a monster. I'm always a monster, and you love that about me. Don't pretend otherwise."

"That's not—"

Nadia waved her hand. "But let's focus on you first. You're the Knight. You know this. Why do you chafe so hard against everything that name brings with it?"

"A knight protects the innocent. A knight doesn't do...whatever the fuck it is I was doing on this planet."

"Fascinating. So, humor me, let's do a little thought experiment together. You've talked to Carolyn, you've heard of some other characters from the first story. Which ones do you remember?"

Marie caught the tease of a trap in Nadia's question, but she thought back anyway, searching her memory as she ticked them off on her fingers.

"There's the Scribe, the Salesman, the Thief, the Paladin—"

Nadia's face lit up in mock surprise.

"Ooh, that's an interesting word! What's a paladin, Marie?" She tilted her head, leaning a little closer. "C'mon. You've been reading fantasy novels your entire life. You know the answer. Tell me. What's a paladin?"

The trap snapped shut.

"A paladin is usually defined as...a crusader," Marie said. "A warrior who fights for the forces of good."

"Mm. So, sort of like a knight, but with an assumed ethical dimension. A *good* knight."

"I guess," Marie said.

"And in the vernacular of the first story, if the Paladin is cast as a crusader for the forces of good, Marie...what does that say about the Knight? What does that say about the *Witch's* Knight? Come on. It's not like you've ever been squeaky-clean outside of your ambitions and your daydreams. You have two constant companions: me, and that rage you're always struggling to keep in check. The darkness bubbling just under the surface, aching for an opportunity to come out and play. But don't take my word for it. You know how long I've had my eye on you?"

She opened her gauntlet once more, and a fresh hologram blossomed. Static flecked a surveillance recording, and tinny audio emerged from Nadia's palm. Marie watched herself, maybe two years younger and murder in her eyes, half dragging a man in cuffs from his apartment.

"I didn't do nothing wrong," he protested. "She knew what she was doing. Little minx came on to me. She seduced me."

"She's *twelve*," Marie's image hissed through gritted teeth.

"Hey, grass on the field, play ball, right?"

She shoved him. The audio clattered as the man in cuffs pitched over, howling as he tumbled down the staircase and hit every step on the way to the bottom.

"Oh, here's a more recent one. Remember this?" Nadia asked.

Her fingers twirled. The footage was blurry, jumpy, shot from a distance, but Marie recognized it at a glance. She'd just gotten done beating the hell out of Beau Kates, bouncing the pimp off every piece of furniture in his 'modeling studio,' and now she was straddling his chest and grabbing at his jaw while the bloody-faced man squirmed beneath her.

"You ever see a man die from an ink overdose, Kates? It's a bad, bad way to go. *Open your fucking mouth.*"

As her partner burst in, Tony's shout echoing just off camera, the image broke into fractal snow. Nadia snapped her fingers and banished it.

"I have an entire demo reel of Detective Reinhart's greatest hits," she said. "Pun intended."

"I did…I did what I had to do. For justice."

"For your liege," Nadia replied. "You mistook the law as your liege, before you met me. And the Knight serves her liege in all things. Faithfully. Diligently. And with no remorse or hesitation. That's who you are, Marie. It's how you were written."

"There are lines I don't cross. I don't kill innocent people."

"Sounds," Tricia murmured, "like a certain barber was running her mouth."

Marie spun around, fixing her with a glare. "Don't you *dare* hurt her."

Tricia held up her hands in mock surrender, smirking. The men of Nadia's black-uniformed honor guard still flanked the red carpet and surrounded the three women, staring in stony silence, living statues with guns on their hips.

"She must have told you about Austin," Nadia said.

"She told me what—" Marie hesitated just long enough to keep the word *I* from falling off her tongue. "What you people did."

"Curious. I assume she told you that you murdered her husband and her son."

"Something like that," Marie said.

"Something like that. Hmm. Did she tell you that her son had evaded a contraband checkpoint by mowing down three people with one of the automatic weapons he'd been hoarding?"

Marie blinked at her. "No."

"Oh. So I imagine she also didn't tell you that her husband, as part of the so-called 'resistance,' was directly involved in planting a bomb at a Liberation Day parade. A bomb designed to target civilians who supported my regime. To terrorize them. Twenty-seven innocent people died that day. I know this because you memorized their names. You recited each one, one after another, with tears in your eyes, to steel yourself before you went out to avenge their deaths."

Nadia's gauntlet drifted down to her side.

"Nothing is ever black-and-white, Marie. The world is a complicated place. You know that."

"I know that you can't kill an entire neighborhood full of people for what a few of them did."

"Hey," Tricia said, "we gave them twenty-four hours to hand the rebels over. They didn't. They knew the consequences."

"You don't remember what this world was like," Nadia said. "Dwindling resources, mass extinction, people starving in the streets. Government by the obscenely wealthy and the obscenely stupid. If I hadn't taken over, this planet would probably be a smoking cinder by now. Is my rule harsh? Yes. Am I cruel? Yes."

"I assume this is the part where you tell me why being harsh and cruel is necessary," Marie said.

"No. Now is the part where I point out the well-documented fact that you *like* it that way."

"No," Marie said.

"You fell in love with me at first sight—"

"With *Nessa*. I fell in love with Nessa. I just *met* you."

"You're still doing it," Nadia said. "Still thinking of our incarnations as different people. I am Nessa. Yes, she and I grew up under different circumstances, in different worlds, but nurture cannot change what nature has decreed. Are we really that different, do you think? Really?"

"Nessa's never done anything like..." Marie flailed a hand, taking in the throne room. "Like *this*."

"Or she hasn't yet. Given my resources, my power, and my reach, can you look me in the eye and tell me Nessa wouldn't do the exact same thing?"

Nessa's voice echoed in her ear. *Let's do it. Let's conquer the entire world.*

"Uh-huh," Nadia said to Marie's silence. "That's what I thought."

SEVENTEEN

Standing in a dark hotel room in the world next door, Nessa had put her lofty ambitions aside for the moment. Tonight she had one mission: find Marie, bring her home, and destroy anyone who stood in her way.

She studied the vial of Hedy's elixir, syrupy and translucent. She uncorked it, held her nose and chugged it down. It smelled like apples and tasted like ashes. The sign, Hedy had told her, of a Shadow infection beyond the point of no return. She felt the fire in her veins simmer down as her magic swelled, and then the sudden rush of the stimulant Hedy had added to the formula. One vial down, and one left.

A knock sounded at the door. Gazelle was outside, waiting.

"They're here," she said.

"Send them up."

Two minutes later, she ushered Janine and Tony into the room, then stood sentry by the door. Janine pulled a rolling suitcase behind her and cradled a tube of thick cardboard, still taped and marked with a Delta Air Lines check-in tag, under one arm.

"Where is she?" Tony demanded.

"Right to business," Nessa said. "Good. You brought the book?"

Janine started to unzip the suitcase. Tony stopped her with a wave of his hand.

"Where," he said, "is my *partner*? And don't give us any bull about magic or other worlds or any of that nonsense. Janine might buy that stuff, but I don't, and I'm not leaving without Marie."

"We don't have a lot of time," Nessa replied, "so in lieu of gently explaining the true nature of reality to you and hoping some of it sinks in...Clytemnestra, would you kindly lend a hand here?"

The knife on the kitchenette counter wobbled. Then it burst forth with a stream of sapphire light, motes glittering on the shaft as it projected the woman's image standing between them.

"How can I assist?" she asked.

Tony staggered backward, bumping his hip against the counter. Janine's mouth fell open and she stared, wide-eyed.

"Holy cats," Janine breathed.

"That's...that's a hologram," Tony said, pointing with his good hand. "Where did you get a hologram?"

"I don't know what that is," Clytemnestra said, "but I'm fairly certain you're wrong."

"That's not a hologram," Janine said.

"It's like that Amazon thing, an Alexa." He leaned closer to the projection and spoke slowly, raising his voice and enunciating every word. "Alexa, what movies are playing tonight?"

Nessa let out an aggravated sigh. "You are a special kind of pigheaded, aren't you? If Marie wasn't fond of you, I'd do something creatively terrible right now. But she is, deeply fond of you, which means I have to be nice. More or less. Now give me the damn book."

Janine produced it from the suitcase. Pages yellowed, cover barely holding on by a strip of spinal glue, it had spent years in Marie's eager hands, soaked in her imagination. Nessa stroked the glossy art, her fingers trailing along the raised bumps of the title. She could feel her there. Before a pang of heartache could distract her, she held it out to Clytemnestra.

"Will this do?"

A translucent hand passed over the book, then through it, her image distorting like a TV with bad reception before it snapped back into focus.

"Absolutely," Clytemnestra said. "I can feel the thread tying her essence to the pages. We can follow it to her, wherever she's been taken."

Janine hoisted the cardboard tube and thumped her knuckles on it.

"I also brought her sword. I mean, it's not a good sword. She bought it off the Home Shopping Network one night after we got blitzed on cheap chardonnay, and I don't think it's even sharp…but it's hers. Knight needs to have her sword."

"Perhaps," Nessa said. "Hang on to that for her. Keep it safe for her return. She *will* be returning tonight."

Three quick, sharp raps sounded at the door. Gazelle opened it and let Daniel in. He barely broke his stride to the heart of the hotel room as he looked Tony up and down.

"What's with the cop?"

"Marie's partner," Nessa said.

"Hold up," Tony said. "How do you know I'm a cop?"

"Because you're a cop." Daniel pointed at him, looking to Nessa. "Is he clued-in?"

"Oh, I've been trying. Janine, Tony, this is Daniel. He does card tricks and steals things. He's with the Mafia."

Janine's eyes darted back and forth between Daniel and the glowing, solemn image of Clytemnestra beside him.

"That's cool. I'm totally cool and not freaking out about any of this right now." She nodded to Daniel. "I do crimes myself. Lots of crimes."

"Uh-huh," Daniel said. He turned back to Nessa. "So here's the deal. The Monaco, just down the street, is under heavy renovation. The entire top three floors are closed off right now, and the director of security over there owes me a favor. I kicked a ghost out of his penthouse once, long story. Anyway, we've got an all-access pass and the green light to use the roof. But we've got to clear out by morning when the construction crews come back to work. Is that do-able?"

"Cutting a doorway won't take long at all," Clytemnestra told him. "Our return is not guaranteed."

"You mean the time of your return, or..."

"Marie could be stranded in any of a thousand possible alternate realities, many of which are inhabited by horrors beyond your mortal imagination. Your eyes would burst at the sight of them, while your blood froze inside your veins. If you were very, very fortunate, you would die quickly."

"Okay," Daniel said, "you ladies have fun with that."

*   *   *

Alton Roth was back at work, glad-handing his way across the ivory-and-beige kaleidoscope carpet of the Hotel Palomar. It was his first fundraiser since his son's murder, and Washington's well-to-do were showering him with compassion and discreet sealed envelopes.

He thought back to what Vanessa had said at Richard's funeral. *This should be good for a few sympathy votes.* If he hadn't been focused on wearing his mask of stoic dignity, he would have cracked a smile. After all, she wasn't wrong.

And according to the text he just got from Rosales, payback was imminent.

Nyx and her team had touched down at an airstrip outside Vegas, armed with Talon's gear and a short list of hotels. By sunrise, his son's killers would be dead and buried. One less thing to worry about.

"You concerned about collateral damage?" Rosales had asked him.

"Madam," he replied with mock gravitas, "I am a senator from the great state of Nevada. Am I concerned about an outburst of sudden, shocking violence at the heart of Las Vegas? Of course I am. After all, such an event would thrust me into the national spotlight, where my swift response and bold initiative would be witnessed by the American people. They'll see that I'm a man of action, and exactly the sort of leader they need at the helm in times of trouble."

It was the first time he'd ever seen her blink, lashes fluttering across her turquoise eyes.

"I have the blood of a murder god in my veins," Rosales said. "I have literally eaten people, and you make *me* look like a decent human being. I mean, you're a real piece of shit. You do know that, right?"

"It's only politics," he told her.

Now he was moving and shaking like old times. He was so busy squeezing a promise of cash out of a blue-haired heiress, parroting her own positions back at her like he was born to agree, that he didn't notice Calypso steaming through the crowd.

"We need to talk," he said.

"It can wait," Alton said. "The Petersens just got here, and they're always good for—"

Calypso's fingers closed on his arm like a steel vise. The sudden bone-grinding pressure stole the words from Alton's mouth.

"*Now*," Calypso said.

He marched Alton out of the ballroom, up the hall, and into the men's room, pausing just long enough to wave over one of the event security guards.

"Nobody comes in until we come out," Calypso told him.

Calypso kicked open the bathroom stalls one by one, making sure they were alone. Alton suddenly felt a rush of heat he couldn't blame on the hard fluorescent lights, his skin going clammy and a pool of sweat dampening the back of his shirt.

"I just had a word with Nyx," Calypso said.

"And?"

Calypso loomed over him. Now Alton realized where the heat was coming from. It was rising from Calypso's skin, his anger rippling out like waves of invisible fire.

"You went behind my back."

"And?" Alton repeated.

He slid one foot to the side, squaring his stance, keeping his chin high. The two prime laws of politics echoed through his mind as he fought to keep his nerve: *never apologize, always double down.*

"*I* called in the bounty on your daughter-in-law and Detective Reinhart," Calypso said. "*I* am responsible for what happens. Do you understand that?"

"What's the problem? Nyx and her crew obviously needed a little help to get the job done. So I helped. Isn't this what we both want?"

"What I want," Calypso said, "is to resolve this situation quietly and cleanly. You reached out to an agent of the Network—"

"Other way around."

"—you took aid and assistance from a daughter of the King of Wolves, and you sent Nyx into a situation that's probably going to end in a civilian bloodbath."

"In my home state," Alton said. "We can *use* this. It's win-win. Again, what's the damn problem?"

Alton stared as Calypso paced back and forth across the pristine tile, too furious to speak. *No*, he realized. *Worried.* He thought back to the conversation on the jet, him and that Scottish redhead, and the bits and pieces he'd been able to overhear.

"The bounty," Alton said. "You shouldn't have called it in at all, am I right? You broke some kind of infernal rule, and now you're afraid your people are going to notice. And the more noise Nyx makes, the more eyes are going to be on her. And you."

"That's *one* problem. You sent Nyx to Las Vegas. *Vegas*, of all the places you could have—"

"That's where Vanessa and her whore are. What should I have done?"

"You should have *let me handle it!*" Calypso roared, rounding on him. "If they're in Vegas, they're with a man named Daniel Faust. You remember Caitlin, that woman who was waiting on your plane? She's the right hand of Prince Sitri, one of the most powerful rulers of hell. She also knows what I did. Daniel is her consort. Nyx wants to kill Daniel, and if he's with Vanessa and Marie, she has a perfect excuse. Can you connect the lines from there, or do I have to draw you a goddamn *map*?"

Alton was sweating hard now. Calypso's naked fury turned the bathroom into a sauna as his voice whip-cracked off the tiled walls. Beads of moisture broke out on Alton's forehead and trickled down. He brushed the back of his hand across his face and stood his ground. If Alton was anything at all, he was a born opportunist, and a new opportunity was unfolding right before his eyes.

"So what you're saying is, if you get found out or if this Caitlin turns you in, your own people are going to…what? Something bad, right? Something real bad. Kill you, maybe?" Now Alton couldn't keep the slow, sly smile from his lips. "Which means, if I understand right, our contract is null and void. So I get my soul back. And everything you've done for me, I get it all for free. I play my cards right, I could probably make it the rest of the way to the White House on my own. I'd be the man who sold his soul, won it back, *and* got everything he ever wanted. Sundae with a cherry on top."

Calypso's voice dropped to a panther growl.

"Better check the fine print, baby. If that's how it all went down? Maybe. But right now, you're still on the hook. And in violation. Contract says if you deliberately do anything that could endanger my efforts on your behalf, or if you go against me, I can punch your ticket on the spot. Go directly to hell, do not pass go, do not collect two hundred dollars or much of anything else on your way to eternal damnation."

Alton had always been a gambler. The bigger the risk, the bigger the reward. Now he stood on the doorstep of the biggest gamble of his life.

"Do it," he said.

Calypso stared at him, uncomprehending.

"Do it," Alton repeated. "Right here. Right now. Kill me. Kill me and send me straight to hell. You're right. Contract says you can. So do it."

Calypso held his silence. The waves of heat rippled and broke, leaving Alton caked in sweat gone cold as ice.

"Little lesson for you," Alton said. "When you go to the negotiating table, never let the other side know how badly you want to make a deal. You do that, they'll bend you right over a barrel."

"That so," Calypso rumbled.

"You tipped your hand long ago. You've got everything riding on getting me into the White House. Your name, your reputation, you staked it all. And we've come way too far for you to back out now. Sure, you can punch my ticket. But you won't. And we both know you won't. I just called your bluff; I've got aces high and you've got *nothing*. Now if you'll excuse me, I've got a fundraiser to get back to."

He turned away, toward the bathroom mirror, and yanked a paper towel from the chrome dispenser by the sink. He dabbed it at his face, mopping up the stray beads of sweat, and crumpled it in his hand. For the first time since his son died, he felt like he was back in control. Everything was going to work out just fine.

"This isn't over," Calypso said to his reflection.

Alton tossed the wadded-up paper towel to the floor at Calypso's feet. It bounced off the polished toe of his shoe. Alton turned his back and headed for the door.

"Just do your damn job," he said. "Opportunity's about to start knocking again. Be ready."

EIGHTEEN

Darkness fell like a cloak over Las Vegas. The skyline erupted in vivid light, a neon carnival where the shadows danced. And the storm rolled in. The rains only came to kiss the desert a few times every year. When they did, they made up for lost time.

On a red rock bluff outside the city, just far enough that the urban sprawl shrank to a razor-thin glow of white light, the first traces of rain dotted the dusty stone. A ragged white hem swayed as the Mourner shook a rattle made of stretched hide and bone, her spine twisting like a rope as she bent her body forward and back. Dora stood near her, face and open hands lifted to the black sky, raindrops pooling in her amber eyes. She had a song on her lips, something ancient, something keening, with words made of forgotten vowels.

A shape emerged from the dark, taking on form and scarlet hue. The Lady in Red wore a secret smile, and the antique key at her throat glistened cold and wet.

"Did I not say, when this all began, where we would meet again?" she asked.

"In a storm of our own brewing," the Mourner replied.

"Before the battle's won," Dora added. "And tonight?"

"You hardly need *my* magic to prophesy what happens tonight," the Lady said. "You hardly need magic at all for that."

"Sure. Some heads are gonna roll. But what about after that? Does Nessa really have a chance of pulling this off? The whole universe is going to be turned against her by this time tomorrow, if she makes it that far. Hell, *she's* up against her. And Nadia literally wrote the book on what Nessa's capable of."

"Can you keep a secret?" asked the Lady.

"That's what we do."

"Yes," the Lady replied with a wink. "It is. Let us focus on the here and the now and the night at hand. My daughters have a difficult doorway to open, and a long journey ahead. We should ease their passage a bit."

She raised one elegant hand, her slender finger pointing toward the black and turbulent sky.

"Shake the rattle and strike the drum. Let's dance down a storm. One to remember."

*   *   *

Hedy came back to Nessa's hotel room with a plastic bag that read *Las Vegas Pawn and Collectibles*. She lugged it in, cradling the bottom of the bag like it could burst at any moment, and dumped it out on the bed. A spill of antique silver and gold, coins ranging from the size of a thumbnail to heavy medallions, tumbled across the pink bedspread.

"Butterfly and Mantis did well," she said. "These should do for the trip. Where's Clytemnestra?"

Janine pointed to the side of the crumpled bag. "Is that blood?"

"Back inside her knife," Nessa told Hedy, shooting a glare across the room at Tony. "*Someone* was being very rude. Anyway, she's resting up for the ritual."

"I think that's blood," Janine said.

"Explain what the coins are for?" Daniel asked. "I wasn't clear on that part of the plan."

Nessa picked up a gold coin. She turned it in her hand and gave it an appraising eye.

"We have no idea where Marie landed, but we know she's still alive, which suggests—hopefully—she's somewhere civilized. But unless we're beyond lucky, our paper money will be worthless there."

"No guarantee that these will be worth anything either," Hedy said, "but silver and gold are valuable both here and on my world, so it's a reasonable bet. I always say it's better to have and not need than to need and not have."

"Wait." Janine stared at her. "Your world? Are...are you an alien?"

"Janine, Hedy. Hedy, Janine." Nessa tossed the coin onto the pile and scooped up another one. "Hedy is my daughter, and yes, she's an alien."

Janine pointed at Hedy, then at Nessa's face, then back again.

"Your daughter? She's older than you."

"I was dead for a little while," Nessa told her. "It didn't stick."

"I am so done with this," Tony grumbled, standing in the corner with his good arm crossed tight over his sling.

Gazelle scurried to answer another knock at the door. The new arrival was cut from rawhide, junkie-thin and grizzled, draped in bikers' leathers. His thin hair was plastered to his scalp, and his rough whiskers glistened as he walked in, hauling a fat canvas rucksack over each shoulder.

"Hey, Winslow," Daniel said. "Just drop 'em here on the bed. Thanks for coming out on short notice."

"Startin' to rain like a mother out there," Winslow said.

Nessa shoved the coin pile aside, making room. The army-green rucksacks rattled as they landed side by side on the edge of the mattress. Without even looking, Winslow jerked a thumb back over his shoulder at Tony.

"What's with the cop?"

"Who says I'm a cop?" Tony replied.

"I do, 'cause you're a cop. I ain't offended, some of my best customers are cops. Still..."

Winslow looked to Daniel. "He's cool," Daniel said.

"*The guy* has spoken," Winslow muttered.

He unzipped each bag and folded the canvas back to unveil a cornucopia of firearms. Nylon straps held pistols snug against taped magazines, alongside a scattering of shotguns and hunting rifles. Tony moved closer, eyes going wide as Winslow hoisted a sawed-off shotgun and sighted its twin barrels toward the rain-slick window.

"Brought the usual goody bags. Just what you wanted, reliable and easy to transport, nothing too fancy. Take your pick and we'll talk pricing."

"Wait," Tony said as Daniel took the shotgun, weighing it in his hands. "What is this?"

"An arms deal," Daniel said. "See, he gives us guns, and we give him money. That's how arms deals work."

Gazelle stepped up behind him and stared over his shoulder, eyes wide.

"Hand cannons. Marie told me about these. Can I have one?"

"Winslow, set the lady up with a pistol, please?" Daniel put a hand on Gazelle's shoulder and ushered her up to the edge of the bed. "She's from a parallel Earth where they haven't invented firearms yet, so give her something a beginner can handle."

Winslow rolled his eyes as he reached into the bag, tugging at the nylon straps. "Supposed to warn me before you get me involved in weird shit, Dan. You know I don't like the weird shit."

"What? She's an alien who wants a hand cannon. That's not weird."

"As much as I agree with this guy," Tony said, pointing at Winslow, "can we get back to...this? The thing that's happening right now? What the hell, man? I'm an NYPD detective. You can't do this shit right in front of me."

"I commit crimes in front of cops all the time," Daniel told him.

"Ones with actual jurisdiction," Winslow added.

"Why. Do we need. Guns?" Tony said, forcing the words out.

Daniel set the shotgun down and turned to face him.

"Because there's a bounty on Vanessa and Marie's heads, and a small army of psychopaths looking to cash in. In about forty minutes, we're all going to march out of the relative safety of this hotel, out onto the Las Vegas Strip, and make our way about a block south of here. We'll be exposed, surrounded by crowds and heavy traffic every step of the way. Then we have to keep these ladies covered while they do a very complicated ritual, which could be the last and only chance we've got to save your partner's life."

Daniel swept his open hand toward the rucksacks.

"So do you want a gun or not? I'm buying."

Tony stared at him. Then he sighed and pushed himself away from the wall, walking up to the bed.

"Yes," he grumbled, "I want a gun."

"There you go. Was that so hard?"

"Got a Glock Nineteen with your name on it," Winslow told Tony, nodding at his sling as he reached into the rucksack on the left. "Has a trigger safety, easier to handle with that busted wing you got there."

Gazelle had a million questions about the matte-black handgun, and as they spilled from her lips, Daniel's phone buzzed against his hip. He took it out and tapped the screen.

"Carolyn, you'd better be able to walk by the time we—" He paused, listening. "Shit. Okay. Stay exactly where you are and keep your head down. I'm coming to get you."

He hung up and shoved the phone into his pocket.

"We're leaving. *Now*."

*   *   *

At first, Carolyn had been annoyed that she'd been assigned an obvious minder. Badger—his real name was Lazzaro, apparently, but he was fine being called by either—trailed her down to the bar overlooking the casino floor and hung on her every word. At first it gave her flashbacks to some of the fantasy conventions she'd been to, picking up overeager fans like barnacles when she just wanted to get a good buzz on.

Of course, Badger had never read any of her books, though he'd lived on the fringes of a couple of them. She was halfway into her whiskey highball when she realized why he was sitting so close to her. His knuckles were white against the edge of the lacquered bar top, squeezing it like he was a passenger on a plane with a blown-out engine and all he could do was ride and pray.

"Is it the crowds?" she asked.

The open bar perched on the edge of the casino floor, overlooking the sweep of flashing, trilling slots. The table games were heating up, every seat filled and shouting gamblers packed shoulder to shoulder as dice tumbled across the green felt. A fresh wave of tourists shambled in through the smoked-glass lobby doors, looking like drowned rats, and Carolyn caught a flash of lightning at their backs before the doors whisked shut.

"The noise," Badger said. "It's quiet at night, back home."

Carolyn sipped her drink. "Yeah, this town doesn't do quiet. I live in a farmhouse. Edge of nowhere is the only place I can hear myself think. How about we go back upstairs? I can hit up the minibar."

"This is all right," he told her, the tone of his voice saying anything but. "The Dire Mother says we're going to be here for a while. Maybe...a long while. I need to get used to it."

"At least order a drink. It'll loosen you up a little. Just charge it to the room."

"That was one of the things Daniel said not to do."

"He says a lot of things," Carolyn replied. "Trust me, doing Vegas on somebody else's credit card is a rare and wonderful treat. Take full advantage. I am."

Badger gave the bartender an uncertain glance and slowly raised one hand—the one that wasn't clinging to the bar—to get her attention.

"Do you think they have honey mead?" he asked.

"I guarantee they do not. Ask for a rum and Coke, that's a good 'welcome to Earth' starter drink."

Carolyn's gaze drifted across the lobby as the doors slid open again, a curtain of rain beyond the glass. More new arrivals. Not tourists.

Water trailed down Nyx's serpentine blond braid, droplets

clinging to her leathers and glistening like her body was sheathed in black eel skin. She had four men with her. They fanned out and moved in military cadence on their way to the check-in desk. Each one had an identical black duffel bag slung at his side, drooping low like they were carrying heavy cargo.

"Cancel that," Carolyn muttered as she dug her phone out.

She slid a little lower on the barstool. Nyx was showing a picture to the check-in clerk. Carolyn's restless fingertips drummed against the bar as she waited for Daniel to pick up.

"Hope you're all packed and ready to go," she said, "because your least-favorite demonic bounty hunter just showed up. I don't suppose there's a back way out of here?"

NINETEEN

"Once," Nadia said, "I thought a perfect plan was all I needed. Then I learned how plans fracture and break when they come into contact with reality. I was betrayed not long after my reign began, by someone I thought I could trust. He slipped a bomb into my first throne room."

She paused, silent, studying her mechanical gauntlet. The mercury-covered plates rippled as she turned her hand. Motes of sapphire light, hologram static, trailed behind her fingertips.

"You died shielding me from the blast. You died, cradled in the one arm the bomb left me. And that taught me the value of trust."

At Marie's side, Tricia scowled at the memory. "It was Ezra. The Overlord gave him *everything*—security, a fortune, a way to escape his fate, and he still stabbed her in the back. He was afraid she was going to turn on him, so he turned traitor first."

Marie looked between the two women. She shook her head.

"But…he still works for you."

Nadia offered Marie a tiny smile.

"No. His image works for me. And the world-class think tank he recruited. You see, I learned early on that some people would never follow me, not eagerly, so I gave them a more palatable alternative. The loyal and tireless genius, and a great *man* who they can look up to. The wizard behind the curtain."

"Obviously," Tricia said, her voice dripping with sarcasm, "the Overlord is nothing but a figurehead. It's really Ezra Talon who's leading New America to glory. Everybody knows that."

Marie thought back to her cab ride that morning. *He's gonna save us all*, the cabbie had said, before reflexively praising the Overlord and offering a gesture of nervous prayer.

"One of the many little games we play, to keep the populace docile and obedient. As for Ezra," Nadia said, "he still has an office at the TAG building. More of a cell, really, with mirrored walls and lights that never turn off, so he has to stare at himself every waking moment of every single day. Well. What's left of him, anyway."

She raised her hand. Her gauntlet's fingers wriggled.

"Sometimes I walk by his window and give him a little wave, like this. He can't wave back, of course. It's the little pleasures in life that matter, don't you think?"

"And you went to all this trouble," Marie said, "hunting across the universe, poisoning Nessa, all of it, for...what? To find a replacement version of Martika?"

"Think bigger, love. Much bigger. For one thing, if you were all I was after, I would have just sent Tricia to grab you the day we found your world."

"Which I suggested," Tricia added.

"For another," Nadia said, "do you really think I'd murder one of my own incarnations, for something so petty as taking her Knight? Ridiculous. If my plans didn't absolutely require Nessa's death, I would have collected her right along with you. Two incarnations of the Witch, working together in the same timeline, on the same world? We'd be unstoppable. As for you, I'm certain I could convince her to share you with me. And let's be honest, the threesomes would be amazing."

Marie folded her arms tight across her chest. The scarlet banners lining the room, spaced between tall Ionic columns, dangled motionless in the frigid air. Lines of soldiers in black still flanked the red carpet down the heart of the chamber, staring straight ahead in stoic silence. The stillness of the hall bore a weight that pressed down on her shoulders. A sense of absolute inevitability, blossoming from the gears of Nadia's machinations.

"Why, then?" she asked.

"I did start out looking for another Knight," Nadia explained. "This world, this version of us, had a unique glitch in the system. You understand our story, yes? Our curse?"

"We die together," Marie replied.

"Or I die, and you follow shortly after. Usually by your own hand." Nadia wagged a mercury finger in mock reproach. "You kill yourself a *lot*. But in this world, I was mortally injured and survived, medical technology and cybernetics to the rescue. So I theorized...if I could find a Knight who had lost her Witch and brought her here to live with me, would the curse of the first story still take hold? Technically, you aren't *my* Knight, and I've already survived the incident that was supposed to end me."

"The story would...break," Marie said. "The universe would stop trying to kill us."

"It's just a theory. But the more worlds I explored, hunting for one where another version of the Witch and her Knight existed at the same time as me, disturbing patterns began to emerge. Signs of a precursor civilization, with language and iconography that spread across multiple parallel worlds."

"You mean like the cathedral under Deep Six?"

"Precisely. And while I've always been happy with the idea of a random, chaotic, and entirely rudderless universe, one devoid of purpose save the purpose we choose to give it...I was forced to face evidence of an architect."

Marie thought back to the cathedral, concealed at the bottom of an alien sea. The mammoth pews of green stone, the carvings of faceless judges standing over cowering, kneeling figures, the condemned burning in a pit of fire.

"God," Marie said. "You're talking about God."

"Not an omnipotent one. Not omniscient, either. We found signs of a civil war. Apparently some of his first children thought a change in management was in order. I don't disagree. Point being, we came across strongholds, temples, caches from both sides of the fight. And many of those caches had locks."

"Like the one at the cathedral. We had to bleed, to open it. It was made for us."

"Ah," Nadia said. "You made the same mistake I did, at first. It *wasn't*, as I discovered after studying a couple and piecing together more of the precursors' language. They were built to keep the talking apes out. You know, stop primitive humans from getting their hands on any dangerous magic. The locks can only be opened by the direct, original creations of God himself. Beings personally crafted by his own divine hands."

The throne-room lights seemed to dim like a storm cloud passing over the sun, as the implication set in. And with it, horror.

"Wait," Marie said. "You're telling me—"

"We thought the first story was created by random chance, an outburst of spontaneous magic in the wake of humanity's discovery of the power of words. A cosmic fluke. We thought the storyteller was some dead, ancient shaman, who likely went to their grave with no understanding of the curse they'd inflicted upon us."

Nadia shook her head.

"God did this to us," she said. "He did it to us on purpose. He created us to suffer and die, again and again, for all eternity."

"But *why?*" Marie asked.

"I'd love to ask him."

Nadia turned her gauntleted palm to the heavens. Golden light spilled from her hand, a new hologram tracing itself in the air. A map of spheres, tied together by luminous and gilded vines.

"The war went badly. God fled and sealed himself up inside one of the first worlds he created." Her opposite hand tapped a golden world at the top of the hologram. It glitched, flooding with static, as her plum-painted fingernail poked through the image. "Elysium. Heaven itself."

"As far as we can tell," Tricia chimed in, "the rebels were confident they could kill him, and he was clearly confident he could *be* killed. They just couldn't get to him."

"But every lock has a key."

New images blossomed around the vine-tangled spheres. A copper bell, engraved with spidery runes. A slim black book. A slender candle, electronic distortion shivering around its tall and steady flame.

Marie knew that bell. It was snug against her side, hidden in Nessa's mirror bag. The realization ignited a spark of hope: not even Nadia had noticed the bag, thanks to the invisibility enchantment. Nadia had mastered witchcraft and the arts of power, and she'd woven a seemingly inescapable trap for them both...but Nessa was stronger than she realized.

"Long story short," Nadia said, "three ritual tools, imbued with the magic of creation and designed to crack open the gates of Elysium. Before they could be used, God's loyalists stole them away. They couldn't destroy the relics, so they settled for the next best thing. They hid them, scattered far and wide across the backwaters of the universe."

"We found that bell in the cathedral," Marie said. "And I don't know if it's the same one, but Hedy almost lost her entire coven over a magic candle she stole."

"Another moment where the master plan went sideways," Tricia grumbled.

"Quite," Nadia said. "My teams recovered the candle, and I sent it to Mirenze, where Hedy was supposed to stumble across it. The Sisters of the Noose found it first. None of Hedy's people were supposed to be harmed. I regret that. Meanwhile, we steered your world's version of Ezra toward Deep Six."

"With the bookmarks inside the suit Carlo stole," Marie said, putting it together.

"Exactly. Carlo 'steals' the prototype armor—he never realized we *let* him do it—then Ezra 'finds' the suit. Tricia had to make some last-minute changes to the plan, thanks to Carlo getting himself killed, but it all worked out. End result: two of the three relics end up in Nessa's hands, while I stay concealed in the shadows."

"And the third?"

"Working on it," Tricia said. "We've got a line on the book, just need someone to go pick it up."

"But you still haven't explained why you poisoned Nessa," Marie said. "What's the point of all this? What are you trying to do?"

Nadia's hologram seethed. The vines twisted, strangling the gilded worlds, crushing them as the golden light turned emerald and black. The spheres became broken gemstones suspended in a net of obsidian barbed wire.

"Shadow sickness is incurable. Nessa has had enough time to come to grips with her impending death. She knows there's no escape, and she's highly motivated to make her mark before she goes. We always are. No one knows myself better than I do, Marie, which is exactly what makes Nessa the perfect instrument of my will. I know how she thinks, how she reacts, what she'll do when given a limited range of options. So, in order for my plan to succeed, I had to do just that: remove her options, taking her pieces off the chessboard one by one until all that remains are the moves I *want* her to make."

One by one, the hologram worlds crumbled to dust. Emerald powder rained down into Nadia's open palm. It pooled, turning liquid, turning scarlet. The image drooled between her fingers like the lifeblood of the universe itself.

"Nessa will find the keys to Elysium. And then…furious, dying, with a rage hotter than the sun and nothing left to lose, Nessa will do the only thing Nessa *can* do."

Marie took a halting step back. She grasped for words, for the breath she suddenly couldn't find.

"She's going to kill God," Marie whispered.

"And you'll be here with me, safe, alive, and at my side where you belong." Nadia's lips curled in a familiar lopsided smile. "Sorry, darling. This time, *I'm* the one who gets to slay the dragon."

INTERLUDE

The interrogator led Carolyn through a bulkhead, the edges of the thick door caked with rust. It whined shut behind them, sealing them into a narrow stretch of corridor between two reinforced doors, the floor lined with a metallic grille and baking under hard overhead lights. Condensation clung to the steel-plate walls, and a smell of mildew hung in the stagnant air.

He had mostly been listening in silence while they walked, with Carolyn trailing behind him. Now he glanced back, looking her over with a glimmer of awareness in his eyes.

"So *that's* why we were never able to find Marie Reinhart. She never went back to her own planet. Out of curiosity, was Nadia's theory about breaking the cycle correct? Is Reinhart still alive, with her, or—"

"No spoilers," Carolyn said. "I thought we were going to see your boss?"

The interrogator gestured to the windowless door before them. A heavy wheel was set into the thick steel, like a bank vault. Or an airlock, with nothing beyond it but the freezing void of space.

"Remember, you asked for this." He glanced down. His eyes narrowed, and he pointed to the sleeve of her sweater. A spot, dark and about the size of a dime, stained the fabric near her left wrist. "You have a cut."

She shrugged. "Might have banged myself up on something when they brought me in. Don't ask what. I had a bag over my head."

"No." The hook of his nose wrinkled. "And I looked you over

when you were brought to the interrogation room. That happened after you arrived."

"I'm in my sixties; if I can go a single day without injuring myself, I'm ahead of the game. Last week I pulled a muscle getting out of bed. And this place isn't exactly up to OSHA standards, in case you haven't noticed." She turned her hand as much as the cuffs would let her, looking it over. "It's shallow, already clotted. I don't need a bandage."

"I didn't offer you one," he replied, turning his back on her.

He took hold of the wheel. It groaned, a high rasping sound, as it slowly turned in his grip.

"I suggest you remember your manners," he said. "You are about to enter the presence of royalty."

Carolyn's stomach clenched, tight as a fist. Her heart hammered, and her fingers squeezed the glass of tepid water between her frail hands. The door swung wide. The interrogator gave her a mocking bow and gestured with a flourish. Like a convict marching to the electric chair with no last-minute pardon in sight, she stepped into the king's chamber.

She had prepared herself for every horror she could think of. Darkness. Fire. Torment and misery incarnate. A creature, foul and twisted beyond imagining.

The room was warm. The air smelled like an ocean breeze tinged with exotic spice, and soft lights cast long shadows along the wood-paneled walls of a modest study. Her feet touched down on piled shag carpet, money green, as a song she knew by heart played on an antique phonograph. Peggy Lee, the venerable songstress, crooning "Why Don't You Do Right?"

"Isn't that," her host asked with a rich baritone chuckle and a nod to the phonograph, "the eternal question?"

The King of Rust reclined in a leather armchair, beside a varnished side table bearing a brandy snifter and cut-crystal glasses. Two more chairs, smaller, sized to fit a human frame, faced him to form a cozy nook.

He was beautiful.

Even sitting, he towered over her, easily twelve feet tall. His appearance was alien, but his individual features echoed the most idealized parts of the human face. His head was long, smooth, like an Easter Island carving, but his eyes were big and rich and deep, his cheekbones high, his features blessed with the kind of symmetrical perfection that supermodels dreamed of. A robe of russet silk draped his body, dangling open to bare the hairless alabaster skin and sculpted muscles of his chest.

A mist clung to his body. It was an aura of faint light, sparkling golden motes following the gentle rise of one long and three-fingered hand. He gestured to the phonograph. It slowed, Peggy Lee's voice drawing out into a long, garbled, single note, distorting until it stopped dead. The room fell silent, save for the soft and relentless tick of a clock.

Behind her, the interrogator shut the door.

"Please," the king said, "won't you both join me? Sit down."

Carolyn settled into one of the chairs, cradling her glass on her lap. Her interrogator took the other. He shifted, uncomfortable, staring down at his shoes.

"We can be comfortable here," the king said. "Uncuff her."

The interrogator gave him a nervous look. "My lord?"

"Do you think an elderly fantasy writer poses you a threat? Because I know you're certainly not saying she poses *me* a threat."

The interrogator wisely held his silence. He leaned over with a tiny key and unfastened the handcuffs before taking his seat again.

"Enjoying the story so far?" Carolyn asked, rubbing her sore wrists.

"Hanging on your every word," the king replied.

"I know. I had my suspicions at first," she said, jerking a thumb at the interrogator, "but once I saw the earpiece, I knew for certain that 'the king is always listening' wasn't just a figure of speech. I'm betting his lie-detector routine was a fake, too. *You* were the one who caught me when I bent the truth, and told him to call me on it. You probably passed him the questions you wanted asked, too. You were my real audience."

"I find it convenient, and amusing, to work through human proxies. Before we continue, I must know something. I'm curious: am I what you expected to see, when you walked through that door?"

"Honestly? I was expecting horns and a pitchfork," Carolyn said. "Something ugly, something gross. In retrospect, though, no reason I should have."

"So you've figured it out? You know what the Kings of Man truly are."

"They say God created man in his own image," Carolyn mused. She stared into the king's golden eyes. "But before he made man...he created angels."

"He should have stopped there," the king replied.

"The carvings in the cathedral under Deep Six gave it away," she explained. "Resting place of one of the 'three faithful thrones.' Through his act of sacrifice, the epitaph said, 'the nine kings are defied.' But the body rotting in that coffin looked an awful lot like you."

The king leaned to his side. His fingers delicately uncorked the snifter. Brandy spilled into a crystal glass, kissing the air with its aroma.

"There were twelve of us, in the beginning," he said. "The Twelve Thrones. Vessels of God's power, instruments of his divine will. Brothers until the bitter end."

"Nine of you tried to pull a palace coup. Three stayed loyal."

"And I mourn them still. Can I interest you in a glass?"

"I'm good with water," Carolyn replied.

The king arched one hairless brow.

"Carolyn Saunders, saying no to a drink? Now that's an unexpected twist."

"We're closing in on the end of the story," she replied. "I need to keep my wits sharp, to tell it just right."

"After, then," he said.

"And before the firing squad. I'm curious, too. Are you going to kill me yourself, or have your errand boy here do the job?"

The king gave her a polite chuckle. He sipped his brandy.

"What's that thing you were saying earlier?" he asked. "Right. No spoilers. Don't want to ruin the surprise."

"Cute," Carolyn said.

"But please, do continue the tale. I assume this is the last we've seen of Marie Reinhart. Taking her final bow, to step out of the story and spend the rest of her life as the consort to a different Knight's Witch."

"Bad assumption."

The king tilted his head. His eyes narrowed to reptilian slits, squinting at her.

"She was stranded on a distant world with no way to return home," he said, "and surrounded by a literal army while her lover was in the final throes of an incurable disease. Surrender was Reinhart's only rational choice."

"Only rational choice, sure, but you're forgetting something." Carolyn cracked a dry smile. "When you run out of rational choices, sometimes you need to get good and crazy. And when it came to fighting for Nessa's life—even stranded a world away—Marie didn't know the meaning of the word *surrender*."

Act II

The Symmachy Encore

TWENTY

Marie was a statue carved from ice, threatening to melt on the red carpet of the throne room. Or shatter into pieces.

"You can't..." she breathed. "You don't even know if Nessa can pull it off. You have no idea what's going to happen if she succeeds—"

"That's the thrill of it," Nadia told her. "We don't, do we? Who knows what happens when the creator of the universe dies? Do we chug along without him? Does the wheel of worlds come crashing down like a house of cards? I'll tell you this, though: I'm done, *we* are done being trapped in this endless cycle."

"What if it's the end? The end of everything?"

"Then we're still set free," Nadia replied. "No more reincarnations. No more needless suffering, no more pointless death."

She took a step closer to Marie, her eyes bright and fervent. Her gauntlet trailed ripples of hologram static, luminous electronic noise.

"No more losing you," Nadia said. "So we still win. In the end, no matter what happens, things are finally going to change. We finally get our happy ending."

"What if nothing changes? What if God dies and the first story keeps repeating without him, and all of this was for nothing?"

"Not for nothing," Nadia told her. "Because if nothing else, we finally get what we deserve. Justice. He did this to us, Marie. Every single time we've been murdered, our love and our memories shattered, our lives erased from the narrative, that's another layer of blood on that bastard's hands. He did this to us.

And he needs to answer for it. He needs to be punished. I *know* you agree with me."

"Not at this cost," Marie said. "Not if it means losing Nessa."

Nadia held out her open hands, one living mercury and the other pale flesh. The fire in her eyes faded to something wistful, almost soft.

"You only say that because you haven't accepted the truth yet, Marie. Nessa is standing right in front of you. Same woman. Different life. Do something for me? Close your eyes."

Marie's world went dark. She stood there, eyes closed, the throne room dead silent. She felt Nadia move against her, hot breath washing across her throat.

"Whose voice is this?" Nadia purred in her ear.

Marie didn't answer.

"Inhale," Nadia told her. "Breathe deep. Who do you smell?"

She smelled clean, fresh linen. The tang of Chanel perfume, and the aftermath of a storm. The mingling of scents carried her a world away, to the bedroom of Nessa's brownstone in the West Village. It was the scent of the first night they spent in each other's arms.

"That's not fair," Marie murmured.

"I'm never fair. You said it yourself, I'm a monster." Nadia's arm curled around her. The fingers of her unsheathed hand trailed slowly up Marie's spine. "I'm your monster. Who touches you like this, Marie?"

With her eyes closed, nothing but scent and voice and touch, she could have been back in New York. Back in a time before her entire world flipped upside down.

"Say my name," Nadia urged her.

"Ness—"

The word slipped from her lips, almost free before Marie caught herself and bit down on it. Nadia's response was a rich chuckle in her ear as her fingers curled around the back of Marie's neck, stroking gently.

"Good girl. Now…would you do something else for me, Marie? Just a tiny thing."

Marie nodded her assent, inhaling Nessa, feeling her presence in the dark behind her eyelids. Nadia's hand tightened on the back of her neck, just like Nessa's often did. Just a little. A proprietary touch.

"I want you," Nadia whispered, "to get down on your hands and knees and kiss my boots."

In the instant before Marie flinched, before her eyes flicked open, one of her knees almost buckled. It was just a tiny betrayal. But she knew it, and Nadia knew it, and Nadia cackled with delight as she pulled Marie into an embrace.

"So close," Nadia laughed. "You see how easy this is going to be? I know this is all strange and upsetting and new, Marie, but all you have to do is give it a chance. Give me a chance. You're going to be happy here."

What scared Marie more than anything was that Nadia was right. Not maybe right. Not probably right. She was right, and when Marie closed her eyes, it was easy to trick herself into thinking she was back in Nessa's arms. After a month with Nadia, a year, would she even know the difference?

And while she was tricking herself, the real Nessa was out there, all alone, dying, and departing to make her final stand without her Knight beside her. Marie's jaw tightened until it shook.

What makes a knight? she asked herself.

She'd grappled with the question ever since her awakening. Was a knight defined by her liege, her cause, the code she upheld? What made those things worthy? She'd spent her childhood reading tales of imaginary knights, stories of valor and chivalry. She had witnessed Gazelle's devotion back in Mirenze, her willingness to hold the line and die in battle so her coven could escape. And Marie's own decision, as she pulled her to safety, that being a knight meant not leaving anyone behind.

She wasn't leaving Nessa behind, either.

Escaping this place was impossible, but Marie knew three things for certain. *A knight always fights, never quits*, she told herself. *A knight never abandons her liege. And a knight finds a way to do the impossible, or dies trying.*

She forced herself to relax. Let her jaw unclench, her hands rising up to rest on Nadia's hips, holding her like they were about to slow-dance.

"It's funny," Marie said. "Back on the road, not long after we left New York, Nessa and I had an argument. She was wild and free, like she is, and I was still acting like I had to follow all the rules. She told me that she thought a little anarchy would be good for me."

Nadia smiled, nuzzling her nose against Marie's shoulder.

"With all due respect to my other incarnation, I think you'll find my empire a much more comfortable fit for you. This is a place of order and discipline. People who obey the rules—my rules—tend to thrive under my wing."

Marie sidestepped, easing Nadia along with her. Turning slightly as they moved a few inches closer to the edge of the red carpet.

"I don't think I took what she said to heart, at first. You know how stubborn I can be."

"Oh," Nadia said, "do I ever."

"But a little anarchy has a practical application sometimes," Marie said. "You know what really decides nine out of ten battles, when you get down to it?"

"Ruthlessness?" Nadia asked. "No. Determination."

"The element of surprise," Marie said.

She bent one knee, sprang backward, and spun toward the closest member of the honor guard, throwing all of her weight into a punch. His nose shattered under her knuckles, spattering her fist with blood, and he crumpled to the floor. Her other hand lunged for his belt as he fell and snatched the pistol from his holster. It was bulky, heavier than her service piece with a texture like ridged cold plastic against her palm.

Marie pressed the gun against the side of her head and put her finger on the trigger.

"I'll do it," she said. "I swear I'll do it. Anyone takes one step toward me and I will blow my brains all over your fancy carpet. What was it you said, Nadia? I kill myself a *lot.*"

The room erupted in drawn guns, confusion, the other guards moving to protect their mistress until Tricia raced to Nadia's side.

"Stand down," Tricia roared. "Everyone *stand the fuck down right now.* Holster those weapons and stand right where you are."

In the midst of chaos, Nadia was a beacon of steely calm. She wore a wicked little smile and held out her open hand.

"Cute. Very cute. Hand over the gun, Marie. We don't have time for this."

"She'll do it," Tricia said, eyes bulging as she swept her gaze across the throne room.

"Listen to her," Marie said. "I'll pull the trigger. You know I will."

"Bold words," Nadia replied.

"I told you we should have kept her under sedation and restrained until Nessa was dead," Tricia said. "Damn it, I *told* you, and you didn't listen."

Nadia glared at her. "Mind your tone."

Tricia took a deep breath. The honor guard stood frozen around her like her sheer willpower was holding them in check.

"Ma'am," she said to Nadia. "Please. Listen to me. Lady Martika was my best friend. I knew her better than anyone, maybe even better than you. And if the situation was reversed—if you were dying a world away, and Martika was here—she would have pulled that trigger in a heartbeat. She'd do it just out of *spite.*"

"Out of duty," Marie said. "As long as my liege draws breath, I have a duty. And I will not abandon that duty. I'll die first. I don't *want* to die, but I will do it. You know I'm not lying. People tell me I'm pretty bad at lying."

Nadia stood there, silent, weighing their words as she stared deep into Marie's eyes. Slowly, her outstretched hand lowered to her side.

"What exactly do you want, Marie?"

"A ride out of here," she said. "You're about to lead Nessa to the third artifact, right? The last key she needs to enter Elysium?"

"That's the plan."

"So send *me*. Nessa isn't going to Elysium. I am. I'm doing it for her."

Nadia pursed her lips. "She's still going to die, Marie. Shadow sickness is terminal. No one can cure it."

"I imagine if anyone can do it, the creator of the entire universe can," Marie replied. "And I can be pretty convincing sometimes. Besides. He owes us."

Tricia leaned in and whispered in Nadia's ear. Nadia listened, then nodded her response.

"You'll give me something first," Nadia said.

"Name it," Marie said.

"I understand your hope, your stubborn need to think you can change things. I understand it. But I also understand reality. You're going to fail, Marie. You're going to fail, and Nessa is going to die."

Marie held firm on the trigger. The fat barrel of the pistol felt cold against her temple, threatening oblivion with the tiniest squeeze of her finger. Her throat was bone-dry and her tongue felt like sandpaper against the roof of her mouth as she danced on the edge of death. She swallowed, hard, her heart galloping.

"We'll have to agree to disagree," Marie said.

"I want an oath," Nadia said. "Your word of honor, which we all know you're not capable of breaking."

"To do what?"

"That when you do fail, and Nessa dies, you'll come home. To me. No tricks, no arguments, no dissent. You will return here and accept your place at my side and at my feet, where you belong."

Marie nodded. The pistol bobbed against her tangled hair.

"All right," she said. "Deal."

Nadia gazed at her, expectant.

"I swear it," Marie added.

Tricia snapped her fingers at one of the guardsmen. "Run ahead to the transit deck, and tell everyone we're coming through. Everyone. Stands. Down. If I see an unholstered weapon, the man holding it is going to lose his hands."

Marie gave an awkward glance to the man crumpled at her feet. Blood from his broken nose spread a tiny mushroom-shaped stain on the red carpet.

"When he wakes up, tell him I'm sorry."

"When he wakes up," Tricia said, "I'm going to personally execute him for gross incompetence."

Marie locked eyes with her.

"No," Marie said. "You aren't."

Tricia lifted her chin and flashed the faintest ghost of a smile.

"He gets a pass, just this once. For old times' sake. You're still her, you know. You think you aren't, but I can see my friend in there. She's hiding just behind your eyes, waiting to come out."

* * *

Marie kept her stolen pistol pressed to her head, all the way to the transit deck. She'd given her word of honor, made her oath, but no one around her was obliged to keep theirs.

"Hang on to that weapon," Tricia told her. "You're going to need it where you're headed."

Tricia walked at her side down deserted steel corridors. Nadia's troops had cleared a path. Nadia led the way herself, with her back stiff and her hand never far from the wand on her hip.

"Where am I going?" Marie asked.

"Your contact," Nadia said, "*my* contact, is a man called the Marquis. He's a smuggler of occult artifacts. Also a thief and an opportunist. Scum, but useful scum. He's already been paid for his services, and quite handsomely."

"So if he tries to shake you down," Tricia added, "hurt him until he cooperates."

"I can handle that," Marie said.

Doors stenciled *01* in block letters whisked open at their approach. Rings of computer terminals surrounded a round, raised dais of stone. Three light-cans aimed down from black tripods at three points of the circle, bathing the engraved rock in shafts of red, blue, and green. Marie recognized it at first sight: it was a streamlined and more stable version of Ezra's shopping-mall laboratory back in Iowa. Instead of rows of chugging, whining generators all daisy-chained together, fat orange cables snaked from the ritual stone to a sleek and softly humming engine against the far wall.

A trio of technicians, all wearing protective goggles and flu masks, rose as they entered the chamber. Nadia lowered them back to their seats with a flourish of her mercury gauntlet.

"As you were. Open a stable portal."

"Yes, ma'am," one replied. "Destination?"

"The Deadknot."

Marie looked between Nadia and Tricia. "Which is where, exactly?"

"What mythology calls a war in heaven," Nadia said, "was not fought in heaven. The rebels staked their claim to territory inside the Shadow In-Between, and that is where their greatest battles raged."

"It's a graveyard," Tricia added. "Thing about old graveyards is a lot of them keep secrets hidden under the soil. Old tunnels. Crypts. Rats. Lots of rats."

"Eaters of the dead," Nadia said.

The standing lights shifted, changing, strobing, circling. Red turned to blue turned to green and back again, spotlights cycling and merging against the face of the ritual stone. The generator's hum grew into a mechanical growl. Tricia stepped back, slipping out of Marie's peripheral vision.

"I wish you wouldn't do this," Nadia said.

"But you know why I have to."

"I know you're going to all this risk and trouble for no purpose. That you're just going to have to watch another of my incarnations die. I know it's going to break you. And I'm the one who's going to have to patch you up and put you back together again." Nadia crossed her arms and stared at the ritual stone. "Exceptionally inconsiderate."

"Sorry for the inconvenience," Marie said.

"I forgive you."

The lights blended, whirling across the stone, taking on sherbet hues of tangerine and lemon-lime. A rough, rectangular outline began to shimmer in the air above the rock, with the impressions of still and ghostly shapes beyond.

Tricia returned, toting a square, hard-edged bag cushioned in black nylon webbing, a little bigger than a pizza box. She offered it to Marie and helped slide a strap over her arm.

"What is this?" Marie asked.

"Return beacon," Tricia said. "Once you're ready to come home, activate it and stay right where you are. We'll see your signal and have a portal open within the hour. I threw in a few extra goodies. Camping gear, protein bars. You get cranky when you don't eat."

"Thank you." Marie turned her head just enough to meet Tricia's eyes. "Seriously. Thank you."

"Never could argue you down from something, once your mind was made up."

The portal took on definition. Marie could see through it now, to a room that looked almost like the deck's twin—but old, abandoned, monitors dead and black, metal siding caked in bilious yellow mold. On her other side, Nadia's voice was an almost inaudible murmur.

"Should have kept you under sedation until Nessa was dead." Her words drifted out like a sigh. "Just...couldn't wait to see you again."

In her downturned face, the deflated gust of her breath, Marie felt the gulf of Nadia's loneliness. It was a shadow bigger and deeper than the world she'd conquered.

"I can't stand by and do nothing," Marie told her. "I'm sorry, but that's not who I am."

"You used to have a very similar saying, when you were Martika. You said it the morning you died." Nadia turned her back on Marie. "Don't you die out there. I won't forgive you for that. I'll never forgive you."

One of the technicians' voices rang out above the generator's whine. "Stable portal, ma'am! We've got three minutes of guaranteed lock, and the destination site is clear of traffic."

Nadia lifted her gauntleted hand and pointed a mercury finger toward the rectangle of light.

"Go. No more words. *Go*. I'll be waiting here, until you return."

Marie approached the stone, her body bathed in strobing candy-colored lights and the stench of ozone. She took a deep breath, held it, and stepped through the door.

TWENTY-ONE

Daniel slapped a magazine into his pistol and sprinted to the hotel-room door, while Hedy scooped up fistfuls of coins from the bedspread.

"If it was any other hunter down there," he said, "I'd say there's no chance they'd shoot up a hotel in the middle of the Vegas Strip."

Nessa was already in motion, plucking Clytemnestra's knife from the kitchenette counter and snapping her fingers at Gazelle.

"Room to room, get the others, everyone leaves *now*." She looked to Daniel. "Is there a back way out?"

"Don't these people have, like, rules?" Janine asked.

"Guidelines," Daniel said. "Technically, as long as it looks like a mundane shooting, Nyx is in the clear."

Brandishing his new Glock in his good hand, Tony squinted at him. "What else would it look like?"

"Well, she could change into her true form and let the whole world see what a rampaging demon from hell looks like while she tears us apart with her bare hands. Good news is, she's not going to do that anywhere she might end up on camera or leave witnesses. Bad news is, she's still pretty much bulletproof. And she doesn't usually leave witnesses."

Winslow was packing up his rucksacks, slinging them over his shoulders, while Gazelle hammered on doors out in the pink-carpeted hallway.

"Bulletproof," Tony echoed.

"I just said she's a literal demon, and that's the part you're having trouble with? Jesus, no wonder Marie's neurotic; she has to work with you every day. Everybody, listen up, here's how we're going to play this. First, let's clear the table. Winslow, hit the elevator and go up to the top floor. Long as you aren't seen with us, you aren't on Nyx's hit list. Just hang out for an hour or two and slip out with the civvies once the smoke clears. We'll settle up the bill next time I see you."

"Already gone," the biker rasped, hauling his rucksacks out the door.

"Same goes for you and the librarian," Daniel told Tony. "Far as we know, they're not after you. Long as you don't give them a reason, you'll be fine. Head upstairs, stay out of the fight."

"We came all the way out here to help Marie—" Tony started to say.

"And you did, admirably," Nessa responded. "You brought what we needed."

She stood in the doorway, poking her head out. Up the hall, Gazelle was herding a gaggle of wide-eyed witches toward the elevators.

"She's our friend," Janine said. "We're not leaving."

"Look, I know you mean well, but—" Daniel looked her way and froze.

No one had noticed when Janine took her own pick from Winslow's arsenal, just before he zipped up the olive rucksacks. She stuck out her bottom lip, standing her ground, and brandished the shotgun in her hands. It was an Ithaca Stakeout model, fat, stubby, and lethal.

"You have got to be kidding me," Daniel said. "Do you even know how to shoot that thing?"

Janine pointed the barrel to the floor and pumped the shotgun, chambering a fresh round.

"I'm a naughty librarian," she said.

"Fuck my life," he muttered. "Okay, you two, go with Gazelle and her posse. Wait three minutes. Head downstairs, keep low and keep moving, and stay clear of the front lobby. There's a corridor just east of the casino floor that leads to an aboveground parking garage. That's your exit."

"What if there are more hunters there?" Gazelle asked, standing out in the hall.

"*No magic.* Every inch of this place is under camera surveillance and being recorded twenty-four seven." Daniel jerked his thumb at Tony and Janine. "Fortunately, you have an ace detective and the Terminator to provide fire support. And you two, maybe cover your faces before you run through a casino with guns? I've got heavy pull with the cops in this town, but there are limits. Nessa, Hedy, you're with me and we're going first. Carolyn and her babysitter are pinned down in the hotel bar, so we're going to grab them and cause a distraction so everybody else can get to the garage in one piece."

"And our way out?" Nessa asked.

They hustled out into the hallway. Up ahead, the elevator banks chimed.

"There's a steakhouse near the bar. We'll slip out through the kitchen. From there, everybody rallies on the Strip and we'll make our way to the Monaco. It's just one block south, opposite side of the street."

"And your friend is waiting to let us upstairs?"

"He'll be there."

The elevator cage rumbled open. He held the door, ushering Nessa and Hedy on board before he punched the glowing *Lobby* button.

"Look on the bright side," he said. "Fifteen minutes from now, this'll all be over. One way or another."

*   *   *

Carolyn and Badger were hunkered down at the open bar, watching Nyx show photographs to the check-in clerk. A discreet, folded bill slid across the counter in one direction. A key card, one plastic corner poking out from under the clerk's shaky palm, slid the other way. Nyx's backup clustered around her, eyes in all directions.

"Do you think we should run?" Badger asked.

"Have you been on this planet long enough to figure out what guns are?" Carolyn asked him.

"Yes. Saw them on the talking box."

Carolyn sipped her drink and nodded toward the long duffels each man carried. The bags were partially unzipped, the shoulder straps buckled high so their hands could slip inside with ease.

"Those aren't party favors," she said. "Just keep it cool. They're probably going to go upstairs and try to corner Nessa and Dan in their room. Once they leave, we leave."

"But...aren't they coming down here?"

Carolyn watched the pack move across the casino floor, cutting a swathe across the tropical-print carpet.

"Yeah," she said. "That could be a problem."

*   *   *

The elevator hummed under their feet, slowly coasting down on a one-way trip. Nessa watched the glowing numbers strobe above the door, offering a hot white countdown.

"Please," Daniel said, "no magic in public. Okay? None."

"No promises," Nessa replied. Hedy stood beside her, silent, and nodded her agreement.

All the same, she had to be careful. She had one vial of elixir left, the only thing holding her infection at bay. It would buy her one more day of strength. One more day to find Marie, bring her home, and set her affairs in order. Nothing was stopping her from unleashing her full power on Nyx and her team—and she *wanted* to—but Carson City was still a fresh memory. She had gone all-out there, and only gulping down one of her dwindling vials saved her from being torn apart by her own wild magic.

She couldn't make that mistake again. If she did, Hedy would insist on going back to Mirenze for more elixir, risking their lives in the process and, at best, devouring time they didn't have. Devouring time Marie didn't have.

She cradled her lover's image in her mind. *I'm coming*, Nessa thought. *I promise. Nothing in this world or any other is going to stop me.*

The cage slid open with a pleasant chime. The casino-level elevator bay was a cul-de-sac, three doors on each side and only one way out, straight across the gamblers' oasis. Another elevator opened on the opposite side of the bay, disgorging a wide-eyed pack of tourists while a small crowd waited to get on board.

They stepped out, turned, and froze. So did Nyx and her men, twenty feet away, headed right for them.

"Let's take it outside," Daniel called out.

It almost worked.

Nyx got the message, pulling her lips back and showing her teeth in a bare imitation of a smile. The man on her left, spotting Nessa, already had his hand buried in his black duffel bag and his eyes on a paycheck. Nyx was turning, about to say something, probably to tell him to stand down, when the bag billowed empty to the floor at his feet.

He braced a bullpup carbine to his shoulder—a sleek blend of black steel and hazard-yellow plastic, like a wasp in the form of a gun—and opened fire. His first three-round burst tore across the casino floor and plowed into the milling crowd. An elderly woman hit the floor on her shattered jaw. A blood-spattered plastic cup fell, bouncing as it scattered bright silver tokens in its wake. The shooter was already firing off another burst as his companions unsheathed their rifles, the screams on the casino floor louder than the bullets. Tourists were falling, some diving for cover, others dead or dying, paradise becoming a massacre in less than five seconds. A hostess tried to run, clutching her drink tray in both hands; a stray round shattered glass, trailing amber droplets as it punched through her pink cocktail dress and out her back.

Daniel snarled and flicked his wrist. A vintage stage magician's wand, concealed in a spring-release sheath, dropped from his sleeve and into his curled fingers. A fresh deck of cards riffled in a stream from his breast pocket, landing in his other hand.

"Canton's Multiplication," he snapped. *"Now."*

He twirled the antique wand and the cards flew. They billowed from his grip, fifty-two, then a hundred, then two hundred and more, pasteboard dancing in an impossible whirlwind. They swept out like a sandstorm. Nessa threw a hand in front of her eyes as they continued to multiply, the storm growing and blotting out the world.

The shooters were blind now, spraying bullets in all directions, screams and gunfire ringing out over the fluttering cards. Daniel's hand closed over Nessa's. Her fingers curled around Hedy's and he gave her a tug, leading them into the maelstrom.

"What happened to 'no magic'?" Nessa called out over the din.

"Sue me," Daniel shouted back over his shoulder. "I like breathing more than I like being right. Let's grab Carolyn and get the fuck out of here."

*   *   *

Carolyn and Badger dropped to the laminate floor when the shooting broke out, just like everyone else in the bar. Then the card-storm erupted, a whirling sphere that blotted out half the casino floor. Carolyn cupped her hands over her head as a wild burst strafed across the shelves, bottles erupting and glass raining down in a razor-edged waterfall. They waded upstream together, battling the human stampede going in the opposite direction. On their left, the lobby was jammed with tourists, squeezed shoulder to shoulder and fighting their way through the smoked-glass doors. Carolyn watched a man fall with a bullet in his spine, bleeding out at the carpet's edge, groaning as panicked escapees trampled him under their feet.

Daniel, Nessa, and Hedy burst from the storm, the shooters lost somewhere in the blurry cyclone behind them. Daniel waved to Carolyn and pointed across the casino to a softly glowing marquee on the far side of a forest of green felt tables.

"Meet us over at Frankie's," Daniel called out. "We're going out through the kitchen!"

They wound their way through the chaos, past bullet-riddled tables and overturned stools, tourists huddling behind the walls of slot machines with their heads down and hands cupped over their ears. The enchantment broke, cards forgetting how to fly and splashing across the blood-soaked carpet in a tidal wave.

Badger looked back. He put his hand on Carolyn's shoulder, shoved her down, started to shout something. She never found out what his last words were going to be. Three rounds from Nyx's rifle raked across his chest. The bullets slammed him back against a slot machine as it shorted out, and he left a slug trail of blood, crumpling to the floor. Another burst was meant for Carolyn, but it went high as she stumbled off-balance. The rounds blew out the faces of a row of slots and showered her in broken glass and electric sparks. She fell to her hands and knees. The ruptured machines spat plumes of acrid gray smoke.

She scrambled on all fours, staying low, trying to keep her bearings in the maze of corpses and trilling machines. She crawled around a roulette table and saw Daniel at the edge of Frankie's Steakhouse, back to the wall at the restaurant archway's edge and brandishing a revolver. Fifteen feet of open ground marked the distance between them, and two dead tourists decorated the carpet in the middle of no-man's-land. Daniel spotted her and held out his free hand.

"C'mon, I'll cover you," he shouted. He leaned out of cover and opened fire as Carolyn broke into a stumbling sprint, her back screaming and knees aching, digging for her last reserves of strength.

*   *   *

Daniel emptied his revolver as Carolyn raced toward the restaurant's arch. One of Nyx's shooters caught a bullet in the lung and went down choking on his own blood. That was enough to encourage the others to dive for cover, at least for a second or two. Only Nyx still stood in the open. She turned, almost casual as she raised her rifle to the glistening shoulder of her leather jacket and took careful aim.

So did he. His last bullet punched into her kneecap.

Her leg twisted and she went down, muzzle flashing, firing a burst into the casino ceiling as she fell. She dropped the rifle and clutched her knee, howling between gritted teeth. Carolyn sprinted across the last few feet of open floor. Daniel reached out, grabbed her hand, and hauled her into cover.

The crumpled bullet was already squirming its way out of Nyx's body, flesh and bone reknitting itself under her torn leathers. She clamped her hands over the wound and screeched, a feral wail of frustration and pain.

The steakhouse was abandoned. A couple of white-shrouded tables had been flipped as a makeshift barricade near the exit. A puddle of red streaked the hardwood floor next to a shattered bottle of wine. Daniel pointed to the swinging door on the far side of the restaurant.

"Let's go, before they rally. Everybody in one piece?"

Hedy looked to Carolyn, then over her shoulder, blinking. "Where's Badger? He was with you, wasn't he?"

"I'm sorry," Carolyn told her.

That was all she needed to say. Nessa watched the light behind Hedy's eyes flicker and die as the reality set in. Another one of her students was gone. From the moment she'd gone to war with the Sisters of the Noose, to their escape from Mirenze, to now, Hedy had watched over half of her coven die. Nessa reached out. Her fingertips rested on Hedy's arm.

"I never would have gotten you involved in any of this—"

"But someone did. Someone made sure we got involved. And there's only one reply when someone sheds our family's blood."

Hedy turned away.

"You taught me that," she told Nessa.

"Hey," Daniel said, "I'm out of ammo, and in about five seconds they're going to figure that out. We gotta go."

Nessa brandished Clytemnestra. The hilt of the Cutting Knife tingled, electric, in her grip. She led the way, shoving through the swinging door and into the kitchen, toward whatever was waiting for them.

TWENTY-TWO

Daniel had told them to wait three minutes. It felt like an eternity. Tony eyed his watch, the seconds draining down. Then he punched the elevator call button. He and Janine herded Gazelle and the rest of the coven on board, then took up stations in front as the door quietly slid shut.

"Seriously." Tony nodded to Janine's shotgun. "*Do* you know how to use that thing?"

"My grandpa has a place in Vermont, used to spend every summer there as a kid. Mostly skeet shooting."

"Clay pigeons don't shoot back," he said.

Janine kept the muzzle low and her eyes high, watching the floors count down.

The elevator opened onto a battleground. Fallen cards and corpses littered the tropical carpet. Janine's first step sank into wet fabric, and the air reeked with a coppery stench. Tony held a finger to his lips for silence, took three quick steps ahead, and waved for everyone else to follow.

Nyx and her men—one of them down and writhing, hands pressed to a chest wound and blood leaking between his fingers—held their ground in the heart of the casino. They had their eyes and their barrels trained on the steakhouse on the far side of the floor and hadn't noticed the new arrivals.

Janine raised her shotgun and took aim at Nyx's back. Tony put a hand on the barrel, gently pushed it down, and shook his head. He pointed in the other direction. An overhead sign showed the way to the parking garage.

They crouched and moved fast, picking their way through the

wasteland of fallen, scarlet-spattered cards and the bodies of the victims, innocent gamblers whose vacation had become a lethal nightmare with no warning. Janine wiped at her face, her eyes suddenly stinging.

The pack made their way down a long, carpeted ramp, untouched by the carnage. Tony broke into a jog, leading the way to the sliding glass doors at the corridor's end, and the others followed in his wake. The doors whisked open and the night air gusted in. Hot, tinged with the smell of gasoline, it carried the sound of thunder and torrential rain.

They emerged onto the parking deck. With concrete under their feet and above their heads, the open sides of the garage were blotted out by darkness and the storm. The rain echoed against the deck and thrummed down like the echo of war drums. It washed in on gusts of sultry wind, painting the far edges of the yellow-striped concrete and the silent cars left behind.

"Okay," Tony said. "I think we're clear. We'll go down, get to the sidewalk, and we'll be home free."

Someone was coming, jogging up the ramp, looking like a tourist until Janine caught the glint of gunmetal in his hand. She shouted a warning and crouched behind a parked pickup truck as his first shots cracked overhead, swallowed by a peal of thunder. Tony answered with two rounds from his pistol, cool and quick. One chewed into concrete and the other landed home, carving into the shooter's guts. He squealed and fell back, bracing himself against a pillar, still in the fight.

He wasn't alone. A bullet plowed into the pickup's side mirror, blasting it into a twist of ruptured metal. Janine spotted movement in a jagged fragment of glass: the shooter's partner was hunkered down behind a sedan about twenty feet to their right.

Gazelle was next to her, eyes wide as she clutched her new weapon to her chest. She leaned out from cover, held the Glock in an uncertain grip, and opened fire. Her shells stitched a line along the side of the sedan, opening potholes in the dusty steel, and her last bullet blew out a window before the gun clicked empty.

"Changed my mind," she said. "Hand cannons are good, but swords are better."

"You have to practice," Janine said.

She rose up at the same time Tony did. His next two shots caught the first shooter in the chest and crumpled him to the concrete. His partner sprang out of hiding, rifle high, but Janine already had him in her sights. She squeezed the trigger. The shotgun's roar rivaled the thunder as it kicked like a jackhammer against her shoulder, and what was left of the gunman slumped over the trunk of the sedan.

She stared, frozen, at the corpse. It slowly slid, tumbled over the bumper and down to the yellow-striped concrete. Tony was right. Clay pigeons didn't shoot back. They also didn't bleed. They weren't men who had names, lives, a history, all erased with one pull of the trigger.

Tony put his hand on her shoulder. He was talking. She hadn't heard him.

"I said, can you hold it together until we get out of here?"

Janine's grip tightened on the shotgun. She wanted to throw it away, as hard as she could. Her rational mind knew better. She nodded, and the gesture sent a tremble down through her body.

"For what it's worth," he said, "what you're feeling right now? That's how it's supposed to feel. C'mon, let's go."

*   *   *

Nessa's hip slammed the stainless-steel island as she jumped back, a butcher's blade catching the overhead lights and slashing the air in front of her eyes. She'd taken the lead, a charge through the abandoned steakhouse kitchen. The back door almost hit her as it flew open and Nyx's backup barged in from the opposite direction.

His gun was down on the stark white tile, fallen in a scarlet puddle. Nessa's knife had been quicker than his trigger finger, and she stole a heartbeat of surprise, using it to carve his wrist open to the tendons. He had dropped the pistol, thrown a punch with his good hand that cracked against her cheek and sent her reeling, and snatched up a knife of his own from a block at the counter's edge.

She swung high. He ducked, jabbed, and a lance of white-hot pain shot through Nessa's hip. Her fury, her grief for her daughter's loss—so many losses, so many of them because she had blundered into Hedy's life—all mingled with the agony of the wound and threatened to send her spiraling out of control. She felt her magic seethe inside of her, a boiling cauldron under a trembling lid.

She feinted, slashing at him then pulling back, and moving with him as he dodged. Her free hand clamped down on the hunter's face.

She couldn't let it all out, but that didn't mean she couldn't dispense a little taste.

The craft surged through her, down her arm and along her clenched fingers, hate-fueled power coursing over him. He stumbled back. The knife fell from his hands, clattering to the tile. He grabbed his face as his eyes went wide with horror and he struggled to speak. Not easy, with lips and a jaw turned to sea-green glass, forever frozen. His shoulders hit the wall and he slumped to the floor, onto his back, struggling to breathe. The magic spread halfway down his throat before Nessa's spell finished its work and burned itself out.

"Just a tiny curse," she murmured. "I've got more."

Hedy grabbed a white linen towel, ignoring the dying man as she pressed it to Nessa's hip and soaked up a blossom of fresh blood.

"Let me look at this," she said, tugging Nessa's blouse up.

"We don't have time—"

"*Mother.*"

Hedy gave her a sharp glare, then crouched down. Carolyn grabbed an armful of fresh towels from the opposite side of the kitchen and hustled them over. The wound was long but not deep, scoring a four-inch gash along Nessa's hip. The instant Hedy stopped patting at it with the towel, it welled up wet and crimson again. Behind her, Daniel rummaged in a utility closet, grabbing sacks and boxes and tossing them over his shoulder.

"It's a goddamn restaurant, they've got to have a—here."

He ran over, slapping a bright blue plastic case on the kitchen island. The first-aid kit was stocked to the brim. He quickly unwrapped a bandage, eyeing Nessa's wound as he tugged at the adhesive strips.

"Ought to disinfect it, and you probably need stitches, but considering Nyx and her buddies are going to burst in here any second—"

"Good enough," Nessa said. She patted the bandage into place, fabric already turning splotchy and damp over the cut, and pulled her top back down. Carolyn grabbed the first-aid kit, clutching it to her chest like a life preserver. Hedy pointed to the floor. The gunman was still alive, the remains of his face contorted in a rictus of agony as his breath whistled through the straw-thin tube of his glassy throat and out the fleshy half of his nose.

"What about him?" Hedy asked.

Nessa thought about it for a second. Then she raised her heel and brought it slamming down.

They charged out the back door, through a desolate storage room where the loading dock doors hung open to the storm. Nessa's nose twitched as she caught the mingled scents on the hot night wind: fresh water, ozone...and the distant hint of roses. The rain embraced her as she ran out into the darkness, sweeping around her and pulsing down. She was drenched to the bone, but she felt lighter than air.

"Do you *feel* that?" Hedy asked beside her. She turned her face up to the jet-black sky and opened her mouth to taste the rain.

Lightning rippled beyond the smoky clouds, brighter than the neon of the Vegas Strip.

The water streamed down Nessa's face, slipping under her glasses, reducing the world to blurry smears of light. Impulse made her raise her hand high, lifting the Cutting Knife like she was presenting it to the storm. Clytemnestra's hazy image wavered within the wet metal of the blade, her arms up and her open hands curled in a gesture of ritual offering.

"No ordinary storm," Clytemnestra's voice echoed from the steel. "The world is thinner here. We have aid, but just a bit of it, and it will not last long. Let us make passage."

They followed Daniel's lead, splashing through steaming puddles, up a dead escalator, and across the sky-bridge that stretched over Las Vegas Boulevard. Traffic below was deadlocked, an endless sea of motionless trucks and taxi cabs, with a chorus of angry horns answering the thunder. Colored lights flashed in the distance, police cars and ambulances struggling to make their way through.

The Monaco was just ahead. Cranes and earthmovers slumbered in the storm, half of the resort penned by tall wooden fencing. A five-story sheet of vinyl, plastered to the side of the building like the bandage on Nessa's hip, depicted happy stock-photo tourists beside a tropical pool.

A knot of paths out front, winding between ornate fence-work and empty stone planters, led the way to the casino's back steps. Hedy suddenly broke ahead of Daniel, racing to the knot of people clustered under a thin green awning.

"We're okay," Gazelle said. She squinted, water in her eyes and her hair plastered to her neck. With Tony and Janine at her side, the rest of the coven gathered around her, they all looked like rats who had narrowly escaped drowning on a sinking ship. Gazelle looked at Carolyn. Then to the empty spot at her side.

"He didn't make it," Hedy told her. Gazelle bit her bottom lip.

Daniel glanced from the gathered survivors to the glass doors at the top of the storm-swept marble steps. He bounced from foot to foot, lips moving silently like he was doing mental algebra.

"Okay," he said. "Cops are going to be swarming this place any minute now. We've got to get off the street."

"You said you weren't worried about the police," Tony told him.

"I said there are *limits*," Daniel said, pointing into the storm. "Shooting up a goddamn casino doesn't just cross the line, it obliterates it with a tactical nuke. Doesn't matter that we weren't the ones who shot it up. We were there. I need to make a lot of phone calls and cash in a lot of favors, and I need to do it *now*. Nessa, take your rescue team, whoever's going with you to...wherever the hell you're going. Everybody else is coming with me."

"Where?" Janine asked.

"I got a place. It's under construction, couple of blocks from here. It's nothing but a drywall shell and a leaky roof, but that's all we need until I sort this mess out."

"Hedy," Nessa said, "you're with me."

Carolyn passed Hedy the first-aid kit from the restaurant, and she took it with a curt nod.

Gazelle stepped up. "And me."

"No," Hedy told her.

"Mistress? You can use my help, and—"

Hedy raised her open hand. Gazelle fell silent. The next words between them didn't need to be spoken. They showed in the look on Hedy's face. She had already lost one apprentice tonight.

"I need you here," Hedy said, "because I have work for you. You'll be leading the coven until I return. Full authority. And if anything happens to me—"

"I should be with you."

Hedy took a deep breath.

"Your task, as of now, is gathering information about those

who attacked us. Nyx, and the men with her. I want their true names, I want to know where they came from, and I want to know where they are now. And don't stop there. I want the man who sold them the weapons they used. The innkeeper who gave them shelter while they planned their attack. Everyone who had a hand in Badger's death, to the smallest degree."

"Everyone," Gazelle echoed.

"One of our own died tonight. Everyone pays," Hedy said. "All of them."

Gazelle clicked her heels together. Hedy turned and gave Nessa a passing glance. Nessa caught the glimmer of uncertainty, like Hedy was a student giving a recital in front of her teacher. Nessa's fingers curled on her shoulder and gave a reassuring squeeze.

"Exactly what I would have commanded," Nessa told her.

While they were talking, Daniel had sprinted up the wet marble steps, carrying on a quick back-and-forth with a man standing inside the casino doors. He was short, with greasy side-slicked hair and a pencil-thin mustache. Daniel waved Nessa up, and Hedy followed on her heels.

"This is Greenbriar. He'll get you upstairs."

"We're square after this, understand? Square." Greenbriar turned his glare from Daniel to Nessa, looking her up and down. "Okay, first, maybe hide that knife before I walk you across my casino floor? Maybe? Swear to God, Faust, I don't know where you find these people."

"They find me."

"Watch over my coven," Hedy told him.

Daniel backed down the steps, into the rain. "They'll be fine. Trust me."

Greenbriar's mustache twitched as he beckoned the women inside.

"Now that," he said, "is terrible advice."

TWENTY-THREE

Greenbriar hustled Nessa and Hedy across the casino floor. News of the shootout down the block hadn't spread to the Monaco's halls yet, half of the ground floor concealed behind plywood and yellow construction tape. The casinos of the Strip were built as a string of hermetic chambers, no windows and no clocks, blocking out the worries of the outside world while the slot machines trilled their siren songs.

He ushered them onto an elevator and stopped a pack of tourists from following them on with a flourish of his security ID badge. Then he leaned in, swiped the badge across a key reader, and tapped the button for the penthouse floor.

"Don't touch anything up there, don't break anything, don't make me regret this," he said as the door slid shut between them.

The elevator began its climb. A video screen set into the wall sprang to life, advertising the casino's renovated theater space. Blue-painted men hammered on improvised drums and spat synchronized ping-pong balls at each other.

Nessa watched the antics on the screen, trying to find something to say to her daughter. Some words that didn't seem trite, pointless.

"I want to ask if you're all right," she finally said, "even though I know you aren't."

"I should be used to losing my students by now," Hedy replied.

"No. You shouldn't. If you ever get used to that, if it ever stops hurting, something's gone terribly wrong." Nessa gave her a sidelong glance as the elevator crept upward. "A coven is a family.

A bastion of support and shared strength, in this nightmare of a universe. Losing family is supposed to hurt."

Hedy stared at the video screen. Now it was advertising one of the casino's restaurants, steaming pork dumplings falling onto a lacquered plate in slow motion.

"How's your cut?" she asked.

Nessa gave her hip an experimental poke. Her lips went tight.

"Stings. I'll live."

Then she giggled. It burst out of her, unbidden. Hedy lifted her eyebrows.

"Mother?"

Maybe it was the aftermath of adrenaline—they'd been shot at and sliced at and drenched by a thunderstorm, and this was the first moment of peace they'd had since the night began—but Nessa's next giggle broke into a helpless laugh. She leaned against the elevator wall, grinning, squeezing her eyes shut.

"We should put some ointment and a new bandage on it. I mean, we don't want to risk an infection." She opened her eyes, damp, and smiled at Hedy. "See? It's funny. It's funny because I'm going to die."

Hedy pulled her into an embrace, clinging to her, her head buried against Nessa's shoulder.

"Not until we get Marie back," she said.

"No," Nessa agreed. "Not until."

The elevator stopped. The door glided open, looking out onto a modern ruin. The penthouse floor was half-demolished, carpets torn up to expose bare stone, once-elegant walls riddled with sledgehammer holes and exposed wiring.

You have to destroy before you can rebuild, Nessa thought. She stepped off the elevator. Her shoes crunched on loose rubble. The fixtures had all been stripped; the only light came from the glowing cage at their backs. The door silently shut, leaving them in darkness.

They picked their way through the labyrinth of half-shattered walls and dangling plastic tarps, following the distant drumbeat of the rainstorm as it grew louder, echoing through the lonely corridors. They found an access stair, steel door groaning open under Nessa's palm. One quick flight of steps, one more door—its stiff push bar fighting her as if it didn't want to let them leave—and they emerged onto the long, flat rooftop of the Monaco.

The storm and the dark embraced them. The water washed down in a monsoon rage, the wind sweeping it in sheets across the concrete, stealing their breath away. They could see the length of the Strip from up here, the hotel neon, the endless snaking sea of red lights on the boulevard.

"Are you ready?" Hedy shouted, trying to be heard over the peal of thunder.

Nessa held the Cutting Knife high, a lightning rod. She felt Clytemnestra's thoughts, her feelings, her heartbeat synchronized with Nessa's own.

We are in accord, Clytemnestra told her, speaking into the depths of her mind.

"We are in accord," Nessa breathed. The rain tasted like electricity. Her skin tingled, her nerves burning.

Think of your lover, Clytemnestra said. *Think of your desire. Gather up your need and kindle it into a fire. And cut.*

Thunder boomed like a cannon as Nessa's hand swept down. And in one swift motion, she sliced a gash in the skin of the universe.

Reality frayed, then snapped. The world buckled and warped like a slashed canvas as the Cutting Knife tore a hole. Beyond it lay a void of perfect darkness and a sudden vacuum, pulling at Nessa, howling as it sucked in the air and the rain and the light to feed its infinite hunger.

Nessa looked back, to Hedy, and held out her open hand.

"Shall we?"

Hedy took her hand. And together they jumped into the darkness.

*   *   *

In the void, there was a moment of silence.

Perfect silence, perfect darkness. Serenity, and the scent of roses.

Then Nessa felt herself flying, propelled as the world blazed back to life and the void cast her out. Her feet clattered onto a corroded steel grille, and sudden light drew blazing streaks across her vision. She was running, almost falling, pinwheeling one arm to catch herself. Hedy's hand yanked her back, both women leaning against each other and fighting for breath as the tear in the universe sewed itself up, whipping shut.

Steadier now, Nessa took a slow look around. They stood in a corridor with angled walls and a flat ceiling lined with burned-out bulbs. Rusted metal and broken sheets of plastic surrounded them. On Nessa's left, a computer screen set into the wall shed soft, trembling light as it spat an endless scrolling feed. Most of the script was alien, letters she'd never seen before, but a single line in mangled Hebrew caught her eye.

"What does it say?" Hedy asked her.

Nessa's fingertip touched the screen, smudging away a line of filmy dust.

"Error, fatal..." Nessa squinted. "Engines gone. Captain lost."

"We're on a ship?"

Hedy crouched down, close to the floor grille, and held out one open palm. She shook her head.

"But no sway. No ocean."

"I'm not sure it's that kind of ship," Nessa said.

She picked a random direction and led the way. Humidity clung to the stale air, thick with the smell of mildew and congealed oil. Nessa felt they were in the bowels of some old and great and dead machine, nothing left of its former majesty but frozen gears and rotten pipes. Not even rats prowled this steel tomb: anything they could have fed on had been devoured long ago.

She heard something. A crackling, electric noise, like the humming of a generator about to burst, and the faint glassy tinkle of wind chimes. The sound gusted down the corridor, washing over them, then faded into the distance.

"This way," Nessa said. It was impossible to judge distance in this labyrinth, but her magic guided her as firmly as her ears. And Clytemnestra joined in, the knife tugging in Nessa's grip. Nessa and Hedy jogged past a long bank of wall screens, half of them shattered and dead, the rest spewing the same endless distress call to an audience of ghosts.

Then she rounded the corner and froze. The figure at the end of the hall might have been a ghost, too, silhouetted in the thin electronic light from a wall screen. But then she broke into a run, and so did Nessa, and they swept each other up and clung tight.

"Don't you ever leave me like that again," Nessa said, her voice breaking as she fought a river of tears.

Marie squeezed her, laughing, wiping a wet smear from her own cheek before lifting Nessa off her feet.

"I'll try," Marie said. "God, I'll try."

Neither one could let go. They held each other like they could stop time and stay that way forever, skin to skin, cheek to cheek, feeling each other's warm breath, the steady and reassuring pulse of their beating hearts.

"You're soaked," Marie murmured against Nessa's neck.

"We were just on a rooftop in Las Vegas in a thunderstorm. Long story. Where did you go?"

"Longer story, but I met the mastermind behind this whole mess. The person who's been pulling the strings since the day we met. Longer than that, really."

Nessa broke their embrace, pulling back just far enough to look into Marie's eyes.

"Do you remember," Marie asked, "when you said you wanted to take over the world?"

Nessa's eyelashes fluttered behind her glasses.

"In hindsight," she said, "I should have seen this coming."

"How do you figure that?"

"Think about it, Marie. Who else would be clever enough to trap me like this? I don't suppose she told you why."

"She wants you to kill God for her," Marie said.

"Brilliant little monster. Not sure what I want to do more, kiss her or kill her."

Standing at her shoulder, glowering with her damp arms folded, Hedy said, "Why not both?"

"It's a long story," Marie said. "I should start from the—"

A *thump*, stout wood against corroded steel, turned their heads. A tall, thin figure stood draped in forest-green robes, face concealed behind a mask of intricate wicker. His hands were the color of the gnarled mahogany staff he clutched, with four fingers and jet-black nails.

He thumped the staff against the floor again and pointed to them. The sound that emerged from under his mask was like a blast of electronic static pushed through a human throat: mechanical, rasping, squeezed out from a bellows of meat.

"I'm…sorry," Marie said. "I'm not really sure—"

He thumped his staff twice more, letting out another rasping blurt.

"I think we're trespassing," Nessa murmured. She slowly pulled away from Marie, turning to the creature, and held up an open palm. "It's all right. We were just about to leave. We're leaving. No problem here."

"We can't leave yet," Marie said.

"I don't think we're exactly welcome here."

"The Marquis," Marie said to the creature. "We're looking for the Marquis. Can you take us to him?"

He paused, leaning on the staff, then nodded. He waved the

staff in a "come along" motion before turning his back, flowing robes trailing behind it on the corroded deck.

Whatever the creature was, he seemed to know the trackless corridors like a native, leading them along twists and turns until they came to a break in the scenery: a broad metal staircase stretching upward. There was light up above, glowing white and azure blue, and the sound of music. Nessa recognized the muffled notes, the voice on the warbling record: it was an old Leonard Cohen tune.

The creature stood to one side, content to stay down in the labyrinth. The tip of his gnarled staff pointed to the light. Nessa, Marie, and Hedy made their way up the stairs.

TWENTY-FOUR

It was a tavern, of sorts.

The stairway led up to a vast, circular room with bulbous walls and dangling globes of light the color of winter snow. Some effort had been made to fight the decay here, with the dark steel walls scrubbed and the floor grilles glistening wet from a recent hose-down. Round tables were flanked by steel chairs not built for the human form, dipping sharply before the backs angled in ways no spine could bend. A bar, sheathed in dented plates with rusted bolts, curved along a quarter of the room.

Nessa felt like she was back in the storm, pulled in every direction at once. The bartender was a squat, thickset man, pouring a rainbow of drinks with a wooden arm. The ornate contraption was varnished, sleek, held together with pins at the joints, a woodworker's masterpiece. It had been grafted to the stump of his elbow, skin inflamed and ragged around the edges, and moved like an arm made of flesh and bone. He was making small talk with a woman—deathly pale, no hair, no eyebrows—who wore a skin-tight Plasticine bodysuit that rippled like oil when she moved.

At one corner table, a motley crew in armor made of rags and scavenged scrap metal hooted and drank, rolling dice. As they tumbled, the runes carved into the dice flashed bright violet. Not far away, two men in prim Victorian suits stared silently at one another, drinking from china teacups. Every inch of their skin, from their foreheads to their delicate fingertips, had been tattooed in precise lines of writing too small to read. An astronaut stood at the end of the bar, waiting for service in a full space suit, NASA mission patches on its bulky white sleeves. It turned its helmet, giving Nessa a look through the visor. Nothing was inside.

Leonard Cohen sang out on an old Wurlitzer jukebox. *Everybody Knows.*

Then there was the window. Nessa saw the long, tall rectangle of glass and felt herself drawn to it, hooked on a line that pulled her across the room. Hedy and Marie followed her, quietly awed by the sight.

Nessa had suspected they were on a spaceship. Wrong kind of space. No stars shone in those inky, endless depths. Just the occasional flicker-flash of a massive sigil in the void lit with burning yellow flame, a storm born of pure and raw magic.

The Shadow In-Between, she thought. She could feel it calling to her, singing to the power in her veins.

Wreckage drifted in the void as far as she could see. Torn, broken metal, girders and dark debris, all tangled in a twisted knot. And the ships. Ships like cathedrals, long and mighty and dead. Stained-glass windows hung ruptured and open to the void, bellies torn wide, hulls crushed like toys in a mad child's hand.

"It's called the Deadknot," Marie said, her voice soft with reverence.

"What happened here?" Nessa said.

Another flash in the deeps illuminated a distant sight. The outline of a body. Titanic, at least twenty stories high, floating motionless. The spear-tip nose of a ship had punched through its chest before breaking apart.

"This is what happens," Marie said, "when angels go to war."

Nessa turned away from the window, facing her. She cast a quick, furtive glance across the room. No one was paying any attention to them.

"I need to know everything," Nessa said.

The song's final note trailed off. The Wurlitzer swung a dusty arm to scoop up a fresh record, dropping it onto the spindle. A new tune warbled over the speaker, Sinatra now, hitting Nessa with a pang of homesickness as he sang his ode to New York City.

Marie knew what she meant. She took Nessa's hand. Hedy knew, too. She turned her back to keep an eye on the rest of the room, standing guard.

Then, in their own little space by the window, Marie and Nessa danced. Slow, cheek to cheek, the world melting away as Nessa invoked the Knot of Venus. And just like it had once before, back in their hotel room in Ohio, her enchantment drew a wreath around them, gently shifting them into Marie's memories.

* * *

Nessa circled her duplicate, standing in a frozen recreation of Nadia's throne room.

"Brilliant little *monster*," she murmured. While time passed at a molasses crawl in the real world, she and Marie danced through the fast-forward flicker of her lover's memories.

"You sound like you admire her," Marie said.

Nessa looked at her from over Nadia's motionless shoulder, surprised.

"Of course I do. Even if her plan frayed at the edges a bit, it still leaves her holding a winning hand. One way or another, with minimal risk to herself, she gets everything she wants. What's not to admire?"

"Poisoning you, for starters."

"She wasn't wrong," Nessa said. "She knows me better than anyone. Which means she knew exactly how to back me into a corner."

They both circled her now, moving slowly counterclockwise, Nadia's image a pillar between them as they stalked one another around the red carpet.

"But you're not going to do it," Marie said. "You're not going to let her win."

"Don't you see? That's the beauty of it. It's not about letting her win; it's about deciding what to do with the time I have left. I'm going to die—she's right, Shadow infection is incurable—and she's handed me the tools to make a mark upon the universe like none of my incarnations ever have or ever will. Why *not* go through with it?"

"We don't even know what we'll find in Elysium. We don't know if any of this is true."

Nessa flashed a wicked grin, darting behind Nadia's back. Almost playing a game now, daring Marie to catch her.

"That's the fun of it. It's one last mystery, one last adventure. What should I do, die in bed?"

"I don't want you to die at all!"

Nessa stopped circling. Her smile faded. She let Marie catch up with her. Then she reached up, her fingertips stroking Marie's cheek as she gazed into her eyes.

"You don't get to decide that, love."

Marie's hands clenched into helpless fists at her sides.

"I don't believe that," Marie said. "I don't believe in giving up."

"That's the thing about reality. It doesn't care what you believe. It simply is. Facts simply are. And you have to play with the cards you've been dealt, not the ones you wish you had."

The vision broke into jagged shards all around them, drifting away like a mirror shattering in slow motion. They fell, scattering, melting, as reality asserted its grip over them once more. Reality was humid, stagnant air. Reality was rusted metal and sharp edges and a battlefield turned into a graveyard.

"And you will keep your word," Nessa told her. They stood face-to-face, just a few feet apart on the corroded, damp floor grille.

"I said I'd go to her *if* you die—"

Nessa's fingertip pressed, gentle but firm, against Marie's lips.

"You will keep your word," Nessa said. "I—she—went to a lot of trouble to make sure you'd survive this, and that you'd have a home waiting for you when it was all over. Knowing that you'll be happy, that you'll be safe, that you'll be with another incarnation of me...that makes this, all of this, what's coming, easier for me to face. Do you understand? It's important to me."

Marie nodded, reluctant.

"I don't know about 'happy,'" she said.

"I do," Nessa replied. "Because you'll be with me. She wasn't wrong about that, either. We're the same woman, love. She was just quicker on the draw, and she beat me in a game I didn't know we were playing until it was all over."

Her fingers brushed the torn fabric of her blouse and came away damp. Her cut was a distant, aching throb.

"Damn. Need to get a fresh bandage on this. Hedy, do you still have the first-aid kit?"

Hedy brandished the bright blue plastic box. It was so mundane here, surrounded by oddities and strangers from a dozen worlds, that it seemed almost surreal.

"Let's grab an open table," Hedy said. "What's our next move?"

"We find this 'Marquis' and claim our prize." As they took seats together, Nessa caught Hedy up quickly with the broad details of the vision she'd just seen. "From there...well, we'll see what happens. Clytemnestra, do you have an opinion?"

Nessa set the knife on the table. Clytemnestra's voice rang out from the blade, her human image a hazy blur along its enchanted edge.

"My opinion stands," she said. "We go, and we...do as you and I discussed, when we entered accord together."

"Agreed," Nessa replied. She pulled up her blouse a few inches, baring the splotchy, dark stains on her bandage, as Hedy opened the first-aid kit. Marie stared, her mouth dangling open.

"I realize I should not be surprised, given—" She finished the sentence with a wave of her hand, taking in the room around them. "But why is that knife talking?"

"Marie, this is Clytemnestra. She's not a knife. She's a witch in the shape of a knife."

Hedy rummaged through the kit, sorting bandages in various sizes and plucking out a slender yellow tube of disinfectant. "Still don't understand why she doesn't just change back into human form."

"You will," Clytemnestra told her. She fell silent, content to leave it at that.

Marie put both of her bags on the table—the mirror bag alongside the cushioned black container Tricia had given her.

"Figure it wouldn't hurt to take inventory," she said. "So, I've got the bell from Deep Six. Did you bring the candle?"

Now it was Hedy's turn to look surprised. She leaned in, staring at the mirror bag.

"Where did that even come from?" she said. Her palm hovered over the bag's face, feeling the invisible, and her eyes widened. "Ooh. Enchanted to go unnoticed. *I* didn't even spot it."

"Thank you," Nessa said. "I think it's arguably my best work to date."

"Nadia didn't notice it, either," Marie told her.

Nessa preened, savoring the small victory. Hedy gently peeled back her bandage and exposed the angry, jagged line of her cut.

"Good chance *God* wouldn't notice it," Nessa said. "Hmm. You know what? Put a pin in that idea, save it for later. What else do we have to work with?"

"The sapphire manacles from the coffin, your spell book—"

"We won't be using that."

"—the gun I took from one of Nadia's guards. Don't even know what it's loaded with, but it's pretty ferocious looking." Marie unzipped the black container and peeled the lid back. "So, *did* you bring the candle?"

"It's back on Earth," Hedy said, "but we can cut a doorway and get it when we're done here. Considering you were the beacon that drew us in, I think leaving this place is going to be a one-way trip. Which is unfortunate, because the silver and gold coins we acquired in case we might need them are also back at the hotel. We left in an unexpected hurry."

"According to Nadia, the Marquis has already been paid. We might have to remind him of that, but he's been paid."

Most of the container was taken up by a lozenge-shaped cube of black plastic. Its smooth, polished face sported only a single pewter button, secured under a hinged shroud like the missile button on a fighter jet's joystick. Marie rummaged through the rest. Tricia had packed a handful of dull orange plastic tubes, a slim coil of rope that felt like flexible steel in her hand, and a few other odds and ends.

"This is supposed to be a homing beacon," Marie explained. "Hit the button, and wherever I am, they'll come to...I mean, they'll know where I am."

Nessa winced as Hedy dabbed her cut with ointment. "This is really unnecessary," she told Hedy through gritted teeth.

"Don't fuss," Hedy told her, unwrapping a fresh bandage. "If by some miracle we all survive this, you'll be thankful I cleaned your wound. This isn't exactly a sterile environment."

Marie kept rummaging. "Looks like she packed some survival tools, basic camping stuff. I'm pretty sure these are light sticks. There's a packet of charcoal tablets for starting a fire, a water filter...a Swiss army knife? I mean, it's probably not a *Swiss* army knife, not sure if her world has a Switzerland, but this could be handy. Oh, and snacks. She said she was packing snacks."

Marie fanned out a trio of Triumph-brand food bars, the stark black-and-white labels promising *oatmeal and raisin-style nutrients*. Nessa and Hedy both held out their hands.

"Give," Nessa said.

They tore open the wrappers and dug in. Halfway through chewing her first mouthful, Nessa looked to Marie. Hedy mirrored Marie's expression as she wrinkled her nose and swallowed, forcing it down.

"Bad?" Nessa asked.

Marie swallowed. Reluctantly. "Can't you tell?"

Nessa's gaze dropped to the table.

"I'm…having a little trouble tasting things at the moment."

Marie understood. The Shadow sickness. She didn't ask for details, and she knew Nessa probably wouldn't give them. Her lover took a deep breath, pushed her chin up, and forced a smile.

"Now I know the true motivation behind Nadia's machinations," Nessa said. "The food on her planet is terrible. Marie, you will deliver her a message when I'm gone."

"You aren't going anywhere," Marie said.

"All the same, remember this, and remember it well. She is not allowed to keep you unless she also abducts a Michelin-star chef from our world to feed you. I'll make a list of suggestions. Everyone is allowed a dying wish, and mine is that you not eat…whatever this is." Nessa turned the wrapper around and squinted at the ingredients. "'Raisin-like substitute.' Really."

Marie stared at her half-eaten bar, her voice flat. "I'm glad you're finding humor in this."

"There are times in every woman's life when you have two choices: laugh or scream. Usually laughter is the more productive choice, or at least more socially acceptable." Nessa reached across the table and took Marie's hand. "I wasn't sure if I was ever going to see you again in this lifetime. If I'm a little giddy, well…you're the reason why."

Marie lifted Nessa's hand to her lips and kissed the curve of her fingers.

Hedy had her eyes on the room, her gaze never resting in one place for too long, avoiding eye contact while she took the lay of the land. She squirmed in her chair and had another reluctant bite of her food bar.

"We should find this Marquis and leave while we still can," she said. "I don't like this place. Too much strange magic swirling around, stray and loose. It's making my teeth itch."

Marie let go of Nessa's hand. She pushed her chair back. "We're in a bar," she said. "I'll go ask the bartender."

TWENTY-FIVE

Marie crossed the room alone, ears perked, senses on high alert. The dented metal curve of the bar was almost empty now, a lull between rounds; the only other customer was the silent astronaut suit with its faded NASA patches. As she walked up, waiting to catch the bartender's attention, the suit's empty helmet turned as if it was staring at her. She pretended not to notice.

The bartender looked her way. His varnished wooden arm set a bottle down, making faint clicking noises.

"Do you, um, understand my language?" Marie asked.

"I only speak 'payin' customer.' So if you're one of those, yeah, sure, read ya loud and clear."

His familiar accent took her by surprise. "Wait…are you from Brooklyn?"

The squat man flashed a big smile at her. "Hell, yeah! Ain't been home in a long-ass time, though. Where you from, doll?"

"Queens," Marie said.

"Represent," he said and leaned over the bar to present his wooden knuckles for a fist bump. "So I gotta ask, how are the Tip-Tops doin' this season?"

Marie furrowed her brow. "Tip-Tops?"

"You know." He pantomimed swinging a bat. "Baseball!"

"Oh. Oh, I think…I think we might be from a different New York."

"Aw, swing and a miss. That happens a lot around here, y'know. Some of those parallels are so close, until they suddenly ain't." He shot a look across the bar and lowered his voice. "Last week, I was sure this lady was from my home turf, and vice versa. We're hittin' it off, she's liking my style, so I make my move."

"Not good?" Marie asked.

"She said she wanted me to fertilize her eggs. I thought she was being metaphorical. She was not. Awkward scene. Very awkward scene."

"Ouch." Marie waved a hand. "So what is this place?"

"This? Just a little patch of solace at the end of the line. This is where people go when they've burned every last bridge and there's nowhere else *to* go. I opened this place a few years back, when a gold rush hit. Bunch of wannabe Idaho Joneses thought they could scavenge the Deadknot, harvest up some magical scrap and sell it for big bucks."

"What happened?" Marie asked.

"Some got lucky and struck it rich. Most got some combination of crazy, crippled, or dead." The bartender glanced to the window. "There's stuff crawling around on those derelicts you wouldn't believe. Angelic war technology. Occult gene splicing. And some of the stuff those crazy mothers built has had centuries to *breed*. Now, my mama didn't raise no dummy. They want to go off and get eaten in search of fortune and glory, more power to 'em. I'll be right here, where it's relatively safe, and make my money keeping everybody liquored up and happy."

"Why is it safe here?"

"Relatively safe. You seen any of the caretakers around? Guys in the green robes and the wicker masks?"

Marie pointed behind her, to the stairs. "One of them found us when we arrived. He led us up here."

"Yeah, they do that. The caretakers keep this place running. Make sure the oxygen flows, keep the dangerous decks welded shut. It's a religious thing. Anyway, we still get a few amateur archaeologists coming through, but the gold rush is dried up and gone."

"Too dangerous?"

"New competition," he said. "The Network got wind of this place and started sending their own salvage teams in. And those guys you do not mess with. So, Queens. What brings you to my humble oasis?"

"Looking for somebody. He calls himself the Marquis."

"Yeah? You don't look like his usual clientele. You a bounty hunter? Because I don't need any Wild West shit in my bar. You want to gank him, I'd appreciate you taking it outside."

"Nothing like that," Marie said. "A mutual friend placed a…special order with him. I'm just here to pick it up and leave."

The bartender gave a subtle nod to the back of the room. Toward the pack of raucous drinkers she'd spotted on the way in, rolling rune-inscribed dice across a battered metal table. They looked like refugees from a medieval war, dressed in scraps of leather and metal, grimy and ragged.

"See the one in back? Big feathered coat and the leather hood, half pimp and half executioner? That's your guy. Just make sure to count your fingers after you shake hands with him."

Marie started to back away from the bar. Then she paused.

"To be clear," she said, "do you mean that literally, or—"

"Nah, I mean he's a sleazy jagoff who'll rob you blind. Now, don't make eye contact, but you see that tubby dude over in the opposite corner? He's got actual mouths in the palms of his hands. Definitely don't shake with him. Really, just a good policy not to make physical contact with anybody in this place." He thumped his knuckles against his wooden arm and grinned at her. "You're talkin' to the voice of experience here."

"Appreciate it," Marie said. "You take care, Brooklyn."

"Stay safe out there, Queens."

As she stepped away, Marie waved to Nessa and Hedy. They got up and joined her in the middle of the room.

"He's over there," Marie said. "Game plan?"

"Let's just be our usual charming selves," Nessa said.

They closed in on the back-corner table. The conversation

ran dry. The dice flashed violet as they clattered to a stop, their upward faces showing twin serpentine runes. The Marquis sat in the heart of his crew like a ruler at a war council, his thin shoulders draped in an oversize gray leather coat. The coat bristled with rows of frayed and faded feathers and sported a long leather hood that drooped low and cloaked his face in shadow. All they could make out was his sweaty, stubble-flecked chin, and lips that twisted into a sardonic smile.

"Gentlemen. We are either in the presence of true royalty or a dead woman walking." The hood tilted toward Nessa. "Which one are you? Nadia or Nessa?"

"I'm ineffably regal and I'm short on time. Do you have my book?"

"Do you have my money?"

"Do us a favor," Marie said, taking a step closer to the table. "Let's skip the part where you try to bullshit us. You were paid in advance. Are you going to follow through on your half of the bargain, or do we have to escalate things?"

One of the Marquis's men flashed a nearly toothless smile. His dirty fingernails trailed along Marie's arm. "Ooh, this one's feisty—"

He yelped as Marie grabbed his arm. She hauled him out of his chair and twisted his wrist behind his back like a perp about to be handcuffed. Dice and beer bottles rattled as she slammed him down against the table, pressing his cheek to the battered metal.

The others jumped to their feet. One pulled a gun made of PVC tubing and brass. He didn't even raise it before Marie's free hand swung up and the barrel of her pistol pressed right between his eyes. Another man leveled a sawed-off shotgun at her while Nessa brandished her Cutting Knife, the air shimmering at the edge of the blade. Static crackled upon Hedy's raised fingertips, like she had a lightning storm in the palm of her hand just waiting to be unleashed.

"That's the problem with people these days," the Marquis said, utterly nonchalant. "Nobody has a sense of humor. Just fucking with you. A little pre-deal banter, nothing to get your panties in a wedge about."

The shotgun stayed aimed at Marie's face. She thumbed back the hammer of her pistol.

"My people are going to put their weapons down now," the Marquis said. "I'd be really happy, and it'd be a good sign for our future partnership, if you did the same. Okay?"

Nobody moved.

"Starting now," he added.

The shotgun barrel dipped downward. Marie eased off, lowering her gun, stepping back. Slowly, everyone put their hardware away. The man Marie had grabbed looked sheepish, brushing himself off and rubbing his arm as he sank back into his chair.

"Good news and bad news," the Marquis said. "Bad news first. I don't have the book. Had a line on it, but my informant turned up with a bad case of lead poisoning. See, this is a hot little commodity, and Nadia isn't the only one looking for it. *Adam* wants it."

Marie shook her head. "Adam?"

"I assume you know what the Network is."

"We're acquainted," Nessa replied.

"Well, he's the big man at the top—and I mean that literally, the guy's built like a brick wall with a bad attitude. The kings allegedly tell Adam what they want, he hands down the marching orders and makes it happen. And he's got a hell of a bee in his bonnet over the keys to Elysium."

"How do you know?" Marie asked.

That got faint snickers from the Marquis's men. One snatched up a half-empty bottle of beer from the table.

"Nadia didn't tell you anything about me, did she?" the Marquis said.

"She said you smuggle occult artifacts."

"Any wand for hire can put his shingle out and play that game," he replied. "What me and my crew do, that's a little more specialized. We fill a…unique niche."

"Which is?"

"The Network is big. You get that, right? They've got outposts on multiple worlds, mobile bases inside the Shadow In-Between. Big money, big power."

"Sure," Marie said.

"That means big bureaucracy. Big waste and big sloppiness, too. Network's got a hundred hands, and fifty don't know what the other fifty are doing. Me and my crew, we exploit those weaknesses. Passcodes? We steal 'em. Guards? We know which ones can be bought and stay bought. I can walk into any given Network base, and they treat me like I work there. Then I walk right out with armloads of loot. Money, precious metals, occult technology. Even alter the inventory logs while I'm there, so they never even know they got ripped off."

"Helps that the kings don't trust each other," one of his men added, digging between his chapped lips with a wooden toothpick. "Technically the Network's a united coalition, but the kings play favorites and their top boys all collect dirt on each other for a rainy day. Dirt that we can use."

"And that's how we get paid," the Marquis said. His men chortled their approval and saluted across the table, clinking bottles together.

"So if Adam's acquired the book, why can't you steal it back?" Nessa asked.

"I said he's looking for it, not that he has it. But in the process, he's doing a real good job of killing off anybody who has a line on the thing. But I promised you some good news, right? I did some digging. Turns out you may not need the book at all."

"We only have the bell and the candle," Nessa said. "We need all three keys."

"You know what I learned in my profession? There's always more than one way to crack a security system."

The Marquis pointed to the window, and to the tangled graveyard of dead ships and debris in the void beyond.

"There's a wreck about six klicks out. The *Logos*. It's a rarity, damn near untouched and unscavenged. Partially because nobody who tried has ever come back alive. Now it's a Network target; they've got the whole area locked down and kill teams on site. And thanks to my little tap on Adam's personal comm line, I know why."

"We're all ears," Nessa said.

"These ships were never meant to land. They were built in the Shadow, they fought here, and they died here. That means there had to be a mechanism for moving troops on and off board, right?"

"With you so far."

"The *Logos* was a flagship, fighting for the three loyal thrones." The Marquis clapped his hands together in a gesture of prayer, bowing his hood. "Faithful unto the creator, for ever and ever, amen."

Hedy was the first to put it together. "A gateway. They'd have a gateway on the ship."

"To Elysium," Nessa said.

"Give the ladies a prize," he said, parting his hands with a finger snap. "Fire that baby up and you'll be knockin' on heaven's door, no keys or relics required. Most of these wrecks are beyond salvation, if you'll pardon the play on words, but the *Logos* still has a functioning reactor. Nobody's home, but the lights are on. Adam thinks that means the gateway still works, and I think, for once, the man's dead right."

"But you told us it's completely locked down," Marie said.

"By the Network. And I can get you in, quiet as a ghost in the machine."

INTERLUDE

"You're not going to interrupt her?" asked the interrogator.

He had been watching Carolyn with a growing air of anxiety, creeping closer to the edge of his chair as she told her tale. The King of Rust, placid, simply sat back with his three-fingered hands twined upon his silk-draped lap.

"And why would I do that?" the fallen angel replied. "We're finally getting some worthwhile information out of her. The last thing I want is for her to stop."

"But she's *lying*." He looked between them, head shaking. "She is lying, isn't she?"

"I hear only truth."

"It's impossible. The idea that anyone could worm their way into our systems, undermine our security..." The interrogator stared at Carolyn. "She has to be lying. It's a distraction. A story to send us on a wild-goose chase for a man who doesn't exist."

The king's chuckle was a basso rumble, the sound of distant thunder.

"Tell me. Are you more afraid for the well-being of our organization...or that I might decide to hold you personally responsible for the breach?"

The interrogator squirmed in his seat. "I'll...I'll carry out an immediate security audit. I'll find him. I'll bring you his head—"

"You will find him, and you will bring him to me alive."

He glanced up. "My lord?"

"He wasn't wrong, you know. We do accumulate certain...useful information about our rival brothers and their chosen emissaries, just in case it might be needed someday. I would like to know what sort of treasures he's found." The king's golden eyes focused upon the interrogator. "And we do, as he said, play favorites. If you would like to become one of mine, then you will find the Marquis and his crew and bring them to me for questioning. And you will say nothing about this to anyone. Not Adam, not anyone. Do you understand?"

The interrogator bowed his head. "The secret won't leave this room, my lord."

Carolyn leaned back and let out a sigh. "Are you two finished? Can I continue, please?"

As if he could smell blood in the water, the interrogator sat up straight and glared at her.

"Speak clearly, correctly, and truthfully," he told her.

"Don't tell a storyteller how to do her job. Do I come down to where you work and tell you how to be an embarrassing failure?"

The king snickered. The interrogator glowered at her, his hands squeezing the arms of his chair.

"Moving on," Carolyn said. "While Nessa and Marie were plotting a one-way trip to the pearly gates, back on my world, Las Vegas was reeling in the aftermath of one long, bloody night. Over a dozen people had been gunned down in the heart of a casino, and the shooters were gone in the wind. Until."

"Until?" the king said.

"They made one tiny mistake. They didn't clean up after themselves. And that tiny mistake was the spark to one hell of a fire."

TWENTY-SIX

The security office at the Flamenco was a nest of eyes. Three walls bristled with screens, capturing every inch of the casino floor. Subtle cameras tracked the servers at the hotel bar and watched the cash-register drawer. The glowing squares of light pursued pit bosses and monitored hostesses as they passed out free drinks. For once, none of it was live footage. The ground floor of the Flamenco was still a crime scene, and emergency crews had worked through the night to tend to the wounded and drag out the dead. The hotel was technically still in operation, but the checkout desk was packed with tourists cutting out ahead of schedule.

One sharp-eyed sentry, in a crisp pink shirt and black slacks, pressed the nub of a joystick on his console. A screen zoomed in to focus on a dealer's hands, tracking moves he made hours before the shooting started. Massacre or not, casino security had a job to do, poring over yesterday's logs.

Those weren't the cards Harmony and Jessie were interested in. They stood behind the casino's security chief as he replayed footage from the camera overlooking the elevator banks. They watched the spray of cards from Daniel's hands, fluttering, multiplying, blotting out the view.

"I don't know how he did it," the chief said. "Had to be some kind of air gun, right? Like a pneumatic tube? Figure he had all the cards up his sleeves and down his pants or something, all strung together. You know, it's like that stage trick with the knotted handkerchiefs."

Jessie leaned close. Even indoors, she wore her dark glasses.

She tugged them down as she hovered inches from the screen, and her turquoise eyes flashed. She was a panther on the hunt.

"Something like that," she murmured. "He's a tricky guy. Show us that other angle again, on the shooters."

A keyboard rattled, and the perspective changed, capturing a bird's-eye view of Nyx and her posse.

"We're going to need the room for a minute," Harmony said. "We also need this footage before we go."

The chief nodded. "Already done. I sent copies over to your office this morning, just like you asked."

She waited until he looked her in the eye. Then she spoke in a voice like velvet over steel.

"And you'll be erasing the footage from your servers before we leave. All of it. If it shows up anywhere, if one frame of it leaks to the media, you'll be held personally responsible."

His head bobbed. "Understood."

"Good. Now, if you please."

She gestured to the door. He gathered his people, told them to take a fifteen-minute coffee break, and shut the door on his way out.

"Well," Jessie said, "this situation is all kinds of fucked."

Harmony took the chief's chair. She nudged a joystick with the tip of her index finger, rewinding the footage. The dead sprang to life on the screen, bullet holes healing, pools of blood evaporating, and flashes of light sliding back into the shooters' guns.

If only it was that easy, she thought.

"Let's work the order of events," she said. "After we parted ways, *something* happened to Marie Reinhart. Next time Vanessa Roth popped up on our radar, she was alone and on a crusade to kill her father-in-law. He wasn't there, but about a dozen bounty hunters—half of them with demonic tats on their wrists, according to the Carson City morgue—were waiting for her. Again, courtesy of her father-in-law."

"And Calypso," Jessie said. "About time to punch both of their tickets for good. But how did we get from there to here? Vanessa's *back* with Faust in this footage. And they've got Carolyn Saunders along for the ride."

Harmony gestured to another bank of screens, capturing a pack of people creeping out across a card-littered and blood-soaked carpet.

"And Marie's ex-partner and her roommate, plus a handful of unsubs." She checked her phone as it buzzed against her hip. "Speaking of."

She tapped the screen and set it on speaker.

"Kevin. What do you have for us?"

The young man's voice echoed over the phone. "Bupkis, boss."

"On any of them?"

"I've been running these stills through facial recognition all morning. NGI system, driver's license archives, passports—hell, I even used my backdoor into Kairos; their database is better than the FBI's. Wherever these people came from, they aren't on anybody's radar. And no joy with the hotel, either. Daniel Faust rented them a block of rooms with a credit card under his 'Paul Emerson' alias. No names, no nothing."

Harmony focused on Daniel's hazy image, a shadow behind a flutter of frozen cards.

"What are you up to?" she murmured.

"You want me to keep looking?" Kevin asked.

"Yes, please. Do what you can."

She tapped the screen and broke the connection. Jessie leaned in at her shoulder.

"So much for 'trust me, I can protect them,'" she said.

"For once," Harmony said, "and believe me, I never thought I'd be saying these words, but I don't think this is Daniel's fault."

Jessie mock-winced. "Ooh. I *felt* that. That had to hurt."

"Uh-huh. Look. Watch what happens here."

She rewound and hit Play. The silent screen captured Daniel's raised hand, his moving lips. Another angle showed Nyx in her human disguise. Her nod, a subtle turn.

"I think he's telling her to take it outside. And Nyx might be an utter psychopath, but even she had to know what kind of heat a gunfight in a casino is going to rain down. Looks like she's agreeing with him."

Jessie pointed to the screen as the man beside Nyx let his duffel billow to the floor, empty as he swung his rifle up to fire.

"And her dipshit buddy was too trigger-happy to get the memo. The second he opened fire, it was off to the races. Wait. Back it up and freeze it."

The footage focused on the terminal moment, the heartbeat before the slaughter. Jessie's fingernail tapped the screen.

"What the hell kind of weapon is that? Looks like a prop from a science-fiction movie."

Harmony squinted at the wasp-yellow and black outline. "Full-auto, not a civilian model. Little blurry, but that's definitely not an AK or an M-16, not military."

"Not even an M-16 does that kind of damage. The casino wasn't shot up, it was *shredded*."

"And last time we crossed paths, Nyx and her gang didn't have anything like that. They had heavy firepower, sure, but all of it was conventional." Harmony shoved her chair back. "That's our trail in the wilderness. We find their dealer, we find Nyx."

*   *   *

On the edge of Las Vegas, half a mile and a world away from the lights of the Strip, the Sunset Garage squatted under a grimy overpass. A neon sign, the tubing burned out long ago and its face caked in soot, depicted a lime-green Studebaker. The grizzled men out in front of the garage, working on their rides, preferred two wheels to four. They tuned up their bikes while guitars wailed on a tinny radio and dogs yowled, hurling themselves at the chain-link fence that guarded the back lot.

Harmony and Jessie rolled up in an SUV with tinted windows.

The bikers stood up straight. Some put their tools down. Some didn't, keeping their wrenches handy.

Harmony stepped out, holding her badge high. Jessie circled around to stand at her side.

"I think you all remember me," Harmony said.

"Good news, everybody," Jessie said. "I hate arresting people. Absolutely hate it. So all you have to do is give us what we want, and we'll go away."

Winslow shambled out from the garage, squinting with a hand cupped over his eyes to cut the glare of the desert sun.

"Well I'll be goddamned," he said. "Agent Black, and you brought a friend this time. Last time I saw you…what'd I sell you, a flamethrower and a refurbished Street Glide? How they treatin' you?"

"Love the bike," Harmony said. "The flamethrower I had to get rid of. I dented the tank."

"Yeah, you gotta be careful with those things. So. I assume this ain't a social call."

The bikers were spreading out, forming a ragged semicircle. There were maybe a dozen of them now, another pair following Winslow out of the garage, and one of them dangled a crowbar at his side. Harmony quietly counted targets and picked out the ones she'd make a priority if she had to.

"I'm not going to tell you about the massacre at the Flamenco last night," she said. "After all, you were there. Security cameras picked you up, leaving in the aftermath."

"Going in, too," Jessie added. "With some very heavy bags. Looked less than heavy on your way out, though. Probably because you stopped in at your buddy Faust's room on the twelfth floor."

"Faust?" He rubbed the stubble on his chin and scrunched his face up. "*Daniel* Faust? Afraid you got some bad intel, Agent. Daniel Faust died in a riot up at Eisenberg Prison a while back. I thought everybody knew that."

"Pick one of your boys," Jessie told him.

"Pardon?"

"Pick which one we're putting in cuffs and taking back with us if you bullshit us one more time."

"We know everything," Harmony said. "We know about 'Paul Emerson,' we know about the New Commission, and we know you and Faust are on the board of directors. We're not after him, for once. We're not after you, either."

"We want Nyx," Jessie said.

Winslow held up his hands. "Hold up. I can't help you with that, and that's God's honest truth. I don't know her. I don't like the weird shit, and I don't want anything to do with it. Besides, I only do business with locals—you being the rare exception, not like you gave me a choice—and she ain't a local. Far as I know, and this is secondhand, she only comes to Vegas when she's on a job."

Harmony opened the back door of the SUV and reached for the blanket-wrapped bundle on the seat.

"What we need," she said, "is your expertise."

Inside the garage, beneath a curtain of shade that cut the arid heat, they clustered around Winslow's workbench. His nicotine-stained fingers hovered over the hard lines of the assault rifle.

"Whoo-ee," he said. "Where'd you get this puppy?"

"Evidence locker at Metro," Harmony said. "One of the shooters died holding it, and the others left it behind when they ran. According to the surveillance footage, all of Nyx's people had weapons just like it."

"Rare, if true." Winslow pointed to the plastic parts on the matte-black rifle, cast in hornet yellow. "You see these? These are preproduction components. Temporary, for testing, until the design's finalized."

"It's a prototype," Harmony said.

Winslow reached across the cluttered workbench for a jeweler's loupe. He fitted it over one eye and squeezed the other shut. Then he turned the rifle in his hands, searching every lethal inch.

"Ain't expecting a serial number, but...here we go." Under the hard-edged, trapezoid shape of the muzzle, his cracked fingernail pointed out a tiny, almost unreadable string of numbers and letters. "We got ourselves a maker's mark. Your wayward prototype walked out of Talon Worldwide's workshop. Big defense contractor, got themselves a handful of sweetheart deals with the government. If I had to guess, this particular weapon—along with its buddies—got jacked in mid-shipment."

Harmony and Jessie shared a glance.

"Thank you," Harmony said. "You've been extremely helpful."

"Do I get to keep the rifle?"

"No," Jessie said, "but you get to *not* be arrested today. How's that for a deal?"

He sighed as Harmony bundled up the prototype in her arms, and gave them a tired wave.

"Pleasure doin' business. Don't come again."

*　　*　　*

On the drive back, Harmony called the rest of the team and handed out marching orders. A machine sprang to life, and calls traced red lines across the map of the nation. An embedded operative in the Department of Defense sent out tracers, hunting down a missing shipment. The Pentagon was involved by midafternoon, and they roped Alcohol, Tobacco and Firearms into the loop. ATF wasn't much help tracking a missing shipment of guns, seeing as Talon Worldwide had never reported one.

A C-130 Hercules descended from an azure-kissed sky. The sun was going down and a midwestern chill hung in the air, the first warnings of a shift in the weather. Ezra Talon was waiting, standing beside his limousine with his hands resting on his silver-tipped cane and a light coat draped across his shoulders. His entire legal team was waiting with him.

"We want you to know," one lawyer said, stepping up at Ezra's side and speaking for him as Harmony and Jessie approached, "that our internal investigation is ongoing."

"But," the woman on Ezra's other side quickly added, "we are fully prepared to cooperate with all legal inquiries, and Mr. Talon is present to answer any questions you may have."

"You gonna let him talk?" Jessie asked, nodding at Ezra.

"He is talking," said a third lawyer, clutching a leather attaché so stuffed with papers it could have been a bowling ball. "He is speaking right now, through us. Metaphorically."

"We've advised Mr. Talon to let us mediate these proceedings and remain silent, considering the...unfortunate circumstances," the first lawyer said.

Harmony's eyes darkened.

"'Unfortunate circumstances.' That's an interesting way to describe a massacre."

"A massacre committed by shooters using your guns," Jessie added. "Guns that aren't for sale yet, with prototype parts."

"Which you didn't report stolen," Harmony said.

"Because we didn't know," said the woman at Ezra's side. She snapped her fingers. The lawyer with the attaché opened up his case. He sifted through it, drawing out a thumb-thick stack of printouts, and pressed them into Harmony's hand.

"It was covered up. Internally, by the person responsible. If one of the weapons hadn't been recovered from the crime scene, it could have been months before we found out. And by then she would have had time to cover her tracks—"

"Angelica Rosales," Ezra grunted.

"Sir, please, let us do the talking—"

He thumped his cane on the tarmac. "My own head of security. She stabbed me in the goddamn back."

"You're certain?" Harmony asked.

"The documentation confirms it," the lawyer with the case said. "Those prototypes were taken from a warehouse in Boston. Ms. Rosales has a company-issued transponder in her car; it places her at a tollbooth less than a mile from the scene of the theft. She then requisitioned one of the company jets."

"Who flew her?" Jessie asked.

"She flew herself. Rosales is a military-trained pilot. She landed at a civilian airstrip just outside of Washington, DC. Her next stop was Las Vegas."

Harmony saw her reflection, doubled up in Jessie's dark glasses. DC. If she hadn't already been certain that Nyx was working with Senator Roth, either directly or using Calypso as a go-between, that would have clinched it.

"She falsified the flight log," said the first lawyer. "Given her status in the company, it wasn't difficult. Not only didn't we know where to look, we didn't know there was anything to look for."

"Until now," said the woman at Ezra's side. "We do hope you'll be noting our full cooperation."

"Noted," Harmony said.

TWENTY-SEVEN

Everything was fucked.

Rosales listened to Ezra on her voicemail. And again, as the reality sank in.

"…whatever you made on your little arms deal, and I have to assume you've done this more than once, I hope it's enough to sustain you in retirement. Needless to say, your access to the office is terminated, as are you, and there is absolutely no need to come in for an exit interview."

Fuck me, she thought, squeezing the phone like a life preserver.

"We're cooperating with the federal authorities. As for you, I suggest you take your ill-gotten gains and hire an extremely talented lawyer. If you're very lucky, you might be able to negotiate a plea bargain."

It wasn't supposed to happen like this. Nyx and her people were supposed to get the job done. Quick, clean, easy. They were not supposed to do it in the middle of a crowded casino. They were absolutely not, under any circumstances, supposed to leave an evidence trail behind.

"This is what happens," she hissed, pacing. "This is what happens when you don't take care of your own business."

Her phone lit up. Adam. He didn't let her get a word out before he started in on her.

"Are you incompetent or insane?"

"I can fix this," she said. "I just need a little time."

"You're going to be *doing* time. More than a little of it. Not only did you lose the women and lose the bell, you managed to get fired and lose your access to Talon Worldwide's laboratory in the process. So tell me something: what use *are* you? You don't seem to be any good to me alive, and at this point I'm contemplating cutting my losses."

"I can fix this. Just...just give me a couple of days, okay? Two days."

"Bring me something, Rosales. Bring me a reason to let you live. Two days."

He hung up on her.

"*Fuuuck,*" Rosales moaned. She paced more. She grabbed a handful of her hair and tugged hard, like she could kick-start her brain. She needed a lifeline.

Yes. She dialed fast.

"Senator Roth's office."

"Yes, hi, hello, this is Angelica Rosales, from Talon Worldwide. I met with the senator just the other day. I was wondering if I could have a quick word with him, please."

She sat on hold for five minutes. The receptionist came back on the line.

"The senator is afraid that you're mistaken."

"Mistaken?" Rosales said. "No, we just talked—"

"He says he's never met you and has no idea who you are. Please don't call back."

The line clicked.

Rosales stared at the dead phone. Then she threw it against the wall. It made a satisfying crunching sound as the plastic casing shattered into tangled shards.

And now I need a new phone. Fine, feds will probably be tracking that one. Think. THINK! What do I have, what resources can I get my hands on? Can't run. I can dance away from the cops, but Adam can find me on this planet or any...

She stopped in mid-pace.

Or any other one.

* * *

Harmony and Jessie never realized how close they came to

their quarry. Rosales returned to the scene of the crime, dressed in white overalls and oversized sunglasses and toting a stolen toolbox. Workers were milling around the casino floor, breaking down bullet-riddled slot machines and lifting out the remnants of a craps table under the watchful eye of cops from Metro.

One of the uniforms waved her to a stop. Her stomach clenched.

"Where you going?" he demanded.

She pointed to the facade of Frankie's, the steakhouse closed. Broken glass and a crusted puddle of red wine still marred the polished floor.

"Cleanup crew," she told him.

He tugged on the radio clipped to his shirt pocket and ducked his chin. "Hey, did the detectives clear Frankie's? Hotel wants to send the cleaners in."

The reply came back on a burst of static, and it sounded like a blurted "*yeahgoahead.*"

"G'head," the cop said to Rosales, nodding her away.

A security guard had made secret backup copies of the footage from the gunfight, thinking he'd sell it to the highest bidder. Rosales had cracked into her rainy-day fund and convinced him to walk away with five hundred bucks and his life. There wasn't any surveillance in the steakhouse or the kitchens, but a camera out back showed Nessa's escape that night.

Rosales watched her run into Frankie's intact, then come out the back door wounded, with the writer clutching a first-aid kit that she didn't have going in.

She found what she was looking for in the kitchen, next to the door. A few spatters of dried blood clinging to the side of a stainless-steel island. She knelt down and opened her toolbox.

"Come to mama," she murmured, uncapping a scalpel. She put the blade to the stain and held a microscope slide underneath, ready to catch.

"Pardon me," said a voice that seemed to echo from the air all around her. "But I'm afraid I'm going to need that blood."

Rosales turned, staring at the empty kitchen. The voice was familiar, but she couldn't place it. "Who's there? Show yourself."

"If you wish, but please, no screaming. *So* many people have screamed at me today."

A slow rope of black tar oozed from the kitchen sink's tap. Rosales watched it plop into the stainless-steel basin, the wet rope coiling and growing as it continued to pour. It overflowed the sink and squirmed up onto the countertop, moving like no liquid found in nature. It finally slid over the side, curling around the bloodstains, and formed the shape of feet as it rained onto the tile floor.

The feet grew legs, then a torso and arms. The last dollop of ink slithered from the tap and rippled its way up the blobby mass, becoming the figure's featureless head.

"What *are* you?" Rosales said.

"You don't recognize me?" the voice asked. "But we used to work for the same company. Not that you seemed happy to see me, the last time we crossed paths."

Now she knew.

"Savannah Cross," Rosales breathed. She backed up, her hip bumping the kitchen island and making the pans rattle. "Holy shit, it's really you. What...happened to you?"

"I've had a breakthrough."

She lifted one fluid hand. The hand went jagged, sprouting a lethal spear. The spear went soft and took on the form of a rose. Then it melted back into the impression of fingers once more.

"You know, lots of people *say* they believe in transhumanist philosophy," Savannah said, "but who *does* anything about it? By replacing my mortal flesh with a stable alchemical matrix, I think I may have pioneered a scientific first. That or Dr. Cross did it, and I'm nothing but a sentient puddle of goo that retained her memories and personality when she died. I'm honestly not sure, and I love that. There's a beauty in that uncertainty. Anyway. Hi."

"Hi," Rosales said. Her mouth hung open a bit. "I'm...having a really bad day."

"Tell me about it. I broke ties with the Network. Adam sent a surveillance team after me, along with a fake surveillance team that was supposed to distract me from the real one. I've been hunting and killing and eating them all morning long, and I am exhausted."

"Eating them?"

"Well, just the ones who were addicted to ink. Keeps my body stocked up on nutrients. I just open them up and slurp it out of them." Savannah leaned in close, her torso stretching as her head hovered an inch from Rosales's. "Just *slurrrp* it out of them. You're not an ink junkie by any chance, are you?"

"Never touch the stuff."

The goo body squished back into place. "Well, I had to ask. You know how it is, never let a good opportunity go to waste. So. I know why *I* want Vanessa Roth's blood. Why do you want it?"

"Because it's my last chance to dig myself out of a hole. Adam had me embedded at Talon Worldwide—"

"I know." Savannah wriggled her oily fingers. "Chief Network scientist here. Former chief. I was recruited after you, but, well, I'm brilliant and you're a thug, so I was promoted a bit faster."

Rosales yanked off her glasses. Her turquoise eyes flashed a warning.

"I never wanted to work for the damn Network."

"But you liked the paycheck."

"Yes," Rosales said. "I liked getting two paychecks for doing half of one job. And now I've got *no* paychecks, and that's just the tiniest part of my problem, considering Ezra's disowned me and the feds are on my tail. Anyway, Adam believed there was some kind of artifact, a really old bell, hidden in the cathedral under Deep Six. I was supposed to snag it, but Marie and Vanessa got it before you and your sidekick crashed that party. I need to bring Adam a peace offering, a big one, or it's my ass on the line."

"And you know that the blood of the first story's characters—in their veins or out of it—can act as a beacon. You're going after them." Savannah flapped an arm at the stain. "Which, unfortunately for your needs, is exactly why I'm here. I want Vanessa and Marie. Mostly Vanessa. In my new form I can slip across worlds. Well, sort of. More or less. It is excruciatingly painful and I boil off a good chunk of my biomass each time and it might kill me, but it's still an impressive skill."

Rosales had a supernatural predator's senses. She could smell the blood in a man's veins and the fear in his sweat. Savannah didn't smell like anything at all, the lack of pheromones like a blind spot in Rosales's vision. All the same, she did catch the scent of something else. An opportunity in the making.

"What if I had a better way?" Rosales asked.

"I don't have actual ears anymore, but I promise I'm listening."

"You want the women, I want the bell. I've got a way to reach them, a better way than yours, and you've got the science and the magical know-how to make sure it actually works."

"You're proposing an alliance," Savannah said.

"I've got nothing to lose—trust me, right now I have *nothing* to lose—and you've got nothing to gain by turning me down. We get the job done and we go our separate ways."

"And you do realize that I'm being hunted by the Network as we speak?"

"I won't tell Adam if you won't. He just wants results, and if I can bring him that bell, I figure that'll buy me back into his good graces."

"That won't help you with your legal situation," Savannah pointed out.

"I can handle that. Worst-case scenario, hey, interdimensional travel. I find a decent parallel world, and I fuck off and stay there. Best-case, Adam offered me a zoo."

"A zoo—" The blob of her head tilted. "Wait. *Vandemere?*"

"It's apparently in upstate New York, in the middle of nowhere."

"Yes. I've been there. I had a bad time."

"I'll just go into hiding," Rosales said. "Live at the zoo, hunt in the forests. The cops'll never find me."

"Sounds like a singularly unambitious life."

"Yeah, well, you know what? I'm down for all kinds of mayhem if it pays well, but at the end of the day, all I want is to lie in bed, eat pizza, and watch shitty reality TV shows. I'm not a complicated woman. So, what do you say? Are we going to fight over that blood, or are we going to team up and get shit done?"

The gelatinous torso stretched as Savannah leaned toward her, invading her space. Rosales held her ground, motionless, as the eyeless head bobbed around her. She had the distinct feeling that she was being *sniffed*.

"Have you ever wanted to be a knight?" Savannah asked her.

"Not even a tiny fucking bit."

"Oh well. Nobody's perfect. We should probably scrape up that blood and get moving. Can I ride in your toolbox?"

"Sure," Rosales said.

TWENTY-EIGHT

On a dying ship, at the heart of an angelic battlefield, the Marquis laid out his plan. Nessa folded her arms, eyes narrow behind her glasses, and judged his every word.

"I can get you past security," the Marquis said. "Fly you right in under their noses. Everything after that, well, that's up to you. Like I said, people have tried to scavenge the *Logos* before. Don't go looking for them, because they're still on that ship. Assuming anything's left of 'em."

"It doesn't sound like we're getting a lot for Nadia's money," Nessa replied.

"She owns most of a planet. She can afford it. Don't act like it's coming out of your own purse. Anyway, you ask me, you're wasting your time."

"Why's that?" Marie asked.

"You're hunting for the biggest game of all, right? You're going after the big man."

"He owes us," Nessa said.

"Elysium's just another word for heaven. You ain't gonna find him in heaven. Of course I can't prove it, but I'd lay serious cash on that bet and sleep like a baby."

"Oh?" Nessa said. "And what makes you so sure?"

"Because God isn't *in* heaven. Hasn't been for ages. First place anybody would look. Think about it." His index finger wagged from side to side like a metronome. "Countless worlds filled with death, misery, plague, war. Unanswered prayers and suffering. You have any idea how many people want that fucker dead?

No. He had to run and hide. It was either that or answer for everything he never did."

They had visitors. Two of the wicker-masked caretakers, forest-green robes trailing behind them, approached the table in silence.

"Thought this might happen. They get touchy when it looks like somebody might start a fight." The Marquis looked their way. "It's good. We're all friends here."

One of them pointed at Marie. A blurt of machine static sounded under his mask, and then a wet, phlegmatic gurgle.

"Really? Sure, I'll tell her." The Marquis turned to Marie. "Our Lady of the Gas Leak wants a word with you. Says it'll just take a minute."

"And...who is that, exactly?" Marie asked.

"The reason we're able to gamble and drink on a derelict angelic war cruiser without getting our faces chewed off. She's the mother hen of the ship. Knows everybody and everybody's business, don't ask me how. Mostly she works through the caretakers, not a lot of one-on-one face time."

Nessa and Marie shared a glance. They both looked to Hedy, who nodded in return, joining in on the wordless discussion.

"We'll go," Nessa said.

The other caretaker shifted his staff in front of him. The sound he made was like ground beef squeezing through a drainpipe.

"Just your girl," the Marquis said. "You two can hang out here in the meantime. It's going to take an hour to get our ride prepped anyhow."

"Is it safe?" Marie asked.

"What? With the Lady?" He snorted. "Safest place on this ship, I'll tell you that for damn sure. Nobody messes with her or the caretakers. Sort of a collective understanding that we've all got a good thing going here."

Marie turned back to Nessa. She reached out, squeezing her forearm, needing to touch her. She could read the look on

Nessa's face and felt it in her bones. They'd almost lost each other once already. It was too soon to be apart.

"I don't think so," Marie said. "We're fine right here."

The caretaker made his squelching-meat sound again. The butt of his staff rapped anxiously on the floor. The Marquis shrugged.

"You want me to tell 'em that? Okay." He slouched in his chair, looking back to Marie. "He says the Lady knows what you are, because she's one too, whatever that means."

Nessa gave Marie a sidelong glance. "Another character from the first story?"

"He says she's got a gift for your girl here. No strings attached."

"No such thing," Nessa said.

"Be that as it may, and I agree wholeheartedly with that sentiment," the Marquis said, "that's the message. And she says if you don't accept it, the caretakers won't try to stop you from leaving, but you're both going to die out there."

Marie weighed the odds. Could it be a real offer? A trap?

"You said this...Lady of the Gas Leak, she's been here a long time?"

"Longer than anybody else has."

Not a ruse by one of their enemies, then. Not Savannah Cross in disguise, not Nadia scrambling to recapture her wayward replacement Knight.

"I think we should risk it," she said to Nessa.

Nessa was silent for a moment. Taciturn. She glanced down, pursed her lips, and thought it over.

"If you're not back in thirty minutes," she replied, "I'm tearing this ship apart."

They kissed, a quick peck, sharing a heart flutter between them, then parted. One of the caretakers stepped aside and gestured with his staff, inviting Marie to the stairwell. They fell in at her sides, silently escorting her into the labyrinth below.

* * *

The caretakers guided Marie through a trackless maze of dark steel corridors, past wall screens flashing their endless and unanswered call for help and banks of dead machinery. Another stairwell down, this one short and ending at a windowless door, marked the end of the journey.

They stood aside. One pointed his staff at the door, and it slid open with the grinding sound of old, unbalanced gears. The room beyond was misty, kissed by a faint and wintery fog, and bathed in dim white light.

Marie stepped across the threshold. The door rumbled shut behind her, sealing her in.

She couldn't see the far edges of the chamber. The floor was marked with pools of light from round fixtures somewhere overhead, illuminating patches of mist while casting the rest in darkness. Fat pipes ran along the walls, coated in faded flecks of venom-green paint and bearing an odd glyph, like the symbol of Venus mounted by the horns of a cow.

She felt lightheaded. Dizzy on her feet, and the more she breathed, the more weightless she felt.

"Do not be afraid," a young woman's voice said. It came from all around her, and Marie turned, fast, almost spinning off her feet. She caught herself before she tripped.

"Who's there?" she called out.

"My appearance may be...disconcerting. But I mean you no harm."

Marie caught movement in the corner of her eye. It was a woman's form, draped in a green silk dress that clung to her slender body. Green scarves dangled from her arms, her outstretched wrists, and wrapped her neck and face like a shawl.

The woman moved out of synchronicity with the world. She walked, circling Marie, and skipped a beat here and there; her leg would suddenly be two inches from where it was, her arms in a different position. Her scarves billowed behind her, rippling in an invisible wind.

Marie rubbed at her eyes. "I'm hallucinating," she murmured.

"We are all hallucinating. What is reality but a shared dream?"

"Hallucinations are a lie," Marie replied. "Reality is real."

The woman jumped in space, suddenly three feet from where she had been walking. Marie turned in place, following her movements. Gentle laughter echoed through the mist.

"We've had this debate before, you and I."

"I've never met you," Marie said.

"Not *this* you and I. The eternal you and I."

"You mean...previous incarnations? Who are you?"

The woman danced as she walked, flinging her arms before her shrouded face, occasionally flickering into a half-glimpsed pirouette. Her footfalls were silent.

"I am Hypatia," she said, "but you would know me as the Psychopomp. A psychopomp is a shepherd of lost souls. And I, in the role that was written for me, am a shepherd of a very particular, small selection of special ones. Like yours."

"So...one of my previous incarnations has been here? On this ship?"

"Why do you separate yourself?"

Marie frowned. "Meaning?"

"There was a time when you welcomed communion with yourself," Hypatia said. "In your darkest hour, recalling your past kept your mind intact and your spirit strong."

Marie remembered the Vandemere Zoo. She remembered the electric surge of agony as she bucked and writhed against her straps, while Savannah Cross's torture machine layered torment upon torment. And the Other, the sickle-wielding knight who stood at her side, mopped the sweat from her brow, and whispered words of strength into her ear.

"But now you wall yourself off," Hypatia said.

Marie saw a faint image in the mist. Distant, a silhouette, but she knew what she was looking at. The statue of Lady Martika.

"Those people, those other lives," Marie said. "They aren't *me*."

"Refusal to admit a disturbing truth does not make that truth go away."

"Now you sound like Nessa," Marie told her. "Why wasn't she allowed to come? Why only me, alone?"

"Because my gift is for you. I don't know if you understand this, but each of us—the creations of the first story—possesses a gift. Mine is perfect recall. I do not lose my memories when I reincarnate. Every lifetime is another book that never closes."

"What's my gift?" Marie asked.

"War," Hypatia said. "You are the tip of the spear, the shield breaker, the one who finds a way. But with my help you can be stronger than you are now. Strong enough—possibly—to face the trials ahead. Would you like that?"

"Will it help me save Nessa?"

"I bear witness to the past, but only a tiny glimmer of the future. I do not know if you will succeed in your quest with my gift in hand. I only know that without it, you will unquestionably fail."

Hypatia's words bounded off the corroded walls and reverberated through the mist. The word *fail* became a thrumming echo in Marie's ears.

"I can grant you the power of the Conversation," Hypatia said, frozen for a moment with her arms to the heavens and her scarves flinging upward. Then she was four feet away, crouched low to the ground like a jungle cat. "It is the power to speak to your past lives. As you have done before, under duress, but now guided by your heart and your needs. You have so many battlefields, so many victories and defeats written upon your scroll, Marie. So much you could learn. There is no reason you should have to keep making the same mistakes, life after life."

She almost said yes. It sounded like a gift with no downsides. Maybe it was her old detective instincts, or maybe Nessa had been rubbing off on her, but she hesitated.

"What's the catch?"

Hypatia flickered again, standing before her, frozen with both hands draping scarves across her unseen face.

"I believe that the story exists for a purpose," Hypatia said. "I believe that we exist for a purpose."

Marie contemplated that. She breathed in, and the mists vibrated around her as Hypatia danced away. She was a string of still images now, frozen and moving at the same time.

"Maybe so," Marie said. "But that doesn't mean it's a *good* purpose."

"All of reality is a dream, and I have appointed myself its priestess. And a good priestess tends to her flock. You would benefit from my gift. You would be made stronger. I have no reason to deny it to you and every reason to wish for your victory."

"But what about Nessa?" Marie asked. "If you can give it to me, why not her, too?"

"Because of her nature. A hundred lives of magic, dread secrets learned once and then forgotten—she wouldn't be able to resist plundering each and every one. That much power would shatter her mind beyond any hope of repair. She would destroy herself. Either that or become a god, and I have no wish to see your lover become a broken god."

Marie had to admit that made sense. "So how do I use this thing?"

"The Conversation will be under your control, conjured by your instincts," Hypatia replied. "When you need it, call to it. Simple as breathing."

Marie hunted through Hypatia's words, sifting for a trap. All she found was gossamer mist. Something about the self-appointed priestess felt worthy of trust, the fleeting echo of a long-forgotten friendship.

"All right," Marie said. "Let's do this."

TWENTY-NINE

Hypatia flicker-strode through the mists, jolting in and out of reality, and stood before one of the fat pipes that lined the walls. Dusky fingers laden with heavy copper rings brushed its face in reverence, and bangles dripped from the curve of her wrist. Her fingertip traced the odd glyph on the pipe, the sign of Venus mounted by a cow's horns, leaving a glistening wet trail in its wake.

She reached down, took hold of a valve, and gave it a sudden, violent twist.

Lime-green gas blasted from the pipe, engulfing her, her scarves billowing. She leaned back, throwing up her arms in a gesture of prayer. It was the first time Marie caught a glimpse of the woman's face. Chains of copper formed a metallic curtain across her high and dark cheekbones, linking clusters of rings in her nose to hoops lining the curves of her ears. Her eyes were white. No irises, no pupils. Just a web of bloodshot veins set into milky nothingness, as if they'd turned inside out in their sockets.

The gas gusted across the room, washing through the mist as it spread. The room spun and challenged Marie to keep her balance. She felt like she was spinning, twirling, even as she stood motionless and her hips rocked from side to side, following the beat of an invisible drum.

Hypatia danced toward her, hovering frozen in the middle of a pirouette, then midway through a graceful bow. Then, in the blink of an eye, she stood before Marie. She clamped hot, clammy palms to the sides of Marie's head and spoke a single word.

"Remember."

Gas flowed from Hypatia's lips, washed over Marie's face, and blotted out the world.

*   *   *

Marie felt time slow to a crawl as she stood in darkness.

The Conversation, she thought. Instinct told her so. It was simply a part of her now, and she sensed she could leave as easily as taking a single step to her left. She stayed, for the frozen moment, and let her need call to the shadows.

She wanted to see her again. The Knight of Mirenze, the perfect warrior who had eased her through the worst night of her life. To thank her, if nothing else. More than that, she needed guidance. A little advice from someone who had walked these roads before her.

A figure appeared in the deeps. Her armored silhouette sauntered toward her.

A glimmer of light turned the armor into mechanized black steel. Lady Martika's hair spilled over the back of her Valkyrie suit, and she cradled her bulbous, insectoid helmet in one arm. She stood before Marie, impassive, and squared her footing.

"You aren't what I wanted," Marie said.

"Should we start a mutual-lack-of-admiration society? Nadia's plan is perfect. Why are you fucking it up?"

"That proves you aren't me," Marie said. "If you were, you'd understand."

"The fact that I'm in your head says otherwise, doesn't it?"

"I didn't ask you to come."

Martika rolled her eyes. "Were you not listening to Little Miss Priestess of the Dream out there? The Conversation calls the incarnation you want. The one you *need*. And here I am."

"Then there's been a mistake."

"Now you're just being stubborn," Martika told her. "Which, to be fair, is one of our most consistent qualities. Come to think of it, as far as magical gifts go, this one is amusingly ironic."

Marie tilted her head. "Ironic?"

Martika spread one gauntleted hand, waving it at the darkness that surrounded them.

"Think about it. Of all the characters of the first story, we're the one who gets the Conversation. The one who universally digs her heels in and refuses to listen to anybody. But I can help you. You've done all right for yourself, given what you've had to work with, but the NYPD never taught you how to fight monsters."

"Pretty sure I'm talking to one right now," Marie said.

"Nature and nurture. We're the same woman, Marie. Only our circumstances changed. If you came from the world I did, if you survived my childhood—"

"We all had shitty childhoods," Marie said. "I had to hide under a bed and listen while my parents were being killed. I didn't grow up and commit mass murder for a dictator."

Martika gave an exaggerated sniff and rubbed her curled finger at the edge of one dry eye.

"Aw, poor little girl." She lowered her hand. "Junker gang broke into my parents' squat because they heard a rumor that we had a food stash. It was a lie; we were eating rats, just like everybody else on the block. They got angry. And me? I had to *help*."

An angry retort died on Marie's lips. Martika's glare was relentless, fixed on her like a spotlight.

"You mean," Marie said, "to help with…"

"Murder was my initiation. See, the gangs liked recruiting children by force. We didn't eat as much, we could slip into places, move around fast, and we were easy to control. They took me with them when they left. I spent six years with that crew. Learning. Studying. Practicing. Then, one night, I cooked them a special dinner. Laced it with a heavy narcotic. Should have seen the looks on their faces when they woke up, all shackled together. And there was me, standing over them with a chainsaw."

Martika's lips curled in a wry smile, eyes distant, savoring the memory.

"Blood in, blood out," she said.

"I'm sorry that happened to you," Marie said. "But it doesn't excuse what you did."

Martika laughed. "Did I *ask* to be excused? I am the Knight. I apologize to no one. I'm trying to make you understand something here. I grew up in hell. My world was devouring itself, falling to pieces, racing toward suicide. It needed a leader to take control, and that leader needed a right hand forged from steel."

"You murdered innocent people."

"Yes," Martika said. "But only the ones who couldn't be brought to see reason or terrorized into submission, and there weren't many of those. I am very, very good at terror. When Nadia took her rightful throne, my Valkyries and I made it clear, to the entire world, what their choices were: kneel or die. Very simple. Very easy. And that is how we saved our Earth. That is how we rescued humanity from itself."

"I would never do what you did," Marie said.

Martika's armor softly whirred as she spread her fingers.

"Proof to the contrary stands before you. You know this is why you haven't been able to answer your question, right?"

Marie's brow furrowed. "Question?"

"The one that's been plaguing you from the beginning. *What is a knight?* We've lived on a hundred worlds, a hundred lifetimes—more than that, to be honest—and we've found hundreds of answers to that question, most of them contradicting each other."

"I suppose you're going to tell me it means being just like you," Marie said.

"No. I would never say you should be like me. And that just shows how far away you are from the answer."

Martika closed in on her, crossing the shadowy void between them. The armor added a couple of inches, and she looked down at Marie with a strange tenderness in her eyes.

"You're talking to your memories, Marie. You're having a conversation with yourself. I'm not a different person, living inside your head. I am you. And everything I did, every drop of blood on my hands—*you* did it."

"I don't accept that. I'm not responsible for what you did in another life."

"You'd better think twice. Because you're going to need me. And once you finally accept the truth of what you are, you'll have your answer. You'll know what it means to be a knight."

Marie backpedaled, trying to get away, while Martika stood stoic and motionless. *That's not true*, Marie thought. *None of this is true, none of this is real—*

She pushed the Conversation aside, and it slid across the top of her brain and tumbled off the edge. The vision wrenched away and sent her crashing blind to the floor, scraping her knuckles on a rusted metal grille.

Her sight returned in blurry slices, reality washing back in. Her head throbbed and her mouth felt like it was stuffed with cotton balls.

The chamber was empty. The clouds of bilious gas had dissipated, taking Hypatia with them, leaving only a fine mist behind. The door was open at her back. The two caretakers waited, faces unreadable behind their wicker-grid masks.

*   *   *

Back in the bar, Nessa threw herself at Marie like a freight train, hauling her into her arms and squeezing tight.

"Are you all right?" Nessa said. "We were about to come looking for you. What happened?"

Marie gently extricated herself and rubbed her forehead. Her vision was still blurry around the edges.

"It's okay. Turns out it was one of us, the Psychopomp. She gave me...something, but I don't think it's going to help. Are we ready to go?"

"They're just finishing up," Hedy said.

The Marquis made his way across the bar, face shadowed

under his dangling hood and the faded feathers of his overcoat ruffling. He nodded back over his shoulder.

"Green light," he said. "We just had to fuel up the centipede and double-check this week's access codes. Getting those wrong would be bad, especially considering we've got a special guest in the vicinity."

"Special guest?" Nessa asked.

"Your competition. Network's apparently getting serious about scavenging the *Logos*, and they're sending in the big boys." Sweat glistened on his stubble-flecked chin as he flashed a smile. "The King of Sorrow just showed up."

THIRTY

Down in the bowels of the ship, past another faceless tangle of dead screens and corroded metal, a tall pair of double doors awaited. They hung open half an inch, one door set at a skewed angle.

"These *used* to open automatically," the Marquis said, curling his fingers in the crack. "These days I'm just glad we have breathable oxygen. C'mere, gimme a hand with this."

Marie joined him, slipping her hands through the crack and taking hold of the door. Flakes of rust rubbed against her palms. One of the Marquis's crew, dressed in scraps of scavenged metal and stitched rawhide, got on the other side with a crowbar. They heaved together, hauling back the doors one grinding, stubborn inch at a time, until Marie's arms ached for relief.

The vast gallery beyond the doors had a vaulted ceiling fifty feet high, and it was at least four times as wide. Open, all but empty now, the ancient docking bay rusted away in eerie silence. The far side of the room looked out onto the endless darkness of the Shadow In-Between, the void held back by a window of shimmering blue light.

Hedy pointed to the curtain of light. "Is that safe?"

"Not even a little," the Marquis said. "Know what happens when a human body is exposed to pure Shadow? That might look like outer space, but trust me, you'd *wish* for explosive decompression. But the warding fields are holding for now, and 'good enough for now' is my guiding philosophy in life. On that note, here's your ride."

At a glance, Marie understood why he'd called it a centipede.

The Marquis's ship was the color of brass tinged with scarlet, and the bulbous, uneven metal glistened like wet stone. It was assembled in segments, four of them standing on struts, each about the size of a delivery van but lumpy and misshapen. Black, rubbery tunnels linked the segments together. Another member of his crew was up on a stepladder beside an open hatchway, spray-painting a fresh serial number with a stencil.

"Centipede's an all-purpose Network vehicle," the Marquis said, running a proud hand along the reddish-copper hull. "Mostly use 'em for hauling cargo. We liberated this one a couple of years back, and they still haven't figured out it's missing."

"Perfect vehicle for someone who makes a living stealing from the Network," Nessa said. "You slip in, you slip out, and you have a place to store your plunder."

"Exactly. Our happy little home on the go."

Marie studied the ship as they walked alongside it. The asymmetrical, willfully chaotic design defied her to hold it in her focus; her gaze slid off it, around it, lacking anything to latch onto. The centipede didn't sport any wings, any engines that she could see, anything that made it look like it could actually fly. She realized there was something else missing, too.

"Is it armed?" she asked. "In case we can't just 'slip in and slip out'?"

The Marquis chortled. "No point. Putting weapons on a centipede is like giving a gun to a squirrel. It ain't gonna help. Nah, if we can't bluff our way in, we're pretty much dead meat. They'll probably tear open a local distortion and kick us out onto some parallel Earth."

"That doesn't sound so bad," Hedy said.

He rapped his knuckles against the hull. "This baby's powered by a Swann-Puthoff drive. Magic, using raw Shadow for power. It can't actually fly. So if they kicked us out, say, two miles up in the air, we'd have just enough time for one good, long scream before crashing to our fiery deaths. Or they'd send us somewhere *real* nasty, like a plague world."

"Or White Nine," said the crewman with the stencil.

The Marquis held up two of his fingers and hooked them in a warding gesture, shooting him a dagger-sharp glare.

"Wash your tongue with salt and spit over your shoulder before you set foot on board. I mean it. You know better." He gestured to the ramp. "Ladies? Shall we?"

They climbed the ramp and squeezed into the front compartment. Tall, tan leather seats sat shoulder to shoulder with a tight aisle between them, and overhead compartments leaned in to choke the cramped space. Patches covered scars in the upholstery, the plastic siding was scuffed and dented, and suspicious-looking wires dangled from an open panel. The ship smelled musty, like an old coffin bound for the graveyard.

The Marquis took the captain's chair, in front of a swirling panel of keys and switches all marked by ornate runes. He cracked his knuckles.

"Just so we're clear," he said, "this is a one-way trip. I'll get you to the *Logos*, I'll drop you off, and that's it. I'm not waiting around, and I'm not setting one foot on that damn ship. Getting back—assuming you live that long, and I'm not betting on it—is up to you. Deal?"

Nessa looked to the bug-eye curve of the window above the console, staring out at the curtain of light and the void beyond. Her fingers curled around Marie's.

"Deal," she said. "Either we'll find a route to Elysium, or Clytemnestra can carve us a doorway home."

"Or you can suffer a horrible and agonizing death," the Marquis said. "You've got plenty of options here."

He flicked a switch. The hatch whirred as the ramp lifted up and folded shut, sealing them in.

"Grab a seat and strap in while I run my preflight checks.

We launch in five minutes, and assuming nothing goes catastrophically wrong, we land in twenty."

* * *

Marie squeezed the frayed edges of her seat as the centipede jerked beneath her, the entire compartment suddenly lunging sideways. Then it slowly lifted, levitating like a magician's assistant, and she heard the reddish-copper struts hum as they folded up under the ship's belly. The rune-inscribed buttons on the console glowed in a neon rainbow as the Marquis's fingers played across them.

"This flight will have no meal service," he said. "Drink service is BYOB, and please do share with your captain."

The centipede glided toward the edge of the bay and the waiting curtain of sapphire light, smooth and perfectly level, as if it was sailing on a greased track. Marie held her breath, counting down in silence. Three, two, one…then they slid through the curtain and out into the dark. A tiny, defenseless speck in the Shadow In-Between.

A mechanical rumble echoed behind them, and the centipede shook on a sudden gust of turbulence. The Marquis reached over and hit a couple of switches on the far end of the console.

"Nothing to worry about, ladies. Old girl's just a little cranky today."

"'Cranky?'" Nessa asked.

"That's the technical engineering term for it."

The centipede pitched its nose downward, but they barely moved in their seats; instead, it felt like the universe was rising up to greet them, rolling around the bulbous cockpit window. Marie had glimpsed the Deadknot from the bar window, but now the sheer scale of it unfolded before her in all of its grim majesty.

The debris stretched on as far as she could see. Torn girders and dead satellites floating in the void, tangled wrecks that had crashed together and died as one. Cathedral ships drifted in the silence with ruptured bellies and shattered portholes, their hulls peeled back in jagged shards as if mammoth clawed hands had wrenched them open.

One of the ships, up ahead and on the right, wasn't dead at all. It looked like an old galleon from the Age of Sail but vast, bloated, built with worm-eaten wood and sails that dangled from leaning masts. The faded canvas, ghostly white, somehow snapped and rippled in the windless void. No one stood upon the outer deck, but down below, through sealed and reinforced windows, Marie could make out signs of movement.

And the swivel of ancient cannons, thirty-two in all, as they took careful aim at the centipede.

"Here we go," the Marquis muttered. "Flagship of the King of Sorrow. And if you'll direct your eyes left, you'll see our mutual target."

The *Logos* dwarfed the other wrecks in the Deadknot. It was the size of three aircraft carriers laid end to end, in a shape that evoked a Gothic castle. It hovered motionless, still but unbroken, with black iron battlements and towering stained-glass windows. The glass depicted burning wheels with eyes, slender and long-faced shadows bearing swords, and a recurring motif Marie recognized from the cathedral under Deep Six: the writhing forms of nine immortal sinners, cast down into a pit of flame.

A speaker on the console squawked.

"Unknown vessel," a voice said over a sudden wash of static. "This is Network high command. Identify yourself at once."

The Marquis tapped a button. The rune flashed violet under his cracked fingernail. "This is centipede oh-niner-six-five. I'm delivering more personnel to join the *Logos* research team, over."

"We don't have any record of new staff."

"Sounds like a mix-up on your end, high command. I've got full clearance here and three salvage specialists who are itching to get to work, so if you don't mind—"

"What's your clearance code?" the voice on the speaker demanded.

The Marquis's finger hovered over the button.

"This is where we either survive or don't," he said. He tapped the button again. "CC of the week is green, echo, armada, futile. Over."

No reply. As they drifted closer to the *Logos*, the galleon's antique cannons followed them, tracking in silence. Marie saw their destination now: a broad rectangle of shimmering blue light down low in the vessel's belly.

"We still don't have a record of additional staff," the voice said. "Oh-niner, change your flight course. Land on the flagship and prepare for a full inspection."

"*Damn* it," the Marquis spat. "These people are usually paranoid, but they're kicking it up a notch. Normally I'd just land, smile, and salute. My cover is bulletproof; I've walked on and off flagships before, right under the kings' noses."

"But," Nessa said, voicing the word he'd left unspoken.

He looked from her to Marie and Hedy. "*My* cover is bulletproof. The second they get a good look at you, they'll know you're not legit. I don't have any choice. I've got to divert and land. You said you had a way to open a portal back to where you came from, right? I suggest you use it before I touch down."

The centipede changed course and the world shifted around it, the shining blue rectangle sliding out of sight. Taking Nessa's ambitions with it.

"No," she said. "Absolutely not."

"Unless you want to die on that flagship—and I mean, these people have invented forms of torture you literally can't imagine—you don't have any other choice. Nice doing business with you. Tell your more evil twin I did my best to deliver."

Marie's mind raced, faster than her heartbeat. *Make it work,* she told herself. *There's always a way to win. Find it.*

"The kings," she said. "Each one has their own ship?"

"Turns out, when you're one of the nine most powerful and evil creatures in the entire universe, you don't really want to hang out with the other eight."

"They work against each other?"

"Not openly," the Marquis said. "That's the point of the Network, keeps them all honest and allegedly on the same team. Ninety percent of Adam's job is maintaining the peace and putting out fires. But the kings'll tweak each other's noses if they can get away with it."

"And the researchers on the *Logos* belong to the King of Sorrow," Hedy said, following Marie's train of thought.

So did Nessa. She lunged forward in her seat, before the Marquis could stop her, and pushed her finger down on the radio rune.

"Command, we are a research delegation from the Vandemere Lodge, here on the authority and direction of the King of Wolves himself. You have no right to interfere."

The line fell silent for a moment. Then the voice spoke up, uncertain.

"We...heard the Vandemere Lodge was all dead."

"You heard wrong, *obviously*. Now let us do our jobs."

"We just need you to land for a quick inspection," the dispatcher said, hesitant now. "It won't take long."

"Oh, so you admit you're trying to stall us? What's happening on that ship? What are your people doing that you don't want us to see? You're hiding something—out with it!"

"N-no, ma'am, it's nothing like that. This is just a routine check—"

"Was our captain's clearance code incorrect? Was one letter, one single digit of it wrong?"

The Marquis slid his fingertips along the glowing console. The centipede stopped flying. It hovered in the void, halfway between the *Logos* and the flagship. The bulbous cockpit window focused on the impossible galleon. And the ancient cannons, locked in on their craft and ready to open fire.

"No, ma'am, it was correct, but that doesn't—"

"So you're trying to delay us. What are those so-called 'researchers' really up to, hmm? Stealing artifacts? Destroying data? The King of Wolves is going to hear about this, and about *you*."

Nessa dropped her voice to a deathly whisper.

"I want," she said, "to *speak to your manager*."

The line went dead. They waited in silence, motionless, watching the cannons and waiting. Then the speaker crackled and the dispatcher returned.

"Ma'am, your pilot is cleared to land on the *Logos*. Have a nice day."

The Marquis puffed out a gust of held breath. The runes ignited under his fingertips as the centipede rolled, aiming for the docking bay.

THIRTY-ONE

The centipede gave a gentle shudder and a muffled whir as it drifted through the curtain of light, its bottom struts unfolding. The docking bay of the *Logos* was a twin to the one they'd left behind, vast and still and waiting for warriors who would never be coming home again. But they weren't alone here. Another centipede sat at the bay's edge, engine cold and windows dark.

"Your competition," the Marquis murmured. He craned his neck, pointing to the roof of the bay and the faint emerald lights, small and round, that shone down from the corroded metal like a field of stars. "See that? Emergency lighting. That and the warding field are proof that the *Logos* still has a little juice in the reactor."

The ship touched down, graceful as a swan, with just the slightest *thump* as the struts kissed the face of the deck. The Marquis leaned over and flicked a switch. The hatch hissed as it opened up, unfolding and becoming a ramp.

"This is where we part ways. I'd say 'good luck,' but you've either got it or you don't."

Nessa unbuckled her harness and rose from the flight seat.

"I believe in making our own luck," she said.

He was true to his word. The second Nessa, Marie, and Hedy stepped off the centipede its hatch was already lifting up, sealing shut with a whisper of air. The ship rose up, its segmented body wriggling, turning, and pointing its nose toward the curtain of light. They watched it sail out into the void, leaving them stranded.

The women didn't break the stillness with a single word. They walked together, footfalls light on the corroded plates beneath their feet, and approached the other ship. The hatch was sealed up tight, no signs of life, and a small pile of crates had been abandoned beside the centipede's back compartment.

"Supplies," Nessa said. "Unopened, by the looks of it. Of course, no telling how long the Network team has been here, or how many there are."

"And when we find them?" Hedy asked.

"Keep one alive, so they can tell us everything they've learned about this ship." Nessa wore an eager smile. "I'll ask them nicely."

They didn't have to search for long. Vast cargo doors hung open at the end of the landing bay, held in place by bright orange clamps. Plastic tubes, the remnants of light sticks used to mark the way, littered the corridor running starboard.

The trail of dead chemlights turned into a trail of debris. Around a bend, open binders and loose, torn paper littered the length of the hall, scattered like a windstorm had hit the place. Marie stepped carefully over puddles of shattered glass, spotting half-broken test tubes and beakers amid the clutter.

"Was there a fight?" Hedy asked, her voice barely louder than a whisper.

Marie studied the dark steel walls, watching her silhouette in the smooth, brushed metal. She shook her head.

"No marks, no bullet holes, nothing that looks like a battle. No blood and no bodies. Just...their stuff."

She remembered what the bartender had told her. *Angelic war technology. Occult gene splicing. And some of the stuff those crazy mothers built has had centuries to breed.*

Nessa crouched down and scooped up a handful of paper. She sifted through the pages one by one, finding nothing but incomprehensible math and text written in an alien script. She opened her fingers and let them flutter to the floor at her feet.

"If they're still alive, they can't have gotten far. Let's keep looking."

Marie felt a trickle of sweat run down her spine, plastering her blouse to her back. The ship was a sauna, the air stagnant and hot. She led the way, careful now, bracing her stolen pistol in both hands and keeping the muzzle pointed to the deck.

She rounded another bend, eyes still adjusting to the twilit gloom, and a shot rang out.

She threw herself sideways, grabbing Nessa and pulling her down, as a bullet chewed into the steel plating at her back and tore open a chunk of wall. A second shot blasted the face of a dead computer screen, spraying the deck with fragments of glass. A figure at the far end of the hall darted out of sight.

"Stay back," a man's voice shouted, quavering on the verge of panic. "Stay away from me! I'll shoot! I'll shoot you dead!"

They backed up around the corner, fast, getting out of his line of fire.

"It's okay," Marie called out. "We're with the Network. We're...reinforcements."

"They're gone," he moaned. "They're all gone."

"Who's gone?" Nessa said.

"*All of them.* Owens, Nineteen, Flack, the triplets, all of them!"

Marie and Nessa shared a questioning glance. Marie leaned closer to the bend in the hall, calling out to him.

"Did you kill them?"

"Did I..." he sputtered. "Are you *stupid*? The *ship* did it."

"We didn't see any bodies. Are you sure—"

"*It ate them,*" the man bellowed. "Owens was first. Everybody thought he just wandered off, but then it came for Flack the next night. Took him right in front of us. We heard him, screaming inside the walls..."

His voice trailed off. Marie took a step out of hiding. Nessa pulled at her sleeve. Marie held up a reassuring hand. Back when she wore a badge, she'd had to calm a dangerously disturbed suspect more than once. She could do this.

"Sir?" Marie said. "We're here to help. I'm coming toward you, okay? I'm not going to hurt you. I just want to come closer, so we can talk without shouting. Is that all right?"

Whether it was all right or not, she was already moving, making her way down another debris-strewn hallway toward the man's voice—and toward his gun. A tattered tent slid under her heel. Another tent was a crumpled pile of canvas and aluminum, beside a clutter of cardboard boxes. She'd found the expedition's base camp. Marie felt a presence and glanced back. Nessa and Hedy were right behind her, standing at her shoulders.

"You need to leave," the man said, the last word breaking into a sob. "It's too late for me. I'm marked. But if you leave, maybe it won't come for you."

"It's all right," Marie told him. Closer now, she could see his shadow on the floor just around the bend. "We're just going to have a talk. Can you do me a favor, first? Can you put the gun down for me?"

His shadow crouched low. Metal clanked against metal.

"Good," Marie said. "That's really good. Thank you."

She gripped her pistol and stepped around the corner.

The man in the middle of the hall stood there trembling, with a needle-nosed gun at his feet and his pudgy body sheathed in a glossy orange jumpsuit. His hair was a rounded chocolate-brown tuft like a soft-serve ice cream cone. He jerked in two directions at once, like he was torn between snatching his weapon up again or retreating. Retreat won, and he staggered back on unsteady feet.

"You're not Network," he breathed. "Who are you?"

"Friends. I mean it, we're not going to hurt you. Can you tell us everything that happened here? From the beginning."

He kept retreating, taking one step back for every step Marie took toward him, like there was a bubble of space shoving him away.

"The gateway," Nessa said. "The way to Elysium. Did you find it?"

He shook his head, shivering "Found it on a map of the ship, but we never made it that far. We found the reactor. Verified integrity. Carted up some loose relics from the war for shipment back to Adam. I think...I think that's when it sniffed us out. Thieves. It doesn't like thieves."

"Focus," Nessa said. "Where is the gateway?"

He pointed a trembling finger down the corridor.

"Just past the reactor room. There's an access hall, but it's blocked. You'll never get through. Even if you did, even if the ship doesn't eat you first, there's a guardian. Old, preserved with Enochian magic, still active."

He kept backing up, until his shoulders thumped against the bulkhead wall. Marie crouched and scooped up his fallen weapon. She still had the bulky handgun she'd taken from Nadia's guard, but right now, more firepower felt like a good thing to have.

"As it happens," Hedy told him, "my mother and I brought a little bit of magic with us. Let us worry about the guardian. What's blocking the corridor?"

"It. It is—"

The man froze. His mouth hung open, eyes in a thousand-yard stare. His tremble became convulsive, like he'd grabbed hold of an electric wire.

"It?" Nessa demanded. "What is 'it'?"

"Nessa." Marie touched her arm. Her eyes went wide as she pointed to the floor. The man stood upon a square of dark metal grating, two feet across.

Something was under the floor.

Spaghetti-thin tendrils, like the arms of a jellyfish, had snaked up from below and lassoed fleshy ropes around his ankles. Hundreds of them. They slid up his calves, coiling, pinning him to the spot. As some of them spiraled upward, others pressed against the glossy fabric of his jumpsuit—and through it, piercing the suit and the skin and bone beneath.

"It's here," he whispered.

Then he began to scream.

Dozens of tendrils snaked out from the tops of his boots, where they'd impaled his feet through the soles. They were fat, wriggling like scarlet worms, siphoning his blood. More worm heads emerged from his legs, tasting the air before burrowing back inside.

He thrashed, trying to break free, but the tendrils held him like steel cables. More whipped up from beneath the grate and lashed onto his hands, sliding in and out of his wrists. Blood guttered onto the grating. Just under the dying man's shrieks—rising an octave as the tendrils slid between his legs—Marie heard a sound like greedy, wet slurps from beneath the floor.

She raised the man's gun, aimed at the grate, and fired. The needle-nosed pistol let out a tiny kick and a spurt of air as some kind of fléchette, silver and blinding fast, sparked off the steel. She tried to get closer, to get a better shot; Nessa and Hedy grabbed her arms and hauled her back.

"He's already dead," Nessa told her.

But that wasn't true. Dead men didn't make sounds like that, half-sobbing, half-screaming, as the worm heads impaled his chest like a pincushion and leaked scarlet trails down the front of his jumpsuit.

An anemone stroked his cheek, almost affectionate. Then it slid through the tender skin, piercing his tongue, and out the other side of his face.

For a moment, the tendrils froze, as if caught in mid-decision. Then, as one, they hauled downward. Bones snapped and the man spat a gout of blood as he was slammed against the grating. Then again. The third time, the square—only two feet wide—buckled and broke. He fell into the gap, middle-first, stuck.

On the fourth yank, it folded him in half. He disappeared

under the floor. There was a wet sound, like a hundred sets of teeth chewing with their mouths open, and then silence.

THIRTY-TWO

The tendrils didn't come back. There was no rustling behind the walls, no sounds beneath the floor. Just the barely audible hum of distant engines, idling for eternity.

"We need more weapons," Marie said.

"We need more *knowledge*," Nessa replied.

Hedy stared at the broken square of flooring. Spatters of blood marred the dark steel of the bulkhead behind it, the only evidence of what they'd just seen.

"There's nothing like that on my world," Hedy said. "Yours?"

Nessa shook her head. She brandished the Cutting Knife. Clytemnestra was a hazy silhouette on the blade.

"You've been around longer than any of us," Nessa said. "Any idea what that was, or how we can fight it?"

The silhouette spread its hands. "This place, all of it, is from before even my time. My sisters and I fought the Kings of Man, but the Deadknot is the ground where they declared their rebellion. This is where they *became* the kings. Either it's some monstrosity that found its way here and made a nest for itself, or..."

"Or it was always here," Marie said. "The bartender told me they engineered things. Living things, made for war."

"Not much prey on a dead ship," Nessa mused. "Presumably it doesn't need to eat to survive. Sustained by some sort of magic."

"But it evidently *likes* to eat." Hedy glanced sidelong at Nessa. "You've got a look in your eyes. What?"

Nessa snapped her fingers. She drew a line from the broken

grating to the warren of corridors behind it, the direction the dead man had pointed them.

"Plenty of plunder in the Deadknot. Some scavengers have presumably struck gold on other wrecks, but not here. No one ever comes back from the *Logos*. It's also the only ship in this entire angelic scrapyard that still has an operational power source."

"Like the centipede," Marie said. "It's not nuclear or electric power. It's magical energy…"

She trailed off as she made the connection.

"That thing is being fed by the generator. That's what kept it alive all these centuries. Alive and…maybe growing."

"Mm-hmm. Kill the power, kill the beast."

"But we need the power," Hedy said. "The gateway won't work without it."

Nessa lifted her chin, resolute.

"Then our only option is to slip past it. There's a chance it's gone dormant. Remember what he said: it took the first of his teammates and didn't come back for another until a day later. Maybe it's full and likes to nap after a good meal."

"We're staking a lot on chances and maybes," Hedy said. "Look, we still have two of the three Elysium keys. We've got the candle and the bell; all we need is the book. Marie, did Mother's other incarnation have any idea where it is? At all?"

Marie shook her head. "None. She was counting on the Marquis to deliver. Which, as we've seen…he didn't."

"So it's the gateway or nothing," Nessa said. "I do not have *time* to go hunting an artifact that could be anywhere on a hundred worlds, if it even still exists."

She took a cautious step forward, then another, keeping her eyes on the floor. Testing it, like she was venturing out onto a frozen lake.

"We advance," she said. "Only up to the generator. We'll see how it looks from there, and if it's truly impossible, we'll cut a doorway home. But only if."

They advanced.

The way forward was a chessboard. Dark metal squares, almost black, interspersed with grillwork. Moving in single file, they carefully stepped from solid floor to solid floor, eyes on the darkness below.

Hedy stepped across sheets of brushed steel, spaced wider than the rest, and her foot slipped. Nessa and Marie froze as she fell to a crouch, catching herself before she could tumble onto the grille. She held up a shaky hand.

"It's okay, I'm—"

The floor shivered under their feet.

Nessa pointed toward her pursed lips. She mouthed the word *sound*. The rumbling slowly settled down.

It's drawn to noise, Marie realized. It hadn't gone after the last man on the Network expedition until he opened fire and started shouting. If he'd stayed quiet, he might have lived.

So all we have to do is stay quiet.

She felt like her feet were made of lead as she eased her way along the corridor. Every step sounded like cannon fire in her ears, but the creature stayed dormant. She gripped the bulky pistol from Nadia's throne room in her left hand, the needle-nosed gun in her right. No telling if they could even hurt the thing, but the weight was reassuring. Nessa was at her side, eyes sharp behind her glasses and studying the floor like a chess master pondering her next move.

Now that she knew the stakes, Hedy didn't step from square to square. She hopped. Light, bounding with long strides and coming down on her toes, impossibly soft. Marie realized that if she closed her eyes she wouldn't even know the witch was there. Hedy turned, a delicate spin on one foot, and flashed a grin at Nessa.

"*Mouse*," Nessa whispered, shaking her head.

The corridor twisted and went black. The emergency lights ahead were dead, turning it into a chasm of darkness. No way to tell what they were stepping on, or falling into. Marie held up a hand. Then she knelt down, opening up her black bag with careful fingers and fishing out some of the survival gear Tricia had packed for her.

She shook a chemlight, snapped the plastic tube, and gave it an underhand toss. It clattered midway down the hall and rolled to a stop. The tube glowed to life, bathing the corridor in hazard orange. They waited a moment, listening, watching, to make sure it hadn't drawn any attention before moving on.

Fifty feet ahead, ship lights returned, pushing through the narrow gap of a half-open doorway. One by one, they squeezed through to the other side.

They stood upon solid floor, in a rounded chamber that narrowed as the walls soared upward, as if they were standing in a giant metallic funnel. Curved screens covered the walls, a mosaic of rectangles in different sizes. Some were dead and dark, some cracked or blown-out, the floor littered with shattered glass. Others flashed waves of alien script and drew neon vector lines, plotting a course laid before the dawn of human history.

And at the heart of the room stood majesty.

A great globe of molten copper hovered above a rounded dais, floating in midair. It whirled, spinning, lightning storms rippling across its face. Marie watched, breathless, as it spat sparks that unfolded in mid-arc and became graceful, shimmering hieroglyphs of gold. The glyphs burned out as they plummeted to the floor.

"The generator?" she whispered.

Nessa circled it, palms raised, closing her eyes as she basked in its hum.

"Has to be. Feels like a hot bath and a glass of red wine."

"Be careful," Hedy told her.

"I know, I know. I can feel it because I'm infected. It's a siphon.

Pulls in the raw stuff of the Shadow In-Between, pure magic, and converts it to energy." Nessa twirled her fingertips, taking in the ancient chamber and the screens all around them. "Imagine it. Limitless power."

Marie drifted across the chamber. There was another exit on the opposite end, another malfunctioning door, this one open a single scant foot with nothing but darkness beyond. She set her bags down and was reaching for another chemlight when Hedy's voice echoed at her back.

"Uh, you should take a look at this."

Nessa and Marie stood behind her. Hedy had found a screen depicting what looked like a map of the ship, in cross section, indecipherable text over geometric slices to mark the *Logos*'s eleven decks. They didn't need to read it: the angry flashing and bright red color was a warning sign in any language.

"I'm guessing," Marie said, "that it says something to the effect of 'large obstruction in the machinery.'"

A bulbous ocher shape glowed on the map. It reminded Marie of a sprouting potato, old and dirty and bristling with tubers. The shape had wedged itself into the heart of the ship, clogging rooms, rupturing entire decks. Its tendrils snaked out through the *Logos*, worming through air vents and access shafts.

"He told us the ship ate his friends," she said.

"He wasn't entirely wrong," Nessa replied. "That creature is…mammoth."

Marie gave an uncertain glance to the metal plate beneath her shoes.

"Still a 'no' vote on the 'shut down the generator' idea?"

"Still a no." Nessa led the way, striding to the opposite door. "He said the gateway was just past this room."

"He also said the passage was blocked and we'd never get through," Hedy pointed out.

Marie hovered at the edge of the doorway, squinting, trying to see anything in the darkness beyond. She picked up a chemlight, shook it, snapped it, and tossed it in.

It was a tunnel of flesh.

The dark steel walls of the corridor had buckled and broken, fallen to land in shards along the grille of the walkway. And all around it, clinging to the skeletal struts, were bloated curtains of gristle and meat. The creature had grown around the corridor, half crushing it, swallowing it inside of its massive bulk.

Its flesh was putrid gray, like steak gone rotten. In the dim light, for a moment Marie thought it was covered in ants. Then she realized the wriggling movement was the hungry sway of anemone, the tiny worm-head growths coating every square inch of its skin.

"Be extremely quiet," Marie breathed.

Hedy took a step back, cupping a hand over her mouth and pointing with the other. The end of the flesh corridor was maybe fifty feet away, the broken door skewed to one side but open far enough to get through, and there was a light at the end of the tunnel. A soft, golden glow that pulsed like the sun's rays rippling off the waters of a pool.

"Gateway," she whispered.

Nessa pulled them both back, away from the door, back to the screen with the map.

"But we can't *get* to it," Nessa said. "Let's figure out where we are on this thing. Maybe we can find a way around."

They found themselves on the map, a point of light in an oval with two exits...and another point of light, this one shining gold, at a dead end.

Hedy drew a line with her fingertip. "If this is to scale, the room at the end of that tunnel is about the size of this one."

"And there's only one way to get there," Marie said, looking back over her shoulder. "Which means there's no way to get there."

Hedy pursed her lips, thinking.

"Not sure about that. Marie, what else did they give you? Do you have any more of those light sticks?"

"Two. And I didn't see anything else in the kit that can help right now. It's mostly stuff you'd want if you were stranded in the wilderness. Apparently, it might take a while to find me, once I activate the beacon, so they weren't taking any chances."

They rummaged through the black bag together, close—but not too close—to the half-open doorway. Hedy held up a plastic-wrapped chemlight.

"Show me how it works?"

Marie walked her through it, tearing open the wrapper before giving the plastic tube a vigorous shake and a snap. This one gave off a bilious green glow. Hedy stood at the doorway, weighed it in her hand, then tossed it into the tunnel. It clattered on the broken flooring, rolling to a stop. She frowned, thinking.

"Something heavier," she whispered.

Marie picked up the Swiss army knife, still folded shut, and passed it over to her. Hedy weighed this one, too, lifting her palm up and down. She nodded. The knife landed midway up the corridor, coming down with a *clunk*.

The corridor exploded. The walls of meat contracted as if trying to swallow it whole, while a razor-wire curtain of anemone burst out from both sides and flailed madly. They tore at the air, at each other, worm heads desperate and starving for prey.

Then it was done. The putrid meat gave one last shudder, relaxed, and fell still. The tendrils retracted, quietly quivering. The knife was gone.

"Now we know," Hedy whispered. "It doesn't care about light. Doesn't care about movement. It might notice being touched, but I'm not going to try and find out. Now we know how much sound will definitely get its attention."

She pointed to the two chemlights, dotting the corridor with their faded puddles of orange and green.

"And how much sound *doesn't*. It didn't react at all when those two landed. You can tiptoe quieter than that, especially if you take it nice and slow. I can *dance* quieter than that."

Hedy gazed at the walls of flesh and steeled herself for the challenge.

"I'll go first, and prove it."

THIRTY-THREE

Nessa's hand clamped onto Hedy's shoulder like a talon.

"What? Hedy, *no*. Absolutely not. That's suicide."

"Do you know why they named me the Mouse? It wasn't because I was the smallest, runtiest kid in the coven." Hedy paused. "Well, actually that's exactly why, but that isn't the point. Names have power. A wise owl taught me that. I turned my name into a strength."

"And if you're wrong? You saw what happened to the knife. What if you're halfway down the hallway and you make a mistake? What if that thing is more sentient than it seems, and it's listening to us right now, just waiting for us to get close?"

"Then you and Marie will know you can't get through," Hedy said. "You'll be safe."

"If Marie and I die, we'll reincarnate. We'll get another chance—"

"No," Hedy said. She held Nessa's gaze, firm. "You know you won't. You'll be reborn, sure, but this—the whole combination of events that brought us all here, this close to changing things forever? This will *never* happen again. This is your one and only shot."

Any argument Nessa could muster died on her lips, unspoken. She reached out and cradled Hedy's cheek in her hand.

"Be careful," she said.

Hedy slipped her shoes off.

She held them in one hand as she stood in the doorway, judging the distance down the tunnel of rotten flesh and the space she had between the wavering walls of anemone. She took a deep breath and held it.

Her toes touched dark metal as she took her first step out into the tunnel. She stood there in mid-stride, watching, waiting. The creature was motionless.

She took one step. Then another. And a third. Standing at the threshold, Nessa grabbed hold of Marie's hand while they watched.

Hedy was a ghost, silent as she made her way. Halfway up the tunnel now. She reached the exact spot where the knife had been taken, swallowed by the walls. Nessa's hand squeezed Marie's in a vise grip, her knuckles turning white.

Hedy was past the point of no return now. She didn't look back. Five more quick toe-steps and she was done. She slipped through the narrow crack of the doorway on the far side of the tunnel and turned, bathed in glowing golden light. She didn't dare shout, but she gave a triumphant wave and beckoned them over.

Nessa's breath gusted out and her hand relaxed, her shoulders slumping.

"Your daughter is crazy," Marie whispered. "You know that, right?"

"Takes after her mom."

Marie crouched down, reaching for her shoelaces. "I'll go next. Let's hope this is as easy as she made it look."

Hedy had her eyes on them, beaming, waiting. They saw the figure looming at her back. She didn't.

"*Hedy!*" Nessa shouted. "*Behind—*"

Her words were swallowed by the sudden violent frenzy of the flesh tunnel, walls slamming together and worm tendrils whipping at the air. Through the chaos, they saw a streak of blue light, some kind of weapon slamming down. And Hedy crumpling to the floor.

No time. No time to wait for the creature to settle down, no time to tiptoe across. Nessa turned, wild-eyed, to the generator in the heart of the room. She brandished the Cutting Knife.

Clytemnestra, she thought, *can we—*

Yes, the elder witch replied, their magical accord finishing the question before it could be asked.

Nessa pointed the tip of the knife toward the tunnel, grabbed hold of Marie's arm, and charged.

She pulled raw Shadow from the generator, from the air, from the endless occult void beyond the bulkhead walls. It funneled through her corrupted, poisoned body, just like it had done back in Carson City. And this time, as it lanced up her arm in a wave of roiling darkness, Clytemnestra was there to catch it and shape it. An oil spill of toxic energy billowed from the tip of the blade like ink spewing into a glass of water, spreading its dark wings.

The magical ward spread, encasing Nessa and Marie like a glistening pearl as they ran headlong into the tunnel of flesh.

The rotten-gristle walls hammered at them, tendrils whipping at the surface of the pearl in a lunatic frenzy. Skeletal metal struts finally collapsed after countless centuries as the creature did everything it could to devour its prey, a mutant giant squirming in the heart of the dead ship.

The pearl held. It held as they burst through the doorway on the opposite side, the tunnel collapsing once and for all in their wake, cutting off the only way out.

Nessa had taken too much, opening herself to the Shadow In-Between. Just like in Carson City, she felt her strength give out as the bubble popped, collapsing to the floor in a shower of purple sparks. She collapsed, too, her legs slipping out from under her as her heart hammered and her stomach convulsed. The world was a smear of golden light, vision fading, and her hands were numb as she fumbled for her final vial of elixir.

She heard Marie shouting, asking her something, but her voice was a thousand miles away.

"Hedy," Nessa croaked. She felt the glass tube under her

fingertips, almost fumbled it, and yanked the cork. "Protect Hedy."

*   *   *

As the bubble shattered and sparks flew, Marie only had an instant to take in the chamber. It was almost a twin to the generator room, round and towering and lined with rectangular screens, most of them dead and broken. Fat pipes wound between the screens, running up and down the walls, disappearing into the floor below. At the chamber's heart, upon a flat-topped dais of dark metal, stood a gateway.

When Ezra and Nadia's machines opened doors to other worlds, Marie had been able to see the destination on the other side. This one...was gold. The purest, richest gold Marie had ever seen or even been able to imagine. The rectangle of perfect light ignited the room in the warmth of its glow. Beautiful.

Elysium, she thought.

She didn't have time for beauty. The dead crewman had warned them about a guardian, and there he—*it*—was, towering over Hedy's crumpled body and reaching back to deliver a killing blow.

It was a statue of living white marble, shot through with veins of jade. Marie caught the traces of a familiar sculptor, the details echoing the cathedral under Deep Six. A long face, vestigial slits for eyes and a nose, not human but a distant cousin with flawless, chiseled muscles. Its three-fingered hands curled around the grips of twin batons carved from some white and frosty wood, each one engraved with runes. Blue light blazed from the runes, and as it lifted one baton high the sweep of light followed, ancient letters etched upon the air for the space of a breath before fading into nothingness.

Marie swung up the needle-nosed pistol and opened fire.

The first fléchette lanced toward the statue's chest. For just an instant, it flickered. The statue was gone, quick as a blink, and the fléchette sailed through the place where it had stood. It crashed into a screen on the wall, shattering glass.

The figure turned its sculpted face toward her as Hedy writhed, barely conscious, at the statue's feet. Marie squeezed the trigger again and again. It flickered as it advanced on her, phasing in and out of reality just long enough to evade every shot. The gun clicked, empty. The first baton knocked it from her outstretched hand, sending it spinning as it slid across the polished floor to land at the foot of the dais. The second baton slammed down on Marie's shoulder, trailing wintery runes, and set off an explosion under her skin.

Every muscle in her body convulsed. The floor shot up to meet her as her legs turned to rubber and she slammed down onto the deck. She struggled to roll onto her back. She clutched her second gun in a death grip but couldn't make her arms lift it.

The statue raised both of its batons and flipped them in its sculpted fingers, as if it was going to impale her on their tips.

"Hey," Hedy groaned, halfway up with one hand against the dais for support. "Over here!"

The statue turned its head. Marie's strength surged back in the aftermath of the shock and she braced the fat, chunky pistol in both hands. The statue's face snapped back toward Marie as she squeezed the trigger. She didn't know what they used for ammunition on Nadia's world, but the gun bucked in her hands like a jackhammer and let out an earthquake boom that left her ears ringing.

The statue flickered and the round went high, harmless, blasting into the chamber wall and leaving a rumpled crater of twisted metal behind.

The batons came driving down. Marie rolled out of the way and they plowed into the deck, denting the floor. A burst of concussive force hit her square in the back, shoving her along the glossy metal and leaving her wobbly as she pushed herself to her feet. In the corner of her eye she saw Nessa gulping down her elixir, still too weak to move, and Hedy was hurt.

All on me, then, she thought as the statue closed in for another round.

She felt a tug in the back of her mind. Or maybe she was doing the tugging. She fired another shot. The statue came at her, faster now, blinking away just long enough for the slug to sail through it and blow apart one of the wall screens at its back. Another brain tug. She felt the Conversation take hold.

The statue swung at her and she ducked under the baton. Frozen runes carved the air above her head. Lady Martika crouched beside her, translucent, mirroring Marie's movements.

"It's phasing in and out of this dimension," Martika told her. "You won't be able to hit it."

Marie dove, throwing herself out of the way, the second baton whistling as it sliced inches from her back. Martika dove with her.

"Thanks," Marie said through gritted teeth. "Figured that out myself."

Martika nodded to the gun. She clutched a ghostly copy of her own. "This is a Talon Ultimatum. Fifty caliber, radical-invasive shredder ammunition, and five rounds in a full magazine. You just wasted two of them. Marie, you aren't experienced enough to fight that thing. Let me take over. I can save your life—"

Marie gave a mental shove, shattering the projection. The statue lunged at her. She darted left, put the muzzle of the pistol to the side of its marble head, and fired.

She didn't even see the flicker this time, gone and back again in a flutter of her eyelashes. Even at point-blank range, it was fast enough to anticipate her every move. She jogged backward, trying to get some distance. The statue strode toward her, heavy feet thudding on the metal sheets, slow and relentless.

It can take its time, she thought, risking a quick look over her shoulder. *Nessa's down, Hedy's dazed, and this thing can chase me around the room until I'm out of breath.* Her strategy wasn't working. She needed a new one, and she had exactly two bullets to execute the plan with.

Even when I was down on the deck and shot at it, it still looked at me before it vanished. Maybe it needs to SEE the attack coming.

"Hedy!" Marie called out, leading the statue in a chase around the dais. "Try to distract it again!"

Hedy waved her arms, shouting, stomping her feet. It ignored her. Marie didn't know if the statue was intelligent, but it seemed to recognize her as the most dangerous threat in the room and zeroed in on her, targeting her for destruction. *Not that I feel like much of a threat.* She looked around, hunting for anything she could use, anything that could sway the odds.

Then she spotted the pipe. One of three that crawled up the walls together, snaking along the tops of the display screens along the rounded chamber. *This ship and the one we left from,* she realized. *Twins. Same fleet, same builder.*

And on the fat middle pipe, the same symbol she remembered from her meeting with the Psychopomp. The sign of Venus mounted by cow's horns, a warning sign in a language she didn't understand.

She would only get one chance. Marie took one last lap around the dais, lining herself up, and let the statue hem her in. Her shoulders bumped the pipe. She froze as the construct loomed over her and reared back one of its lethal batons. She waited for it to swing, aiming for her skull—and then dropped to her knees.

The baton smashed into the pipe, buckling steel. A blast of emerald-green gas billowed out in a torrent, exploding in the statue's face and blotting out its vision.

Marie's first bullet plowed through the statue's chin and blasted the top of its head off in a rain of white marble shards. The second punched through its chest with enough force to chop it in half. The torso hit the floor, cracked down the middle, and the rest followed. One frozen leg snapped at the knee, wobbling on the deck. Then it fell still.

She rolled to one side, keeping her head ducked and holding her breath. Her vision was throbbing, blurry from the gas. She rushed over to Nessa. Hedy was helping her up, with Nessa's arm slung around her shoulder.

"I'm all right," Nessa said. She eyed the empty vial in her hand. "Had to use the last of the elixir."

"We should go back to Mirenze," Hedy said.

"We've been over this. It's too dangerous. The Sisters of the Noose will be waiting for us."

"Mother," Hedy said. "You *need* that elixir."

Nessa lifted her chin. Her owlish glasses caught the portal's bright, pure glow, turning them into circles of molten gold.

"What I need," she said, "is on the other side of that gateway. You were right, Hedy. In a hundred lifetimes, we've never come this close. And if we turn back now, we'll never be this close again."

She pointed the tip of her Cutting Knife toward the rectangle of light.

"I'm still breathing, and I've got a little fight left in me."

Marie dropped her empty gun. Then she looked back to the broken remnants of the portal's guardian. She crouched low and scooped up the fallen batons. The varnished grips were firm in her hands, balanced, stout. As she walked, they trailed twin streamers of winter mist and sapphire runes that broke and dissolved in the air at her back.

"So," she said to Nessa, "we're doing this."

Nessa cracked a lopsided smile.

"We're doing this. Let's go."

THIRTY-FOUR

The glass doors of Talon Worldwide's corporate tower opened onto a sweep of gray granite, polished to a mirror shine. Two men in blue uniforms and caps, Talon logos stitched to their shirt pockets, sat behind the check-in desk and waited for lunch to roll around. The lobby was empty.

"Hot one out there," one of the security guards said.

"Yup."

"Nice and cool in here."

"Yup."

"I'm thinking...burritos."

"Burritos," the other said. "Nice."

The automatic doors whisked open. Rosales strode in with a toolbox in her right hand and a pistol with a sound suppressor in her left.

One of the guards lurched forward, eyes bulging, and fumbled for the phone. Rosales shot him twice in the chest. The other scooted backward in his rolling chair until it thumped the wall behind him.

"Carl," she said, "get your fat ass out of that chair. My access cards are all deactivated. I need you to open up the security room."

"Are you going to shoot me?"

"Are you going to piss me off? I don't know. Same answer to both questions, probably."

He hustled up a short hall off the lobby floor, fumbled with a lanyard, and half leaned against a secure door. He rubbed his plastic-sheathed key card against the lock like he was trying to start a fire with it, until the display finally clicked and flashed green.

She shoved him through the doorway. The room beyond was a little bigger than a walk-in closet, and two men monitored the building's cameras through a bank of grainy screens. One saw her, jumped up, and reached for the pistol on his hip. She shot him between the eyes. The other one froze.

Rosales pushed the dead man onto the powder-blue carpet. Then she shoved Carl into his chair, lining the two survivors up side by side.

"Oh hey, Rick. Didn't think you'd be working today. Now, here's what I need. First get on those screens and find my former employer."

Rick stared at the corpse at his feet.

"You...you shot Joe."

"Yeah, well, he was kind of a douche. I've been wanting to shoot him for a while. Carl, tell Rick the consequences of pissing me off, please?"

"She's gonna kill us," Carl said out one side of his mouth. "Please don't."

"Now don't freak," Rosales said and set down the toolbox.

She pulled back the lid. Savannah burst from the container, a wave of inky tar springing to her full height as she took on a watery human outline.

Rosales cringed as both men let out shrill, full-throated screams.

"I said do *not* freak. Jesus. Learn to follow instructions."

She leaned in and snatched Carl's key card, snapping the strap of his lanyard with one sharp tug. She stuffed it into the pocket of her jeans. Then she grabbed the only other thing in the toolbox: a stainless-steel hatchet, fresh from the hardware store down the street.

"That's the Blob," Carl sputtered, on the verge of tears as a damp stain spread across the seat of his pants. "You brought the Blob in here. We're gonna get eaten by the Blob now."

"I have a name," Savannah said. "I mean, *rude.*"

Rosales snapped her fingers at the bank of monitors. "Ezra. *Now.* First one who finds the old man gets to live."

They raced each other, flicking through camera feeds, eyes fixed on the screens. Rick won. He almost sprang from his chair—then thought better of it and pointed to the upper-left screen. Ezra limped his way down a mahogany-paneled corridor, then turned into an open doorway.

"There. He's in his office on forty-three."

"Perfect. Seen Bran today?"

"Should be in the labs on twenty-one," Rick said. "So, you're not going to kill me, right?"

Rosales looked between Rick and Carl. She ran her fingertip across the hatchet's blade, testing it.

"Here's the thing," she said. "Remember last week when I forgot my lunch and I didn't have a dollar for the vending machine and I was like, 'I'm super-hungry, does anybody have a dollar?' and you told me you didn't have any cash on you, and then ten minutes later I saw that you in fact *did* have a dollar, which you used to buy yourself a Coke?"

Rick's head bobbed, just a little.

The hatchet was a blur as it came down. A gout of blood arced across the security monitors and spattered Carl's face.

Rosales braced a knee against Rick's chest and wrenched the hatchet out of his forehead. She ran her thumb across the dripping blade, testing the edge, and nodded her approval.

"Nice."

Carl clung to the arms of his chair and let out a faint whimpering noise. She glanced his way. Then she poked the head of the hatchet against his uniform shirt, leaving a scarlet smear.

"You bought me a burrito, Carl. I didn't even ask you to. It was an act of genuine thoughtfulness, and that, my friend, makes you one model motherfuckin' employee."

"T-thank…you?" he said.

"Doc," Rosales said, "go and cut the comm trunk. We don't need anyone calling the cops and making this more complicated."

"That won't stop them from using cell phones," Savannah said.

"Then we'll just have to be fast. I'll head upstairs, get what we need, and meet you in the subbasement. And my man Carl is going to sit right here and count to ten thousand. You cool with that, Carl?"

Carl was cool with that. Savannah's human form wavered and broke, splashing into a puddle of ink on the security-room floor. She flowed toward an air vent, climbing the wall, making a slurping sound as she slithered into the grate.

Rosales rode the executive elevator. The hatchet dangled in her hand, slowly dripping onto the carpeted floor. She hummed along with the elevator music. The elevator stopped on the fifth floor and a woman she vaguely recognized got on, toting an armload of binders.

She didn't notice the hatchet until the doors slid shut. She clutched the binders to her chest.

"Anna, right?" Rosales said. "From accounting?"

Anna nodded, mute.

"Cool."

The elevator slowly glided upward.

"Whatcha got there?" Rosales asked. "Some accounting stuff?"

Anna stared at the hatchet. "Payroll," she said.

"Cool." Rosales looked up at the glowing numbers. "Very cool."

Rosales tapped her feet in time with the elevator music while Anna pressed herself into the back corner of the cage.

"*Man*, this elevator is slow," Rosales muttered.

It ground to a halt on the forty-third floor and the door slid open. Rosales was humming a jaunty tune as she wandered up the hallway. Behind her, Anna lunged for the control panel and pounded the *Door Close* button until it shut.

* * *

Ezra Talon's desk was a monument of dark-varnished oak, its U-shaped sweep taking up half of his office. He needed the space. Like most days he had two laptops open at once, an in-box choked with papers demanding his attention, and a technical blueprint spread across the grainy wood. He sat in a tall leather chair, his silver-tipped cane resting against the desk beside him, and clicked through his email with executive efficiency.

A thumping sound echoed from the next room, like something slamming against the door. He glanced up.

"Cora?" he called out.

Another thump, and then silence.

His door swung open. Rosales sauntered in, casually toting her hatchet. Now it was wet from the tip of the blade all the way down to the rubberized grip, leaving her hand gloved in rivulets of scarlet.

"Bitch tried to pepper-spray me, do you believe that?" Rosales looked genuinely perplexed. "I was going to let her go, she was halfway out the door, then she went all kamikaze on me. What were you paying her? I mean, what's an admin make, like fifteen, sixteen bucks an hour?"

Ezra sank into his chair. One hand slowly reached for the telephone.

"Rosales, wait. We can talk about this—"

"What kind of a dumbass makes sixteen bucks an hour and decides to literally die to protect her boss? I didn't even have to kill her, but after a move like that, I figured I was cleansing the gene pool."

"Rosales, *please.*"

He had his hand on the receiver. She waggled her hatchet at him, spattering crimson drops across the blueprint.

"That ain't gonna work. Anyway, I had a long think on the

way up here. Slow elevator. You ever think about destiny, Ezra? I mean, it's gotta be weird for you, this whole 'fated to die over and over again' deal. But do you think about destiny in terms of the big picture, the grand scheme of...everything?"

"What do you want?" he said. "Money? I can get you money, assets, a jet—"

"See, I didn't really get it until today, the whole 'first story' concept. Oh! Right, I should explain. This is a robbery. We're stealing the Golden Saint."

"Okay," Ezra said. "I can—I can help you. That's very, um, reasonable of you."

"You know what's not reasonable, Ezra? You know what just blows my mind? Okay, so you know you're the Salesman. You know that according to the first story, you're condemned to be imprisoned for the rest of your life after you get your hands and your tongue chopped off. Inevitably, it's going to happen. That's the part I never got. Like, just don't put yourself in a situation where it's possible and you'll be fine, right?"

Ezra swallowed, hard.

"But there I was," Rosales told him, "standing in line at the True Value, buying this hatchet. I'm not a part of this story, but it was like some cosmic force was just *steering* me. And then I'm thinking on the elevator up, you're the one who decided to keep the Saint behind a biometric lock keyed to your personal handprint. Why would you *do* that? Were there no red flags? Did you think, for one second—"

"Rosales, you don't have to do this!"

She grabbed his arm and hauled him out of his chair, halfway across the desk.

"I know I don't," she said, "and that's the fucked-up part. I mean, I could just take you hostage, walk you to the basement, and make you open it."

The hatchet plunged down. It split through the folded cuff of his dress shirt, through flesh and bone, splintering the wood beneath his wrist. He howled as his blood pooled out across the desk. She grabbed his other arm as he thrashed, pinning it down and holding him in an iron grip.

"But here I am," she said, "cutting your hand off. Hands. See, all of a sudden I don't remember if it was keyed to your right or your left, so I have to take both. I've seen you open that door a million times; there's no reason I shouldn't remember this."

The blade caught halfway into his wrist bones. She had to wrench it free and give it two more chops to finish the job. She tossed the hatchet aside, letting it fall to the powder-blue carpet. Then she forced Ezra's jaw open, reached in, and took hold of his tongue.

"What I'm saying is, this is not rational behavior, and intellectually I know that." His frantic screams were muffled by her curled fist as she *pulled*, shoving her other hand against his chest for leverage. "And now I need to jump to another dimension, and while I have absolutely no reason to set Roth and Reinhart on fire when I find them, I have a really strong compulsion to do just that."

Ezra fell backward as his tongue ripped free. He hit his chair and pulled it down with him, crashing to the floor, choking up gouts of dark, syrupy blood. Rosales glanced at the ragged strip of meat in her hand and tossed it onto the desk.

"I feel like such an asshole right now," she muttered.

She locked his office door on the way out. No reason, but it seemed like the right thing to do.

*   *   *

A police cordon surrounded the parking lot. They'd tossed a phone into the lobby, wanting to talk to the madwoman with the hatchet and hear her demands. Rosales didn't even know they were there. She'd taken the elevator to twenty-one, rounded up Bran and a couple of his more competent minions, and ferried them straight down to the subbasement.

She pressed one of Ezra's severed hands to the biometric pad.

It flashed red. She tried the other one and the pad let out a happy beep.

"*Left* hand," she told Savannah. "See, there's no reason I wouldn't have remembered that."

She didn't worry about keeping Bran and his people in line. One look at the living blob of ink at Rosales's side, and they'd been paralyzed into compliance.

The vault door rumbled open, one slow inch at a time. Rosales tossed both of the severed hands over her shoulders.

"You do understand," Bran told her, "you're mad as a box of frogs. The Saint isn't *finished*. She's halfway peeled."

Rosales gave the Irishman a sidelong glance. "You know who else could be halfway peeled, real soon now?"

After that he didn't say anything. The door shuddered to a stop. In the heart of the test chamber, surrounded by coiled hoses and mottled olive walkways, stood the Golden Saint. The insect-like armor, coppery metal spaced out between segmented black joints, had been opened for maintenance. Runes of binding and warding lined the inside of the breastplate, laser-etched with mathematical precision.

Savannah splashed into a puddle, flowed across the room, and rose up again beside the crane arm that held the armor. She stretched out, bending like a spring made of black water as she studied it from all sides.

"How much of this is based on my work?"

"Forty percent," Bran said.

The impression of a head turned toward him.

"Eighty percent," he said.

Rosales handed him a microscope slide, with a crust of dried blood fixed to its transparent face.

"We're tracking Vanessa Roth," she said. "Can you key the gateway to this?"

He twisted his wiry beard as he stared at the slide. "Maybe? Possibly? We know our tech *can* hone in on first-story blood, but 'can' ain't nowhere near a mathematical certainty. This suit is an untested prototype based on somebody else's prototype. You're taking a hell of a risk."

Rosales approached the armor. "I'm wanted as an accessory to a mass murder. Also I'm not exactly in a position to ask for my old job back. What I'm saying is, I'm pretty much out of good options at the moment. Suit me up."

"Suit *us* up," Savannah said.

"I'm trying to figure out where you can ride," Rosales told her.

"Simplicity. My current form is not only highly compressible, it's eminently malleable."

Savannah turned into a geyser of ink, splashing toward her and then washing over her body. As Rosales staggered back, surprised, the oily tar engulfed her. The ink went taut. It compressed around her, forming a thin layer from Rosales's neck to her toes, a suit made of ink.

"I'm a scientist *and* a fashion statement," Savannah said.

Rosales curled her now-glossy fingers, her hand and arm coated in a sheen of what looked like wet latex.

"Okay, that's weird as hell, but I can roll with it." She looked to Bran. "You heard the lady. Suit us up."

THIRTY-FIVE

Nessa, Marie, and Hedy stepped through the golden rectangle of light.

They emerged under an overcast sky, the noonday sun a faintly glowing orb behind the clouds. The cool air smelled like the aftermath of a springtime rain, and dirty puddles collected here and there on the scalloped pavement around them.

"This can't be right," Nessa murmured.

Heaven, if this was heaven, was an abandoned carnival.

The portal had placed them at the tip of a midway, the concrete boulevard lined with shuttered games. A cotton-candy machine stood empty, near a hot-dog stand where cheap stuffed animals and pennants dangled from a length of cord. Up ahead, off to their left, a Ferris wheel stood dead and silent. The skeleton of a wooden roller coaster rotted away like the bones of some ancient and misshapen beast.

They advanced up the midway. Marie's gaze swung left and right as they walked, her batons trailing wisps of frost and magic as they swayed in her hands. She couldn't shake the feeling of being watched. The skin on the back of her neck prickled.

Something rustled, behind a shuttered booth. They stopped walking.

A shape peered around the corner of the painted wood. Its three-fingered hands, tipped with dirty claws, slowly curled around the booth's edge like a child trying to hide. Then it poked its head into sight. It had stringy, greasy black hair and wore a theatrical mask over its face, the grimace of Tragedy.

Comedy emerged from the opposite side of the midway. The

second masked creature shambled into sight, back hunched and twisted, its neck craned at a spine-breaking angle.

The figure in the Tragedy mask stepped all the way out of hiding. The wings of a dove, tattered, feather tips soiled and twisted, ruffled upon its back. Comedy only had a single wing, and a stump of old, broken bone that jutted from its left shoulder blade.

The three women stood together, back-to-back, forming a triangle. Marie brandished her batons.

Four more of the winged creatures crept out of hiding. Their masks were baroque but ravaged by time, flecks of once-golden paint clinging to bare and half-rotted wood. They circled, slow, claws making curious snatching gestures as they kept their distance.

Against Marie's side, the mirror bag began to quake, squirming like something was alive inside. She blinked at it. "Uh, Nessa? My hands are full. Could you—"

"Right." Nessa reached into the bag. She came out with the sapphire manacles they'd taken from the cathedral beneath Deep Six.

They suddenly bucked in her grip, chain twisting, manacles snapping like angry twin mouths. Comedy was the boldest, and the one-winged figure lunged at Nessa. She let go of the chain. It flung itself through the air between them and the manacles clamped down on Comedy's wrists. The creature fell to the pavement, thrashing in a puddle of water and making low, keening noises behind its mask as it struggled against the chains.

"That," boomed a voice from the end of the midway, "is enough of that."

The figures threw up their hands, covering their masked eyes, and parted like waves. The new arrival was an elderly man, deep brown skin with a mole on one side of his thick nose. Long ashen hair spilled down the shoulders of his plain linen cassock, and he walked with a gnarled staff in his grip, using it for a cane. He crouched down at Comedy's side, voice low now, soothing.

"There, there. They didn't mean it. They're just stupid humans."

The man's fingers brushed the manacles, and the sapphire coils snapped open, clattering to the pavement. He helped the ragged creature up and brushed him off.

"Go along, then. You're good boys. Go along, all of you."

The masked figures scattered in all directions, loping back into hiding without a word. The man frowned, picked up the manacles, and slipped them under his cassock. Then he turned away. He started to leave, paused, and looked back.

"Heaven's closed," he said. "Go away."

His staff thumped the wet concrete as he walked. Nessa took a step forward and raised her voice.

"*Excuse* me," she said.

He turned to face her and leaned on his staff with both hands, letting out a tired sigh.

"We. Are. Closed. I don't know how you people got here, but there's nothing here for you. *Go away.*"

"Are you God?" Nessa asked.

"If I say yes, will you go away?"

"No."

He rolled his amber eyes. "If I say no, will you go away?"

She took another step toward him. Marie and Hedy followed at her side.

"My name is Nessa Fieri. This is Marie Reinhart. We have been cursed, we have been mistreated, and we have been wronged. We *will* have justice."

He squinted at them. Then he rose up and nodded, as if he was seeing them for the first time.

"Ooh. You're a couple of *those*. Figured one of you would make it here eventually. Well, hate to disappoint, but I'm not God. I just work here. Used to work here, when there was work to be done.

Now I just…maintain the place. I keep watch over these poor, broken souls and occasionally tidy up a bit."

"Then you'll take us to him," Nessa said.

"Can't. He's elsewhere. Locked away. Doesn't answer my letters anymore. Nobody can get to him. Impossible."

Nessa's hand snaked into the mirror bag. It came out gripping the copper bell. She flicked her fingers and it let out a crystal chime that rang along the midway.

"Oh," he said. "Don't suppose you found the candle, too?"

"It's not with us," Hedy said, "but we have it."

"You asked about the candle, but not the book," Marie said.

"Did you find the book?"

Marie latched onto the mistake like she was getting a confession out of a perp.

"You know we didn't. Same reason you didn't ask us if we found it. Because *you* have it."

"Bell, book, and candle," the old man said. "You know what that means? Any of you girls raised Catholic?"

"I'm not from their planet," Hedy said.

"Excommunication," he said. "It was a little joke, on the part of the Kings of Man. The relics could have looked like anything, or nothing at all. They chose those forms to make a point. Anyway, the Demiurge—that's what I always called him, you'd call him God, or a thousand other names, doesn't matter really—fled to a very tiny world of his own creation and locked the door when the civil war began."

"The nine kings against the three faithful thrones," Nessa said.

"Exactly. The keys were designed to crack their way in. Drill a hole straight to the Demiurge's hiding place. The thrones stole them. Couldn't destroy the things, so they scattered them across the cosmos." He paused. "Not a bad plan, there's a *lot* of cosmos out there. Of course, the kings could hone in on the keys—they crafted the damn things, after all—so the thrones made a sacrifice play."

"When we found the bell," Marie said, "it was inside a coffin. *Inside* the corpse."

The old man took the sapphire manacles out from under his cassock. He gave them a rattle before slipping them away again.

"Angel-forged. Potent magic. Some of the oldest magic. Powerful enough to bind even a throne and steal his powers away."

Hedy's lips parted as the implication sank in.

"Wait," she said. "You're telling us they chained themselves up?"

"Each of the three faithful crafted their own tomb. They sealed the keys inside their bodies, to hide them from the sight of the Kings of Man. Then they chained themselves, becoming reliquaries, and waited to die. Such was their love for their creator, and their desire to save him from harm." The old man leaned on his staff and frowned up at the overcast sky. "*Fools.*"

"You have the book," Nessa said. "That's the last key we need, and I don't have much time. So I'm going to ask nicely. Hand it over."

His eyes narrowed. "Are you threatening me?"

"Absolutely," Nessa replied.

"What would you do with it if you had it? If you could open a doorway right now and stare the Demiurge right in the eye—the creator of worlds, the father of man and mankind—what would you actually do?"

"Demand that he free us from this endless cycle."

"Don't know if he can do that."

"She's Shadow sick," Marie said. "We'd ask him to heal her."

The old man shrugged. "Maybe he would, maybe he wouldn't. Fifty-fifty."

"And if he's that useless," Nessa said, "there's nothing left to do but punish him for his crimes."

"You're not selling me on the idea of cooperation," the old man said.

Marie took a step forward, hands clenched around her batons, suddenly desperate.

"He *owes* us," she said.

His bushy eyebrows lifted. "Does he, now? What does your creator owe you, do you think?"

"He owes us an answer," Marie said. "He wrote the first story. He made us, cast us in these roles. You want to know what I'd do if I could look him in the eye right now? Nothing. He needs to look *me* in the eye. He needs to see my face and hear my voice. He needs to admit what he did to us."

Her eyes glistened as the words burst out like water from a breaking dam.

"He needs to answer for it. And if he can't fix it, if he really can't set us free, then at the very least he has to *tell us why.*"

The old man fell silent. He studied Marie. Then he gave a tiny nod.

"I'll take you to the book," he said. "One condition."

"Name it," Nessa said.

"I want to tell you a story along the way. Might change your mind, might not. Will you listen?"

"Lead the way," Nessa said.

He turned and they followed, guided by the unsteady thump of his staff on the puddle-streaked midway.

"First thing you have to know," he said, "the Demiurge isn't the first being you'd consider a god. In the beginning—the beginning I know about, and for all I know there was a beginning before the beginning and a beginning before that one—there was Sophia."

He raised his staff and waved it at the sky. The day tore open down the middle.

The clouds and muddy blue sky parted, opening like a zipper, exposing the night beyond. It was dark over the carnival now, and they stood bathed in the inky blackness of space, lit by a thousand twinkling stars.

"Now *she* was a goddess," the man said, resuming the walk. "A being of pure ascended spirit. Perfect. Luminous. She made the light and saw that it was good. Not the starlight or the sunlight, the inside-you kind of light."

"I'm not much for inner light," Nessa said. "Sounds a little too close to peace and love."

"There was a time, young lady, when such things were not food for mockery. There was a time when peace and love were things a being *was*, not things you momentarily felt or ached for in their absence. Anyway, Sophia was lonely, so she created herself a son."

"The Demiurge?" Marie asked.

"Mm-hmm. He had her spark, but not her skill. He wanted to create, just like mama did. And he made himself a world."

He raised the staff once more as they walked and pointed to a spot in the distant heavens. A shape was racing toward them, billowing from the void between stars. Then it jolted to a halt. The Earth, bigger and closer than a full moon, hung above their heads. *An Earth*, Marie thought, realizing the mist-shrouded continents of lush green didn't match the ones she knew.

"The first *material* creation. And he made dogs and cats and serpents and the first ostriches—" He paused, glancing back over his shoulder. "Ostriches didn't always look that dumb. There were ill-advised revisions later. And then he got really inventive. He made beings that could think and feel and love, just like him and Sophia."

"Humans?" Hedy asked.

"Not yet. Gods, tier three: angels. The thrones were the greatest and most powerful, built with the purpose of helping him to manage these new creations. After all, he couldn't be everywhere at once. Then humanity. A garden, a woman, a man."

"You're telling us the Garden of Eden was a literal place," Nessa said.

"You have to understand that the myths and legends of your world are mostly wrong. Of every world, honestly. Not your fault, but you received bits and pieces of truth filtered through eons of mistranslation. So yes, there was a thing *like* what you picture as the Garden of Eden, but there was no snake tempting Eve with an apple. It ended...differently."

High above their heads, the Earth curdled and died.

A flash of light erupted in the heart of the green. And from it, in all directions, spread a sickly yellow rot. Marie watched as it consumed the planet, the clouds turning vomit-brown, the oceans churning and dark alien shapes writhing beneath the poisoned waters, so vast they were visible from space.

"The first human family," the old man said, "was an epic shit-show on every level. You'd think that would have deterred him, but no. The Demiurge tried again. New planet. New humans. But remember what I said? He had his mother's power, but not her skill, and his hopes of perfection fell short. So he tried again. And again."

Nessa pushed her glasses up on her nose. "All of these parallel worlds, all these alternate realities...they were *do-overs*?"

"He just couldn't get it perfect. And he couldn't see that since he was working with mortal clay, he never would. Life was never meant to be perfect. So while he was crafting Earth after Earth and screwing up the ostrich, trouble was brewing. See, the thrones were supposed to become the spiritual guides to humanity. A perfect ideal. He wanted humans to look up and say, 'We will strive to become like them.'"

"I assume that didn't work out," Nessa said.

A lamppost near the midway's end cast a pale arc of light across the concrete. The old man stood in its glow, resting for a moment, leaning against his staff. Off to one side, bumper cars rusted away in the dark. Across from them, the cages of a petting zoo were open and empty, a musty smell like old hay hanging in the air.

"Nine of the thrones," he said, "looked down upon the worlds he'd built. And they said, 'No. We should be like them, and they will worship us as gods.' Thus were born the Kings of Man. They looked at humanity and saw only your worst natures, the flaws that hound you, the burdens that drag you down. Greed, hatred, bigotry, cruelty. You didn't choose to have those things in your hearts, you're only human. But they...they *embraced* them. They chose to become those evils, to embody them. And they twisted themselves inside out, becoming a parody of their former selves."

"Why?" Nessa asked. "What could they possibly gain from that?"

The old man looked back at her.

"Because that's how they feed," he said. "Every time a human being gives in to their darker nature. Every time you people raise your fists to one another, or destroy something beautiful, or lie or cheat or steal or break a lover's heart, the Kings of Man grow stronger. And, oblivious to what was happening right under his nose, the Demiurge just kept building more Earths."

"More humans," Marie said. "More power."

"I'll never know where Sophia was, all that time. She'd gone somewhere. Maybe she'd gone to sleep. Or she'd slipped off, stepped sideways into some *other* multiverse. All I know is that one night she came home, and the kings were waiting."

The lamplight turned the old man's face into a map of weariness and pain. Every wrinkle, every furrow in his brow was deep as a chasm as his eyes went distant.

"They combined their strength. And they tore her apart."

He waved his staff and banished the night. The starry dome ripped like a sheet of paper, crumpling up and tumbling over the edge of the horizon. Beyond it was absolute darkness. An endless, eternal void. Then a lightning storm flashed in the impossible distance, with alien sigils etched upon the onyx in gold, flaring and then dying. They left outlines that hovered in Marie's vision when she shut her eyes.

"They killed her," the old man said, "but they couldn't destroy her. Sophia's blood spilled out and filled the space between worlds. A realm of pure and absolute spirit, winding between her son's flawed, material creations."

Marie was about to say something, but then she noticed Nessa. Her lover was staring up at the void, eyes wide, mouth open, frozen where she stood.

"Nessa? What is it?"

"All along," Nessa breathed. "We had the answer all along and we didn't know it."

The old man chuckled. "The scholar among you knows. Go ahead. Tell them."

Nessa tore her gaze from the darkness and looked to Marie.

"Sophia. It's a Greek name," she said. "It means 'wisdom.'"

Marie blinked. "Wisdom wasn't the first witch. She was the first goddess."

"And all these years," Hedy said, "all this searching—"

"We already knew," Nessa said.

"The Shadow In-Between is Wisdom's Grave." Hedy raised her hand and pointed to the void. "The wellspring of magic. Wisdom's Grave isn't a place. It's *every* place."

"It wasn't always so dark, you know," said the old man. "No. When Sophia died, and her death and her blood gave birth to magic...there was *light*."

He lifted his staff in both hands and brought it driving down, thundering against the carnival pavement. In response, the sky exploded. It erupted in gold, in white, and then a rainbow, dizzying colors dancing upon the firmament. It was riotous, joyous, all-encompassing, and Marie felt a tear roll down her cheek as she stared up at its glory. Nessa's hand curled around hers, holding her close.

"A cunning creator, betrayed by venal men who cut her down," Nessa murmured. "Sophia was *absolutely* the first witch."

Slowly, the colors and the light faded. They went pale, then gray, then dark. Marie felt her heart ache, her stomach clench as they drained away. She felt like a love she'd never known, something pure and absolute and unconditional, was being stolen away moments after she'd discovered it. She felt like she was watching her mother die.

Then there was nothing but the darkness. And the loveless ache in Marie's chest became a slow, simmering boil of anger.

The old man didn't speak for a moment. He hobbled ahead, leading them down dark paths, past shuttered and abandoned rides. They came to the tent of a sideshow attraction. The marquee was faded, almost unreadable in the dark, but it still showed the caricatures of carnival acts from days long gone. A strongman hoisting a dumbbell, a woman wearing a snake around her shoulders like a shawl.

He pulled back the tent flap with the head of his staff. Dust danced in the shadows beyond the entrance.

"But our tragedy's not done yet, so neither is the show. Step right up, ladies. I'll tell you what became of hell, and show you what became of heaven."

THIRTY-SIX

At the far edge of the darkened carnival, a spark ignited. It hovered in midair, spinning, and stretched out razor-wire lines of hard light. The lines curved and stretched. They took on form and definition as they carved the impression of a suit of armor, etching it like a pencil sketch.

Then, with a gust of ozone stench and a distorted burst of static like a speaker blowing out, the image turned sideways and stepped into reality. The Golden Saint set one mechanized boot down on heaven's midway.

Rosales tapped the side of the helmet. Metal shutters over her face clicked, telescoping back and opening wide. She took a deep breath.

"Got all my fingers, all my toes, and nothing inside of me is outside. I'll call that a successful test run. How about you, Doc?"

An arc of tar spat from the neck of the armored suit like a toxic fountain, splashing onto the wet concrete. Savannah put her body back together, rising to her full height as the last of her spurted out.

"None the worse for wear," she said. "Or for being worn. You were right: that was *so* much easier than my last few attempts at interdimensional travel."

Rosales took in the shuttered booths, the black void sky. "Now where the hell are we? And where are they?"

"Assuming we followed her blood trail correctly, Nessa can't be far."

A rustling sound drew their attention. From the shadows of

the Ferris wheel, a broken and hunchbacked figure with a single dirty wing shambled toward them.

Then another, and another, the creatures circling as they became a pack.

"I believe we're trespassing," Savannah said, stepping closer to Rosales.

Rosales tapped the side of her neck. The helmet shutters snapped down, sealing her in, and she slapped one gauntleted fist into her palm.

"*Yeah* we are."

"You seem...eager."

"Doc?" Rosales said. "I'm wearing a prototype suit of mechanized armor built for combat, with an interdimensional jump drive, magical shielding, and jet thrusters. Is there any reason I would *not* be eager right now? C'mon, let's take this baby for a test drive."

* * *

The space beyond the tent flap wasn't a sideshow attraction. Not in any sense Marie expected. It was also impossible.

They stood upon a stretch of white marble floor in a hall of gold, its walls wider and soaring taller than the tent outside. Thick, rounded arches reached up to the vaulted ceiling, like the gilded bones of a great whale. Here and there, plush sofas and divans upholstered in snowy white formed conversation nooks. Small tables of gold and glass stood abandoned, their faces kissed with dust.

"I try to keep the place clean." The old man's staff clunked on the marble as he led them along. "Not really sure why. Nobody's ever coming back. Gives me something to do, I guess. That and take care of the wayward boys."

"The things outside, with the masks?" Hedy asked.

"Those *things*, missy, are angels. Nothing on par with a throne, mind you—that's like comparing an ant to an elephant—but still. A little respect for the broken and the lost. They were purpose-built, you see. All they understand is taking care of this place and the people who live here. Then the people all left and took their reason to exist with them."

"Where did they go?" Nessa asked. "What *happened* here?"

"You have to understand that reincarnation was baked into the original design for humanity. *All* humans reincarnate. Difference is, a human can reincarnate into anything, become anyone on any world. Each life is a completely new story."

"While ours are written for us." Nessa shared a sidelong glance with Marie. "Along with our endings."

"But the Demiurge was frustrated. Kept seeing humans cycle back into the system and make the same mistakes over and over again. Figured there had to be a way to force some kind of spiritual evolution."

A man brushed past Marie's shoulder. She jumped, spun—and stared down the empty hall.

"I saw it too," Hedy murmured.

"You might catch a few echoes, here and there," the old man said. "Don't worry, they're harmless. Just memories of the souls who lived here. Anyway, we picked one world, a single random choice out of the countless he'd built, for an experiment."

He glanced over his shoulder at Nessa and Marie. There was something wistful in his eyes, wistful and bone-tired.

"As it happens, same one you two were most recently born on. We put a wedge in the reincarnation process. Most people still recycled, but for people who fit a certain ethical standard—"

"You keep saying 'we,'" Nessa pointed out.

"Me and Lucifer. I was in charge of building heaven. Lucifer was in charge of building hell. Humans who lived lives of compassion and caring for their fellow mortals came here when they died, and, well, you can guess what kind of people went downstairs. I'll admit, the whole judgment system was sketchy and vague, and a few folks ended up in the wrong place once in a while, but we figured we'd fine-tune it once we got the system running smooth. Never really got around to fixing that."

"But if a bad person can reincarnate and become a good person in their next life, just by random chance," Marie said, "what's the point of condemning them to hell? They could be a saint next time around."

"Remember what I said: human conceptions of the cosmos are based on *mis*conceptions. Forget what you've been told, hell was never meant to be a place of eternal punishment. See, we'd spotted trends. People reincarnated as blank slates, but they seemed to bring certain traits along with them. A kind-hearted person usually remained kind. And if someone was a miserable bastard, nine times out of ten they'd be a miserable bastard the next time around. Hell was meant to be a place of rehabilitation."

"Like a prison?" Marie asked.

"Like a prison that actually did its job and tried to teach criminals a better way to live. Punishment with compassion. The idea was, souls would stay down there until they'd cleaned up their act. Then they'd get kicked back into the system. We'd watch their reincarnations and see if they turned out to be better people. If it worked, given a few thousand years of steady evolution, we might actually get a world filled with reasonably decent human beings." He snorted. "Should have known right there that it was a lost cause."

There were more echoes around them now. Ghostly figures, like living glass, sitting on the divans and strolling along the golden concourse. They wore togas of white, and laurels sat upon their brows like grape-leaf halos.

"I take it that the experiment failed," Nessa said.

"The experiment never *started*. I went down there after a while to see how he was doing. And to catch up—we were old friends from way back. Best friends, once. Anyway, he never even tried. He was just warehousing the humans, leaving them to run riot all over hell. You ask me, subjecting them to each other was the worst punishment he could inflict on them. He'd decided that humanity was hopeless, so he had spent all his time handcrafting what he hoped would be a new and better version. Humans two-point-oh."

"Demons," Nessa said.

"Mm-hmm. You ever meet a demon?"

"Unfortunately, yes."

"Then you know how well that turned out. Even at the time I think he knew how badly he'd messed up, but...well, pride's a hell of a drug. We had the shouting match to end all shouting matches, and he told me he'd show me just how wrong I was. We haven't spoken since. Far as I'm concerned, my door's open, but again. Pride."

"So demons aren't fallen angels," Marie said.

"Not remotely. I'm sure some demons *claim* they are, but demons lie. They're a totally different species, different creator. And Lucifer had nothing to do with the thrones' rebellion. His only rebellion was refusing to do his damn job. Last I heard, he got fed up and abandoned hell entirely. It's still running, but nobody's in charge anymore."

"You haven't told us your name," Nessa said.

The old man stopped walking.

He turned to face them. He seemed taller than he was, and a cold and distant fire burned behind his amber eyes.

"I've had hundreds of names on hundreds of worlds. You would recognize two or three yourselves, but I won't give them to you."

"Why not?" she asked.

"I would come down, now and then over the centuries. Just pick a world at random, wear a mortal face, and try to teach you people a little something. Lessons about compassion, about empathy, about taking care of each other. Nothing complicated. Love is simple. Then I'd leave. A few hundred years later, maybe a thousand, I'd check in. See if the seeds I planted bore any fruit. And do you know what I found, each and every time?"

A hot wind gusted through the golden hall as his voice rose. His hand clutched his staff, raised it, then slammed it down against the marble floor with a *crack* that echoed to the vaulted arches.

"They built things in my name. Temples and statues and laws. But only a rare few built anything in their hearts. No. What I saw were the wealthy, and the hateful, and the cruel using my words and my name to justify doing whatever they *wanted* to do. They would slap a book against their open palm and preach on my behalf, conning their congregations, conning nations into believing that they should despise their neighbor, turn away the needy, and persecute anyone different from them because *I told them to do it.*"

The wind died down. The fire in the old man's eyes flickered and died. He leaned against his staff, his voice softer now.

"It got to the point that hearing my name on a mortal's lips made me *sick*. And I know that wasn't fair to the ones who were trying to do right, trying to listen. But a man's heart can only be broken so many times before it stops healing. I just don't go by any name at all anymore."

He turned his back on them.

"And I don't go down there anymore. Anyway, I like it better here. It's quiet here."

*   *   *

Rosales shot across the wet pavement, holding a mad angel by its throat. She hurled it into the cotton-candy stand, where it snapped a wing and fell limp in a pile of broken glass and splintered wood. To her left, Savannah had sprouted arms of black tar from her shoulders, arms tipped with jagged spears and scalpel blades, punching through bodies and filling the air with a flurry of torn, bloody feathers.

"How many of these fuckers *are* there?" Rosales shouted.

They fought in the heart of a circle of corpses. The masked angels kept coming. More closing in now, from the bones of the roller coaster and behind the Ferris wheel, drawn to the sounds of battle.

Rosales was a whirling dervish, muscles aching and caked with hot sweat in her armor, the suit translating her punches into sledgehammer force. Another angel lunged at her, three-fingered hands hooked into dirty claws. She hoisted it into the air like it was weightless and then brought it down onto her steel-clad knee. Its spine shattered with a hollow *crack*. She tossed the twitching body aside just in time for another to leap onto her back, clawing at her helmet.

A synthesized voice spoke calmly into her ear: "Warning. Suit integrity at seventy-seven percent."

"Doc," Rosales called out, "this'd be a good time for some insight."

Savannah was performing field surgery, scalpel-tipped tentacles whipping through the air like the blades of a blender. A masked angel fluttered toward her, claws out. Before it could grab hold, her human shape broke, splashing to the pavement in an inky puddle, then flowed across the midway before popping up again.

"Insight," Savannah murmured. Her ink arms twisted around an angel, coiling like ropes, pinning its wings and dragging it close. "In. Sight. Yes. Good time for an experiment."

She sprouted another black tendril, this one thin as a needle. It slid, probing, into the captive angel's ear.

Rosales staggered past her, still trying to shake the maddened creature off her back. "No, it is arguably a *bad* time for an experiment."

Rosales wrenched herself free. She spun and snapped out one plated boot with a bone-shattering kick, crushing her attacker's emaciated ribs. Two more had already sprouted up where the first had come from, latching onto her arms, trying to drag her down. She smashed their skulls together and dropped them to the pavement.

Filthy wings fluttered. Rosales cocked back her fist—and then the creature shot past her, throwing itself onto one of its cousins in a flurry of mute rage. Claws tore into tattered robes and feathers. Rosales blinked at it, confused, and then the traitorous angel turned its face. Its eyes, burning through its featureless wooden mask, were blots of ink.

She turned on her heel. Savannah had one tentacled arm coiled around a captive and an inky needle-probe sliding into its ear. Her other tentacle whipped loose and set a third test subject free, darkness spreading and blotting out its eyes.

"I believe in working smarter, not harder," Savannah said. "Now watch my back while I make us some more friends."

THIRTY-SEVEN

The old man led the way up a winding spiral staircase. The banister was made of one continuous strip of crystal, and it chimed when Marie's fingers brushed across it. On the floor above, another boulevard of marble and gold awaited. High, arched windows looked out over a sprawling city below. It had been grand once. Mansions of gold stood tarnished and abandoned, windows broken. Dusty streets wound around copper statues caked with green patinas.

"Just like hell wasn't purely a place of punishment, heaven wasn't purely a reward," he said. "We wanted to see what would happen when a spiritually evolved person had longer than a human lifetime to study and grow. The hope was that they would enrich one another, and in a few hundred years we'd have an entire golden city filled with the best your species could offer. Then they would be recycled again—just like the inmates of hell, bringing their positive traits to the mortal world."

"Antibodies," Nessa said.

Off by a cluster of plush white chairs, the echoes of the past were gathering. A throng of them sat, wide-eyed, while a man in a toga delivered a silent lecture—his lips moving, his words lost to the mists of time. Across the hall, a painter was at work, his brushstrokes delivering invisible paint to a blank easel. Students, young and old, etched notes onto tablets of crystal and gold.

"Think of it as...spiritual genetic manipulation," the old man said. "If the experiment worked, we'd weed out the traits we didn't want in humanity and encourage the positive ones. Then we'd expand heaven and hell to all the other parallel worlds, not just one. Perfecting the cosmos and, if we were lucky, starving the Kings of Man."

"So why is it empty now?" Hedy asked. "Where did all the humans go?"

The old man pursed his lips. "I made a mistake. A simple misunderstanding of human nature."

Marie's eyebrows lifted. Off to her left, shed togas and fallen laurels draped the floor at the foot of a sofa. A woman and two men writhed together, primal, biting at each other as their bodies thrust and bucked. Another echo with a crystal tablet walked past, not even seeming to notice.

"Mortal lifespans aren't a bug," the old man said. "They're a feature. Do you know what happens when you take someone who only expected seventy good years and hand them all of eternity?"

Two echoes were fighting, rolling across the ground, hands tearing at each other's togas. One man grabbed the other by the ears and silently slammed the back of his head against the polished marble floor, leaving smears of ghostly white blood.

"First, the boredom sets in," he said. "You can only contemplate the universe and study virtue so many times before you've had every thought you're capable of thinking ten times over. Familiarity breeds contempt."

A long, gilded counter had been set for a party, with plates of snacks and a punch bowl. Echoes clustered around it, all smiles, nobody fighting. Marie almost sighed with relief, until she noticed the man on the counter. He'd been stripped and hog-tied, wrists and ankles bound behind his back.

"Then," the old man said, "the decadence sets in. Nothing left but the pursuit of sensation and pleasure."

One of the partygoers shoved the bound man's face into the punch bowl. He held it there, laughing, as his captive fought and squirmed. The bound man went limp. His killer grabbed a fistful of hair and yanked his head out of the punch.

A moment later, the drowned man sprang back to life, eyes flickering open, taking a deep, wheezing breath of air. The partygoers cheered like they'd just seen a clever magic trick. And the man gripping his hair slammed his face back into the bowl, drowning him all over again.

"In a world where no one can truly die," the old man said, "and where every wound is healed, decadence quickly becomes a thing more terrible than you can imagine."

"The best of humanity," Nessa said, her voice dry.

"It wasn't their fault. They weren't equipped for immortality, and I didn't know how to give them that strength. Well, the Demiurge was in hiding, locked away, and even I couldn't hear his voice anymore, so I had to make a judgment call."

"You shut heaven down," Marie said.

"And kicked everyone out. Heaven was a disaster. We had good intentions, but you know what they say about good intentions. And here we are. End of the tour."

The arch ahead drooped low, gilded marble formed in scalloped waves like a theater proscenium. The room beyond it was a tomb.

Bas-reliefs upon the ivory walls echoed the carvings in the cathedral under Deep Six. The burning wheels, the tall and slender thrones, the images of the kings curled and writhing in eternal fire. Alien letters ran from top to bottom in careful rows, like Egyptian hieroglyphs. At the center of the room was an open-faced sarcophagus of solid, gleaming gold.

The old man stood at the proscenium arch, venturing no farther. He gestured with his staff.

"Two of the three faithful thrones picked the farthest, most remote places in the universe they could find and went to die alone. The third trusted the fortifications of heaven to keep his key safe. I stayed here with him while he starved to death. Mopped his brow, prayed with him. Promised I would stay behind and guard his resting place, keep the book safe."

"And yet you've led us here," Nessa said. "Explain yourself."

"I think I'm just tired," the old man said.

"So you've decided to betray God."

His lips curled in a wan smile. "Does it ever get exhausting, assuming the worst about everybody? No, handing it over to the kings, that would be a betrayal."

"Do you really think what *I'm* going to do to him will be any kinder?"

"Do you?" he asked. "I'm not so sure. I knew Sophia. Did I tell you that? I walked with her once. And then she created the Demiurge and from there...everything just went wrong. Went rotten. World after world of misery and hate and broken dreams, on and on. Gave you people free will, and you can't go ten minutes without using it to bash each other's skulls in. Maybe it's time to end it all. The universe is broken. Maybe the best thing we can do for the sorry thing is burn it all down."

He held his staff in both hands, leaning on it, and turned his gaze to the gilded ceiling.

"And maybe, just maybe, Wisdom's not dead in her grave. Maybe she's just sleeping. And if we clear the slate, maybe she'll come back and start all over again. Get it right next time."

Marie stood over the golden sarcophagus. The mummified figure within was a twin to the one in the ocean cathedral, nothing but jerky-hide skin and moldering bone, bound by manacles of sapphire. In its rib cage, upon a bed of dust, sat a slim black book.

"You're wrong," Marie said.

The old man lifted an eyebrow but said nothing. She turned to face him.

"Free will means that people can be good. People can *choose* to be good. But they need inspiration. They need heroes to look up to. They need to see great deeds to remind them that they can be great, too."

"You really believe that, don't you?"

"I believe it because it's true."

She set one of her batons on the coffin's rim. Then she reached into the sarcophagus and took hold of the sapphire chain. The manacles snapped open, twisting in her grip as she slipped them into the mirror bag.

"And you might have given up," Marie said, "but I haven't. And I *won't*. We'll find a way to fix this, to fix everything. We'll set the universe right."

The old man studied her. There was a faint twinkle in his eye.

"Been a long time since anyone gave *me* faith. You haven't yet. But keep on like that...you just might." He looked to Nessa. "You wanted to know why I brought you here? One word. Hope."

"Hope," Nessa echoed.

"Besides, you might surprise me. It's been a long, long time since anyone managed to surprise me."

Windows along the great hall exploded. Sprays of glass showered the marble, glittering like diamonds, and the air erupted with a flurry of dirty gray wings. A masked angel hurtled toward them like a screaming missile, claws out and curling. The old man spun and waved his staff, its arc drawing a trail of luminous white mist. The angel glanced off the mist like it was a brick wall and went tumbling, rolling across the marble floor. One of its wings broke with a hollow-boned snap.

"What are you *doing?*" the old man roared. "Stop this foolishness!"

An angel with two broken stumps on its shoulders grappled with Hedy, throwing her against the bas-relief wall. She shoved her hands against its chest and tried to force it back. Marie ran in, her baton drawing wintery runes in the air as she brought it down against the back of the angel's skull. A blast of concussive force slammed it to the ground and it rolled onto its back, dazed.

"Nessa," Marie said, "its eyes!"

The black orbs fixed upon her. Then it spoke, from behind its mask, in a familiar voice.

"Just who I've been looking for," Savannah said. "Surprised to see me? That's 'me' in the plural now. You could say there's plenty of me to go around."

The ones who could fly were circling in the hall, while more clambered in through the broken windows. They tore their hands open on the sills and crawled across shattered glass, relentless. A flying angel broke from the pack and folded its wings back, diving toward Nessa hard and fast. She brandished her Cutting Knife in both hands, jumped aside at the last second, and drove the blade upward, slicing the possessed creature open from its chest to its sexless crotch. It landed, facedown and dead, in a pool of spreading ink. As Nessa watched, the puddle took on a life of its own, turning serpentine as it wriggled away from the corpse.

A new figure loomed at the far end of the great hall. Marie recognized the rough outlines of the armored woman: it was a Valkyrie suit, coppery-red instead of black, and its engines thrummed with eager anticipation. Rosales's voice spoke over amplified speakers.

"Is that another throne tomb? Holy shit. I just came for the bell, but if you've got another Elysium key in there, you know what that means? I am going to get *paid* tonight."

Nessa reached in, punching through brittle rib bones, and snatched up the slim black book.

"Get your own," Nessa shouted back.

The suit's thrusters ignited with a hiss of blue flame.

"Normally I'd say hand over the goods and nobody gets hurt," Rosales told her, "but as you can see, I've got Dr. Cross with me and, well, I'm pretty sure you're all going to get hurt real soon now."

The old man's staff drew another crescent of mist, driving off an ink-maddened angel. Its wings flapped, shedding dirty feathers, as its claws scrabbled at the magical shield. The man looked back over his shoulder, face strained and beading with sweat.

"Get out, now, while you still can!"

"What about you?" Marie said.

Rosales triggered her thrusters. The armored suit streaked toward them, one metal fist cocked back to deliver a killing blow. The old man raised his staff high in both hands and brought it slamming down. It hit the marble hard enough to draw a hairline crack down the heart of the gallery, and with it, a blast of sheer force that roiled through the air like an invisible tsunami. Angels and broken glass went flying, and Rosales flipped end over end, thrown off-balance and off course as her suit's thrusters slammed her into the wall.

She picked herself up and brushed herself off. Around her, the possessed angels slowly did the same, shaking their dazed heads in unison.

"I can hold them off a little longer," the old man said to Marie. "And if they get their hands on those keys...never mind. Just *go* already."

"Clytemnestra," Nessa said, "are you ready?"

Let us cut, the ancient witch said, speaking into Nessa's mind. *Where would you like to go?*

"Where?" Nessa asked. She looked to Marie, and they locked eyes.

"There's no place like home," Marie told her.

"No place like home," Nessa echoed. Then she stabbed the Cutting Knife into the open air, dragged it downward, and tore open a hole in the universe.

THIRTY-EIGHT

The tear in reality spat Marie out. She lunged, stumbling, almost tripping over her own feet. Hedy and Nessa were right behind her. The tear whipped itself shut, frayed edges of the world sewing themselves up with the sound of crystal chimes.

A laugh track rippled over a laptop's tinny speaker. Janine was sitting on the futon, legs curled, watching a sitcom with an open pint of Ben & Jerry's on her lap. The spoon in her mouth slowly slid free, then clattered to the apartment floor.

"Holy cats," she breathed.

Then she leaped off the futon, grabbed Marie, and pulled her into a ferocious hug.

"Don't you *ever* scare me like that again—" She paused, pulled back, and stared down at the batons in Marie's hands. They wavered, trailing mist and snowy runes. Her jaw dropped. "What are *those*? Are those magic? Can I hold one?"

Hedy was looking around the apartment, from the cramped living room to the kitchenette with a sink full of dirty, mismatched cups. "This is...charming," she said.

"Marie's old apartment," Nessa told her.

"Is this Vegas still?"

"Queens," Nessa said.

"Daniel put me and Tony on the first flight out of town," Janine said. "First class. Ritzy. He figured a ton of cops were going to be poking around, asking questions, and it'd be better if we were elsewhere."

"And my coven?" Hedy asked.

"Still there. Not at the hotel, obviously. He's got his own

nightclub, but construction isn't finished yet so they're all camping out there, sleeping bags and everything. Sort of like a really messed-up slumber party, and I don't want to know what their version of spin the bottle looks like. Carolyn's with them, too, since she can't exactly go home until this all blows over. Ezra already had her kidnapped once."

"I need a phone," Hedy said. "And someone needs to remind me how to make phone calls."

Janine helped her. On the other end of the line, Daniel barely got a word out before Gazelle yanked the phone from his hand. Her breath was a gust of relief.

"Mistress, you're all right! Did you find Marie? Is the Owl safe?"

"We're all here. And we need you. Can you gather up the coven and come to us? We're in a place called Queens. I assume Daniel knows where that is."

"Daniel," Gazelle said, "you need to steal another bus and drive us to Queens."

His voice was muffled, somewhere a few feet from the phone.

"Or I can *rent* a bus, like a normal person—oh, shit. Ask if they're watching the news. If not, they need to be."

Hedy passed it along, and Janine grabbed her laptop. She pulled up her favorite news site, and the lockdown at Talon Worldwide's headquarters was the top story on the banner.

"Former chief of security Angelica Rosales," Janine muttered, "with a hatchet? Ew. Okay, so half the building is evacuated, the place is locked down, and they assume she's barricaded in there."

"We just saw her five minutes ago," Marie said, "so obviously not. Does it say anything about Ezra?"

Janine shook her head. "'Conflicting eyewitness reports,' it says. Not a lot of details."

"He's dead," Nessa said. "Judging from that suit she was wearing, it looks like Ezra was trying to build his own version of the Valkyrie armor."

Marie rubbed her chin. "Well, it works. So she teamed up with Savannah Cross, stole the suit, and came gunning for us. She must have had something to locate us with."

"The kitchen, at the Flamenco." Nessa grimaced, patting her bandaged hip. "They found some of the blood I lost. *Damn* it. If they tracked us all the way to heaven, they can track us back here, too. We have to move fast."

"Wait." Janine blinked at her. "Did you say 'heaven'? You actually went to heaven."

Hedy pressed the phone to her chest. "Daniel says he can drive everyone here in three days, maybe a little less."

"*Fly* out," Nessa said. "We'll find a way to reimburse him for the tickets."

She shook her head. "Says you need identification to get on a plane. That's fine for him and Carolyn, but my people aren't exactly lawful residents of this planet."

"Fine, fine, just tell them to leave *now*. We need all hands for this, and time is not on our side."

"Can we circle back to the 'heaven' thing?" Janine asked.

"Make sure they bring the candle," Nessa said. "They need to guard it with their lives. We're playing for *all* the marbles now."

*   *   *

A few blocks from the Vegas Strip, a nightclub stood frozen in mid-creation. A motionless earthmover stood beside a drywall shell, tarp over brand-new windows, a week or two away from the club's first coat of paint and a month from the grand opening. The construction crew had been told to take a few days off. A sign out front read, *The American, where Old Vegas meets New, coming this summer.*

Inside, an explosion of activity was underway. Hedy's witches were breaking camp, rolling up sleeping bags and boxing battery-powered lamps, as Gazelle supervised the evacuation. She passed along everything she'd been told; Daniel was tapping his phone as he strode for the door, hunting for the closest rental place.

"Everybody sit tight," he called out, "and I'll be back in half an hour with a bus—"

He pulled open the door. Harmony and Jessie were standing right outside.

"—ted," he added.

"Relax," Harmony told him. "We saw the footage from the casino. We know you tried to stop the fight before it started."

"We're looking for Nyx," Jessie added. "Figure you are, too."

"Not even a little bit. Look, I'm going to make a really long story short: the Kings of Man made three keys to open the way to the sealed pocket-dimension where God is hiding. Keys stolen. Keys lost. Keys found again. We have one, Vanessa and Marie have the other two, and we've got to drive to New York and get the band back together."

"You'll be handing that over," Harmony told him.

"I don't think you get the magnitude of this situation. This is the first time in history that all three keys have been present on the same world. This one. And the Network wants these things like a cop wants donuts. As soon as they find out, they're going to send all the assets they have. *All* of them."

"All the more reason my people should confiscate them," Harmony said. "We have a secure artifact vault."

"You have a vault. They have thieves, spies, and assassins from a dozen alien worlds, and zero restraint. Want to know who I'm *not* betting on in that fight?"

"You got a better idea?" Jessie asked.

"Damn right," Daniel said. "We give Vanessa Roth what she wants. As far as I know, the portal is a one-time, one-way trip. No keys, no reason for the Network to tear this planet apart looking for 'em."

"And you're not worried about what Roth is going to *do* on the other side of that portal?"

"I believe in risk mitigation," Daniel said. "Vanessa's dying, but Marie's with her. Wherever she was, I'm told they just pulled her out alive and intact, which greatly reduces the chances of Vanessa going nuclear again. Look, I don't even know what she's going to find over there, much less what she can do. But I do know what the Network is capable of, and if you think Nyx shooting up a casino is bad news, just wait. At least Nyx follows some kind of code. They don't, and they've burned planets bigger than this one for *fuel*."

Harmony and Jessie stepped back from the front stoop. They leaned close to each other, conversing in low voices. Then Harmony glanced toward him.

"We have a plane," she said. "Get your people and let's go."

"Got room for one more on that flight?" he asked.

"Who did you have in mind?"

He hit the autodial and put the phone to his ear.

"Hey, hon, how's work? Good, yeah, same here. Long day. Hey, so, looks like the apocalypse might be happening, so I'm teaming up with the good guys and some witches from a parallel Earth to try and make that not be a thing. Uh-huh? Yeah. Love you too."

He hung up.

"Caitlin says she'll meet us at the airport."

*   *   *

Janine put on a pot of coffee. Hedy was perched on the futon next to Nessa; the two of them leafed through the slender book, seeking insight from the runes scribed along its brittle pages. Marie was touching things around the apartment, the old ritual Janine recognized. Every time the past swallowed her in a bad memory, making her live it all over again, she would touch things. Reminding herself of where she was.

"So, you going to keep that promise?" Janine asked.

She blinked at her, jarred from her thoughts. "Promise?"

"Back when you called me from the road, you said that when this was all over, you'd tell me the whole story. The real story."

Marie cracked a faint smile. "It's not over yet."

"Have you got something better to do?"

"Guess not." She came over, opened the kitchen cabinet, and stood on her tiptoes to pull down a mismatched pair of mugs. Janine poured the coffee while Marie hunted in the cluttered fridge for the creamer.

They clinked their mugs together.

"Cheers," Janine said.

"Some of it I'm still trying to understand," Marie said. "And some of it…some of the things we learned…you're not going to like it."

"I'm a big girl. I can take it."

"I know," Marie said.

While they talked, Nessa watched from the futon, silent. She put her hand on Hedy's arm.

"I need a little air," she said. "Be right back."

The apartment window was cracked. Street air and street sounds blew in through the cheap, gauzy curtain. Nessa opened it up all the way and clambered out onto the fire escape.

* * *

"Penny for your thoughts."

Nessa had been alone with those, all racing and tangled behind her eyes. She thought the city might ground her. It was afternoon in Queens, under a hazy, dusty sky, and she stared down at the cars and the pedestrians and the line of bars waiting to roll their shutters up. Real, concrete things. The world she used to take for granted.

Now there were two people on the fire escape. The Lady in Red lounged beside her, leaning with one elbow against the metal railing like a femme fatale in a speakeasy. Nessa answered by tugging up her blouse and peeling back the bandage over her cut.

Black veins spread from the wound in all directions, carving spidery lines across her torso.

"I don't have much time left," she said. "The last dose of elixir saved me when I went all-out on the *Logos*, but the infection is worse now, spreading faster and faster. Can't taste anything."

She cupped the air and waved at her nose.

"Can barely smell anything. The world is...muffled. What's next? If I can't hear and see, I can't fight. And sooner or later, Hedy tells me, the mind goes too. She says that when a witch succumbs to Shadow infection on her world, they usually have to put them down for their own good. Too dangerous otherwise."

"You've died before," the Lady observed.

"I'm not afraid of dying. I'm afraid of *losing*. I feel like I'm on a tightrope, and I can see triumph ahead, and under me is this vast chasm of failure. One single wrong move, and down I go."

"Is that what's troubling you?"

Nessa tilted her head. She stared out at the street.

"If I want to win, I have to do something I don't want to do. I have to hurt someone."

"You enjoy hurting people."

Nessa gave her a sidelong glare. "Not the people I love. Do something for me?"

"Perhaps. Ask."

"When I'm gone, watch over Marie."

"When you're gone," the Lady replied, "*you* are going to be watching over Marie. That was part of Nadia's plan from the beginning."

"I don't know if she knows what she's in for." Nessa forced a chuckle. She curled her hand into a fist and rapped it against the railing. "I just want her to be happy. Damn it, I just want her to be happy."

"Mother?" Hedy said.

Nessa turned around. She was alone on the fire escape. Hedy crouched at the window's edge, poking her head out.

"Gazelle just called me back," she said. "They found a plane. They'll be here in a few hours, which means we can do the ritual tonight."

"*Can* we do it?" Nessa asked.

Hedy held out her hand, and Nessa helped her climb through the open window.

"I think so. The glyphs, the ritual poses, they're all pretty basic—"

Hedy froze. She stared up and into the distance.

"That's Manhattan," Nessa told her.

"It's...tall. And large. I thought Vegas was large."

"After this is over, have Marie take you to the top of the Empire State Building. I wish I had time to show you myself."

Nessa stopped talking. She squeezed her eyes shut.

"Mother?" Hedy put her hand on the small of Nessa's back.

"I just—" Nessa took her glasses off, rubbed her eyes, and put them on again. "There are a lot of places I would have loved to show you."

"We don't know what's going to happen. The Demiurge might be able to heal you. He might end the cycle."

"Anything *might* happen, Hedy, but we have to prepare for the worst-case scenario. The odds are I won't be coming back tonight. Or ever again. And I apologize, because you aren't going to like it, but I have a task for you."

"Name it. Anything."

She told her. Hedy listened, her face growing grim, and nodded. She went back inside.

Nessa took a deep breath, a long last look at the city, and followed her.

THIRTY-NINE

Nessa pulled Marie aside. She sat her down on the futon and nestled beside her. Hedy was puttering in the kitchen, while Janine sipped what was left of her coffee and contemplated the impossible.

"We have to talk about tonight," Nessa said.

"I'm ready," Marie told her. "Whatever's waiting for us on the other side, whatever happens, I'm with you."

"You can't come," Nessa said.

Marie shook her head a little, like she wasn't sure she'd heard her.

"What are you talking about?"

"Marie, there aren't many ways this ends in a victory. The Demiurge might kill me the second I walk through that gateway, or worse."

"So we die. At least we die together."

"*No,*" Nessa said. "Damn it, Marie, for once you have a chance to survive. I'm *already dead*, don't you get that? Even if I survive whatever happens tonight, I'll be dead in days. Nadia wove her trap for me, and she wove it well. All I can do is make the most of it."

"I won't go to her."

"Yes, you will," Nessa said, "because you gave your word and we both know you won't break it."

"*If* you die. I said I'd go to her *if* you die—"

Hedy interrupted, stepping over with a pair of mugs. Light steam wafted from the rims, carrying the scent of chamomile.

"I think we could all use a little tea," she said. "Good for the nerves."

"I'm not nervous," Marie groused, but she took the mug.

"Well, I'm nervous enough for both of us," Nessa said. She blew across her mug and took a sip.

"Easy solution for that." Marie cradled the warm mug in both hands and raised it to her lips. "Take me with you."

"And then I'll be worried about your safety."

"I'm supposed to be worried about *your*—"

"Marie. I know. I know."

Nessa reached over. She stretched out her fingers and rested them on Marie's thigh.

"That ship has already sailed," she said. "Let's look at it mathematically, hmm? Think of it as a logic problem. If we go together, and the Demiurge destroys us both, you've died for nothing. If he refuses to help and we can't force him to, I'm still going to die and there's no guarantee you'll be able to return to this world. Again, you die for nothing. If he *can't* help, same scenario. If a miracle occurs, and he's able and willing to heal my sickness and return me here, I'm fine, we're reunited, and we both live."

They argued, and drank their tea, and argued. Marie thrust her fists against Nessa's iron walls of logic until her arms grew tired. Trapped downrange of a lovers' quarrel, Janine found some questions for Hedy and asked them in the kitchenette, both of them trying to stay out of the way.

Marie kept fighting, long after she'd run out of punches to throw. She circled back, repeating herself, and Nessa gently but firmly reminded her that she'd already given her answer. Steering Marie back onto a one-way path that led to acquiescence. With nothing left, Marie spoke the truth into Nessa's eyes.

"I'd rather die," she said. "I'd rather die than live without you."

"I knew you would say that," Nessa said. "And I hope you can forgive me."

Marie squinted. She set the empty cup down and rubbed at her eyes.

"Nessa, what—what is—"

Nessa reached out, taking gentle hold of Marie's cheek. She was out of words too, so she just touched her, until Marie's eyes rolled back and her eyelids fluttered shut. She slumped against the futon, sliding halfway onto the floor. Nessa caught her and waved Hedy over.

"Help me get her into bed."

She took Marie by the shoulders and Hedy grabbed her legs. Janine ran over, following as they hoisted her up and carried Marie into her cramped and cluttered bedroom.

"What's wrong with her?" Janine said, her voice on the edge of panic. "Is she okay?"

"She's sleeping," Nessa said.

They laid her down on the lumpy mattress, propping a pillow beneath her head. Nessa took one last look, her fingertips trailing along Marie's brow, and turned away.

"Sleeping charm on her tea," she said to Janine. "By the time she wakes up, I'll be gone."

Janine stared at her sleeping friend, then at Nessa, then back again, the depth of her treason sinking in. She searched for something to say, some way to release the sick horror that felt like a lead weight in her heart.

Janine's hand whistled through the air and cracked against Nessa's cheek.

Behind her, Hedy went tense. Nessa raised one slow hand and rubbed her reddened cheek.

"You can't possibly hate me any more than I hate myself right now," Nessa said in a soft voice. "But if you have any honesty in you, you'll admit this had to be done. For her. I'm doing this for her."

She pointed to the open doorway.

"Now fetch me a pen and some paper, so I can write her a letter."

* * *

The C-130 Hercules descended fast from a stormy, darkening sky, banking hard and aiming for LaGuardia Airport. It touched down on the tarmac with a rough, rattling thump and screaming breaks, throwing its passengers sideways in their jump seats. Then it taxied for a private hangar with a government registry.

The cargo ramp began its slow, whirring descent. Jessie and Harmony stood at the ramp's edge, the fold of metal exposing the world beyond as it inched downward. Daniel and Caitlin—the latter stoic, her scarlet hair in a French braid that draped over one shoulder of her white leather trench coat—stood beside them.

Carolyn was at Caitlin's shoulder. She gave the demoness a tiny arm nudge. Caitlin glanced back and arched a sculpted eyebrow.

"Isn't it a little warm for that coat?" Carolyn asked.

"As you know perfectly well, because you've written about it in your little books, my prince's domain is the West Coast. I'm not necessarily welcome in New York, and with the locals hostile, Nyx and her hunters on a rampage, and the Network afoot, I chose to wear a symbol they're well familiar with. The white coat is a message."

"What's the message?" she asked.

Caitlin pulled back one side of her coat. A coiled bullwhip, old and supple leather, its cold brass handle inscribed with jagged runes, dangled on her hip.

"I don't come for parley," Caitlin said in her Scottish burr. "I come for war."

Carolyn fell silent for a moment. Then she said: "So…does your prince read my books?"

"You renamed him 'Citron.'"

Carolyn nodded. "I change all the names."

Caitlin folded her arms and stared dead ahead.

"My prince," she said, "is not a lemon."

On her other side, Daniel leaned closer to Harmony.

"Been meaning to ask you something."

"Hopefully not a favor, under the circumstances."

"Something like that," he said. "You stole my car last year."

"Your car was impounded after you were arrested. Considering you're legally dead, it's not your car anymore."

"But then you stole it," he said. "My fixer got me the impound records."

"Putting in a legal requisition form for a vehicle is not 'stealing' it."

"I'm just saying, you don't mess with a man's wheels. You just don't do it."

"You faked your own death," Harmony said.

"Well, now you know better." He paused. "So?"

Harmony gestured to the plane's cavernous cargo bay.

"Do you see a car here?"

He couldn't argue with the empty space. He faced the ramp, tapping his foot.

"Really want my ride back," he said.

"We'll see," she told him.

Behind them, Gazelle was corralling the last survivors of the Pallid Masque. Butterfly, Vole, Roach, and Mantis clustered around her. Half of them were visibly shaky and pale, Gazelle foremost among them.

"We are all agreed," she said, "that metal cages that fly without magic are terrible, and we never need to do this again."

She drank in the chorus of nods.

"But we're here now," Gazelle said. "The Dire Mother is counting on us, and the Owl is counting on us. We can't let them down. No matter what happens tonight, we stay strong and we hold the line."

They agreed with that, too. By silent accord the witches formed a circle and joined hands, the five sharing their strength between them, feeling it flow.

When they broke ranks, Jessie stood at the circle's edge. She waved Gazelle over with a casual flip of her hand.

"You in charge of this crew?" Jessie asked.

"The Mouse is our leader. It's my honor to serve as her knight."

"My partner and I are wondering about your intentions, when this is all done and the dust settles."

"Intentions?" Gazelle asked.

"Specifically, are you planning to return to your world of native origin?"

Gazelle glanced to the ceiling of the plane, head tilted, thinking.

"Well, that's going to be up to the Mouse, but we're largely in agreement that we'd like to settle here. For one thing, there's a murder cult trying to kill us back in our own world. For another, this world has hot running water and minibars and barbecue potato chips."

"These are compelling arguments," Jessie said. "We're gonna have to talk about this. After."

The ramp touched down. They moved out.

*   *   *

A convoy of yellow cabs snaked through the streets of Queens. The passengers disembarked outside a plain brick apartment building over a convenience store.

They met on the roof. Nessa was already there, Hedy at her side. Night had fallen, and Manhattan was a glowing beacon in the distance. The bars across the way were lighting up blue and white, shutters rolling open, and the streets were clogged with slow-motion traffic. Ordinary people, trying to get home from another ordinary day.

That was me once, Nessa thought. She could barely remember the feeling of a life without magic, a life before she got onto the roller coaster and climbed to the first crescendo before the fall. A time before she'd embraced the role she'd been cast in against her will.

And tonight, my final scene.

All eyes were on her. She felt like she should say something. She decided to keep it simple.

"I don't know what's going to happen tonight," she said. "I wish I could offer you some certainty, some solace, some glimmer of what the world will look like come dawn. I can't. All I know is this. Once upon a time, God wrote a story. A story about two women who met and fell very much in love, and would move worlds for one another. And for one of those women, a miserable, evil, and most wicked witch, this love was the only good and pure thing in her entire life."

Nessa's grip tightened on her Cutting Knife. Clytemnestra's silhouette wavered upon the dark steel blade.

"And then he killed them. Over and over and over again. Two women fell in love, and he killed them for it."

She took a deep breath.

"Our author has wronged us. And tonight he's going to hear from me." She looked to her daughter. "Hedy, hold the book. Gazelle, take up the candle."

In her other hand, Nessa brandished the copper bell.

"Let's get started."

*   *   *

The world swam back to Marie in slow, gentle waves, like her bed was rocking upon a tropical pool. She opened her eyes, squinting, rubbing the blur out of them.

Then she remembered how she got there, and shot bolt upright.

She jumped off the mattress, frantic, and spotted the folded letter on her bedside table. Nessa's precise cursive spelled out *Read Me*. She grabbed it and unfolded it, her heart sinking with every word.

Marie, my love,

First, don't be angry at Hedy. She hexed your tea, but it was by my command. She wasn't happy about it. Janine had no idea, either. This betrayal is mine alone.

I can only hope that you'll forgive me, and that someday you'll understand why I did it. I meant every word I said, love. There is a time for romantic and doomed last stands, but this...this is not that time. We have a once-in-all-our-lifetimes chance to make a change, and part of that change is a twist in the tale. This time, the Knight lives.

I won't be entirely alone. Clytemnestra is with me. We have a plan. An idea, more than a plan, and I'd mark our chance of success...I don't even want to write down a number that small. But it's better than nothing.

And you'll be with me, too.

Hedy told me something that I taught her, when I was the Owl of Mirenze. All successful witchcraft begins in passion. In hunger. In fury and darkness. When you approach the altar of magic, you can't just come with a wish cupped in your open hands. You have to bring the fire.

You are my fire, Marie.

You gave me love I didn't deserve. Strength I never knew I needed. You came into my life and brought magic with you.

You were always the best part of me. I love you. And I always will.

Nessa

Marie bolted out the door. Janine was on the futon, hands clasped in her lap, staring at the floor like a patient in a doctor's waiting room.

"Where?" Marie demanded.

"Marie, she already—"

"Where?"

"The roof," Janine said. Her head hung once more as Marie dashed out of the apartment. She took the old wooden stairs two at a time, feet pounding on the dusty risers, and threw open the access door at the top.

Everyone was there. Everyone but Nessa. And at the heart

of the rooftop, a shadow in the shape of a woman had been scorched black upon the dirty concrete.

Marie fell to her knees and pressed her hands to her face, fighting back the tears.

FORTY

Nessa stood upon a silver walkway, ten feet wide and polished to a mirror sheen, suspended in a murky abyss. The world around her was a void of molten mercury, shifting, lights glimmering beyond misty clouds.

Crystal statues flanked the walkway. They were towering, brandishing wickedly barbed spears. As she strode toward them, their heads turned her way.

"No god's design will bar my path," Nessa hissed. "No locks, no wards."

She raised the copper bell high and brought it slashing down. A shock wave erupted along the walkway and caught a statue head-on, blasting it into a shower of crystal shards.

"No hopes, no dreams," she said.

The bell swooped down. It clanged with the sound of a cannon shot, and a second statue exploded.

"I am the night wind," Nessa said. "I am inevitable consequence."

The bell's merciless echo rained destruction down upon the path. Ancient guardians crumbled, blowing off the lip of the walkway and plummeting into the endless void in pieces. Crystal heads and hands and spear hafts littered the road ahead as she walked forward, relentless.

A mammoth shape rose from the deep, looming alongside the path and hovering there. It was a wheel of flesh a hundred feet across, whirling and spitting gouts of blue-hot flame from its spokes. Eyes sprouted from the wheel's face, countless, all sizes and colors and all staring at Nessa with a single emotion: hatred. She turned to face the wheel and raised the bell high.

"And I will *not* be denied," she shouted and whipped the bell downward. The wheel's flames turned to ice under the sheer force of her fury, and it spun, falling, plummeting back into the mercury abyss.

Nessa strode onward.

A door stood at the walkway's end. Simple, plain, wooden. The grainy knob yielded to the turn of her wrist, and she let herself inside.

*　*　*

A small, grassy lawn surrounded a small, humble cottage. A trickle of black smoke leaked from a brick chimney, poking through the crude thatched rooftop. The smoke coiled up to a bubble-dome of sky. And beyond it, the endless dark void of the Shadow In-Between. Nessa looked in all directions, seeing where the lawn suddenly cut off at the bubble's edge. It was a very small world.

The air was cool and crisp like a perfect fall morning. She caught the scent of home cooking, some kind of comforting stew. She walked up to the cottage.

Outside the front door, a mound of bare earth marked the length of a grave. A simple pylon of stone stood at the grave's head, with simple letters etched into the rock: *Sophia*.

"She's not really in there," said a small voice at Nessa's back.

"I know." Nessa turned, raising her hand, taking in the void above. "She's out there. She's everywhere."

The voice belonged to a child. Maybe twelve or so, towheaded and dressed in a white linen robe. Grass stains clung to the robe's hem and knees. He kept his distance, uncertain.

"You aren't one of the kings."

"Don't you know who I am?"

He shook his head, and a fresh spark of anger fired in Nessa's heart. She fought to keep it under control.

"But you are him," she said. "You're Wisdom's child. The creator. The Demiurge."

"I don't do that anymore," he said.

"How can you not know who I am?"

The child squinted at her. "You don't have a human soul. What are you?"

"Look *harder*," Nessa said through gritted teeth.

"Oh." He took a halting step back, sandals scuffling in the tall grass. "Oh. I wrote you. I remember now."

She closed in on him. "You remember? You mean you *forgot* about us?"

"It's not that simple. I made so many things..." He looked to the void. "I made too many things. I just wanted to be like my mother. She was perfect. I wanted to make something perfect."

"World after world after world," she said. "And because humanity didn't live up to, what, some arbitrary standard of perfection, you abandoned them."

"I didn't mean to!" he said. "I mean, I tried. But I could hear them. I can still hear them, praying to me. Imagine eight billion voices in your head. A million times eight billion. And they're all hurting and they all need something and I *can't*."

He paced across the grass, keeping his distance, his face twisted in a grimace as he slapped at one of his ears.

"Imagine hearing a child dying of hunger, and you're trying to pick out their voice, just one voice, while ten thousand people are shouting that they want you to make their football team win, and ten thousand more are shouting for the other side. In my other ear I have a policeman who wants me to help him catch a criminal, and that same criminal is begging me for help because he stole bread to feed his family. Every second of every hour of every day, they all want me to be judge and jury, they all want me to fix everything, fix their lives, fix what hurts, and it's too *many*. I can't. I just can't."

"You took on a responsibility when you created humanity,"

Nessa said. "And you left us all on our own out there, while you hid away in here and did *nothing.*"

"What could I do?" He waved to the darkness above. "That's my mother's blood. And it isn't supposed to look like that. The Kings of Man *infected* it when they planted their flags and built their kingdoms. They corrupted the heart of magic. They've only been getting more powerful since then."

"Are you telling me that you, the Demiurge himself, can't stand up to them? Honestly? You created them."

"And I could uncreate them, one by one, given the chance," he said, "but I'd never get close enough. The second I leave this place, they'll sense my presence. And they'll come in force. You don't think they've been planning for that, working toward it? I'm the only thing holding the kings back from becoming gods themselves. The best thing I can do for humanity is to stay locked up in here, where they can't steal my power. Because if they took it...you think you know what darkness is? Suffering? You have no idea what they'd do to this universe. All of existence would become an eternal hell, just to keep them fed."

Nessa fell silent for a moment. Taciturn.

"And what about us?" she asked.

He shook his head. "You?"

"The characters of the first story."

His gaze dropped to the grass.

"It was a long time ago."

"I'm very aware of that," Nessa replied.

"I wanted to give something special to humanity. I wanted to give them the power to make things, like I do. So I started with stories. I moved on to song, and sculpture, and dance, but all art starts with a story. I didn't really understand what I was doing, what I did. I made it up as I went along. Later, a lot later, I had some glimmer that you'd all come to life and I knew I should fix it, but..."

"But?"

The child turned his back on her, standing at the edge of the lawn.

"I got distracted," he said.

It took Nessa a moment to find her breath, to find her words. Her hand squeezed the grip of her knife.

"You...got...distracted," she said. "All this suffering, this death, this pointless misery...because you got distracted."

She took a step toward him. Her knuckles squeezed the knife tighter, turning white. He didn't look back.

"For what it's worth, I'm sorry—"

"It is worth *nothing*," she said.

"Just...too many voices," he said, his voice distant. "Not long ago, I heard so many of them screaming out at once. I looked. There was a war. An entire world, blanketed by plague bombs. I guess things had been bad there for a while, and then I remembered hearing so many of them praying for help before the bombs started to fall, and I knew I could have stopped it, but...there are so many voices."

Nessa stood behind him. Slowly, like the blade of a guillotine, the Cutting Knife rose in her hand. She knew she was committing suicide, but she was beyond caring, beyond anything but rage.

"I didn't mean it," he said.

And those were the last words of God, as Nessa drove the dagger down into his back, piercing his immortal heart.

INTERLUDE

"You're lying," the King of Rust said. The giant, draped in golden mist, leaned forward in his elegant chair. His silken robe shifted around the chiseled muscles of his chest. "I smell the lie on you. That's not what happened."

Carolyn lifted one hand, offering a casual shrug. Her other hand cradled her nearly empty glass of water.

"You brought me here to tell you the story of how God was murdered. How else could it have gone? I mean, Nessa—the Witch eternal, dying and trapped by fate, brought to the end of her rope and her sanity. A helpless and imprisoned Demiurge. A knife in the back. Tell me, and be honest: from the moment I first sat down to begin my story, is that not *exactly* the ending you expected?"

"It is," the king mused. "And yet, you're not telling me the truth."

"I see the problem," Carolyn said. "It's the expected ending, but it's not a very satisfying one, is it? I mean, you saw it coming from page one. What kind of a story is that? I could have just jumped right to the ending and saved us all a lot of time."

"Which I believe I asked you to do in the first place," the interrogator said. He looked to the king. "My lord, she's obviously wasting time, drawing out the last hours of her life. You can let her play Scheherazade all you like, but may I suggest it's time to prepare...the alternate interrogation room?"

The king's nostril slits flared. He flicked one three-fingered hand at his human servant.

"See to it."

As the interrogator rose, wearing a sadistic smile, he leaned in to whisper in Carolyn's ear.

"Your uncle," he breathed, "is going to be *so* happy to see you again."

Then he was gone and the bulkhead door swung shut, leaving Carolyn alone with the King of Rust.

"So," Carolyn said. "Torture. How lovely."

"I can be generous," the king said, "so I'll grant you one last chance. Tell me the true story. What really happened when Vanessa Roth faced the Demiurge?"

Carolyn studied her fingernails, taking her time. And counted silently under her breath.

"Like I said," she told him, "I knew right away that you were my real audience. The interrogator was just a proxy. You were the one I was talking to, not him."

"And?"

"And I hope you appreciate that I played fair. Just like I told you, I gave you all the clues."

The king leaned forward in his chair. He loomed over her, glowering. The golden mist turned a dark and violet hue, rippling with his anger.

"Explain yourself."

"Let's begin with this: you assumed Nessa died when she cut down the Demiurge, didn't you?"

"Naturally. And?"

"Now, this wasn't one of those aforementioned clues. It's just a literary technique I'm fond of. Foreshadowing."

Carolyn took her time, dragging it out. Still counting, and praying her timing was perfect.

"You didn't read the writing on the wall," she said. "The Owl *lives*."

FORTY-ONE

The air above the rooftop crackled. Just a spark. A glint, a ripple of wind, and the scent of roses.

Then a rent of raw darkness tore open, reality wavering around the edges like a ripped sheet of paper, and Nessa stepped through. Marie looked up, still on her knees, cheeks glistening wet. Nessa held out her hands.

"I'm sorry," she said.

Marie threw herself into Nessa's arms, squeezed her close, smeared her tears on the collar of Nessa's blouse. Nessa held on tight. When they could both breathe again, Nessa gently pulled away. She turned, slow, taking in the motley crew of allies they'd found along the way. The criminal, the demoness, the agents, the writer, her daughter's ragged coven.

"Clytemnestra and I have a plan," she said, the night wind carrying her voice across the rooftop. "A plan to change things. A plan to change history, to change *everything*, and it begins tonight. But we can't do it without your help. Are you in?"

"What happened over there?" Hedy asked.

"Nothing less than what you should expect from the Witch," Nessa said.

Her lips curled in her familiar lopsided smile.

"I made a deal with God."

INTERLUDE

The king's fists slammed down on the arms of his chair, and the violet mist flashed around him like a camera bulb.

"*What?*" he roared.

Carolyn leaned back, casual. "Am I lying?"

"No, but…" He rose from his chair, pacing, taking heavy strides across the vintage office and back again. "It's not possible. Our intelligence confirmed the Demiurge went dark. They confirmed Roth and Reinhart were involved, that both women went missing—"

"Am I lying?" Carolyn repeated.

He spun, pointing an accusing finger at her.

"Tell me the rest. *Now.*"

FORTY-TWO

Preparations were made. Calls went out, from Las Vegas to Quantico to Washington, DC. Favors were cashed in and resources were counted.

Marie went to Inwood Hill Park, alongside the Hudson River.

She had never been there, but Nessa knew a perfect spot. It was the very same one, lush, secluded, a patch of primeval forest in the heart of the world's greatest metropolis, that she used to haunt in her early pursuit of power. Marie stood in the exact spot where Nessa had made her final offering, conjuring a guide to teach her. Above her head, the branch where she'd seen her vision of the Owl was a jagged black line in the moonlight.

Marie set the beacon down on the grass, hit the activation button, and stepped back. Then she waited, listening to the crickets and the night birds trill.

The minutes dragged on, molasses-slow...and then a rectangle of light shimmered into existence above the beacon, hovering a few inches in the air. The rectangle became a doorway, stable and strong, with the blurry impression of shipboard machinery and generators on the other side.

Tricia stepped through the doorway, clad in her Valkyrie armor, helmet dangling at her side. She saw Marie and a flicker of emotions passed over her—joy, relief, sympathy.

"Marie," she said, "I'm so sorry for your loss. But I promise, everything is going to be better now. Let's get you home and—"

Nessa stepped from the shadows. The words died on Tricia's lips.

"What loss?" Nessa asked. "We're here to win."

The blood drained from Tricia's face.

"Oh," she breathed. "Oh, *shit*."

"I think you know who I want a word with," Nessa said, nodding toward the gateway. "Go get her."

Tricia swallowed hard. She slapped her gauntleted fist against the shoulder of her armor in salute. "Yes, ma'am."

Then she slipped back through. She was gone long enough that Marie almost expected the doorway to collapse, shutting tight from the other side before Nessa got impatient and invaded their world. But soon enough, a new arrival pushed through the rectangle of light.

Nadia stood there, imperious, in her military uniform and a wooden wand in the custom holster on her hip. She studied Nessa for a moment, looking her up and down. Then the two women began circling one another with identical strides, mirror-image movements.

"Well, well," Nessa said. "Look who went all fascist."

"You know we look good in this outfit," Nadia replied.

"We do. So, hatch any devious plots lately? Any elaborate schemes I should know about?"

"I won't apologize."

"I wouldn't ask you to," Nessa said. "It was brilliant. It worked perfectly, and your plan had only a single, fatal flaw."

"Which was?"

"Me," Nessa said.

"I suppose you found a way to heal yourself?"

Nessa lifted one corner of her blouse. The black spiderweb of veins seemed to glow in the moonlight.

"Still dying, and time is running out," Nessa said. "But I have a plan of my own, and you're going to help."

"I am?"

"Oh, yes," Nessa said. "You most certainly are."

Then she told Nadia what she had in mind and what she

needed. Nadia's eyes grew wide as her fingers rapped against her wand, deep in thought.

"I like it," she said.

"I naturally assumed you would."

"I'll put the wheels in motion," Nadia said. "You'll have exactly what you need, when you need it. Consider it..."

"I won't call it your apology," Nessa said, "because you won't apologize."

Nadia showed her teeth. She turned to go, then paused.

"I hope we meet again," she said, hesitant.

"But there's a very good chance I won't survive this."

"True," Nadia said. "I was just...well, this is a strange question, but meeting oneself is a rare treat and I was wondering if—"

Nessa's hand shot out, grabbed hold of Nadia's collar, and yanked her close. Their lips met, locked in a smoldering kiss that went on and on, until Nessa roughly shoved her away. Nessa grinned, taking a deep breath, and nodded.

"You're absolutely right," Nessa said. "It was just something we had to experience."

Nadia took a stumbling step back. Her eyelashes fluttered.

"Agreed." Nadia pointed an unsteady finger to the gateway. "I'll, um, I'll be—"

"Doing what I tell you." Nessa wriggled her fingers in a dismissive wave.

Nadia disappeared through the rectangle of light. A moment later, the gateway snapped shut. A faint wisp of white smoke coiled from the burnt-out guts of the beacon.

"Wow," Marie said.

"Do you object?" Nessa asked.

"Honestly, I'd probably do the same thing in that situation. I think you impressed her."

Nessa curled her arm around Marie's.

"Of course I impressed her," Nessa said. "That wasn't even

my best effort. I save that for you. Now let's go get Carolyn on board."

*　　*　　*

"You want me to do *what?*" Carolyn said.

They were back in Marie's apartment. Just her, Carolyn, Janine, and Nessa. Everyone else had been sent on their tasks, racing against the clock. Carolyn sat on the futon with a mug of tea in her lap, and the others stood, surrounding her.

"This plan doesn't work without you," Nessa said. "You're the key to everything."

Carolyn held her mug out to Janine. "Do something for me, hon? Throw this out, make some coffee, and Irish the hell out of it."

"We know it's a lot to ask," Marie said.

"A lot to ask." Carolyn stared at her. "I could die. I could be horribly tortured, then die. I told you, you saw what happened to Carlo: we Scribes are supposed to write about adventures, not go on them. It always ends badly."

Marie sat down beside her.

"Hey, I know, it's scary." She forced a nervous smile. "Believe me, we're all scared. When I think about all the parts in play, everything that could go wrong...Carolyn, I'm terrified. But that's not going to stop me. You know why?"

"Because you're an idiot?"

"Because it's the right thing to do. We can't make you help. You can walk out that door and never look back. But what we've got here...it's beyond a once-in-a-lifetime chance. It's a once-in-*all*-lifetimes chance. And it will never ever come around again. So yeah, I'm scared, but I'm going to be brave and I'm going to do it anyway. We all are. Will you stand with us?"

Carolyn looked into Marie's eyes, gazing for a long, quiet moment. Then she let out a bitter sigh.

"You know, what I said to you, when we were in Deep Six—"

"You were in a bad mood. I don't hold it against you."

"I was wrong," Carolyn said. "Marie, do you know why I wrote those books about you, about your past lives?"

Marie shook her head.

"Because deep down, one thing in life is simple: people need stories about heroes."

"I know," Marie said. "I know I did, when I was a girl."

"And you were a hero in those other lives. I think you still are. I think you've got a chance here to carve out a legend nobody's ever going to forget."

Carolyn's gaze dropped to her lap.

"You're a hero. But I'm not."

Marie touched her arm.

"Wouldn't you like to be?" Marie asked. "Just once?"

Carolyn took a slow, deep breath.

She looked up again and met Marie's eyes.

"Fine. Fuck it. Let's do this." She looked to the kitchenette and called out to Janine. "Hey, kid. Forget the coffee, just bring the bottle. I'm not doing this sober."

Marie pulled her into a grateful hug. Carolyn squirmed out of it, wincing.

"Ugh, no, no, we are not doing touchy-feely right now. Feelings are another thing I don't do sober." She looked up at Nessa. "So let me get this straight. You want me to be…"

"A Trojan horse," Nessa said. "You're going to fly home to Bloomington, go about your normal life, and wait for a day or two while we lay the seeds of an irresistible mystery. And then, you're going to be kidnapped."

FORTY-THREE

The King of Rust froze in mid-pace. His nose slits flared like he was hunting for the scent of a lie.

"I've been thinking of this entire affair in literary terms," she told him. "Foreshadowing, laying seeds, following the rules of a trilogy. Sometimes life really does imitate art, especially when you're dealing with the characters of a story made real. We can't help it—it's in our nature. On that note, I've been thinking about these little moments—the bits where my story is interrupted or a digression occurs—as interludes, until now."

The king stared at her, silent.

"The interludes are over," Carolyn said. "We're in real time now."

"What did you people do?" he whispered.

"Now here's another literary technique. Irony. Actually, I have to confess, I've never really grasped irony for one-hundred-percent certain. I know that everything in that Alanis Morissette song is actually not ironic, it's just a list of things that suck, but beyond that I'm honestly in the weeds—"

"What did you *do*?" he repeated, looming over her.

"When the Lady in Red's daughters were ambushed, mutilated, turned into Cutting Knives, do you remember that day?"

"Vaguely," the king said. "It was a long time ago."

"Do you remember Clytemnestra?"

He waved a restless hand. "Why would I? We made a point of taking their names away from them. Slaves don't have names."

"You and your brothers each picked one knife to take home as a trophy of your cruelty," Carolyn said. "Clytemnestra was yours. And if you'd known that—if you'd known that, or if you'd kept track of which of your minions you'd lent her to or where she ended up over the centuries, well…you might not be in this situation. Because she never forgot you, and she never forgot her vow to see you pay for what you'd done to her. Tell me…is that ironic?"

"How is this possible? Our intelligence network is flawless. The Demiurge is *dead*."

"If my estimate is wrong," Carolyn said, "yes, he is. But it didn't happen when Nessa visited him. And if my timing is absolutely perfect…"

She tilted her head, eyes distant, as if listening for a whisper on a dying wind.

"If my timing is perfect," she said, "it's going to happen roughly six minutes from now."

"*What?*"

"And as for the question of how we were able to inject fake information into your flawless intelligence network, well."

She cracked her knuckles and savored the moment.

"It's time for my favorite literary technique of all," she said. "The twist ending. Are you ready for it?"

*   *   *

The flagship's command deck was a small, rounded disk near the top of the vessel, at the far end of the long, slender gooseneck that separated the King of Rust's elite from the drones, soldiers and beasts toiling in the belly of the ship. Three men in slate-gray uniforms worked a rounded bank of consoles, taking in telemetry from the Shadow In-Between. A radio squawked now and then, blaring something in an alien tongue, and the men would make subtle adjustments to the bank of controls.

The door hissed open and a figure stood in the doorway. The closest man expected a visit from the king. He jumped to his feet, eager to salute faster than the others. Then he blinked.

"Wait, you're the fleet interrogator. What are you doing up here? You don't have clearance—"

The interrogator drew his Luger and shot him twice in the chest. He fell back and slammed into the rolling chair, momentum carrying him across the steel deck. Another man spun, reaching for his sidearm. The Luger spat fire twice more, tearing out his throat and drilling a hole between his eyes.

The third showed his open hands, frozen.

"Who *are* you?" the man breathed.

"Oh, me?" he said. "You can call me the Marquis."

He held his gun steady on the pilot. His other hand twirled, brandishing a scrap of paper, and handed it over.

"Change course to these coordinates and prepare to enter terrestrial space."

"You can't be serious," the pilot said. "This...this is..."

"A hijacking," the Marquis said. "We're stealing this ship."

"You can't take a ship this size out of the Shadow! It has a Swann-Puthoff drive—without a total saturation of magical energy, it can't even *fly!*"

"Don't worry. We're not stealing the whole thing." He pressed the long, slender barrel of the pistol to the back of the pilot's head. "Now key in the coordinates and set a five-minute timer for the jump."

He watched, covering the pilot's every move.

"Good. Now lock it in."

The pilot swallowed hard as he turned a key on the console.

"There. It's done. Five minutes and—"

The Marquis pulled the trigger. The pilot slumped against the console, blood guttering down the back of his uniform shirt. The Marquis briskly walked from the command deck. The door whisked shut behind him.

* * *

The King of Rust dashed to his credenza. An antique telephone rested beside his phonograph. He snatched up the receiver.

Through the walls, Carolyn heard the distant echoes of his voice, magnified through the entire ship.

"Red alert. We have an impostor on board. The fleet interrogator is a spy. Capture him and bring him to me at once. Lock down all hangars immediately. Do *not* let him escape."

"A while back," Carolyn said, "I asked Daniel if he could teach me a thing or two about stage magic. He told me that the most important thing, when it comes to sleight of hand, isn't the moves. It's about assumptions. Give people an assumption, sell it hard, and they'll believe it right up until you pull the rug out from under them. We gave you a few assumptions. First of which, that I wasn't a willing hostage who wanted to be here all along. Second, that your 'interrogator' was real, not a fake personality the Marquis has been using to rob you people blind for over a year now. He had to play rough with me a few times, to sell the act, but that's all right. See, we knew you were listening, so we had to be careful."

Carolyn reached under the neck of her sweater and tugged out a tiny antique key, dangling from a brass chain. The key's teeth were sharpened to a razor's edge and crusted with flecks of dried blood.

"So for instance, when I needed to cut myself, I asked him to leave the room so he wouldn't see it, even though he knew that was the plan. And later he made a point of noticing the cut. Why? Because if he pretended not to notice and *you* spotted it, you'd want to know why he'd been so imperceptive."

"Why would you..." The king's voice trailed off as the answer sank in.

"Because just like I told you—repeatedly—the blood of the first story's characters is special," Carolyn said. "And with the right blend of technology and magic, you can track it."

*   *   *

Far below on the detention level, inside the pea-soup-green

confines of the interrogation room, a puddle of Carolyn's blood lay crusted beneath the brushed-steel table.

With a pop of displaced air and a sudden violent gust of wind, the table flipped on its side. Chairs slammed against the cinder-block walls as a rectangle of light erupted.

Tricia was first through the gateway, helmet on, the bulbous, insect-shell grip of a rifle in her hands as she led the charge. Her sister Valkyries followed. Bandoliers dangled over their shoulders, slung with fist-sized black disks suspended in elastic webbing.

Two guards were on patrol in the hallway outside. The nozzle of Tricia's rifle spat a gout of white-hot fire that washed over them, engulfing them in a living inferno as they fell and thrashed against the deck. She drew her pistol as she strode right past them, not even looking as she delivered a pair of kill shots to the shrieking men's skulls.

The king's warning blared from concealed speakers as they rode a lift upward. *Good*, Tricia thought. *Green light.*

The lift gate rattled open. A security squad was running their way, but the Valkyries were faster and washed the corridor in merciless flame. Tricia led the way to the long, slender gooseneck of the ship, with its windows gazing out upon the Shadow In-Between. More flagships hung in the frozen void, the King of Rust's brothers come to savor their victory.

The Valkyries unslung their bandoliers. They slapped their black disks against walls, windows, support struts, giving each one a firm press and a twist. The disks beeped in unison, and a tiny green light flashed beneath their black plastic faces. While they worked, the Marquis speed-walked down the corridor from the other direction.

"Time?" Tricia asked.

"One minute thirty."

She slapped her last disk in place, looked to a readout on her armor's wrist, and tapped in a ninety-second timer. It strobed once and began to count down. The Valkyries retreated back to the portal, taking the Marquis with them.

*   *   *

The king stood over Carolyn, the purple mist dancing like a coat of fire as he seethed at her.

"Whatever this 'plan' is, whatever you think you're going to accomplish here, you aren't going to succeed. There's no escape from this ship. Your little friend is going to be found, he's going to be captured, and the two of you are going to spend the next ten thousand years suffering for even thinking of challenging my authority."

He stormed across the room. The sweep of his arm sent the phonograph slamming to the floor, its antique box smashed, spilling mechanical guts across the money-green carpet. He wheeled around, snarling.

"Who do you think you are? I'm a throne. The first of the Demiurge's own handmade creations, invested with his power and his strength. *I am a god!* And you, you...barely evolved monkeys, you sniveling little maggots, you *accidents*—what makes you think you can stand up to me?"

"I can't speak for all humans everywhere," Carolyn said. "But I've found there's one thing that most people, decent people, have in common. We don't like bullies. And really, that's all the reason we need to stand up to you. Because take away your power, take away your armies, your fancy ship, and that's all you are. Just another bully who needs to be knocked down a few pegs."

"Well." The king's voice dropped, dangerously soft. "I don't see how you're in a position to take away any of those things. So you lose."

"You know, there was a point—it was close, I was almost sure the jig was up—but there was a point in this story where I did blatantly lie, and you let me get away with it."

He frowned, uncertain. "When?"

"When Clytemnestra and Nessa first met, and they entered

each other's minds. Passing your questions through the interrogator, you asked me what the secret of poison was. I told you I wasn't there, then I gave you the reasons I couldn't have heard them speak, and you took that for my answer. But the truth is, I know the secret of poison."

Carolyn sat back, cupping her glass of water between her hands.

"Want to hear it?"

FORTY-FOUR

Standing inside the misty void, Clytemnestra whispered her secret.

"Every herbalist, healer, and witch should know the secret of poison. Very few herbs are naturally good or naturally evil; that which can heal, in large enough doses, can kill, and some dangerous ones—when used properly, in the right measure and for the right affliction—can drive impurities from the body."

"There's no cure for the poison in *my* veins," Nessa replied.

"I was here before the Kings of Man staked their dominions inside the Shadow In-Between. They corrupted it with their own essences. That is the source of your ill."

"I don't see how that knowledge aids me."

"You've shown a knack for siphoning Shadow itself, haven't you? When you needed it, in Carson City, you turned yourself into a conduit. You devoured it and turned it into fuel for your magic. Yes, the ordeal nearly killed you, but most witches couldn't do that."

"I'm not most witches," Nessa replied. "But again, not sure how that helps."

"Shadow isn't entirely fatal to all who imbibe it without wards. After all, there are nine living creatures who are utterly saturated with it."

Nessa pulled back, squinting.

"The kings."

"They suffer the ultimate Shadow infection," Clytemnestra said, "and yet they live and thrive, unharmed and even immortal. They've attuned themselves to the winds of raw magic, to such a degree that it can no longer harm them. That which normally kills, in their case, heals."

"And you're saying...there's a way I could take that power for myself?"

"Perhaps," Clytemnestra said.

The ancient witch leaned close once more, whispering into Nessa's ear.

"If," she said, "you devoured the very essence of a king."

*   *   *

A convoy of black SUVs roared down the back roads of upstate New York. Trees shivered in their wake, the underbrush cast in the glow of red and blue strobes as shrill sirens sent animals scurrying for cover. New York City was a distant memory. Up ahead, one hundred and eight miles north, was their final destination.

The abandoned ruins of the Vandemere Zoo.

A procession of emergency units—ambulances, a fire-rescue truck, and a mobile command center with FBI markings—followed in their wake. By radio command they broke off a quarter mile shy of the staging ground, setting up a triage station and preparing for imminent casualties.

The SUVs flooded the parking lot, curling in a semicircle like an armored wagon train. Doors slammed and black suits moved out with military precision. Hatchbacks swung up as they dragged out heavy crates of gear. On the other side of the wall of cars, the gates of Vandemere—one flat in the dust, the other hanging on one twisted hinge—marked the way forward.

"Get those floodlights set up," Harmony called out, striding through the controlled chaos. "Beach Cell, on me. Redbird, establish perimeter. Panic Redux, I want every piece of that arsenal checked and double-checked in the next five minutes. Jessie, are we—"

Jessie walked past her in the other direction, nodding sharp as she held up a finger, talking into her phone. "—no-fly zone for

five miles around our coordinates in every direction. *Everyone.*
No commercial flights, no law enforcement, *nothing* flies over
Vandemere tonight—"

"Where do you want us?" Janine asked, cradling a long
cardboard tube in her arms. Harmony sighed, looking between
her and Tony.

"Not here, at all. But seeing as you insisted and your roommate
insisted right along with you—stay behind the cordon at all times
and keep your heads down."

One of the newer recruits waved to get her attention. "Ma'am?
Question?"

"Shoot," Harmony said, not breaking her stride. He scrambled
to keep up.

"Um, over by the end of the convoy—" He pointed to the
figures standing in a tight circle at the perimeter's edge. "That's
Daniel Faust and Caitlin Brody."

"Yes, it is."

"They're on our target list."

She turned, studying him. "Janssen, right? How long have you
been with Vigilant, month and a half?"

"Yes, ma'am."

"You're going to find, Agent Janssen, that there are some ops
where we have to toss out the rulebook. This is one of them." She
cupped her hands to her mouth. "Everybody, focus front!"

She waited until the din of conversation simmered down and
all eyes looked her way. Jessie finished her call as she walked up
to stand at Harmony's side.

"In a minute, Jessie will give you your squad assignments and
firing positions. First, let me say this: we're hunting big game
tonight. The biggest game anybody's ever hunted. Under normal
circumstances, Vigilant's mandate is to confine and contain
supernatural threats."

"That's off the table tonight," Jessie said. "They won't be taking any prisoners. Neither are we. All Network operatives are to be terminated with extreme prejudice."

Harmony held up a pair of fingers.

"We have two objectives. Primary: carve a pathway for Ms. Fieri and Ms. Reinhart to reach their target. Secondary: extract Carolyn Saunders and ensure a safe evac to the medical staging ground."

One of the gathered agents, a broad-shouldered woman with hard eyes, raised a hand. "Ma'am? What kind of OpFor are we expecting here?"

"Expect anything and everything," Harmony said. "What we're doing tonight has never *been* done, in the history of humanity. But that doesn't mean the other side hasn't trained for the possibility. Whatever happens out there, I want you to remember one thing. Tonight, we are sending a message to the Kings of Man."

She stepped forward. Her gaze swept over the gathered teams, slow and steady. Making eye contact with each and every one of them.

"And that message," she said, "is going to be loud, direct, and crystal-clear. You *do not fuck with our planet.* Time's running out. Let's get this welcoming committee underway."

*　*　*

"Everything had to be timed perfectly," Carolyn said. "It helps that while you were listening in on me, my friends on Earth were listening in on you."

The king shook his head, his giant shoulders clenched, torn between fury and panic. "How?"

"How many times in this story," she asked, "did a witch use a puddle of stagnant water to communicate with her sisters?"

The king's gaze shot to the glass of water in Carolyn's cupped hands. Just a quarter inch left, the last few sips she never drank but insisted on carrying with her, with a sliver of wilted lemon floating on the surface.

And for just a moment, upon the water's face, the image of the Lady in Red. She winked as she vanished in a fluid ripple.

"I gave you all the clues. But that's not the big one. The one I mentioned time and time again."

The King of Rust loomed over her, one hand drawn back like he might strike her down, but frozen, trapped in indecision.

"Nessa's greatest enchantment," Carolyn said. "Even Nadia wasn't powerful enough to notice the illusion she laid on that mirror bag. What did Nessa say, in the Deadknot? 'Good chance *God* wouldn't notice it.' Marie was even searched while she wore it, patted down twice, and no one found it."

The king's eyes flared, a second pupil blossoming inside the first, as he looked to Carolyn's side.

And to the mirror-coated bag that had been there all along. The one Carolyn had patiently carried for two days while she waited to be kidnapped. The one no one, not even him, had been able to see until now.

Carolyn snatched up the water glass and hurled it in his face. He reflexively threw up his hands to protect himself, surprised—which gave her enough time to reach inside and yank out a length of sapphire chain. The manacles bit at the air, smelling the presence of a throne, eager to do the job they'd been enchanted for.

She let them fly, and they snapped around the king's wrists.

* * *

"What if I offered you a better way?" Nessa had asked him.

The Demiurge stood alone on his tiny disk of a world, outside his humble cottage, on his overgrown lawn, and stared up at the void.

"You want the endless voices to stop. You want to shed this burden."

"I can't," he had told her. "I can't even leave this prison. If I do, the kings will devour me and all of creation will be lost. I...I know I'm not a good caretaker. I can't be what humanity wants me to be. But I

won't abandon them like that. I can hold the line against the kings. That much, that little good, I can do for them."

Nessa had pointed to the flickering, endless gulf of darkness above their heads.

"That darkness...that's an infection in your mother's blood, yes?"

He nodded. "It's not supposed to look like that. They corrupted it."

"You are your mother's son," Nessa said, and she rested her hands on his shoulders. "What if a fresh infusion of divine blood is just what it needs to become healthy once more?"

"You mean..." His voice dropped to a whisper. "...if I died?"

"I don't think Sophia is dead," Nessa told him. "I think she's only sleeping. You know, I died once upon a time, and Hedy told her followers that I'd return to them—but only once they built a world I could return to. And so I did. Maybe that's what Sophia is waiting for, too. Maybe Wisdom will return to us, once we show that we're ready for her."

"But they're waiting for me. The second I open the door—"

"Trust me," Nessa had said. "I think I can provide a tiny distraction."

Far above, he could feel his creations in confusion. A distress call had gone out from the flagship of the King of Rust. His brother-traitors were scrambling, trying to react to a crisis none of them had ever anticipated, a threat they were too arrogant to imagine.

It was time.

In one hand, he brandished Nessa's parting gift. Her slender little quill blade. She had offered him a trade. This blade in exchange for a few drops of his divine blood to feed her Cutting Knife. Granting it the power it would need for the battle ahead.

With his other hand, he reached toward the sky and opened the firmament.

The dome over his pocket world cracked and parted wide, and the Shadow In-Between rushed in to claim him, devouring all. As it did, he gazed upward. He'd thought about last words, but they seemed pointless. Last deeds were infinitely more important.

Maybe he could make something beautiful. Maybe, just once, he could make something perfect.

He slashed the blade across his throat. His blood erupted from the wound as his head fell back, a gout of golden droplets that soared upward, blossoming, and spreading wide to meet the darkness head-on.

FORTY-FIVE

The King of Lament's flagship, like half of his brothers', had flown in for the special occasion. The celebration of the death of the Demiurge, their hated father, and the last obstacle to their triumph. They'd taken on a holding pattern, waiting for the King of Rust's invitation to board.

Now the command deck had gone mad, hooded figures with flashing eyes racing from console to console, scarred fingers slapping against mold-crusted controls and levers of jagged metal. Radio chatter squawked from the neighboring ships, everyone talking over each other at once. The captain rose from her spiked command throne, a third eye peering from a crack in her radiation-blistered forehead as she bellowed orders.

"I want centipedes loaded and an armed boarding party over there *now!*"

"Sir," one of the hooded pilots said, "without an invitation, that could be construed as an act of war—"

Her lobster claw of a hand gripped him by his throat.

"No idea what's going on over there, but that distress call can pretty damn well be construed as an invitation. And where is *Adam?*"

"Monitoring the situation," the deep and gravelly voice rumbled over the ship's speakers. "I'm coordinating an emergency response now. Everything is under control."

Through the grimy windows of the deck, the void flashed vivid white as the King of Rust's flagship exploded. The neck of the vessel detonated with the force of a sun going nova, blasting debris in all directions, running lights flickering and going dark.

They barely had time to react before a second explosion washed over them.

An explosion of pure light, from a dying god.

A mammoth shock wave of liquid gold blew across the horizon like a tsunami. Wave after wave of shining light rocked the ship backward, tossing it out of control. The golden light bloomed as alarms screamed and every readout flickered, overloading. A console exploded and blasted its operator backward in a shower of sparks.

"Get us out of here!" the captain screamed. "Terrestrial transition, *now*! Pick the nearest habitable world. I don't care which one!"

"Ma'am," one of the pilots called back, "we could be stranded. And the drives won't be able to fly outside of the Shadow—"

She pointed at the command deck windows. Cracks were starting to form along the glass, the flagship crumbling under the onslaught of gold.

"Does that look like the fucking Shadow to you?"

On the endless horizon, for the first time in uncounted eons, shone the bend of a rainbow.

One by one, the flagships of the Kings of Man blinked out of sight. Banished from their own dominion, and scattered across the wheel of worlds.

* * *

Suited agents armed with bullpup rifles and sidearms scrambled along Vandemere's outer pathways, taking up firing positions. Hedy led her coven to the gates, making their stand by the abandoned carousel. The sight of the zoo sparked old memories in Marie, old aches. But more than that, a quiet appreciation of the road behind them. Her batons dangled from her belt, ready for the fight ahead.

She took Nessa's hand.

"We've come a long way," Nessa said.

"We have." Marie looked up to the starry sky. "For a moment, I thought this was the calm before the storm. It's not."

"No?"

Marie shook her head. She looked at Nessa.

"It's the eye of a hurricane. We passed through one side of it. Now we have to get through the other."

"Well," Nessa said, "don't go dying tonight. I still owe you a wedding. If...you still want to, I mean."

Marie pulled her close. Her hands squeezed Nessa's shoulders, traced the curve of her back, as their lips met. One last kiss before the fight. She pulled back just a little and nuzzled her forehead against Nessa's.

"That answer your question?"

"Admirably," Nessa replied.

The sky erupted.

A jagged chasm opened in the night and spat out the remnants of the King of Rust's flagship on the heels of a shock wave of blinding golden light. The light washed over the battlefield, floodlights bursting, electronics shorting out as the wave of raw magic hit the ground.

Then came the wreckage. The remnants of the flagship, all that remained after the Valkyries' explosives split it in half, were two stories of twisted metal and exposed, smoking engines with a circular command deck barely clinging to life. It hovered for a moment and then came down hard, power dead, almost all hands lost. The command deck slammed into the ground nose-first. Windows exploded and its front end crumpled on impact as it crashed into the walkway near the old monkey house. It dug a four-foot trench in the path, spraying dirt and broken concrete, sheer momentum propelling its massive weight. One rumpled slice of a wing carved into the monkey house, caving the wall in and bringing the ceiling down, while the deck jutted out over the pit of a tiger den.

For a moment, there was silence.

* * *

Another smaller rent in space tore open above the roof of the zoo's lodge. Adam's massive foot, textured like raw clay, thumped down on the broken shingles. Then the other, as the crack in space whipped shut at his back.

He brandished the copper blade of his own Cutting Knife in one hand. In the other, the chrome neck of a vintage microphone. He swung it down low, like a crooner from the forties, and spoke into its art-deco grille as he surveyed the battlefield.

"All hands," he said. "The King of Rust is under direct attack. Need reinforcements to my location immediately. Network elites. Open gateways to parallels alpha-eight-zed—"

"Say again?" a response crackled from the microphone. "Direct attack? Sir, that's not possible—"

The ship's debris spat sparks, the frayed steel cables twisting like a nest of angry snakes. Coolant fluid pooled across the overgrown walkways and filled the musty air with a scent like ripe jungle fruit. Hazy blue smoke wreathed the wreckage; nothing moved inside.

"And yet, I am standing two hundred yards from what's left of his command deck, with heavily armed mortals closing in. Abandon doubt, embrace faith, and *do as I say*. Open gateways to alpha-eight-zed, delta-blue-triskelion, and ninety-seven-minor."

"Sir," the dispatcher's voice crackled, "we're reporting unprecedented turbulence inside the Shadow. As it is, do you realize how much that will cost? We'll have to strip-mine an entire planet's worth of resources to power those gateways, even if they're only open for a minute or two—"

Adam put the microphone against his wormy lips. His voice dropped to a deathly growl.

"I take full responsibility. These humans have given us unprecedented insult. Our reprisal should be no less historic. Open the gates."

* * *

Like cancerous rose blooms, portals erupted across the abandoned zoo. As they waited for Ezra to perfect his dimensional gateways, the Network's own experiments had borne instable, erratic fruit. The tunnels blossomed from pinpricks of light to giant and gaping toothless maws of inflamed flesh, their exposed gums bleeding fractals made of violet light. The fractals tumbled to the weed-infested pavement and shattered into bouncing sparks.

Harmony and Jessie had commandeered an overlook by the gates. A line of old tourist binoculars still stood on candy-painted rods at the overlook's railing. Harmony dropped a quarter in the slot and leaned close, swinging them around for a better vantage on the distant flashes of light.

She watched a squad of men jog from the gaping tunnel in perfect synchronicity, moving two by two and six deep, bracing sleek assault rifles against their digital-gray camouflage. A second squad followed moments later. Then a third. Jessie stood at Harmony's side, sunglasses off; her turquoise eyes glittered in the dark, radioactive, and she didn't need binoculars to see that far.

"Full battle rattle," Jessie said. "Looks like the contingency plan just showed up."

An old map of the zoo lay spread across a picnic table, pinned down at the corners with empty ammo cases and sliced with a precision grid drawn in bright red Sharpie. Harmony jogged over, checked the map, and got on the radio.

"All teams, we have enemy movement at C1 and F4, arriving via some kind of teleportation. There's another portal at E2, but it appears dormant. Hold positions and continue to provide cover. If Roth and Reinhart don't make it through..." She put the receiver back to her lips. "Get them to the target. No matter what."

"Uh, Harmony?" Jessie waved her over. "E2 isn't dormant anymore. What the hell are those?"

Harmony dropped another quarter and swung the binoculars around. Through the dusty lenses, she watched a horde of gray and ragged figures swooping through the fleshy maw. Their funeral gowns and thick veils gave them a shapeless, flowing outline, and their fingers—too long for any human hand—twisted like boneless worms at their sides.

*   *   *

Harmony's lead team, Redbird Cell, made their stand by the reptile house. The air was thick and musty, the stench baked into the old, bleached stone. Out front, a ten-foot statue of a gecko on a long, low dais had once marked the hub of a roundabout in the path. Now the gecko's paint had all but faded away, leaving the paper-thin shell a dull gray flecked with green, and the statue had crumbled in spots to expose the wire armature beneath.

Redbird took up firing positions behind the three-foot stone dais, lined up their sights between the gecko's patchwork legs, and waited.

In the country night air, the tromping of boots carried for miles. The team leader kept his eyes on his iron sights and one fist to his shoulder, curled. *Wait for it.* The first wave of Network reinforcements came into sight. They'd slowed their pace, lead troopers sweeping the dark with halogen lights fixed to their rifles, hunting for mortal prey. Every passing second brought them closer to Redbird's hiding spot.

The clenched fist held steady. *Wait for it.*

Lights played across the gecko's pallid tongue and its wirework ribs, then moved along.

Two more heartbeats, and the team leader gave the order. His clenched fist became two outstretched fingers, pointing sharply at the men in digital-gray camo.

The night erupted with gunfire and muzzle flashes, as Redbird hit the Network's elite like a pirate ship delivering a lethal broadside barrage. Bodies dropped, riddled with high-velocity bullets, and stray gunfire shredded the underbrush at their backs.

The team lead sliced the air with his hand, calling for a cease-fire. The last report echoed into the distance. Then there was no sound at all but the metallic clatter of fresh magazines sliding into position.

"That's all they got?" muttered an operative at the team leader's side. "Thought these guys were supposed to be scary."

One of the corpses twitched. Then it jerked, spasmodic, like someone had jolted it with an electric cable. Others were moving now, lurching to their feet, and one turned their way with a wheezing groan. His left eye was a gelatinous ruin from the bullet that had killed him. The other blazed with a light brighter than the one on his rifle barrel, as the dead man raised his weapon to return fire.

FORTY-SIX

Marie unholstered her batons. Standing beside her, Nessa took a deep breath. Their prize, their only shot at survival, was on the opposite side of the Vandemere Zoo. All they had to do was get there in one piece. Hedy and her coven stood at their backs, an honor guard, while a fresh stream of playing cards riffled into Daniel's outstretched hand. Caitlin's eyes glittered like dying embers in the dark as she studied the pathways ahead.

Everyone waited for Marie to give the word.

She felt the power of the Conversation calling to her. The faint, demanding voice of Lady Martika, insisting she have her say. *Battlefield tactics are what I DO*, Martika told her. *Let me take command.*

She pushed the voice aside. She didn't need a general's skill to know how to tackle Vandemere. She'd been here herself once, back when it all started, and she'd run these twisting paths with her own two feet while a murderous cult hunted her down.

Gunfire sounded in the distance. First contact.

"There are three ways to reach the monkey house from here," Marie said, pointing the way. "Hedy, take your people around by the southern path. It goes by two of our support positions, and they might need your help."

"We're not here for *them*," Hedy said.

"Those men are risking their lives to help us tonight," Marie told her. "All they have are guns and bravery, nothing else, and they're still holding the line. For us. We will *not* leave them unprotected. You'll be close enough to reach us if we need you, and you'll draw some enemy attention away from us."

"How about me and Cait?" Daniel asked.

"You're on the northern trail. That one goes high, and about midway across it runs right through the old food court, overlooking the whole central zoo. You'll have overwatch on us for most of the route, and you can call out any trouble you see coming our way."

"On it," he said.

"And speaking of drawing attention?" Marie looked between him and Caitlin. "If you get a chance, make some noise. Make it loud, make it flashy."

Caitlin gave Daniel a sidelong glance. "Apparently she knows you well, pet."

"As for me and Nessa," Marie said, "we're going right up the center aisle. Fastest way between point A and point B."

Nessa gripped the Cutting Knife and held it high. Clytemnestra's silhouette shimmered on the blade, one hand raised to catch the stars.

"We have one shot at this," Nessa said. "Let's make it count. And whether we win or die tonight...let's make them remember our names."

* * *

They broke in three directions, feet pounding the weed-infested walkways to the staccato beat of distant gunfire. Past the carousel, Nessa and Marie's path was a straight shot through the heart of the abandoned zoo.

The last time she'd been here, Marie had been defenseless, hunted, on the run. Now she brandished her batons, the enchanted rods trailing winter-wisps of glowing light in her wake, and smelled blood on the night wind. Nessa was at her side, stars shining bright above her lover's face, moonlight burning down.

Fifty feet ahead, square in their path, another ragged, raw hole in space tore itself open. Marie expected soldiers. The figures it disgorged, one after another until nearly a dozen stood in their way, might have been soldiers once. They were mannequins of flesh and metal in tattered uniforms, the fabric clotted with dried blood from the wounds that killed them long ago. Titanium plates and rods had been hammered into mottled flesh and drilled through bone, holding them together and armoring them like metallic beetles.

"Not dying here," Marie said. Their old refrain, one last time.

Nessa nodded, sharp.

"Not dying here."

Marie ducked low and lashed out with one of her batons, shattering the first trooper's knee with a blast of concussive force that flipped him off his feet, sending him flying in a rag-doll somersault. She stayed on the move, fluid, her other baton thrusting out and stabbing a second attacker in the stomach. The shock wave knocked him backward, straight into another trooper and sending them both to the dirt.

Nessa didn't hold back. There was no reason now. She was out of time, and she'd either seize victory in the next few minutes or die trying. She called the power of raw Shadow into her, through her, using her body as a conduit. As one of the dead men lunged at Marie from the left, trying to blindside her, she brought her curled fist sweeping down.

Five feet ahead, a wave of billowing violet energy echoed her gesture. It slammed down from the heavens with the weight of a marble pillar and crushed the man beneath it, smashing him into a blood-soaked mass of pulped flesh and twisted metal.

* * *

Hedy tried to keep Nessa and Marie in sight as she led her coven along the southern trail. She saw their battle begin, watched them fight their way down the center boulevard, then lost sight of them behind the frosty white paint of the penguin house. Up ahead, to her left, the gunfire was closer. So were the screams of the wounded and the dying. Harmony's men were losing their fight.

She froze a moment, eyes darting left and right, forced to decide.

Gazelle watched her, uncertain. "Mistress?"

"My mother can take care of herself," Hedy said. "These men can't. Let's go, we're helping them."

They made it ten feet before a dark figure plunged from the trees to land squarely in their path. More figures boiled from the tangled underbrush and rounded the bend at their backs to cut off retreat.

"Thieves," hissed a Sister of the Noose.

"Thieves and blasphemers," said another, clutching a silken garrote in her squirming fingers.

The witches clustered in a tight circle as Hedy swallowed a surge of terror. She'd lost so many of her apprentices to these monsters, watched them die for the choices she'd made, and she'd thought that nightmare was over. Now she was going to lose the rest. It was a hopeless fight, no way out, and—

Gazelle took her hand.

Hedy blinked. Gazelle squeezed her hand, tight, and locked eyes with her.

"We believe in you," she whispered.

Other hands were on her now, touching her back, her shoulders, her arms. Her students, her children, telling her without words that she had never lost their faith. She was still their Dire Mother, and they were counting on her to lead them.

Hedy raised her head high. She rolled her shoulders, and her free hand curled in a ritual gesture, beckoning a curse to her fingertips. The air above her hand shimmered like a heat mirage.

"We are the Pallid Masque," she said to her coven. "And as the Owl taught us, sacrifice is what happens to our victims. Not one of you is permitted to die tonight."

Gazelle let go of her and clenched her hands into eager fists.

"Understood," she said.

"Then prepare for battle. And victory."

"*Not alone,*" said a new voice from the shadows.

The sisters turned, heads raised and veils rippling as if they were sniffing the air. The Mourner was a ghost walking, luminous in her white gown and gloves. The sisters hissed as one, a furious rattlesnake sound.

One pointed her gloved finger. "*Traitor.*"

"I tried to show you the glory and beauty of freedom," the Mourner said. "You refused to listen, blinded by your devotion to a false god. It seems the only way you'll find freedom is in death. And so, my old sisters, I love you so much that I've come to grant it to you."

Two sisters dove toward her. The Mourner's leg shot out in a whip-crack kick, ribs snapping under her heel; then she spun and threw a flurry of punches so fast the air blurred in her wake. The coven moved as one. Hedy unleashed the curse on her fingertips, lancing toward the closest sister like a dart made of bubbling acid, as her apprentices broke in all directions. Butterfly dropped to her knees, choking, as a silken noose dropped over her head and cinched around the slender woman's throat. Gazelle was there in a heartbeat, slicing through the line and cutting her loose, while Mantis hurled herself onto Butterfly's attacker and plunged a dagger straight into the assassin's veiled face.

The Mourner dropped low, gloved fingers to the stone, and swung herself into a circle kick. She put her entire body behind it, brute force and sheer momentum, throwing two more sisters off their feet. She raised her veiled face and called out to the witches.

"I can hold them off—the humans up ahead need your help. *Go!*"

* * *

Daniel and Caitlin had made it as far as the old food court, an elevated plaza atop a long-drained fish habitat, when a portal ripped open in their path. The things it spat out were barely human. They had skin like beef jerky and distended jackal jaws, segmented eyes glittering like faceted opals as they loped on long, jagged-clawed hands and feet.

Daniel brandished a brace of playing cards in his right hand and a .45 automatic in his left. He let the cards fly, his razor-edged opening argument, and followed up with three quick shots. Muzzle flash lit the darkness and one of the creatures hit the plaza floor, kicking and thrashing in its death throes. Another tumbled over the railing, plummeting to die in the dry aquamarine veins of the fish habitat below.

Caitlin slung back her coat. Her bullwhip slithered free. Inside the other half of her coat, snaps broke loose and she tugged out a foot-long shaft of tempered bronze. She gave it a shake. It sprouted a long haft and bloomed a wickedly barbed tip, becoming a full-fledged spear in the blink of an eye.

The whip slashed down upon the pavement with a crack of thunder, and blue flame raced from the handle to its tip like a trail of lit gasoline. Then she twirled the whip above her head and lashed out, snaring one of the creatures around its neck and dragging it close. The tip of her spear punched through its chest and out the other side.

They were coming too fast, too many of them. One bowled Daniel over, knocking him onto his back. He pointed his automatic toward the moon and pulled the trigger, blasting the creature off him and rolling to the side as another pounced claws-out toward his head. He flicked another playing card, barely looking, and slashed its throat wide open.

Caitlin dove into the fight, gleeful, laughing as the creatures tried to swarm her. She lassoed one with her burning whip, its body igniting like a torch, then swung it like a wrecking ball. It slammed into three of its brothers, sending them scattering, plummeting over the railing, braying as they burned like dying stars.

"Oh," Daniel called out, dodging backward as claws sliced at his face. "*Who* is loud and flashy in this relationship?"

She rolled her eyes. "Behind you, pet."

He turned, pulled the trigger, and blew a creature out of the air in mid-pounce. He used its corpse as a springboard as he ran to get some distance. There was movement to the east. A brick wall of a man standing atop the old lodge building, gesturing and talking into a vintage microphone. As he pointed the tip of a copper blade, another cavernous maw ripped open on the far side of the zoo.

Down below, he spotted Harmony and Jessie on the move, running to support their team. He let another two cards fly, dropping his closest attackers, and shouted out to the agents.

"Hey, looks like the asshole on the roof over there is the one opening these portals—take him out!"

*   *   *

Redbird Cell was overrun by the reptile house, two men down and waging a fighting retreat against the Network's undead soldiers. Beach Cell wasn't doing much better; they were lighting up the radio, screaming for reinforcements, and Harmony heard the *crump* of a flashbang grenade detonating in the distance.

They heard Daniel's shout, and they were closer to the lodge, but a wordless glance between them settled it. Priorities. They had to take care of their people first and hope someone else could get up on the roof. They rounded a bend and hit the ground as automatic-rifle fire chopped the air above their heads. Redbird's operatives were pinned, trapped behind the bullet-riddled gecko statue, and their leader was doing battlefield triage on an agent with a sucking chest wound.

Harmony called to her magic. The air turned to congealed syrup, trapping a hail of bullets and slowing them to a crawl. She held the weave as her partner sprang past her, turquoise eyes blazing, and hurled herself onto the shoulders of one of the Network zombies. She grabbed him under the chin, twisted, and pulled. The flesh of his neck stretched, then ripped wide, his head tearing free with the crunch of splintering bone.

Another grenade went off, over by the swan lagoon. Beach's team leader was screaming over the radio, begging for reinforcements. Harmony fought to hold her spell, to hold the line, but she couldn't be in two places at once.

A blur of purple mist blazed over her shoulder. It plowed into the gaping mouth of an undead soldier.

A second later, his head exploded in a storm of shattered bone and blood.

Hedy and her coven formed a line, the air crackling with magic. She gave Harmony and Jessie a nod.

"We've got your people here. Go. Help the others."

*   *   *

The Mourner was a dervish, a lethal blur delivering pinpoint strikes and bone-crushing kicks. The corpses of her former sisters littered the path around her, their funeral-gray gowns turned to burial shrouds.

It wasn't enough.

There were too many of them, and even as she whittled their numbers down, she was running out of strength while they were still fresh and ready to fight. A gray-gloved fist plowed into her gut, doubling her over, and a silken noose dropped over her head from behind and yanked taut around her throat. She clawed at it as it yanked backward, hauling her off her feet. Two more were on her as she rolled and struggled to get free, their sandals stomping on her belly and ribs. Her air was gone, vision clouding in a blur of pain as something snapped inside her chest.

A buzzing sound filled her ears. She thought it was her own blood, boiling as she suffocated, but then the knot around her throat went slack and the kicking stopped. She coughed and rolled onto her knees.

The sisters were thrashing on the ground, batting their worm fingers at the air as a storm of gnats washed over them. The gnats choked out everything, turning the air flickering gray like static on a dead television, forming a protective barrier around the

Mourner. They chewed into gray gowns and ate through the lace holes in the sisters' veils, devouring the corrupted flesh beneath.

Dora strolled up, uncorked soapstone cask cradled in her arm, and offered the Mourner a hand. She helped her to her feet and they watched the last of the sisterhood die.

"Really?" Dora said. "You don't even invite me to the party?"

"Old and unfinished business," the Mourner said. "Needed to handle it alone."

"How'd that work out for you?"

The Mourner didn't answer. One of the sisters raised an arm that was little more than scraps of silk glove clinging to bloody bone and half-eaten tendons.

"We're a coven. You know better. You *call* me before you go looking for trouble." Dora glanced over her shoulder. "And speaking of knowing better, we should clear the scene before our Lady gets pissed off."

"We can help them."

Dora shook her head.

"Sure," she said, "but this is their day. We're creatures of an older world, sis. We gotta let the kids win this one on their own."

"Do you think they can?" the Mourner asked.

Dora thought about that.

"I'd say they've got a fair shot," she said, "and that's more than a lot of people ever get. C'mon, let's watch the fireworks from a distance."

*   *   *

A small rip in space billowed open and spat the Golden Saint onto the roof of the lodge. The suit of armor landed in a kneeling crouch, white-hot steam leaking from its battered joints, and the runes along its copper-red breastplate scattered sparks across the broken shingles.

The helmet telescoped open, and Rosales gasped for breath. Savannah's oil-slick body sprayed from the neck of the armor, landing with a splash at her side. They'd just battled their way across a city of gold, tearing the wings off angels and leaving a trail of blood and feathers behind.

"Open a portal on my mark, to delta..." Adam looked to his left. One eyebrow slowly lifted.

"I can explain this," Rosales told him.

"At the moment, I genuinely don't care, and I'll take any help I can get." He pointed across the zoo, down to the heart of the labyrinthine paths where two small figures were plowing their way along the boulevard like twin juggernauts. "Roth and Reinhart. Stop them, and all is forgiven."

"Doc?" Rosales said.

"I get Vanessa."

Savannah oozed over the side of the roof and splashed to the pavement below. Rosales shrugged. Her helmet rattled back on, concealing her face. Then she triggered the jump jets, her armor propelling her like a shooting star into the night.

FORTY-SEVEN

Nessa and Marie had cleared a path, leaving the first wave of opposition dead and dying at their backs. The boulevard ahead was clear, all the way to the smoking ruins of the King of Rust's command deck.

Then Rosales streaked down from the sky, landing in a crouch with one steel-jacketed fist punching cracks in the pavement. She rose up, her voice amplified by the speakers in her helmet.

"Did you *see* that shit? Perfect superhero landing. I love this armor."

Savannah oozed down the path behind her, and her oil-slick form billowed upward to take on the shape of a woman.

"I saw," she replied, unimpressed.

Marie brandished her batons, one foot sliding a few inches to the left as she dropped to a fighting stance. She was already winded from battling her way up the path, and she stole a few stray breaths while she could.

"You don't want to stand in our way tonight," she said. "You get one warning. Leave. Now."

Rosales's laugh rode on a blurt of electronic distortion.

"Are you kidding me? I've got an eighty-million-dollar suit of power armor. You've got a couple of sticks. What are you going to do?"

To Marie, the answer was obvious.

"Fight you."

"Talk about wanting to do things the hard way," Rosales said. "Eh, whatever."

She charged at Marie, throwing her servo-enhanced strength

behind a haymaker punch. Marie ducked under it and lashed one of her batons across the back of the armored suit. It connected with a thunderclap of concussive force and a shower of rune-words that fell from the air and hit the pavement as a spray of blinding sparks.

Nessa moved to help Marie—and twin whips of black oil locked around her wrists. They hauled her across the rough pavement and hoisted her in the air.

"I'm afraid not, Professor," Savannah said. "We have our own score to settle."

Rosales reeled from the impact but rallied in a second, spinning, driving one armored heel into the dirt at the edge of the path and catching herself from falling. She came at Marie, relentless, punch after punch whistling as they split the air. Marie dodged left, then ducked, moving as fast as she could but playing pure defense now, no opening to hit back.

"I can do this all day," Rosales said. "I'm not even tired. The armor does all the work for me. How about you? Getting a little winded? You look worn out. You wanna take a break or something? I could go get a sandwich, come back later."

Marie jerked her head to one side, steel knuckles so close she could feel them slicing the air beside her cheek. Her lungs were burning, arms like lead weights. She kept fighting.

Ten feet away, Nessa summoned twin bursts of raw magic, lancing down the veins of her wrists like a pair of live wires. Savannah's shoulder tentacles jerked, spasmodic, and let her go. Nessa hit the ground hard, landing in a sprawl, pain jolting up her leg as her ankle twisted.

She forced herself to rise.

"So what is it?" she asked Savannah. "Do you want to study me, capture me, kill me? Is this science or revenge? Do you even know anymore?"

The tentacles quivered as the woman's oil-slick face seemed to lose definition, becoming an uneven blur.

"Are you familiar with the story of Theseus's Paradox?"

"I'm an anthropology professor," Nessa said. "Of course I am."

"An educated woman. *God*, why couldn't we have been friends?"

"Because you're a homicidal maniac who tortured my lover."

"Everything I did," Savannah said, "I did for a higher cause."

"What?" Nessa pointed toward the distant figure on the roof of the lodge. Adam raised his knife, brought it slashing down, and another portal ripped open on the far side of the zoo. "For him? You claim you're following the cause of knowledge, but all I've ever seen you do is take orders from men who use your gifts for themselves. And now look at you. Was it worth it?"

Savannah wavered on her oily feet, trapped in a moment of indecision. And as Nessa mentally flipped through the arsenal of magic at her command, she knew exactly what spell to use.

"I don't remember things that I should remember," Savannah said. "It never bothered me before. And it bothers me that it never bothered me."

"I've got a fix for that," Nessa said. Fingertips of thought ran along the spidery lines of an incantation, internalizing it, sparking a fire in her heart.

"Too late. I'm sorry, Professor Roth, but there's only one way this can end now."

One of her tentacles lashed out, cutting the air with a razor's edge. Nessa dove under it but instead of trying to escape, she darted in close, almost toe to toe with the figure of living ink. Another tentacle slammed down, smashing against the pavement, and she sidestepped it with feline grace. Nessa held the Cutting Knife tight but didn't even try to strike her.

"Why aren't you fighting back?" Savannah asked, confused. "Are we dancing or fighting?"

"Dancing," Nessa told her.

Then her free hand shot out and plunged deep into Savannah's oil-slick face, fingers digging in, and the world flashed like sunlight on a bed of diamonds.

*   *   *

There was pure, perfect light, then darkness.

An end-table light snapped on. Nessa and Savannah stood side by side, gazing into a cutaway section of a bedroom, like the set of a television show. A ruffled bedspread, a stuffed black cat propped up on the pillows, a framed poster of the first space-shuttle launch on a pastel-pink wall. A teenage girl sat at a desk with a bulky old computer monitor and a sheaf of handwritten pages at her side, the receiver of a corded phone tucked between her shoulder and her ear.

"I can't go," she said. "No, the science fair is next week. I need to get this—no, it's not stupid, it's important. It's important to me."

"What is this?" Savannah asked.

She slithered at Nessa's side as they stepped into the bedroom, unseen by the girl arguing on the phone. Nessa pointed to the screen, and to the title of the presentation: *Genetic Crop Modification and the Potential for Ending Famine*, by S. Cross.

"Is that..." Savannah's body bent and stretched as she coiled around the girl. "Is that me? Why don't I remember this?"

"I read up on you, after we first crossed paths," Nessa said. "This is you, age sixteen. You won the science fair, by the way. Got you scouted by a half dozen colleges."

"Biochemistry," Savannah murmured. "I remember an early interest in biochemistry."

"You were going to feed the world," Nessa said.

The image unraveled, slid, spun around them like a record before it whipped back into focus. Savannah, age twenty-six, sat on the far side of a mahogany desk. The man's face was in shadow, lost to memory, but his voice was crystal clear.

"Dr. Cross, you're a talented young woman—"

"Then why did you deny my grant request?"

He folded his hazy hands.

"Because as admirable as your goals are, there's no money in giving food away. Can I offer you a word of advice? Learn to be more pragmatic. Use that big brain of yours and join us in the real world."

Another blur, another lurch forward in time. Just a couple of years, but her eyes were harder, her lips more tightly pursed, as she perched on the edge of a chair in a hotel room. Ezra Talon sat across from her, bracing his cane between his knees.

"As I said," he told her, "we're big fans of your research. There's a place for you on our team. Your own lab space, lots of leeway, and you won't get a more competitive offer."

"Talon Worldwide," Savannah said.

"That's right."

"Weapons," Savannah said. "That's what you want my research for. You want me to make weapons for you."

"The Romans salted the earth when they went to war. Denying resources to the enemy is a time-tested tactic, and I think it's ripe for modernization. Look, I know it might be...distasteful at first, but think about the big picture. You help me, I help you. I'm happy to put funding behind a side hustle or two if I think it'll bear fruit, pardon the pun. You come on board, show me some solid results I can peddle to the military sector, and we'll talk about your passion project in a year or two."

A year or two passed in the blink of an eye, like they so often did.

Savannah perched on a stool and squinted into a microscope, watching bacteria wage war against each other. Her custom-made microorganisms launched a blitzkrieg and tore through the enemy forces.

"The fuck is this, Cross?"

It was Ferguson, head of the division, standing at her shoulder. He rattled a plastic-sheathed binder at her.

"Oh, that's—that's my project proposal," she said, straightening up. "I was hoping Mr. Talon would reconsider—"

"You don't hope. You don't think. You do the job I give you." He waved his hand at the bustling laboratory. "Look around, Cross. Do you notice anything different between you and everybody else here?"

She shook her head. "Well, we come from an array of technical backgrounds and schools, but some commonalities exist. You and Dr. Bloch both received degrees from Rensselaer Polytechnic, while—"

"Jesus, you're fucking thick." He leaned in, dropping his voice. "You were a *diversity hire*, Cross. You're the team mascot, so we've got a nice pair of tits around for photo ops. You're the Smurfette."

He dropped the binder onto her lap. It slid onto the floor, pages jolting loose and scattering.

"And we don't have time for this bleeding-heart crap. Get with the program, toe the line, or you're going to be out of here and another girl exactly like you will be filling that seat by lunchtime."

The sun vanished. The moon sprang up on the far side of a plate-glass window. Savannah was alone in the lab, one side of her head shaved down to the scalp, watching herself on a feed from a tripod-mounted camera.

"My work in neuroscience has pointed to methods of...focused behavioral modification," she said to the camera. "Obviously untested on human subjects, for ethical reasons, but my science is sound. I know it is. And if I'm going to keep this job long enough to replace Ferguson, long enough to force my own agenda through the pipeline, I have to take risks. Make sacrifices."

The tool in her hand was unique. She'd built it herself. It had a pistol grip and a hair-thin filament mounted on a nozzle, the sleek titanium probe computer-linked for flawless precision.

She squeezed the trigger. The tip of the probe glowed red, hot as a branding iron.

"I'm going to attempt a slight modification of the part of my brain that controls empathy. Just enough to...fit in with my team.

To act like they do. I've administered a local anesthetic. There shouldn't be any pain. Shouldn't be."

She focused on a screen at her side, a cross-section of her skull in deep blue and neon orange. She raised the probe. It felt like she was putting a gun to her head.

"When I save the world, it'll all be worth it."

The probe sizzled as it slid through flesh and bone like a knife through butter. It smelled like roasting pork. The next day she came back to work. She wore a wig. She did her job and built a better plague.

The sun and the moon battled, spinning like the wheel of a slot machine. It landed on the moon. Savannah in the lab, surrounded by surgical tools, more cameras, more monitors.

"Diligence alone is not serving my purposes," she told the camera. "Ferguson isn't going anywhere. Promotion is a distant hope. I need to improve my productivity, improve it in a way he can't dream of equaling. I've developed a procedure to eradicate the need for sleep. Imagine it: eight extra hours, every single day, to dedicate to my work."

She lifted a shining scalpel. It caught the laboratory lights, gleaming.

"I won't dream anymore," she mused. "But if you have the power to change the world for the better, you have to do it. I've always believed that. No matter what it costs, no matter what you have to sacrifice. And I have that power."

She made the first cut and used a tiny hissing vacuum to suck down the blood.

The sun and the moon danced again and the brief, scant light died out once more.

"He stole my work," Savannah seethed into the camera. "He stole my work. Put his own name on it. I now realize drastic measures have to be taken. Ezra will never fund my anti-hunger project, not until I've taken control of the research division."

She drummed her fingers on the arm of her surgical chair. The probe sat out on a swing-arm tray.

"Ferguson has to die. I'm not proud of that. I'm ashamed, just saying it. But he's standing in the way of saving countless lives. If you could go back in time and kill Hitler, you'd do it, right? Of course you would. But I...I'm not a violent person. I'm afraid I'll hesitate."

She picked up the probe and watched as its tip glowed red-hot.

"I can't risk that. So I have to make a more radical modification. Destroy my capacity for pity, for compassion. Anything that might stay my hand. My work is too important. The funny thing...you know what the funny thing is?" She looked into the camera as she lifted the probe to her shaved scalp. "If this works the way I think it will, I won't even know it's gone."

Ferguson took a fall out a twentieth-floor window. She took the lab. Then Ezra came to her, proposing she join his skunkworks division.

"It's...special research," he told her, leaning on his cane. "Secret research. A personal passion project of mine, and it's on the absolute cutting edge of science. We're redefining what we know about the universe in ways I can't begin to tell you. I'd love to bring you on board; you've earned this promotion ten times over. Unless there's something you'd rather be working on?"

At long last, she'd clawed her way to the top, and now she could ask for anything she wanted. The lamp had been rubbed and her personal genie was waiting, ready to grant her dearest wish.

"I accept," she said. "I'll need access to a larger lab and a bigger budget for equipment requisitions. Also, a raise would be appreciated."

The roulette wheel of time spun and landed on a different night in a different laboratory. Savannah had a visitor.

"We've been watching your work for some time," Adam told her. "We're impressed. We'd like to recruit you for our team."

She was mostly annoyed at her research being interrupted. "And I'd be interested, why?"

"A lab that makes this one look like a child's first chemistry set, and unlimited project funds, subject to my discretion."

"Unlimited," she echoed.

"We see great potential in the work you've been doing with Carlo Sosa's blood. The synthesized form, and the psychic-resonance effects it seems to hold. Tell me, do you think you could find a way to spread it to a greater segment of the population?"

Savannah thought about it for a moment and gave a careless shrug.

"Simple. Add a narcotic component and make it addictive. I could do that in a week, and we'll have a bumper crop of infected junkies by this time next month. Let's talk more about this lab you're promising me. And the money."

Nessa broke the mindwalk. Their connection snapped and the real world lurched back into focus with nauseating speed. The musty smells of the zoo, the warm night wind, and the distant sound of gunfire and screams all snapped back at once.

Savannah stood, frozen. Her oily face rippled, and Nessa realized it was mimicking the flow of a single tear.

"*I remember now,*" she whispered.

"You made yourself forget," Nessa said. "It was you. It was always you. One small step at a time, one sacrifice after another...until you forgot what you were making those sacrifices for."

"I thought I was doing the right thing."

"You bought into a lie," Nessa said. "The system was designed to ruin women like you, Dr. Cross. It's made to take all those idealistic dreams and snuff them out, and turn you into another tool for profit. You played along until you became a part of it."

Savannah looked down at the ink blobs of her hands. They burbled as they curled and twisted.

"And this is all that's left of me."

"Is it?" Nessa asked. "Are you sure?"

Savannah's oily head lifted. She silently tilted it at Nessa.

"You are the ship of Theseus," Nessa said. "So tell me...are you the same ship that sailed to war all those years ago? Or are you a brand-new vessel that can plot its own course? Maybe I gave you your memories back. Or maybe you're a unique form of life, almost a newborn, and I gave you the memories of the dead woman who you patterned yourself after. But now you have to decide: who do you *want* to be?"

She pointed at Adam's muscular bulk in the distance, shouting commands from the roof of the lodge.

"Are you his tool, or are you your own woman?" Nessa asked. "You know, it's not everybody who gets a second shot at freedom. It's not everybody who gets one at all. Make your choice."

FORTY-EIGHT

Nessa and Savannah's mindwalk only took a handful of seconds in the real world. It felt like minutes to Marie, her muscles aching, lungs searing as she struggled to evade blow after blow. She ducked under one of Rosales's swings and drove one of her batons upward, catching her on the shoulder of her armor. The shock-wave blast sent both of them staggering back, breaking the momentum. It gave Marie a quick second to rally, gulping down air, before Rosales launched herself to deliver a fresh salvo of punches.

"Seriously," Rosales's amplified voice said, "why are you doing this? Adam didn't say I had to kill you, just stop you. So just run away already, not like I'm going to waste effort chasing you down. You don't have to die here."

Marie crouched low and drew both arms back, bending her elbows, then thrust. The twin batons connected with the armor's breastplate and both ignited at once. Rosales blew back off her feet, landing hard in the dirt. Her helmet shook from side to side as the suit's engines whined and she pushed herself back to her wobbly feet.

"Jesus, that *hurt*, you fucking psycho. But if that's the best you got, your best ain't gonna cut it. Not tonight."

I can help, Lady Martika hissed in Marie's ear. *Her suit is based on Valkyrie armor. You know everything about that armor, from when you were me. You know how to counter it—*

I was never you— Marie didn't get to finish the thought. Rosales came at her like a jet-propelled battering ram. She thrust the batons and Rosales's open gauntlets shot out, anticipating the attack.

Runes shuddered and erupted into scarlet and white spark showers as Rosales grabbed hold of the batons. They shook in Marie's grip and she clung on for dear life as the weight of the powered armor bore down on her.

Then the batons shattered. They flared in twin retina-searing blasts of wild light and then died. The splintered wood tumbled to the pavement, leaving Marie with nothing but two powerless and broken grips.

A sledgehammer punch to the gut sent Marie flying. She hit the ground, tumbling, dropping the grips and coming up empty-handed as she struggled to stand again. Just drawing breath was a losing battle, and she fought for the strength to rise.

"What *is* it with you?" Rosales said, incredulous. "This would be a real good time to stay down, just saying."

Marie forced herself to her feet. Her back was burning, and she could barely straighten up. She curled her empty hands into fists.

* * *

Up on the overlook, beyond the outskirts of the fight, Janine and Tony had been left behind with a stern warning to stay put. Janine watched the battle unfold through a pair of post-mounted binoculars, after scrounging for change to open the rusty old lenses. She saw the batons burst in Rosales's armored grip, and she saw Marie fall. And rise again, unarmed, wobbly, but still determined to fight.

"Tony," she said.

"I know."

She held up the cardboard tube in her arms.

"You're crazy," he said. "You know that, right?"

"We promised we'd be there when she needed us." Janine pointed. "She needs us *now*."

Tony still had the Glock 19 he'd gotten off Winslow in Vegas. Jessie had scrounged up a fresh pair of magazines for him, traded for the promise that he'd stay put and use them only for self-defense.

He'd apologize for breaking his word later, if they lived through this.

Janine tucked the tube under her arm and led the charge. He was right behind her. Ten feet down the path an insect-eyed, dog-jawed monster pounced from the underbrush, smelling fresh meat. Tony gunned it down with shooting-range precision and they kept on running, deeper into the fight and past the point of no return.

*   *   *

Lady Martika was insistent in Marie's ear, inside her brain.

We are one, Marie. Take my hand. Accept it. What is a knight? What is THE Knight? That's the question you've been asking for so long, but you already know the answer.

I'm not you, Marie thought.

Answer this, Martika countered. *If we're so different, how can we both be the Knight? What do we both fight for?*

"What do you fight for?" Marie murmured, speaking aloud.

"Me?" Rosales said. "I don't, if I don't have to. Way too much work. I like to collect my paychecks with the minimum possible effort."

"What do you stand for, then?"

Her chuckle rode a tiny wave of electronic distortion. "Principles are another thing that require way too much effort. C'mon, Reinhart. Grow up. Heroes only exist in storybooks. Nothing is true, barely anything in this life is worth much effort at all, and none of it is worth dying for. Save your own skin and run away. Last chance. What are *you* fighting for?"

Then Marie saw it. The answer she'd been looking for.

She heard Janine shout her name. Turned, as her roommate tugged open a fat cardboard tube, but then she kept turning in her mind and sidestepped into the Conversation.

*   *   *

"You see it now," Lady Martika said, standing imperious in her midnight armor.

"Truth," Marie said.

Something so small, so pure, so clear. It fell into her cupped hands like a flawless pearl.

"A knight fights for her truth."

She remembered. She remembered the nights of fear and hunger and endless squalor, looking up at the distant Miami skyscraper lights in the middle of a summer heat wave. She remembered the night she took slow vengeance on her parents' killers. The night she vowed that society had to be forced to change, by any means necessary.

She remembered the moment she met Nadia Fields and fell head over heels in love with the woman who shared her dream of a better world. A world of order, of discipline, where no child would ever suffer like she had.

She remembered it, because she was Lady Martika. And she was Mari Renault, and Marie Reinhart, and all the rest, a string of lifetimes and choices and decisions. Her choices. Her decisions. Her nature never changed, but nurture transformed her and she rose to the occasion, molding herself to fit the worlds she walked upon.

"She fights for her truth," Marie said. "That's what we all have in common. That's what it means to be the Knight. The things you—the things *I* did, we were fighting for the values we believed in our heart to be true."

"Yes," Martika said. "And now?"

＊   ＊   ＊

"A knight fights for her truth," Marie told Rosales. "And here's mine. I believe that people need heroes. I believe that the weak are meant to be protected by the strong, and that dragons are meant to be slain. I believe that love is real, that *hope* is real, and any battle worth fighting is worth fighting until the end. Because it doesn't matter if you win or lose. What matters, in the end, is that you *fight*."

Janine dropped the empty tube to the ground and lifted what she'd brought with her, hurling it to Marie. A gleaming arc of steel flew through the starry night sky. Marie held out her hand and caught it by the hilt.

She'd bought the sword off the Home Shopping Network, one night after too much cheap wine and too many poor decisions. It had hung on her bedroom wall ever since. Now she clutched it in a two-handed grip and bent one aching knee, brandishing the blade like it was Excalibur.

"You have got to be fucking kidding me." Rosales laughed and thumped the chest plate of her armor. "That thing isn't even sharp. See this? Eighty. Million. Dollars."

"A knight fights," Marie told her, trembling on the edge of exhaustion. "A knight doesn't quit."

The suit's afterburners fired a gout of blue flame as Rosales hurtled toward her, aiming to end her with a single rocket-fueled punch. Marie slid into the Conversation. Into herself. She remembered walking through the other Ezra's labs, before his ill-advised betrayal and her own death. Studying the Valkyrie schematics and his early efforts at building a transdimensional drive into the suit.

"Here," he'd said, tapping a slide rule against the lower back of the armor. "The existing internals are already as compact as possible. We have to build out a little bit, a separate compartment for the drive, just below the jets."

"Is that safe?" Martika asked.

He was kind enough to muffle his patronizing chuckle behind his hand. "None of this is *safe*, my lady. It's a transdimensional drive bolted onto a suit of armor. Danger is assumed. Most of the compartment will be taken up with ceramic heat shielding, and that should protect against most hazards as well as your own propulsion system."

"Most?"

"I would avoid direct impact," he said. "And until we work out a better method of protecting the internals, definitely watch these seams."

As Rosales swept in for the kill, it was Marie who threw herself to one side, rolling on her shoulder, drawing on her last reserves of strength to jump back to her feet and charge. It was Martika who drew Marie's arms back, took precision aim, and struck the final blow.

A blunt sword could still serve as a spear. The tip drove through a hairline crack along the back of the armored suit, sliding home, and into the guts of the dimensional drive.

Rosales whirled around, ripping the sword from Marie's grip. "What was that? Seriously? Did you just try to *stab* me? Okay, playtime's over. I'm getting—"

She paused as an electric shimmer washed over the armor. It rippled along the coppery hull, sparking off the engraved runes.

"Oh," Rosales said. "Oh, this is bad."

The shimmer became a web of wild lightning, encasing her in a crackling cocoon of sapphire light. Marie threw a hand over her eyes and staggered back, pushed by a wave of heat as the crippled drive went out of control. The light flared, brighter than the moon—

—and the world tore open, sucking Rosales and her armor through the crack before sealing itself up with a hiss of air that made Marie's eardrums pop.

Marie stood there, dazed, squinting against the smears of light on her retinas until they faded. Nessa pulled her close.

"Are you okay?" Marie managed to ask, leaning against her. "Where's Savannah?"

"She made her choice," Nessa said.

She pointed to the end of the boulevard, the monkey house, the tiger pit where the ruins of the king's ship teetered over a twenty-foot drop.

"Way's clear," Nessa said. "Let's finish this."

FORTY-NINE

Adam watched the humans press forward, rally, fighting back against everything he could throw at them. He held his microphone in a death grip, beads of sweat breaking out on his squat brow.

"More portals! I want gateways to parallel fifty-two, gamma-epsilon-eight—"

"Sir," squawked the response, "we *can't*. Our systems are blowing out right and left. They were prototypes as it was, and you've overloaded them past any hope of repair."

Adam took a deep breath. He studied the field. Weighed his own odds of survival if he let a king fall into human hands.

"One more portal," he said. "On my location. Give it everything you've got. Open a gateway to White Nine."

"Sir?"

"Do it," he growled. "If the King of Rust falls, *I* fall. Might as well take this entire insufferable planet with me. Open the gate."

Another gristle-flesh maw ripped open at his side. White mist boiled from within, spilling around his feet, a harbinger of the horrors about to arrive.

"Mutual assured destruction," Savannah said. "I approve."

He turned just as she hit him full-on, her oily form splashing across his chest and face, clinging to him like a second skin. She sprouted arms, tipped with jointed blades of hardened ink. Then the arms drove home and stabbed him in the back. He staggered, flailing as her blades pierced him again and again, turning his body into a slab of bloody ground beef.

"The things I've done are beyond making amends for," Savannah told him, "but that's no excuse not to try."

He teetered dangerously close to the edge of the yawning portal, struggling to catch himself. The microphone toppled to the shingles at his feet as he clawed at Savannah's body, his thick fingers passing harmlessly through her. It was like trying to fight an ocean.

"You don't know what you're doing!" he shouted, flailing at her.

"Quite to the contrary," she said. "I know exactly what I'm doing. I'm choosing for myself."

A whip-thin line of ink wrapped around his ankle and gave it a bone-cracking twist. He lost his balance, tumbled, and they fell into the mouth of the gateway together. A blast of energy rippled from within, disrupting the conduit. The maw slammed shut.

* * *

The survivors converged on the wreckage. Nessa and Marie, Hedy and her coven—ragged, bleeding, but all of them still on their feet. Daniel and Caitlin ran up from one side of the path to join them. Harmony and Jessie were the last to arrive; they'd tasked the able-bodied operatives from their fire teams with shepherding the wounded to the medical staging ground a quarter mile up the road.

Blue mist wreathed the twisted steel and shattered engines. The pools of spilled coolant smelled like ripe fruit mixed with chlorine. Nothing moved.

Then a girder shifted. Metal groaned as it slid aside, a figure squirming from the wreck. The King of Rust rose, his wrists still trapped in the sapphire manacles, his silken robes in tatters and his flawless form flecked with cuts that oozed golden blood. He towered over them as he stood at the ruin's summit, armored in disdain.

"It's over," Marie said.

"*Nothing* is over." The king strode down the wreckage, the sapphire chain taut between his wrists. "You think this cheap trinket can contain me? You're all going to die here. And look what your little rebellion cost you. The Demiurge is dead, exactly like my brothers and I wanted. You did our bidding, and now you are a species without a god. Alone, utterly alone."

"That makes two of us," Nessa replied.

"I *am* a god."

He flexed his arms, twisted, groaning as he pulled. And one by one, the links in the sapphire chain began to stretch. Then they snapped.

The manacles died, falling open, clattering to the pavement at the king's feet. He singled Nessa out and closed in on her, one clawed hand rearing back to strike her down.

"Now prepare to face the consequences of your—"

Nessa thrust the Cutting Knife forward with both hands, outward and upward, and speared him through the chest. The blade punched through his immortal skin, broke through unbreakable bone, and ruptured his angelic heart.

He froze, trembling, as if his muscles had turned to stone. "*How?*" he croaked.

Clytemnestra appeared as a flickering blue projection at Nessa's side. "Speaking of consequences."

"It would take the Demiurge's power to unmake a king," Nessa told him. "And that's what he gave us. He infused this knife with some of his blood. Just enough to get the job done."

"I've waited centuries for this moment," Clytemnestra said. "Dreaming of it. *Preparing* for it. Do you know why I never changed my form back when I was freed from your power? Because I wanted you to see me like this. I wanted you to see what you did to me. So you'd remember. And I wanted you to know something else, too: you *never* broke me."

"Oh, but we're not just going to kill you," Nessa added. "You have something I need."

Clytemnestra's image clasped hands with Nessa, their powers conjoined, their souls made one.

"Indeed. Now let us feast."

Thick mists swirled around the women as they moved in on the King of Rust, embracing him like lovers. Then Nessa sawed his chest open. His golden blood spilled out and she bathed in it, washing herself in its corrupted light. It coated her arms like gloves of melted wax, matted her long black hair, droplets plastering her owlish glasses as it ran down her cheeks and into her upturned, open mouth. Clytemnestra dug her luminous fingers into the meat of his wound and ripped it wide as the king began to scream.

The mist swirled faster, turning to smoke now, thick and radiant from within, like a lightning storm roiling behind shadowy clouds. It enveloped the three of them, blotting them from sight as a hot, violent pressure filled the air and shoved everyone back from the wreckage. The pressure built to a screaming, thundering crescendo.

Then it stopped. The smoke cleared, blown free on a stray gust of night wind.

The King of Rust was gone. Destroyed. Wiped from the face of existence.

And so was Nessa.

Marie stood there, motionless, staring at the spot where they'd been as if she could will them to come back. If she wanted it badly enough, prayed hard enough. Then she remembered. There was no god left to pray to.

Harmony was the first to shake off the stunned silence that had fallen over the battleground. "C'mon. Can I get some help here? We have to find Carolyn."

The others moved, climbing up and combing the wreckage, pulling back debris and tossing the smaller bits aside. Marie didn't. She couldn't.

It was supposed to be easy. Kill the king, take his power. Nessa had miscalculated. Maybe she'd been too greedy, taken too much, and the king's destruction had taken her with it. Something had gone wrong. For the first time in a hundred lives, they'd had the chance to break the cycle, to escape, to be free and together at long last. Their happy-ever-after.

Ruined.

She stared, and fought back the sting of tears, and dug her short-chopped nails into her palms until they threatened to bleed.

"Over here," Daniel shouted. "She's over here!"

The sound jolted her into movement. She climbed up, numb, making her way through the debris as the others scrambled to help. They peeled back fallen girders, broken furniture, and found Carolyn beneath. A fat slab of steel pinned her from the waist down, one of her arms was bent the wrong way, and blood crusted her mouth like lipstick. Her eyes tried to focus on Marie.

"Hey, kid," she croaked. "Did we win?"

Marie looked to Daniel, to the slab of steel. He gave her a tiny shake of his head.

"We won," Marie told her. She'd gotten better at lying. It felt like the right time for it. Carolyn closed her eyes.

"Worth it, then. You take care of that girl of yours. Don't let her conquer the world or anything crazy."

"I won't," Marie said, her voice breaking. "I'm...I'm sorry I got you into this."

"Nah," Carolyn breathed. "Don't be. You were right. Nice to play the hero, just once. 'Sides, I'll be back somewhere, sometime. Sooner or later, everything comes round again."

She let out one last, rattling breath and died.

Tony put his good arm around Marie's shoulder and eased her away from the wreck. No one said a word.

The survivors of the Battle of Vandemere left in a long, ragged, and silent line. They walked in twos and threes, abandoning the wreckage and the bodies of the dead but carrying the memories with them, etched bone deep.

They had won, sort of.

FIFTY

Marie turned herself in.

A night in hell didn't change the hard facts of reality come morning, and she was still wanted for Richard Roth's murder. Tony drove her to the station. Captain Traynor met them at the back door, cleared the hall, and kept a fatherly hand on her shoulder as he steered her into an interrogation room.

Then she waited. No one came to question her. No one asked her anything at all. The clock turned, slow, leaden, and the hours dragged on. She didn't really care what they did to her now.

The door swung open. Harmony poked her head in and nodded back over her shoulder.

"You're a free woman. Hit the road."

Marie pushed her chair back. "How?"

"Politics," Harmony said. "The dirty, off-the-record kind. Long story short, Senator Roth exerted some pressure on a few city officials to get you indicted. We exerted a little pressure of our own. My partner is really good at pressure. Anyway, the charges are dropped. I can't get you your badge back—I'm sorry, that's outside my reach—but you're not setting foot in a courtroom."

"Thanks. Thanks anyway."

She walked out of the interrogation room and turned toward the exit, numb on her feet.

"Hey, Marie?"

Marie turned.

"I told your partner once," Harmony said, "that sometimes in life, people make a wrong turn. They open a door that should stay closed, hear a secret that wasn't meant for their ears. Then, before they know it, they find themselves in a world they weren't prepared to face."

"The real world," Marie said.

"The real world." Harmony nodded. "Dealing with that, that's my job. Finding people before they can slide too deep, and pulling them out before they drown."

Harmony looked her up and down and let out the ghost of a sigh.

"You and Vanessa...I wasn't fast enough to save you. And I'm sorry for that."

*   *   *

Marie walked through Midtown, listless, swallowed by the electric canyons of Times Square. The city moved around her. She was a face in the crowd, a walking shadow, seen and instantly forgotten by ten thousand eyes.

It was a week after Vandemere. Janine had taken her back in. Her old bedroom was just the way she left it. Yesterday Janine had suggested maybe it was time Marie thought about looking for a job. Cosmic adventures or not, the rent was still due next Tuesday.

Marie had walked with witches and angels, seen the golden city of heaven, and battled nightmares spawned from the pits of hell. And now it was over. It was all over, and she was back home again. Without Nessa. It almost felt like she'd been yanked back in time, back to the day before they first met, when the only inkling of magic she'd had was found in the pages of a yellowed paperback.

Now she knew better. But she was back from the Land of Oz, without so much as a pair of ruby slippers to show she'd been there. And now she had to find a way to live in an ordinary world all over again.

No wonder there were no stories about retired heroes. In the myths and legends, they came onto the stage, fought their titanic battles, and then faded into the mists. No one talked about the aftermath, and now she understood why. Once you'd tasted ambrosia, how could you go back to microwave dinners? Ex-heroes had to shave their legs and balance their checkbook just like everybody else, and the world didn't care where they'd been or what they'd seen.

She had promised to go to Nadia. She couldn't keep her word. The beacon had burned out when they used it at Inwood Hill. She assumed that sooner or later, Tricia would come hunting for her. And she'd go with her. *Or I could just die*, Marie thought, and she didn't really care which. Dying wouldn't be so bad.

She took the train back to Queens. She didn't have anywhere to go, really. The sun was long gone and it was Janine's game night, so she'd have the apartment to herself until well past midnight. She picked up a bottle of gin at the store on the corner. Drinking herself to sleep kept the dreams away.

Her key jiggled in the lock. She let herself into the apartment and shut the door behind her.

The lamp by the futon clicked on.

Alton Roth sat on the futon, patiently waiting for her, with Nyx at his side. The demoness was curled like a cat, leather-clad legs nestled beneath her. She uncoiled them and raised her arms, indulging in a slow and languid stretch.

"You didn't think I was going to let you get away, did you?" he asked.

Marie set her brown paper bag down on the kitchen counter. She didn't try to run. She'd seen how fast Nyx could move.

"What amazes me," Marie said, "is that you still think you're the good guy here."

"You murdered my boy."

She didn't have the energy to try to talk him down. No, she did, but she wasn't going to. She decided in that moment that if she was going to die tonight, she'd do it standing on her feet and telling the truth.

"He had it coming," Marie told him. "Richard was an abusive, manipulative, murderous piece of shit who carved up women for fun. He had it coming, and I'm *glad* I killed him. It was a public service. And you know what? I *enjoyed* it."

Alton's eyes narrowed to slits. He flicked his gaze toward Nyx. "Do it. Kill her slow. I want to watch. Peel her fucking skin off one inch at a time."

Nyx rose from the futon, flashing a shark-toothed grin.

Marie had thought about dying, but something stopped her. She didn't want to die. Not really. That was the easy way out. And she didn't take the easy way out.

And she wasn't going to die here. Not like this. Alton didn't get to win. Not tonight, and not ever.

"You won't get paid," she told Nyx.

That stopped the hunter in her tracks.

"It's a joint contract," Marie said. "That's what they told us. Isn't that right? You have to get me and Nessa, or you don't get paid."

"This one doesn't have to kill you both at the same time," Nyx replied.

"You don't get it. Ask anyone who was at Vandemere. Nessa is gone. Forever. She disintegrated along with the King of Rust when they killed each other. You know what that word means? Disintegration?" Marie chopped the air with the flat of her hand. "*No body.* She's dead, but good luck proving it. It doesn't matter what you do to me: you won't get a single red cent out of it."

Nyx glanced back to Alton. "Is the prey correct?"

"Does it matter? I'll pay you myself, out of my own pocket. *Kill* the little bitch."

Nyx sniffed. She folded her arms.

"It is not a matter of coin. It is a matter of prestige. This one makes her name by fulfilling bounties. A bounty that cannot be fulfilled is a waste of this one's time."

He fumbled in the breast pocket of his jacket, tugging out a slim, squat-nosed pistol.

"Fine," he grumbled, "I'll do it myself."

The apartment door opened. Marie turned, about to shout a warning for Janine to run, but her roommate wasn't home.

Calypso entered, with Caitlin at his side.

"See what I mean, baby?" Calypso pointed to Alton and Nyx. "Give a man a taste of power, and it goes right to his head. Some people just can't handle their high."

Alton scowled at him. "The hell are you doing here?"

"I could ask you the same, daddy-o."

"I'm doing what you couldn't, obviously." Alton took shaky aim, framing Marie in the sights of his gun. "Cutting the loose ends. Paving my way to the White House."

Calypso reached into his own jacket. He came out with a cellophane packet and a gold-plated lighter. He shook out a cigarette.

"I had a long, hard think about things, thanks to a little help from a friend." Calypso nodded at Caitlin. "Made me realize something. See, I'm all about the stories. Souls may be my stock in trade, but stories make the world go 'round."

"And this is how hers ends," Alton said, still aiming at Marie. His finger brushed the trigger.

"Well, see, that's my problem. Because that'd be a low-down and dirty way to end it. I couldn't abide an ending like that. So I suppose I've got to do something about it." Calypso turned to Nyx. "Sweetheart? Alton's in violation of his contract with me. I'm calling it due. The bounty is live, and I'll pay your usual fee. Ought to make up for what you're losing on Marie and her dearly departed."

Alton's eyes slowly went wide as Nyx turned toward him.

"You—you can't mean that," Alton said. "We had a *deal!*"

"Sure did. With clearly stated terms that you agreed to. Signed in blood, no less."

He dangled the cigarette between his lips, lit it up, and tucked the pack and lighter away. His hand emerged with a slim, folded piece of parchment, bound with a scarlet wax seal.

"You chose the terms, you agreed to 'em, and you broke 'em when you went behind my back, baby." Calypso shrugged. "That means you get nothing. Nothing but your final reward. And believe me, it's exactly what you deserve."

"But what about you? Your reputation, everything you staked on getting me in! You'll be *ruined*, you dumb bastard!"

"Suppose I will," Calypso said. "Nyx? Take him."

Alton leaped off the futon. Marie threw herself to one side, diving out of the way as he opened fire. His bullet drilled into the backsplash over the sink, spitting powdered tile onto a pile of dirty dishes as Marie's shoulder slammed against the fridge. He didn't get another shot. Nyx's hand lashed out, grabbed his gun hand, and gave it a vicious twist.

His wrist shattered. Shards of bone tore through the skin, jutting out and gleaming scarlet as he screeched in pain. Nyx dragged him close and clamped one hand over his mouth.

"This one finds the screams of humans often delightful, but in this case, irritating. Compared to what is waiting for you in hell, this is like crying over a stubbed toe."

She yanked him off his feet, dragging him backward, toward the open door of Marie's bedroom. The last thing Marie saw were his bulging eyes, his red, sweaty face and look of absolute terror, before Nyx hauled him out of sight.

A wave of heat boiled across the threshold, carried on a shifting crimson glow and the crackling roar of an open furnace. Then came the sound of an iron door clanging shut, swallowing the light and the sound all at once. The heat wave broke against Marie's skin, leaving a thin film of sweat in its wake.

"Suppose we should leave you be," Calypso said. He gestured to the bullet hole in the backsplash. "Sorry about that."

Marie stood there, mute.

"Just one thing," Calypso added as he turned to go. "You got all the look of a woman thinking about cashing in her chips."

"I'm still here," Marie said.

"For now. But I know how thoughts creep in, in the small hours of the night. And all that pain you're carrying around? You might be tempted to make it all go away with a bullet or a bottle of pills. Now, seeing as I just saved your life, I think you owe me a favor."

"Which is?"

"Wait," he said. "I know stories, see. And when I look at you...I see one that isn't quite finished. Not just yet. So wait for it. You'll know the real ending when it gets here."

"Do you know something I don't?" Marie asked.

"Nope. Wish I did, wish I could tell you so, but no. I'm just a humble gamblin' man, and a gambler has to believe in hope. Always room for a twist ending, right?"

"Okay," she said. "I'll wait."

Marie never broke her word. So she'd wait. She felt a bit of strength in that resolution. Something she could cling to, something to keep her standing on her feet.

*   *   *

Calypso and Caitlin left. Caitlin spoke for the first time once they were out on the landing, door closed at their backs.

"That was kind."

"That was dumb and self-destructive, and you know it." He puffed his cigarette and eyed the contract in his hand. It ignited in a sudden gust of flame, like flash-paper lit by an invisible match. He tossed the last scrap from between his fingers and watched it turn to black ashes, drifting to the dirty stair runner.

"Not mutually exclusive concepts," Caitlin said.

"True. True. So. Let's see how fast word travels."

He took out his phone and dialed up his favorite restaurant.

"Hey, friend. Webster Scratch here. Listen, I was wondering if you could rustle up a couple of seats for tonight. I've got a—"

They hung up on him.

He hit another few numbers. An electronic voice told him that his line of credit had been shut down for non-payment. Another refused to admit his account ever existed. Fontaine picked up on the fifth ring, the hunter's New Orleans drawl drifting over the line.

"Son, you stepped in it."

"Word travels fast indeed," Calypso replied.

"Let's just say some very unkind words are floating about hither and yon. Not from my lips, but I've never been much for high society. You bet the house and you lost it all."

Centuries of stories, centuries of pride. Gone in the flash of one irrevocable choice. There was something smaller about Calypso now, something less, but he forced himself to keep his chin high.

"Good lookin' out, Fontaine."

"Same. Call me sometime. We'll get those drinks I owe you. Just...after the smoke clears a little, okay?"

Calypso hung up. Caitlin studied him, motes of copper dancing in the whites of her eyes.

"You want to get a cab with me?" she asked. "I'm headed to the airport."

They left the apartment building, stepping out onto the sidewalk under a slate-black sky. City lights chased all the stars away.

"Nah," he said. "I'm gonna take a walk, collect my thoughts a bit. Something poetic about midnight in New York."

She hailed a taxi and he left her behind, walking alone. He was busted. Back to ground zero, square one, clean slate, no different than any no-name fledgling bargainer with a blank contract and a razor-tipped pen.

Maybe that was all right.

He'd been a clean slate once, when he was knee-high to a grasshopper. He'd learned. He'd gotten good at his trade. He could do it again.

The sound of music jolted him from his thoughts. It was a

harmonica, dense-woven notes drifting from an alley, dulcet and full of soul. Calypso's feet steered him around the corner.

A grizzled hobo was slumped in a makeshift camp, back to the wall, half-empty bottle of rye at his side. He played the harmonica like he was born to the stage, making it sing the blues.

Calypso rapped his knuckles on the crumbling brick wall. The man stopped playing and looked his way.

"Sorry to interrupt," Calypso said. "Just had to show my appreciation. You're damn good with that harp, old-timer."

The hobo chortled, a laugh that became a phlegmatic cough. He grabbed the bottle of booze at his side and tossed down a swig of hard medicine.

"I'm better than good, boy. I'm the best that's ever been."

Calypso had to smile. "Is that so?"

"Used to be somebody. I was gonna be one of the greats. I could play better'n anybody. Made some bad choices, fell down hard, but I still got the music in me."

Calypso's hand slipped into his breast pocket. His fingers curled around his lighter. But it wasn't a lighter anymore.

"You sound pretty sure of yourself. You could outplay *anybody*?"

The old man snickered and took another pull off the bottle.

"The Lord upstairs and all the saints," he said. "Hell, bring the devil himself down here. I'll kick his ass, too."

Calypso opened his hand, showing off a harmonica made of solid gold.

He put it to his lips and played a few notes. He was rusty. That was all right. The old man's eyes glittered in the dark, a fish on a hook.

"Tell me something," Calypso said. "Are you a bettin' man, friend?"

He'd gone back to the very beginning, but that was just fine. Beginnings were always better than endings, and besides, the journey to the top was the fun part. He could do it all over again. Get it right this time.

FIFTY-ONE

Morning brought a light rain, kissing the air with the smell of diesel fumes. It clung to Marie's face and hands, cooling her down as she drifted through the streets once more. Supposedly looking for a job. She'd filled out a half-hearted application at a liquor store and called it a day.

Her stomach grumbled. She had a dollar in her pocket and fifteen cents change. She walked until she found an ATM. She slotted her card, punched the keys, waited. It spat out a twenty and a paper receipt. A blurb of text on the receipt caught her eye. *"Now open: Sunrise Café, serving breakfast all day long. Free cup of coffee with the bottom half of your receipt!"*

She shrugged. The address was on 30th Avenue, not far away. She wasn't sure if she was in the mood for breakfast food. She folded the receipt and kept walking.

The next block up, a mural had been painted on the side of a brick apartment building. It was an ad for the Sunrise Café, showing a smiling sun rising over a steaming cup of coffee.

"Weird," she muttered and moved on.

She waited at a corner for the light to change, no particular place to go. Across the street, a scrolling LED sign hung in the window of an electronics store, reading off a stock ticker. As she idly glanced over, reading the meaningless jumble of acronyms and values, the sign flickered and died. Then it sprang back to life.

Marie, it read.

Stop being stubborn.

Go to the goddamn Sunrise Cafe already.

The light changed. She speed-walked across the street, heart pounding. Then she broke into a run. The café was on the next block, with an open face to the street and outdoor seating under white-and-black striped umbrellas. A lone customer sat under an umbrella's shade, sipping a cup of coffee.

Nessa turned to her, raised her cup, and smiled.

It was her, alive, in the flesh, and she set her cup down and stood and opened her arms wide to meet Marie as she ran in. Marie threw her arms around her and pulled her close and lifted her off her feet, spinning her around, tears streaming down her cheeks.

"I'm sorry it took me so long," Nessa told her. "I had a little trouble out there. Had to put myself back together on an atomic level, and I mean that literally."

Marie pulled back, just a little. Behind her owlish glasses, Nessa's eyes had changed.

They were pits of darkness. Globes of absolute night, windows into the depths of outer space.

And in that darkness, there were stars. Nessa's eyes were like tiny universes, infinite and deep and glimmering with diamond pinpoints of starlight.

Marie clutched Nessa's shoulders, touching her like she had to reassure herself that this wasn't a dream, wasn't a mirage. "What happened to you?"

"I did what I set out to do." Nessa flashed her lopsided smile. "I ate the King of Rust, down to every last little morsel. And he was *delicious*. Clytemnestra is inside me now, too. That's by her own choice; she's committed to this crusade and plans to see it through."

"Crusade?" Marie asked.

"One king is down. The rest are scattered, in confusion, cut off from their former dominion. But cornered rats bite hard. Besides, I'm hungry for seconds. And thirds. And fourths." Nessa reached up, cradling Marie's cheek. "I have the power of a king now, love. Plus my own unfettered potential as the Witch, plus Clytemnestra's gifts and the spark that the Demiurge gave us before he died...you know, they call themselves kings, but they clearly never read their fairy tales."

She leaned in. Her lips, painted a deep plum, brushed against Marie's. An electric tingle passed between them.

"Kings are so over and done," she murmured in Marie's ear. "It's high time that they all made way for the evil queen."

"Nessa," Marie said, hesitant. "If the Demiurge is dead, and you have his last spark and one of the kings inside you, along with everything else..."

"Yes, love?"

She gazed into Nessa's eternal eyes.

"Are...are you God now?"

"You know," Nessa said, "I do believe I am. The closest thing to it, anyway. Which makes me—and I say this with no shortage of resentment—responsible for the safety of humanity. I think my top priority is doing what my predecessor couldn't. We're going to hunt the Kings of Man. Every last one of them. I won't have such creatures running amok in *my* universe. And of course, as I devour each of them, my power will grow...exponentially, I believe. Until such time as my will is absolute, my control over reality is unquestioned, and I will unleash a tidal wave of darkness and despair, ruling over humanity as its eternal, cruel, and merciless goddess, worshiped and dreaded by all."

Marie quirked an eyebrow.

"You know I'm going to fight you on that, right?"

"Maybe I'm just looking forward to the arguments." Nessa winked. "And the make-up sex. All right, maybe the darkness and despair is negotiable. But I'm not going to be a *nice* goddess."

"I wouldn't ask," Marie replied. "I know you too well. So what's the plan? Just...saddle up and go hunting?"

Nessa shook her head. "No. Direct force is out of the question. These creatures have had eons to learn their craft, Marie. They know what I've done, and they've already gone to ground, plotting their retribution. They fight by proxies, and we're going to do the same."

"Like the Network?"

"Exactly so," Nessa said. "It's time for us to slip into the shadows, too, and build a network of our own. This war will be waged on a thousand battlefields. We'll infiltrate societies on every contested Earth. Our agents will undermine institutions wherever they go and lay the seeds of secret societies, covens, cults, all serving our will. Whatever suits our needs and wins the fight."

Her fingertip stroked the nape of Marie's neck, sending a shiver down her spine.

"You're my perfect knight," she said. "Can you be my general, too?"

"Always," Marie said.

"Let's go see Hedy and end her mourning. I have work for her. Then I suppose we should pop back so you can say goodbye to your friends; you may not see them for a while. How do you think Janine will take it?"

"I think she's either going to freak out or start your official fan club," Marie said. "Probably both. What then?"

Nessa took Marie's arm. She led her away from the café, down a dead-end alley.

"Then, my sweet, I'm going to take a little of what I am and put it inside of you. So you won't ever grow old, and you won't ever die. And then...how about we catch up over lunch? I don't have to eat food anymore, but I still enjoy it. Anyway, I spent about a week bouncing from reality to reality, trying to put myself back together, and I found a world next door where the Mayan Empire never fell. The food is *amazing*. Spices you've never dreamed of."

"One thing we should do first," Marie said.

She shared her idea, and Nessa broke into a grin.

"Yes," she said.

Then she curled her hand in the air. Her fingernails matched her eyes, jet-black, and stars glittered in their depths. She raked her fingers downward and tore a hole in reality.

On the other side was the Light In-Between. A sea of radiant gold, with the bend of a rainbow shining in the distance. Then Nessa took Marie's hand, and they were gone.

*   *   *

On a desolate, frosty plain, a woman in deerskin and furs beat her fists against a drum. Tears stung her cheeks as she hammered out the song of mourning, pouring her grief and despair into every thudding note and sending the sound echoing out over the tundra. A funeral pyre of logs and twigs stood before her. It was small. She'd had to build it herself, cast out of her village and her clan. Her scalp still stung to the touch, from the rock her own brother had thrown at her.

And on the pyre, the body of her wife, hands folded over the gash in her heart. She had been sentenced to torture and death for practicing the witch's craft. The woman had only been able to save her by killing her herself, driving a horn-knife into her wife's heart to protect her from the pain to come.

The woman stood, clutching a pair of spongy stones covered in russet mold. The stones struck together, the mold spat sparks, and the pyre ignited. She stood there, watching her wife burn, and steeled herself for the pain as she prepared to join her in death.

A hole in space tore open. Marie jumped from the gap, waving her hands as she gasped for breath.

"Hold up! *Wait.* Wow. You have no idea how hard it was to find you."

The woman's eyes went wide. "You're..."

"I'm you, yes. Look, I'm about to change your story."

Marie held out her hand.

"Do you have anything to lose?"

*   *   *

Another portal erupted in the heart of a throne room. Marie, her twin, and Nessa emerged, stepping out onto the red carpet as black-uniformed guards jumped back in surprise and shouldered their rifles.

"*Hold!*" Trisha shouted, raising a clenched fist as she stood beside the throne.

Nadia rose. Her lips parted as she stared at the new arrival.

"But—" Marie's twin said, shaking her head. "You...you just died. You died in my arms."

"And you in mine," Nadia said. "But it's all right now. Come here. I'll explain everything, but first, come to me."

Nadia pulled the woman into her arms and squeezed her tight, holding her close as the pall of bitter loneliness lifted from her at long last. She looked over to Nessa and Marie. Her eyes glistened.

Thank you, she mouthed.

"Behave yourself," Nessa said. "Best believe I'll be checking up on you. Consider this incentive to cooperate with my future endeavors."

She turned to Marie, basking in the pleasure of a job well done.

"Shall we?" she asked. "There's a whole wild universe out there. Can't wait to share it with you."

Marie looked to the golden portal and prepared herself.

Their fight wasn't over. Maybe it never would be. There were eight kings still standing, more dangerous than ever now that they knew they could be hurt. The battle ahead would rage for years, decades, centuries and beyond, as they moved across worlds and turned entire nations into chess pieces.

That was all right. Marie was a decent chess player. And she would never say no to a good fight. Whatever waited for them around the next corner, no matter the challenge, she and Nessa would face it together.

She held her lover's hand, they shared a smile, and then they took a running leap, diving into the golden light side by side.

And, more or less, they lived happily ever after.

AFTERWORD

Shortly after *Sworn to the Night* came out, a friend asked if the trilogy was going to have a happy ending. I had to think about that. I believe I replied, "It's going to be a complicated salad." In retrospect, a fair summary.

After building a multiverse spread across three (now four) series and over a dozen books, continuity can feel like a weight. I had two goals for this trilogy, beyond the story itself: to answer a lot of long-running questions and mysteries (which I hope I did to your satisfaction) and to shake things up on a cosmic level. Nessa promised she was here to change things, and she did not lie. But change can be messy, and bloody, and demand sacrifice. When night falls and we fight for our passions, for justice, for our freedom, the sun may rise over chaos and disarray.

But the sun does rise. And if you believe, and if you're willing to fight, sometimes you can get your happy ending.

After all, if a college professor from the West Village can become God, imagine what *you're* capable of. On that note, if missionaries show up on your doorstep and ask if they can talk to you about the divine word of the Owl, you…are probably living on a contested parallel world and should really let them in. In any event, your life is about to get interesting. Be safe out there, owlets.

Speaking of divine beings, I have to offer thanks to my editor, Kira Rubenthaler, who hammered this saga into shape. Also thanks to James T. Egan, my ace cover designer; Susannah Jones, my always-incredible audiobook narrator; and my steadfast assistant Morgan Faid. And thank you, for taking this strange journey with me. We're only getting started.

Want to know what's coming next? Head over to http://www.craigschaeferbooks.com/mailing-list/ and hop onto my mailing list. Once-a-month newsletters, zero spam. Want to reach out? You can find me on Facebook at http://www.facebook.com/CraigSchaeferBooks, on Twitter at @craig_schaefer, or just drop me an email at craig@craigschaeferbooks.com.

Also by Craig Schaefer

The Revanche Cycle

Winter's Reach
   The Instruments of Control
   Terms of Surrender
   Queen of the Night

The Daniel Faust Series

The Long Way Down
   The White Gold Score
   Redemption Song

The Harmony Black Series

Harmony Black
   Red Knight Falling
   Glass Predator

11534056R00261

Made in the USA
San Bernardino, CA
05 December 2018